IN PRAISE OF PATRICIA KENNEALY'S KELTIAD SERIES

"In a class with the Pern, Amber, or Darkover novels
. . . as good as the work of Janet Morris and
Julian May."
—*Fantasy Review*

"Remarkable indeed—full of color, imagination,
and innovative plotting."
—*Irish Echo*

"Kennealy expresses in loving detail the magic and
wonder of Celtic legend . . . highly recommended."
—*Library Journal*

"Those who like their fantasy and SF well blended,
as with Marion Zimmer Bradley and Julian May,
should eat it up."
—*Isaac Asimov's Science Fiction Magazine*

"Everything comes together, and readers will be
reluctant to abandon the adventure once they have
been hooked."
—*Dragon Magazine*

"A highly effective combination of Celtic
mythology, science fiction, and fantasy . . .
absorbing . . . an imaginatively wrought and
scrupulously detailed series."
—*Booklist*

The Silver Branch

A Novel of The Keltiad

Patricia Kennealy

A SIGNET BOOK

NEW AMERICAN LIBRARY

A DIVISION OF PENGUIN BOOKS USA INC.

Acknowledgment

The sequence of Aeron's immram of initiation was lifted from *The Voyage of Maelduin*; all praise, thanks and honor to Aed Finn, king's bard, who composed it long ago.

To my grandmother Agnes McDonald

In the Earth year 453 by the Common Reckoning, a small fleet of ships left Ireland, carrying emigrants seeking a new home in a new land. But the ships were not the leather-hulled boats of later legend, and though the great exodus was indeed led by a man called Brendan, he was not the Christian navigator-monk who later chroniclers would claim had discovered a New World across the western ocean.

These ships were starships; their passengers the Danaans, descendants of—and heirs to the secrets of—Atlantis, that they themselves called Atland. The new world they sought was a distant double-ringed planet, itself unknown and half legend; and he who led them in that seeking would come to be known as St. Brendan the Astrogator.

Fleeing persecutions and a world that was no longer home to their ancient magics, the Danaans, who long ages since had come to Earth in flight from a dying sun's agonies, now went back to those far stars, and after two years' desperate wandering they found their promised haven. They named it Keltia, and Brendan, though he refused to call himself its king, ruled there long and well.

In all the centuries that followed, Keltia grew and prospered. The kings and queens who were Brendan's heirs, whatever else they did, kept unbroken his great command: that, until the time was right, Keltia should not for peril of its very existence reveal itself to the Earth that its folk had fled from; nor forget, for like peril, those other children of Atland who had followed them into the stars—the Telchines, close kin and mortal foes, who became the Coranians as the Danaans had become the Kelts.

Yet Brendan himself had said that a day must come at last when Kelts and Terrans should meet again as cousins; three thousand years later, that day had not yet come, and many there were among Brendan's people who prayed it never might.

Until one was born in Keltia to cause that day to dawn . . .

CAERDROIA

EASTGATE
LANDGATE
IRONGATE
WOLF GATE
SEAGATE
SANCTUARY

TANA BARRISONS

THE STEWPONS

LIT PORT
SOME STEW ROOM
EROTHOU
TEMPLE HILL
HOUSE STEW ROOM
THE STEWS

PALACE
KEEP
ARRUSTEROIN

DRAGON KINSHIP
DOCKWAY

THE WAY OF SOULS

MOUNT EAGLE
THE BATTLEROCK

Main Characters

Aoife Aoibhell, High Queen of Keltia; known as the Shan-rían, the Old Queen

Lasairían, her son, Tanist; later High King

Gwyneira nighean Brega, his wife; later queen-consort

Fionnbarr, their son, Prince of the Name; later Tanist and High King

Elharn Aoibhell, called Ironbrow; son to Aoife, brother to Lasairían

Budic, King of Fomor

Bres, his son and heir; later King

Basilea (Sovay), Bres's betrothed; later queen-consort

Errazill-jauna, Emperor of the Cabiri

Strephon, his son and heir; later Emperor

Celarain, High Justiciar of Ganaster

Faolan, Master of Douglas, later Prince of Scots; friend to Fionnbarr

Emer, youngest daughter of Farrell Prince of Leinster; later queen-consort to Fionnbarr

Keina, her sister, a Ban-draoi Domina

Aeron, daughter to Fionnbarr and Emer, Princess of the Name; later Tanista and High Queen

Rohan, her brother; later Tanist

Ríoghnach, her sister; later Princess of the Name

Kesten Hannivec, Ban-draoi Magistra, abbess of Scartanore

Morwen Douglas, daughter to Faolan; later Duchess of Lochcarron and Taoiseach to Aeron

Arianeira Penarvon ferch Gwenedour, daughter to the Prince of Gwynedd

Roderick, Master of Douglas, son to Faolan; later Prince of Scots

Arawn Penarvon ap Kenver, Prince of Gwynedd

Gwydion, his son and heir; later Prince of Gwynedd, Pendragon, and First Lord of War to Aeron

Tybie Vedryns ferch Eilir, Ban-draoi anchoress, spiritual advisor to Aeron

Sabia ní Dálaigh, friend to Aeron

Duvessa Cantelon, schoolmate of Aeron and Sabia
Struan Cameron, swordmaster of the Fianna
Denzil Cameron, his brother, Fianna Trialmaster
Donal mac Avera, Captain-General of the Fianna
Vevin ní Talleron, friend to Aeron
Elathan, Prince of Fomor, son to Bres; later King of Fomor
Jaun Akhera, Prince of Alphor, grandson to Strephon; later Cabiri Emperor
Helior, his mother
Slaine, daughter to Elharn, cousin to Aeron
Melangell, cousin to Aeron
Kieran, brother to Aeron
Declan, his twin
Gwyn ap Nudd (or Neith), King of the Sidhe

and various Personages.

Ny yl blyth gul ken ages avel blyth.
(A wolf can act but like a wolf.)

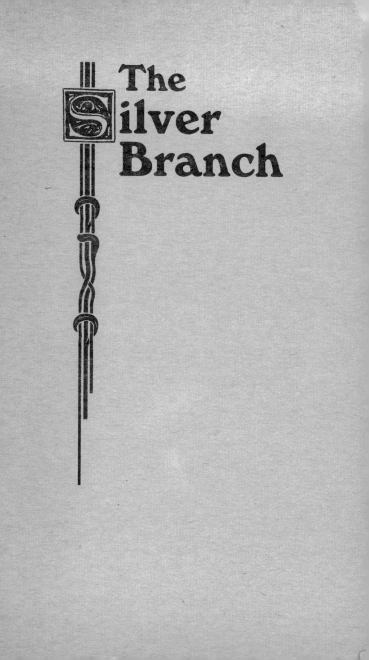

The Silver Branch

Prologue

Queen Aoife was dying. For a hundred years and near half that again—longer than any other had before, or ever would after—she had ruled Keltia, with an iron hand and a stiff back and a mind that could work at computer speed; had given the realm four sons, four princes to follow her; had seen the father of those sons dead long since, in a battle far from his home; had gone on alone, to make Keltia stronger than the kingdom had ever been in all the centuries of its existence; had lived to see the name of Keltia respected and feared and honored far beyond the Pale of its protection, a power among the stars. Now she was dying at last, and knew that she was dying, and was more than content that it should be so.

The vast spaces of the state bedchamber were thronged with people, subdued, watchful, conversing in whispers when they spoke at all; the witnesses custom required to attend upon the passing of a monarch—family, friends, ministers of state, ambassadors of foreign worlds, Druid priests and Ban-draoi priestesses to offer the withdrawing soul the grace of ritual, and guidance for its passage.

Aoife herself had cared little enough for most of those present, had never stinted to show it in life; good luck to them if they thought to get other of her now . . . But the laser-green eyes, still piercingly perceptive for all their growing dimness, picked out the ones among them she had truly cared for, and who had cared for her in return. To her othersight, far sharper than her physical vision with her nearness to her change, they stood out like torches in fog, bright amid blurriness, their souls clearer to her now than their faces: the friends of a lifetime, the helpers

1

who had shared with her the burdens of a long and already legendary rule, and, among a large and diverse family, those few she had loved the best . . .

"Barraun. Barraun, come here to me."

The whisper was surprisingly strong in the room's rustling silence, and it carried every ounce of the old command; the murmurs of the watchers suddenly ceased. At the foot of the great bed, where he had been standing for nearly an hour now, the youth Fionnbarr smiled at the pet-name, and came round the bedside to kneel by his grandmother's head.

Aoife laid a claw-fingered hand—the big emerald ring that was Keltia's Great Seal looking larger than ever against her finger's new gauntness—on the untidy thatch of red-brown hair, met the clear hazel eyes, wide and steady and warm with love, beneath the straight-trimmed glib.

"Ah, my Barraun, *you* have never been afraid of me, have you, not even as a little lad; not like the rest of these quaking slinters. That is well, for you are a prince, Prince of the Name, soon now to be Tanist, and then High King after your father; and after you—" Her strength began to fail her, and her voice cracked and faltered.

"After me," said Fionnbarr, trying to help her, to comfort her with that royal continuity he sensed she had such need to hear reaffirmed, "after me, another prince for Keltia."

"Nay." Aoife's voice came clear and strong now, like a sudden north wind in the room, and those sensitive to such things shivered like willows in that wind, for they knew that the Sight had taken hold upon her, as happened so often near the end.

"Nay," she said again, as clearly. "No prince to be your heir, Prince Fionnbarr, but a princess; a princess who will be such a sorceress, and such an Ard-rían, as Keltia has never yet known. You shall call her—aye, you shall call her Aeron."

A stir ran round the chamber. Deathbed seeings were far from uncommon among Kelts, but they were invariably strongly omened, one way or another; and for the dying High Queen to foretell the birth of the next High Queen, and one named for the Kymric battle goddess, was not the sort of portent those present were longing to hear. But, they consoled themselves in thought, Fionnbarr himself was as yet only a stripling, barely three-and-twenty, far from being wed or even betrothed; and maybe the princess would never come . . .

It seemed that Aoife had heard their thought, for the green eyes gleamed wickedly, and the face, scarcely lined for all its years, flowed into as wicked a smile.

"Ah, you may hope against her as you please, but she will come all the same: Aeron. In the old speech, the bardic meaning of that name is 'the sword flashing downward in the stroke.' She will earn that name, then lose it, then take it back again greater than before. Though I shall never know her in this life, she will be more truly a child of mine than any son I bore."

"As you say, dama-wyn," murmured Fionnbarr soothingly, taking her hand in both of his and kissing it, "and as you have Seen. May your journey thrive," he added, tears at last springing to his eyes.

Aoife smiled again, this time a smile of satisfaction and farewell, and seemed to relax back upon her pillow, still looking upon her grandson. Presently her Taoiseach of thirty years' service—Mathuin, grave, white-haired, militarily erect of posture, last of the many who had been her first servant down the decades as she had been Keltia's—came forward to stand on the other side of the golden-pillared bed, beside Lasairían and Gwyneira: Lasairían, who would in a matter of moments now be Ard-rígh, High King of Keltia, after waiting longer for the Copper Crown than any heir in history; and Gwyneira, who would be his queen.

"Lady?" said Mathuin softly. "Before you leave us, leave us one last word: If Keltia must change with the coming of this princess, is the change for good or for ill; and does Keltia survive it—or her?"

But Aoife spoke no word more, and in a moment the rich silk coverlet, embroidered with the royal arms, fell over her breast and did not rise again. Then came that sound which all present had known that they should hear: Through the open casements, falling down the slopes of Mount Eagle high above them, came a terrible descant—the mournful howl of a wolf. The chamber's stillness rang with it; then, one by one, as trees bend beneath the blast, those present went each to his right knee in token of respect, and heads were bowed for Aoife's passing, while the keen throbbed in the hushed air.

Rising presently from where he had knelt by the bedside, his face hidden in the coverlet, the Ard-rígh Lasairían reached out with a shaking hand to slip the Great Seal of Keltia from his mother's finger, and the smaller Unicorn Seal of the House of Aoibhell also; and, half in guilt, as if he feared she might even now sit up and beshrew him for his haste, he placed the rings upon his own hands. Then he reached out again, to close forever the eyes that had looked upon so much for so long: the green eyes of the Shan-rían, that had struck such fear, and sparked such fealty, in so many hearts.

As he did so, bending then to kiss his mother's brow, Lasairían was himself struck by the expression plain upon the countenance of the dead queen.

Aoife—oldest monarch in Keltic history and longest to reign— Aoife had died smiling.

Book I: Fionnbarr

Chapter 1

The gold-bound diplomatic diptych lay upon the Council table, glowing softly against the granite's dark grain. Though not one of the dozen or so people seated round that table would look at it directly, still it occupied the center-place of all their attention, and their whole minds were filled with it and with its import.

"Well," said Lasairían at last, and the sound of the King's voice seemed to free his companions from their strange stasis, "the mills of the law grind exceeding slow on Ganaster, but in this they have ground slower and finer even than usual." He picked up the diptych, breaking the thin gold seal with the device of the High Justiciary stamped upon it, and held it up to read. "My eyes are not so good as once they were, and this Englic the galláin all use of late comes not so easy to me as once it might have. Do you, Barraun, read to us what this thing may say."

From his place at his father's left hand—traditional seat at the Council table of the heir of Keltia, as the Taoiseach, First Minister to the Crown, sat always upon the monarch's right— Fionnbarr Aoibhell reached out to take the tablet from his father's hand, and scanned the message matrix within.

"Naught but what we have heard already through less official channels," he said presently. "It is of course our formal notification from Ganaster of the coming to trial of the Lykken matter, that the Ard-rían Aoife bequeathed to us upon her death these twenty years since." When no response was immediately forthcoming, he added, "Surely we knew that this brangle would someday fall to us."

Surely they did . . . Around the room, the mood had perceptibly altered, and not for the lighter. Of all matters of interstellar consequence that might have occupied their attention, the Ard-eis, the High Council of Keltia, could think of none just now that they would like less to deal with. Yet the Prince's word carried truth: Deal with it they must, like it or loathe it. It had been long delayed, and for that they had been long grateful; but now the grain that had sprung of the seed Aoife had so arrogantly sown had come to full harvest, and it was for them to make of it what sheaves they might.

Fingers thoughtfully stroking his beard, the Ard-rígh Lasairían, third of that name and fifteenth of the House of Aoibhell, let his glance move down the table over the faces of his advisors. Almost he could tell from those faces alone, or from their still or tapping fingers, or even from the very postures in which they sat, what was passing through what it pleased most of them to call their minds.

As to those closest to him, he had no need even to look, for he knew their minds already, as their friend rather than as their King, and those minds were of the same cast as his own: Sighile of Ossory, his Taoiseach, who faced Fionnbarr from her seat on Lasairían's right; at the far end of the table, Donlin O Talleron, First Lord of War; over against the western wall, among the members of the Privy Council, Elharn Aoibhell, called Ironbrow, both for the silver-gray hair and the war-helm that so often covered it—youngest of the four sons of Aoife, and named by Lasairían his brother to be Fionnbarr's tutor.

And as for Fionnbarr— Lasairían looked casually away to the left, where his heir was staring at the fateful diptych as if it could be made to yield up to him that instant the Rúnachanna, the Secret of Secrets that shall be revealed at the end of time. *Ah, no mystery there, amhic,* he thought. *Only politics, and long enmity, and in the end without a doubt yet another goaround with the Fomori* . . . He sighed, and tapped twice on the table to catch their attention.

"For those of us who have not kept abreast of this old matter," he said aloud, "do you, Ossory, run it out in brief. And for those who are up with it, a retelling can only serve to make it clearer. Begin, Taoiseach."

"Well then," said Sighile, as the others settled back to hear her account. "Some years before she died, the Ard-rían Aoife, upon whom be the peace of the gods, gave offer to the planetary system of Lykken, that they should become a Keltic protectorate. Now Keltia had at that time but few protectorate worlds by compare to what we have now taken upon us, and Aoife—rightly or wrongly, it is not for us here to decide—sought to increase these both in their numbers and in their possible future usefulness to Keltia.''

''Oh, come!'' snapped Dahal Hendragoth, from his place beside O Talleron; Dahal, the red-bearded giant who was Master of Sail in the Keltic starfleet. ''No coyness here, Ossory; let us feign no innocence as to why Aoife did what she did. Some are in this room this very minute that helped her to it; myself among them, and not shamed to say it. Plomine is none so thick in the ground anywhere in the galaxy for her, or for us, or for anyone else, to pass up so rich and gleanable a source—or to scorn suppliers who are so eager to offer it. The Lykkenoi were never anything other than hopeful of gaining our commerce and anxious to be sheltered by our shield.''

''And that is where the Fomori come into it,'' remarked Elharn. ''For they did have their own designs on Lykken as a future subject world of the Phalanx, and for the same reasons. Never would they have it that Keltia should be so favored and they should not.''

''More even than that,'' said Sighile. ''In addition to the plomine moon-mining operations, Lykken is situated at an important wayscross, and is of both military and economic desirability: equidistant for refueling of warships and merchant vessels both, and on the trade routes for many of the most profitable galactic markets. No blame to the Fomori that they were so wroth with Aoife for her high-handedness in seeking to annex the system.''

''But the plomine is the meat of it,'' said Lasairían. *Was then, and still is now* . . . Plomine, the bright blue halogen gas so essential to the manufacture of the hyperdrive motivers that made interstellar travel both possible and easy. *Nay, they would never have given that up without a fight* . . . It was only by grace of the might of Aoife's fist—an iron hand in an iron glove, as her daughter-in-law Gwyneira had once acidly, and accurately, characterized her—that Fomor had chosen to fight the matter out before the court of the High Justiciary on Ganaster rather than upon the field of war. *Though it might yet come to that, as it has* done so often before . . . And if it did, Lasairían knew he would not shirk it; but for the moment it seemed that words, not swords, would be the weapons to settle this newest turn of the ancient quarrel, and he had a thought as to who should be Keltia's chief champion in the contest.

But Sighile was speaking again. "Any road, Aoife offered to Lykken, which offer was contrary to all right practice, and she had no right to make it, for by law of galactic covenant and law of true dealing, she should have waited until such time as Lykken came petitioning to *her* . . . and they would surely have done so. The spurs to her hasty offering were, of course, Fomor's own designs upon the Lykken system, and the further threat of seizure by force on the part of our other longtime foes, the Cabiri Imperium, should Lykken manage to evade the Fomori grasp."

"Not much room for choosing there, Taoiseach." That was Fionnbarr, who looked up to give Sighile—a connection of his foster-kindred, and, despite the great difference in their ages, a friend as well—a wry grin.

The First Minister matched it. "As you say, Tanist . . . And the Lykkenoi were very much of that same mind, choosing overwhelmingly to accept Aoife's offer. Then Budic, King of Fomor, chose to challenge both Keltia and Lykken in a brief submitted to the Justiciary. For that no actual war did threaten, and since such cases are frequent through the settled galaxy, it has taken until now for the suit to come to consideration before the High Justiciar."

"Such delay is by no means unusual," said Tujen Kerival, seeking to reassure them on that count; and, as Chief Brehon since before the coil of Lykken had begun, he was one who should know. "Nor does the timing bear any relation, one way or another, to the merits of the case. But the Justiciary works in its own way, to achieve its own ends, and delay is but one tool of many."

"Still, *we* shall not delay, surely, in accepting of this summons." That was Dorn Straffan, and Lasairían threw him a look of mingled relief and gratitude, for bringing the Council so featly to the point. *Else they had debated it from now to Nevermas, and I wish this acceptance swiftly made* . . . But Dorn, called Dorn Arghans, "Silverfist," for the hand fashioned of that metal to replace the one lost in battle, could ever be relied upon to collect his fellows when they strayed from the trail—it was as much for that knack and daring as for his military skills that Lasairían had appointed him Earl Marischal—and no surprise to any that he did so now.

"Nay, surely we shall not," said Lasairían. "For one thing, I wish to give Fomor no more time than he has had already to prepare his case against us; and for another—well, even I must think on it a little longer, and before I take any action I must consult with Tujen and with several others as to what our best defense shall be. Let us meet again, then, in the morning. Barraun—"

"What you mean more truly is that you must consult with my mother," remarked Fionnbarr as he accompanied his father from the Council chamber.

Lasairían laughed. "Did I not so, on so grave a matter, no doubt but that I would have more trouble with my Queen than ever I had with Fomor, and you would likely come to be Ard-rígh sooner than you might otherwise expect to . . . But jest aside, Barraun, your mother is a more astute counselor of state than most of those who have just now left the chamber behind us."

"I know that," said Fionnbarr, all teasing gone now from his voice. He knew, too, the belief among the people that it was in truth the Queen Gwyneira who ruled Keltia, for that she ruled the Ard-rígh Lasairían. And the truth was perhaps not so very far off the mark: There was very little Gwyneira nighean Brega, daughter of the Lord of the Out Isles, ever wanted that she long failed of getting. Her great grace was that whatever she sought, she sought for Keltia and not for herself. Not that Lasairían was so weak a king or so doting a lord that he would have indulged her even had she been a rapacious strumpet; but Gwyneira was a queen in the true Keltic sense of partnership in sovereignty— more than the breeder of heirs, more than the companion to the monarch—and she filled that part more strongly and surely than any consort, king or queen, had done for long years. No question but that she had a far stronger say in governing than had Aoife's own partner, Graham Drummond . . . Fionnbarr grinned. It would have taken Lugh, or Fionn, or the great Dagda himself, to have any kind of sway, save the most superficial, over Aoife;

no doubt but that even now she was disputing with the lords of dán. *They will be wanting to send her back straightway, if only to rid themselves of her for another turn of the Wheel* . . .

"What are you looking so mirthful at, Barraun?" said his mother as they entered her grianan. "From what I hear of the Council meeting, this is no laughing matter."

"It is clear and simple enough, Laisren," said Gwyneira to her husband. "You must go to Ganaster yourself to give Budic a flyte to his face over this coil; and you, Barraun, must conduct the case for Keltia."

"I!" Absurdly, Fionnbarr blushed, and his mother lifted a questioning brow.

"Well, had you not thought of it? I see that the idea had already occurred to the Ard-rígh, for he looks most unsurprised to hear me say so. Am I not right, anwyl?"

"As ever," agreed Lasairían, amused at his son's reaction. "But, you know, Barraun, it is full time you began to act for the future, and the reign of Fionnbarr XIV Ard-rígh. You have been formally invested Tanist these fifteen years now; time you donned that cloak before the worlds outside the Pale as well.

"Have they not felt my hand hard enough in war?" muttered Fionnbarr, stung at what was doubtless a nonexistent implication: that the King thought his heir lazy, or lacking in responsibility.

"They have indeed, and have been much the worse for it," said Lasairían approvingly. "That was not what I meant: You have acquitted yourself there well indeed, none better. But there is more to kingship than war; and sometimes more victories, and longer-lasting ones, may be won by other means. That is the kind of victory I intend to win here, and you, my son, shall be the sword I wield to do so."

"Besides, Barraun," observed Gwyneira, "it is not as if you have had no training for such a task. Did you spend all those years at the Hill of Laws for pastime only?"

Fionnbarr laughed, his momentary chagrin forgotten. "Nay; rather for that I was advised I had but little future at every other training establishment to which you two did send me: not as Fian, nor Druid, nor bard. I turned brehon novice by default; had I not been born Tanist, I should have had no employment at all to hope for."

His parents laughed too. "Now that is entirely untrue," protested Gwyneira. "Though I will admit that your sister, Orlaith, made a better sorcerer than you might have done; and Deian your brother did excel you somewhat as a Fian . . . Still, Tujen Kerival himself told me that you would have made a most worthy brehon, and that he was only sorry he could not offer you consecration to the Chair of the Law, for you were as fine a student as ever he had trained up."

Fionnbarr had blushed again at the relayed praise. "And kind it was of my master Tujen to say so. But if you will give this trust into my hands, Ard-rígh," he continued with sudden formality, "my word upon it that I will do my uttermost best to win; and, at the very least, my word that I will do naught to disgrace Keltia, or you, before the bar of the High Justiciary."

"Then be it so," said Lasairían, matching his son's manner. On the morrow we shall tell the Council, and meet with Tujen to plan out our case."

In her chair beside the great hearth, Gwyneira smiled, and went contentedly back to her book.

Chapter 2

"So they have accepted."

Budic, King of Fomor, laid down the diptych his prime minister had just brought him—gold-bound, as only the most very important of diplomatic messages merited, and bearing the sixfold knot of Keltia upon its cover.

"Did you think that they might not?" Credine seated himself across from his master with the air of one preparing for a long, perhaps disagreeable, surely unavoidable debate.

Budic snorted. "Not likely! I am only sorry Aoife is not here to face us herself, that paramount harpy. But she has been gone to her gods these twenty years now, and I am pleased enough to have to deal with Lasairían."

"With his heir, Fionnbarr, more likely," predicted Credine with some gloom. "Lasairían is perhaps not so clever as he should be, and certainly he has not the low cunning of his mother; but his son has been trained up as a jurisconsult, from what we know of him—clever enough for his father's purposes. It would be in Lasairían's rights to designate him to argue the Keltic case, and it would be very much more in Lasairían's interests."

Budic had caught the behind-thought. "As it would not be in *my* interests to name my own son . . ."

"I did not say so."

"You did not need to." Budic shifted in his chair, looked at his prime minister with despair in his face. "Ah, my old friend, what are we to do with him? Bres grows more intemperate with every passing year, or so at least it seems—for all that his mother and you and I and everyone else who had a hand in his

14

upbringing have tried to do to change it. What he will do to Fomor when I am gone—it freezes my heart to imagine.''

Credine looked more uncomfortable than ever, though he and Budic had had this same discussion many times before, to the same end . . . ''Perhaps if you were to give him some real responsibility—''

''Can you say in honesty that I have not tried? Recall if you please the results; any disaster you like, there were enough of them . . . No, Bres has some kind of malign touch, that everything to which he puts his hand turns to grief and sorrow. Even Basilea—I had such hopes of her when I allowed the betrothal, you remember; I thought that if anyone could bring him from that manner of headlong unreason it would be that sweet and lovely child—''

''Yet she was betrothed first to your elder son, not to Bres at all.'' Credine spoke without thought, then swore inwardly at his own stupidity: After nearly ten years, Budic had still not recovered from the loss of his first heir, his namesake and only child of his first, beloved queen. *Not the best of times, moreover, to remind him of such*, thought Credine with a fresh pang, *for young Budic died under the guns of the Kelts themselves; and now here we go to court against them . . .*

But Budic gave him a searching look, and nodded; he had picked out the same trail of thought among all possible thickets.

''And it will be a very great satisfaction to do so, I am nothing loath to admit . . . But as for Basilea, it seems from what my son has *not* told me that she is unwilling to go through with the marriage.''

''Can she—?''

''Oh, she has no choice in the matter, of course; her family and ours have agreed long since, especially for that she was never wed to Bres's brother. She is the daughter of a proud and noble house, she will do her duty to them and to Bres, I have no fear of that. I had only hoped that if she could come to care for him—well, no matter. It will never be, and that is a sorrow for them both, for I think he truly loves her.''

''But Ganaster?'' asked Credine, gently returning his king to the matter at hand.

Budic sighed. ''What choice have I? No more choice than that poor child Basilea . . . Bres must of course conduct the defense.

He will have to deal with Fionnbarr of Keltia when he himself is king; he might as well begin now. I should tell him today, I suppose; where is he? Now I think on it, I have not seen him for some days.''

"No one knows his whereabouts,'' admitted Credine, concealing his own misgivings. "He took himself off from Tory with only a few words to the Queen and to his friend Corsin Letro, about some tiresome chore that needed to be attended to. It was assumed—upon what ground I have no idea—that he had gone south to the Mirregaith; but he has not been seen there, and now the thinking is that he is off-planet. He took half his household troops with him, so I think we need not fear just yet for his safety.''

"No, well, perhaps you are right there. All the same, Credine, I like not the thought of him wandering around the system; or, gods forbid, some other system . . .'' Budic seemed to collect himself. "See what you may learn of his whereabouts—before he does something that I am sure to regret.''

Far from Fomor, on the desert world Alphor, seat of the Cabiri Empire, yet another monarch was in receipt of yet another diptych. This one, however, came from Ganaster itself, and contained news of a very different sort.

"We are called to serve as legists,'' said the Emperor Errazill-jauna to his son, Strephon. "In the matter of Fomor against Keltia for the possession of the Lykken system.''

Strephon looked genuinely shocked, as indeed he was. He was a man in early middle age, with the wiry grace and night-black hair and amber-gold eyes that graced so many members of the Imperial house of the Plexari, and he had a full measure of that house's cunning.

"And they call *us* to sit?'' he asked. "In such a case? This is the first time Ganaster has ever deigned to ask a Cabiri to one of its empanelments.''

"Well—effectively the first,'' replied his father. He himself was surprised at the summons: For all the antiquity of the race that ruled it, the Cabiri Imperium had not long been established—as such things are reckoned—as a galactic entity. Over the millennia, the Terran root-race of Telchines who had founded it, and the Coranians who had sprung from that stock, had themselves been subject to the tides of conquest and conquering that have washed over every nation since nations had begun. Yet somehow this nation had held together through all of its trials, and now, after a long period of military and political reverses—more than a few of which had been dealt them by Keltia itself, admitted Errazill-jauna—the Cabiri were clearly once again in the ascendancy. For all that, though, he was only the eleventh ruler of his house; with any luck, and the help of the gods, Strephon would be the twelfth. After Strephon—well, that need not be faced just yet . . .

"Shall you go, then?" asked Strephon, his eyes on the diptych.

Errazill-jauna let him wait a little longer. Then: "The summons is not for me. They ask for you."

"*Me*! But why—"

"—has the Justiciary summoned the Cabiri at all, and why has it summoned you in especial," finished Errazill-jauna for him. "You are right to wonder. I have been wondering myself."

"And?"

"Ganaster has its own dark reasons for everything it does. But still it strikes me strange that they ask us to sit, knowing our past history with the Kelts—on Terra as well as after—and our present dealings with the Fomori and the Phalanx alliance that Fomor rules. Whatever Ganaster's reasons, though, we shall learn as much about Keltia and Fomor—more, even—by fulfilling this legist's chore as ever we have learned in battle. It is almost that by seeking to throw all three of us together, Ganaster thinks to gain something for its own secret purposes. But what those may be I have no idea."

"To learn something?" mused Strephon aloud. "Or to teach us something?"

"That sounds more like it," said his father grimly. "For all their pious claims of disinterest, Ganaster has meddled before now in more than a few galactic brawls that it would have become it better to have refrained from."

"And you think something of the sort is afoot here."

"I cannot say that it is not," said the Emperor of the Cabiri. "But it is you, Prince of Alphor, who will find it out for us."

"If I cannot?"

Errazill-jauna smiled his slow smile. "Then perhaps you had best not trouble yourself to come home."

*   *   *

When the news came to Keltia, it was at first simply not credited, and Lasairían sent out at once those who could more accurately ascertain of its truth: spies and ferreters, in the guise of merchants and bards and harmless travellers; and they came back every one of them to Tara to tell their King that it was so.

"But what in all the hells can he have hoped to gain by it!"

Fionnbarr, closeted with his father and Tujen and Sighile and Dorn Arghans, shook his head, still astounded by the facts now proved beyond a doubt: Bres, heir of Fomor, acting alone and apparently unsanctioned by king or council, had led a lightning raid on Lykken. Not a very large raid, it was true, comprising only several cohorts of his own personal guard, and not doing very much damage to Lykken itself. But as that world was, and had long been, a planet protected only by the Keltic garrisons it had itself welcomed there, Bres's actions could be construed in one way only: a deliberate attack on Keltia.

"It draws us more than ever into Fomor's sticky web, Ardrígh," Dorn Arghans was saying. "To summon us to Ganaster for lawful process on the one hand, and then to attack Lykken on the other—it makes no sense. It is as if they try to cut the ground from beneath their own feet. Can even Fomori be so stupid?"

"So it would seem," said Fionnbarr. "They would have done better to keep to one battlefield or the other: Either defeat us before the Justiciary, or else take Lykken with sufficient force to hold it against us."

"To attempt both is to fail to win at either," agreed Sighile. "What can Budic be thinking?"

"At the moment he is thinking what I would be thinking," said Lasairían, "were it *my* son and heir who had acted so. I think Budic knew as little of Bres's intent as did we here . . . But, Tujen, how might this new development bear on Keltia's case before the High Justiciar?"

The Chief Brehon's face, alone among those in the room, was wreathed in delight. "I cannot see how it could work against us, Lord. If Bres's immoderate and well-known rashness has led him to do this—as plainly it has—then let us give thanks for it, and prepare our own case accordingly."

"And let us give thanks also," said Dorn Arghans, "that our own prince is made other wise."

* * *

When Bres of Fomor returned to his home planet, the word was there before him, as it was by now in every palace of every government throughout the settled galaxy. Striding through the halls, he could see that the courtiers knew already, for they drew back for him, and from him, though they bowed at his passing as mannerly as ever. And when at last he came into his father's presence, he saw that Budic had known first of all, and he altered his demeanor to suit.

But by the gods I will not *apologize for it, and no more shall I admit shame or error of it, for it was no error, and by those same gods I feel no shame . . .*

"Sir and father—"

"Silence!" roared Budic. "At this moment I wish I were neither! Dare you speak to your King before he speaks to you— you who have broken law and reason as well as honor? Who told you to bring force against Lykken?"

"No one tells me, and no one told me." *King and father though he be, he has no right to speak so to me . . .*

"Then why did you? And consider well that your life, my son though you are, may hang upon your answer."

"If my lord the King will recall," said Bres, biting off each word as he spoke it, "he was himself advised to give me charge over the Lykken matter and anything that might bear upon it, and it was Credine who is Prime Minister to this realm who informed me so."

"To handle in the Justiciary on Ganaster!"

"To handle as I thought best! And it seemed best to give the Lykkenoi and their Keltic bravos a touch of what they should have felt long since: the strong hand well applied."

"Bonehead! All you have succeeded in doing is prejudicing our case; if case we still have . . . Or did you think perhaps to raise that same hand to Ganaster itself? Or to me?" Bres was sullen and silent, and Budic paused to take a deep breath. "I'll confess I myself have long wished to give Lykken—yes, and Keltia too—a significant thrashing; but my wishes, and yours, Prince Bres, are not the only consideration here. Not only has our case been severely compromised in the eyes of the High Justiciar and the chosen legists, but Fionnbarr has gained immeasurably by your action."

Bres hardly heard, spoke his sole and blinding thought. "But I may still manage the defense!"

"By rights you should not now be given the management of a fish-stall in the lower city . . . Do you think you still deserve to be allowed to defend Fomor's cause?"

"I think none deserves it more, and it was that I thought to prove . . . But I swear by all gods, if you permit me this, you will have no cause to think the worse of me."

"Not hard," said Budic dryly, "for I can scarcely think worse of you than I do this instant . . . Well, let it be so. If I remove you now, I merely give more cause for ridicule; enough folk are laughing at us as it is. Prepare your case; call upon whatever jurisconsults you like for assistance. But hear this, Bres, and hear it well: If you lose us this case, or give way yet again to rashness of any sort, you will lose yourself Fomor after me."

"I will not lose."

Alone, Bres closed his eyes and leaned back against the wall, in a passion of relief so great that his knees sagged under him. That had been much too near a thing for comfort; Budic would have been well justified in depriving him on the spot of his heirship, or even his life, let alone the defense, for so endangering Fomor's interests. But now all was well: There was no road down which lay defeat, not for him, not on Ganaster. And perhaps this task could work to his own advantage in another matter that had not been going well of late: Basilea, his betrothed, should come with him to Ganaster. His reluctant betrothed . . . perhaps she could be made to see at last in what mold her future lord was cast, and perhaps he could even win her to him, as so far he had not managed to do: to win her will, if not her heart, to the fact of their marriage that must be. For wed her he would, and wed him she must; their families had arranged it. But if he could win for Fomor on Ganaster, he might also win for himself in her eyes. The chance was his. There was no way he would not now take it.

Basilea was in the garden-room—winter now in this half of the planet, and beyond the greenglass an icy rain was beating down upon Tory—cutting blooms of spear-lilies and king's bryony, snowstars and the great shaggy summerbyes, for the Queen's chambers, when Bres came quietly in. She saw at once that beyond the quietness he was immoderately pleased with himself, and she guessed almost as swiftly that it had to do with Lykken.

He came to her, threading through the fragrant damp rows of flowers, and she offered him a cool cheek to kiss.

"I have great news for you," he said, baffled as ever at her continuing indifference.

"What news is that?"

"The King my father has given me charge of the case against Keltia; when we go to Ganaster it will be I who argue it before the High Justiciar."

"In spite of your recent doings on Lykken?" she murmured, pinching the heads off a few dead blooms.

"That has naught to do with it!" he snapped, nettled by the sarcasm she scarcely bothered to veil. "I came to ask if you would not wish to come with me to Ganaster," he said after a moment's pause. "If you do not care to—" He was even more astonished by the swift change in her: Almost she seemed to wake to warm life before his eyes.

"I should like to, very much," was all she said, but she did not pull away as she so often did when he put a hand on hers; encouraged, he pressed on.

"Basia, I would do more than that to please you—to make you think kindlier of me, and of the marriage."

"There is no need." Her voice was cool again, and she withdrew her hand from his. "I have made myself think so— kindly, as you say—long time now."

"That is not true. You may have accepted the fact of the alliance, but well do I know that I have not engaged your heart." She did not trouble to refute him, and Bres smiled bitterly. "So it was in my mind," he went on with dogged persistence, "that if we were to be together, away from Fomor, perhaps you might incline to me a little more—"

All at once she took pity on him, and put the thought of her own bleak future resolutely aside. There were worse fates far than being Queen of Fomor, consort to a king who seemed truly to love her . . . *But I will have to be his princess first*— Basilea took a flower from the sheaf before her, and folded it gently into Bres's hand, and looked up at him.

"Perhaps, indeed, I might."

Chapter 3

So the two kings and their heirs and their queens and their entourages journeyed to Ganaster, to the High Justiciary, there to settle between them the grievance that had festered for more than a score of years.

On the morning after the Kelts' arrival in the white city of Eribol, only city of size on all that planet, Fionnbarr rose before dawn, and having dressed himself in clothing that might have been worn by a man of half a hundred races or a dozen social stations, he went out of the palace where he and his parents and the rest of their company were lodged, to walk alone through the empty streets.

The sky was still gray, though with a rapidly growing rosiness to one quarter that betokened sunrise; the stone-paved streets were wet underfoot, with the dampness of dew and with the washwater which the early-rising merchants of Eribol sluiced over the pavements in front of their shops, in preparation for the day's trade.

Fionnbarr, who had been shivering a little under his thin russet mantle, welcomed the warmth that the sun began to throw upon his face and into his eyes. He was walking slowly now, getting hungry for his breakfast, having arrived by winding ways at the market district of the city: shops where the wares spilled out into the street, fruit and flowers and fresh-baked breads; tented stalls that purveyed everything from jewels to carpets to caged songbats. But the morning walk had more purpose to it than exercise, or even the satisfaction of curiosity: Fionnbarr had been taking careful meticulous note of all he saw, for anything and everything that might possibly be of use to him in the days of the trial to come.

The first thing that had struck him had been the number of aliens in the streets, and their sheer variety: In twenty minutes' strolling, he had seen representatives of surely a double score of races, humanoid and not in roughly equal proportions—nonhuman races that ranged from the blueskinned Thallo that dwelt on Inalery and nowhere else in the known worlds, to the Dakdaks, the biped furred marsupials who lived a nomad's life on the steppe-deserts of their hostile and beautiful planet. And human-oids aplenty: Already Fionnbarr had glimpsed several Coranians, and had passed them by on the far side of the street, lest he betray himself by the cold anger caused by the ancient grievance— many centuries older than the squabble with the Fomori that would be settled, one way or the other, here and now in Eribol. And of course there were the Ganastrians themselves, a small, agile, dark and handsome people; every one of whom, reflected Fionnbarr, probably had more of galactic law canon in a smallfinger than Keltia's Chief Brehon had in the whole of his massive mind. It was a question of what one lived in and with and among; and here in this city that was a sanctuary of the law, statutes and precedents and arguments breathed from the stones and hung like woodsmoke in the very air.

Coming round a corner in the market square, where the cano-pies of the stalls cast the footway into shadow, Fionnbarr found his sight suddenly dazzled by the full glare of the system's blazing white primary. Blinking in the light, he went forward blindly a few steps more and abruptly collided with an unseen figure. The force of the impact knocked him off his feet; as he rose, though his blurred vision, now jarred as well, still could not focus properly, he was aware that whoever—or whatever—he had blundered into had managed to remain upright, standing silhouetted against the sunlight.

"My sorrow for my clumsiness," he began politely, then his sight cleared and he found himself looking down into the face of a young woman. Tall she was, and so he had not so far to look as was usual with him; but it was well worth the looking. Some would think her not pretty, and they would be strictly correct to think so: Her face was too narrow, her brows too strongly marked, for prettiness. But beautiful she surely was; strikingly original, her hair and eyes a rich deep brown with touches of gold, her entire face alive with intelligence. Now, though, there was an overlay of apprehension, and apology, and interested attention, and excitement too, as at the doing of something new and daring, something possibly even forbidden . . .

"You have torn my skirt," she said; in that sweet low voice it was an observation merely, not a reproach.

Fionnbarr dragged his glance from her face to the hem of her skirt; yes, he could see it was undoubtedly torn, the heavy band of fine embroidery hanging away from the fabric.

"Then the honors are about even, lady," he said smiling, "for you have blooded me."

The girl looked in her turn where he indicated—the heels of his hands, rawscraped and bleeding from his violent contact with the paving-stones—then blushed and made some small sound. Deftly lifting the corner of the ruined skirt, she ripped off the hanging embroidery, tore it in two and neatly bound the halves across Fionnbarr's skinned palms.

"I hope that will suffice it, sir, until you come to your home and may better tend to it." She looked up into his face again, wondering at him: who was he, where was his home—for surely he was no man of Ganaster—and what business had he here . . . "It was my fault, truly; I was not watching where I went, being on an errand for my mistress—" She had begun to babble, and knew she was babbling; and since that was a thing she was most unused to do, the fact of it only flustered her the more, and she turned as if to flee.

"Wait—what is your name, lady, and where from?"

Fionnbarr had caught her, rather discourteously, by the sleeve; though she kept her head turned from him, her voice came clear.

"Sovay—I am called Sovay. I am a maid of honor to the Queen of Fomor. You may know we are here on Ganaster for a case to be heard before the High Justiciar."

Fomor . . . The word was like a knell in Fionnbarr's brain. As if from a great and echoing distance, behind the bell's clangor, he heard himself answering, and answering with a lie.

"And I am Kian, in the service of Prince Fionnbarr of Keltia. It seems that our master and mistress are unfriends, but that does not mean you and I must follow their example."

"Does it not?" She had turned back to him, and he was

entranced anew by her face, and absurdly delighted at the struggle he saw upon it: the knowledge that he must surely be a Kelt, and thus her people's enemy; set against that, the shy and undoubted attraction she was feeling.

Fionnbarr was feeling much the same struggle and attraction in his own mind. Ladies of Keltia had there been for him before now, most of them of higher birth and greater loveliness than this; but with none of them had he ever felt such instant and innate affinity, and by comparison to hers their prettiness seemed to his memory suddenly gaudy. *Yet is she a gallwyn, not only foreign but* Fomori! *What can I be thinking . . . moreover, if she is in service to Queen Melaan, she is of no lowly rank, and in no manner the sort for a light tumble—and nor would I wish her to be . . .*

"Sovay," repeated Fionnbarr, in the lilting accent that a tongue bred to the Gaeloch will give to Englic, with a smile at which her heart turned over. "That is like a word of ours, 'syvy'—the wild flowering strawberry that is shy and sweet and lovely. It is perhaps a blunt and graceless thing to ask you, but— I would meet you soon again, under perhaps less painful"— he turned up his bandaged palms, and she blushed anew—"circumstance. There is little time for us here as it is, and none to waste on protocol."

She seemed to share his determination, and for all her shyness she met his glance full on. "And I you," she said, and now she did not blush. "But send not to me; a message to my own maid—she is called Kathelin—will find me; we lodge in the palace at the head of the Street of Steps. Or, better, I will contrive to send to you, with word of where we may meet."

She gave him one quick incredulous smile, then hurried away, to vanish almost at once into the crowds now thronging the marketplace. Fionnbarr watched her go, himself dumbstruck at what had apparently been wrought here, then ran a hand unthinkingly over his beard. The touch of the embroidered silk, and the stinging pain in his scraped palm, called him back at once to reality, or at least to what seemed just then to pass for such.

With a sigh Fionnbarr began his own long walk back through the streets of Eribol, to where the Kelts' hired palace stood in spacious grounds beside the river. *Better it is I tend these scrapes myself,* he thought. *A skinfuser will make quick work of them, and it will save no end of explaining.* He paused, half-turning back to the square. *But though they be the first, I think these are by no means the worst wounds, nor yet the last, that I shall take here in Eribol . . .*

As she fled through the marketplace, dodging nimbly past any number of other possible collisions, Basilea's mind was in turmoil. She had, she freely admitted to herself, slipped out unchaperoned that morning in hopes of an adventure. A *small* adventure, nothing alarming; and now this was already so far beyond anything she had ever planned, or even imagined. *A Kelt* . . . The first man she had ever seen to make her heart beat, and more beside; and he must be one of an enemy race. *But he is not* himself *the enemy* . . . Still, there had been some secret about him, something kept back that had not been said; which ordinarily he might have, for he seemed as attracted to her as she to him, and that also was a new and wonderful thing.

And there was her own secret, which, sooner or later, if he were truly in the service of the Keltic prince, he would come to learn; and when he did, would he then turn from her in anger and disgust at her untruth? She did not think she could bear *that*; it had been a lie of sheer desperation only, for if she *had* told him the truth—that she was Basilea of Rhanos, *Lady* Basilea; not only a noblewoman of Fomor but the affianced of Fomor's heir—he would have been away up that street in an instant, to be seen again, if at all, only at a cold, correct distance. *Aye, when Fionnbarr his lord faces my lord before the High Justiciar, and I must be there, then. But I had sooner be torn by bears than lose my chance with him; whatever price be put on it after, and it will be a high one, this is more surely worth its cost than anything I have ever known, or likely ever will . . .*

And so thinking, Basilea went on up the wide cobbled street, to the Fomori lodgings near the Eastgate, composing her face and her mind alike to face her mistress—and her lord.

The Kelts and the Fomori, though of chiefest interest to the general populace, were by no means the only new arrivals on Ganaster. Even then, in a room of yet another palace not far from that same street, Strephon, Prince of Alphor, was preparing himself for his legist's duties.

I had not realized there would be so much with which I must be conversant, he thought, staring dismayed at the high-piled texts and computer billets that had been delivered to him by a servitor of the Justiciary. All of it was mere background information to the case he would so soon be helping to determine. He smiled, thinking of his father's last instructions, in the gold-walled stoa back at Escal-dun.

"What do you think they are up to, on Ganaster?" Errazill-jauna had asked his son, and Strephon had answered at once, as if he had conned this matter throughly, and had long had his answer ready.

"I think there are reasons within reasons within reasons," he had said to his father. "Like a set of those nesting boxes from Kuthera . . . I think that Ganaster would see an end to the hostilities between Fomor and Keltia; but Ganaster knows too that Keltia and the Cabiri have had enmity between *them* for longer far. Yet still they have asked us to sit upon the panel that will judge between Keltia and Fomor."

"And why is that?"

"They hope to force some sort of result," Strephon had said, "and are willing to bide the issue. Ganaster would like well to see a clear-cut siding here, that we should reveal ourselves for Fomor and against Keltia for all the worlds to see. And they think that by dragging us all to Eribol they will achieve that end."

In spite of himself, Errazill-jauna's old eyes had sparkled. "How right you are, and how dearly I would love to go to Ganaster myself to see it! But you, Strevi—you learn what you may of them both, and of Fionnbarr and Bres in especial, as they will be the ones with whom you must deal when you yourself are Emperor of the Cabiri. Take Azaco with you; she will be useful as always, and may find out as much or more from the royal ladies of Fomor and Keltia as you may from their lords. Helya too; it is time she began to learn politics, since she is to be your heir; or rather, since her sons are."

Strephon had wondered at that; wondered now, remembering. How had his father known? He had only come to *that* decision in his own mind barely two days before that farewell audience. No denying his father had been entirely correct, if prescient, for as yet Strephon's daughter Helior had no children at all, being but lately wed. But Strephon had indeed already determined to name her future offspring as his ultimate heirs. She would herself succeed him, of course, should he die untimely, but it was her unborn sons he looked to—one of them, the eldest most likely, though not of necessity, would be the next Cabiri Emperor after him. It had been a good match Azaco had made for her only daughter: Phano, scion of an ambitious Alphorian house, whose progeny ran to boys.

With an effort Strephon turned his attention back to the legal tangle that lay before him, and staring again at the horrid texts he began to laugh quietly. Whichever way this matter went in the end, it would be a blow to the loser of no mean proportions: whether for Bres, whose colossal stupidity in attacking Lykken had without doubt altered his case, or for Lasairían, who after the difficult start his reign had suffered had nevertheless managed to preserve Keltia's peace for more than a decade, and who would certainly wish to see that peace preserved longer still.

But even kings must know they cannot have all things their own way always, mused Strephon. *And that is something I must never forget for my own reign to come . . .* One way or another, the next fortnight would see a balked and angry monarch; not a pretty sight under any circumstances. Whether that monarch would be Lasairían of Keltia or Budic of Fomor depended now on the skill of their heirs and the luck of the law; on the consensus of the legists and the judgment of the High Justiciar. And it would not be long now before all that intricate, inevitable process would be put irrevocably in train: Tomorrow morning, at the third hour, the trial would begin.

In the meantime, he had much to read; time it was he made a start on it. Strephon settled into his chair and opened the first text.

As challenged party, the Kelts were the last to arrive at the great justice-hall that crowned Eribol's central hill like some majestic fane or high palace. But neither king nor god could command in that place the due that was the law's alone, and would have been fool to try.

Entering the barrel-vaulted Lawchamber, Fionnbarr, pacing behind the ceremonial usher—as chief defender for Keltia, he took precedence on this occasion over even the King his father—

saw the Fomori contingent standing in their place before the law-seat, waiting upon their adversaries' arrival.

Fionnbarr's gaze travelling onward lifted then to the Chair itself, and he came up short at the sight. He had known of course of the race of the present High Justiciar—it was certainly no secret, and made no differ whatsoever to his case, or to Fomor's, or for that matter to anything else—still, the knowing was but foreshock to the seeing.

Behind the stone rostrum, flanked on either side by the empanelled and red-robed legists, sat the High Justiciar herself: Celarain, a daughter of the Hail, the Eagle-people. She was thin to emaciation, or what would be so in a human; and very tall, taller than the Kelts, taller almost even than the Cheryth, and they the greatest of stature in all the known galaxy. The fine short feathers that covered her body were for the most part white, with metallic silver filaments and golden rachides that caught the light from the chamber's many lamps, and the long shapely fingers ended in tapering steel-colored talons. And then of course there was the amazing, the tremendous thing: the wings, folded now, their tips tucked neatly in behind her back, the great bowed double curve of them rising above her head, white with a blue flush, faintly pink where the morning light touched them through the windows.

Her face was humanoid, and massively intelligent: long, thin, with high prominent cheekbones; the eyes were dark with flecks of fire rimming the slitted irises. She was five hundred years old, in full prime for one of her race, who saw a thousand oftener than not.

Fionnbarr, bowing first to her, then to the legists, last of all to his adversary Bres, felt the depth of those eyes as they touched on him, and the weight of that intelligence, and wondered briefly what it would be like to be alive for a thousand years and more—such a being would have a very different outlook on life from that held by lesser-lived creatures; and how might that not affect her judgment?

But Celarain gave no sign that she had noticed his attention, and at her infinitesimal nod an officer of the court struck a silver bell with a silver hammer, the melodious chimes signalling the start of the session. *It has begun*, thought Fionnbarr with a thrill, and turned as Bres turned to face the court.

The legal preliminaries took up most of that first morning: introducing and affirming the principals' acceptability before the Chair—legists as well as plaintiffs, for all that Ganaster itself had summoned them; then the charges must be read out, suit and countersuit—and even at this late date Celarain could choose to dismiss the case . . . As the morning droned on, Fionnbarr found his attention wandering farther, and more often, than was probably good for him or for his case. *Still,* he thought, *these are but juristic protocols, and Tujen and our other brehons will mark if there be aught I need to mind . . .*

He ran a covert gaze down the line of legists sitting on Celarain's either hand, in stone chairs behind a long marble railing. Only about half those seated there were humanoid in form; the remainder were aliens of various races. However different they might be, all had been chosen by the Justiciary itself to sit upon this most unusual of courts. For the legists empanelled before Celarain were not as other, common jurists: Only half their number were impartial, for one thing; the others were sworn partisans of either litigant party, to such number as must equal that of their impartial colleagues. And it was these impartial legists, of course, that each petitioner would do his utmost best to sway.

Fionnbarr's glance paused on one who sat three places down on Celarain's left. *Strephon, heir of the Cabiri . . .* Fionnbarr knew the face well from the dossiers he had been given to study. Knew the policies and the politics behind the face: Though his particular dynastic house had not long been seated upon Alphor's throne, and none too firmly seated there at that until just the last reign or so, Strephon would in time inherit from Errazill-jauna his father a strong and ever-expanding empire.

And a greedy one too, thought Fionnbarr with all the old distaste rising up undiminished. *In all the centuries from Atland to Alphor, whether they call themselves Telchines or Coranians, that race has never changed and never will so. No planet too poor or too small for them to scoop up, like piggish children at a feast, stuffing rather than savoring. Well, if they think to try to gobble down Keltia, they will find themselves choking on too difficult a morsel. Unless they should invite Fomor to help them carve us up . . .* But such a union was on the face of it most unlikely: Neither the Coranians nor the Fomori pulled well in double harness, and they would not be like to prosper as yokemates. Still, unlikelier pairs than that had in time past made common cause against a common foe, and Keltia was surely that to both . . .

Bres was holding forth again, Fionnbarr noticed with irritation, and he himself was in no mood to pay heed to the Fomorian prince's pre-trial bombast; there would be enough of that in the days to come. Looking sidewise to where the spectators sat in the outer court precincts, Fionnbarr saw Bres's mother, Melaan, a handsome dark-haired woman, where she sat among her ladies. Then, with surprise and gladness quick and sharp as a slap, he saw Sovay, small and quiet beside the Fomorian queen, dressed in a plain blue cloak and dark red gown.

He knew that she had seen and recognized him, for her head was lowered and her eyes cast down to her lap; but her cheeks slowly reddened as he watched her, and her fingers twisted nervously in her long brown braids, and after a while she dared a quick glance up at him. He smiled, but she only flushed the more and dropped her eyes again. Then the queen leaned over to whisper somewhat to her, and with an air of thankfulness plain to Fionnbarr even at that distance, Sovay rose from her seat and slipped quietly from the chamber.

Though he watched for her return from her errand for her mistress, Fionnbarr did not see her again that day. After the daymeal recess, the session wore on, and Bres continued to monopolize the jurists' ear, and the Kelts' patience wore thinner, and she did not come.

But when Fionnbarr returned, tired and peevish, to his lodgings that night, he found a message waiting for him. The tightly folded billet was scribed to one Kian, and left in care of Prince Fionnbarr, and for a moment he stared at it in total bewilderment. Then he remembered, and his face lighted, and he broke the seal to read the few lines within.

The message was from Sovay, directing him to an inn—not one of the palatial establishments in the center of the city, but a humbler place, as he found when he went there an hour later, old and small and cheerful, on a tree-lined square in the oldest quarter of Eribol, where the plashing of seven fountains was the loudest sound to be heard.

When Fionnbarr entered the inn, and gave the name of Kian to the master, he found that he was indeed expected, and an incurious servitor conducted him upstairs to a chamber in an inner courtyard wing, removed even from the square's infrequent traffic—a well-appointed room where a fire burned on the hearth, and heavy draperies hung at the windows.

When the door closed behind the servant, the curtain to the inner chamber was suddenly pulled back, and Sovay was there with him. She had changed her attire from the morning's plain red gown, he saw with approval, and was now clad in a rich chamber-robe of gold brocade and a fine silk shift; her hair, newly washed, fell loose and curling almost to her knees, and smelled of roses and fernwater.

"I am still Kian," he said softly, as if in apology to a protest she had not made, and taking her hand he raised it to his lips.

She shivered at the touch, but her fingers tightened around his, and with her other hand she brushed back his long hair where it had fallen forward over his face.

"And I Sovay," she answered. "No other names in this place . . ."

"I did not think to see you in the court today," he said, "though I hoped that I might, as much as I feared to have you see me . . . to have you learn that I was—" But her eyes widened with denial and warning, and instead he heard himself asking, "Did you complete your errand for your lady?"

"My lady! Oh, you mean the Queen's grace . . . yes; yes, I did so. No great chore, she is not a difficult mistress; but by the time it was done, the hour was late, and I was clear across the city, so I did not trouble to return to the court." She had moved away from him a little as she spoke, to stand near the fire, and herself now spoke the name she had just forbidden him to say. "To learn you were the Prince himself— Almost I did not come here tonight."

"But you would have come here to meet the Prince's man . . . and for all that, you did come in any case." Fionnbarr closed the distance between them again. "I swear to you it shall make no differ."

"No!" The cry was sharp and full of warning, and he looked down at her, astonished. "No, swear me no swearings, I pray you. No promises or pledges. This is enough, this now."

"*Is* it enough?" asked Fionnbarr.

She took both his hands and drew him behind the curtain to the inner alcove. "It must be."

She woke when he did in the cool rainy dawn; startled at first to find herself there, then snuggled down next to him again, loath to leave the bed's soft warmth, doubly reluctant to leave him.

So, then, that is done, she thought, with a kind of half-dazed wonder; the wonder was not unmixed with desire renewed, and she caught the echo of a triumphant little mocking thought: *I have chosen my own man, and it was not Bres. I chose as I desired*—I, Basilea, *not my father's obedient daughter nor yet Bres's ratified betrothed, and I am not sorry but so very glad, and perhaps Bres will now no longer want me . . .*

Fionnbarr, aware of none of this, slid an arm beneath her and pulled her closer. "What is the hour, lady?"

"Nearly dawn, and time we were gone from here."

His arms did not loosen. "A little longer."

She returned his kiss, then unwillingly freed herself. Already, though he did not know it and she chose to ignore it, she was becoming Basilea again, and Sovay was beginning to fade as the light grew outside the windows.

"Nay," she said tenderly. "There is the court, and I must return to my mistress before my absence is noted."

"Shall I see you at today's hearing?" he asked, flinging back the coverlets and yelping as his feet touched the bare cold floor.

"I think not." Basilea gave him a teasing smile. "Else I might begin to cheer for your victory, and not my own Prince's. Not that I think he *deserves* to win, but I must not say, nor show it in public."

Fionnbarr had nearly finished dressing. "Do you know the Prince well, then? I hear such a note of misliking in your voice when you do speak of him."

She stiffened momentarily, then reached out for her undergown and pulled it over her head. "I know him only from proximity," she said carefully, "for that I am near to the Queen his mother . . . But I have seen how he deals with others, and I do not think well of him for it." *There; that should ring honest enough . . .*

It seemed that it had, for Fionnbarr turned to her with sympathy in his face. "Then I can find it in me to pity him." He looked away, suddenly shy again, and so he did not see the look of radiance that flashed over her face, enough to light the dim room. "Shall I see you again?"

"If you do wish it."

Fionnbarr took her hand again and gravely kissed it, but with a tenderness and an insistence together that the gesture had not had the previous night.

"I can think of naught I might wish more greatly."

Chapter 4

Ah, gods, the everlasting disproportion of it all, thought Fionnbarr, waiting for Celarain to call the day's session to order. *Twenty years and more to get this quarrel to Ganaster, and the inside of a fortnight to settle it. Surely there must be a better way than this . . .* But he knew that there was not, and that such delay was a tool and strategy of the Justiciary, only the gods and the Justiciars themselves knowing the hows and whyfors of it.

He cut his glance sidewise, to where the legists were filing in to take their chairs. It had been ten days since the case had begun; both sides had had a chance to speak and a chance to refute, and now today Fionnbarr would begin the summation of Keltia's case. By Tujen Kerival's tally, more than half of the legists were by now inclined to Keltia, and also according to Tujen—a veteran observer of such matters, after all—more than half of those had been so from the first. Even some of the sworn Fomori partisans had over the past few days exhibited a plain and undisguised exasperation with Bres and with his actions concerning Lykken. *And that is no real surprise either; by no means is it the first time that Fomori stupidity has worked to Keltia's advantage, and surely it will not be the last . . .*

Fionnbarr allowed himself a moment's thought of matters closer to his heart than that: Sovay, and the memories of the time they had spent together; and despite his best efforts his face betrayed the tenderness he felt. *Never did I think I could feel so for anyone; and thrice never so for a gallwyn . . .* But though his days were spent in the courts arguing the case against Bres, his nights had been passed in the upstairs chamber at the little inn, with Sovay in the wide curtained bed. He shifted a little in his chair. *Ah, soon there will be an end to this sleeve-and-cover stealth, my Syvy; I know you detest it as surely as do I. It has been necessary, but soon, perhaps, no longer—you will see, and you will know that I am right . . .*

But Celarain had fixed him with a certain glance of hers—the one that seemed to bore straight through its victim into the midst of the week yet to come—and Fionnbarr reddened, absurdly certain that she had read his thought, and knew his secret.

"My lord of Keltia," came the silvery voice, calm as ever, though the wings rustled a little behind her head. "You may begin your argument."

Another three days, and it had come to the day of closing argument. It took most of that morning for Fionnbarr to restate his chief points: the long history of Keltia's side of the Lykken matter; Aoife's admittedly indiscreet actions; Lykken's undeniable pleadings, attested to under oath in this very court; Fomor's unsubtle pressurings; Bres's utterly illegal show of force. He argued cogently and he argued well; most Kelts possessed the gift of easy persuasion, and Fionnbarr had allied that natural fluency to twelve years' schooling at the Hill of Laws.

Concluding his remarks—and nicely timing it for the customary daymeal recess—he risked a glance at the legists. Their faces revealed nothing, as usual; save only for Strephon's, and his face showed, again as usual, cool amusement. *That one is trouble,* thought Fionnbarr, *trouble now, and trouble when he comes to be Cabiri Emperor . . .* And that last just might not be so very distant an event, according to many informed sources: Strephon's father, the aged and ailing Errazill-jauna, had taken a turn for the worse over the past fortnight. Only the summons to sit as legist, which could be declined only for extremely grave cause—and which in practice was almost never refused, for fear of a time when those who begged off legist's duty might themselves stand before the High Justiciar, and would need then all Ganaster's goodwill—only that summons had brought Strephon to Eribol, and kept him now.

And I wonder what will happen when the old jackal has gone to his gods at last, mused Fionnbarr, gathering up his books and notes and rejoining his own father. Not that Strephon and his Imperial sire were especially close, so that the heir would be inconsolable when it fell on him to take the Cabiri Throne. As to after that—Fionnbarr had heard tales of Strephon's own progeny: a pair of princes of very little brain; a few younger demiprinces, sons of co-wives and concubines; and a princess, the eldest of all of them—Helior, her mother's pet and her father's pride, here now with them in Eribol. Fionnbarr had glimpsed her at a distance: a dark-haired beauty, not overly tall, who looked as clever and as vicious—and as full of sleek grace—as a firead.

He was not the only one, he knew, to make such a judgment: But on Alphor, the Imperial heirship—etcheko-primu, it was called, in the Coranians' own barbarous tongue—was solely in the gift of the Emperor. He could bestow it upon a pigkeeper if he thought it best for the realm; it was no surprise that Strephon, in the opinion of many, should favor his daughter as etcheka after him—or if not Helior herself, then surely her sons to come.

Fionnbarr shrugged inwardly. That would be for his own heir, and Bres's, to deal with; for now, it would be the three of them here present—Strephon and Bres and he himself—to carry on the ancient rivalries.

His mother had come up behind him, and he turned to salute her with a smile. "Your Majesty."

Gwyneira laughed, and tucking her hand into the crook of his arm led him out of the bench enclosure. "My majesty has been spending some very instructive hours listening to the opinions of the old-hand observers," she said. "You would be surprised, I'd wager, how many folk come here to listen, or to study, or simply to be entertained."

Fionnbarr grinned. "I hope we are found good value; I should hate to bore or weary anyone, though by this time doubtless these same watchers know more of the law of the case than I. Certainly more than Bres—"

"That *would* take but little . . . Still their opinion is that you will win most handily. Keltia has too clear a case, they say, and you are presenting it too eloquently, *I* say—though they concur on that also—for Fomor to have much chance with Celarain."

As they emerged into the strong noon sunshine, Gwyneira gave her son a searching look. "Are you well, Barraun?" she asked, touching the back of her hand to his forehead in the age-old gesture of a worried mother. "There have been times these past days I have thought you sickening for something, and other times when you have such a look about you as I have never before seen you wear. Is it that you have met someone to take your fancy?'' she added teasingly. ''I have noted some very handsome lasses here in Eribol; no surprise—or displeasure—to me or to your father if you have found one to suit you.''

Fionnbarr blushed.

That night for the first time he arrived at the trysting place before Sovay; when she entered the chamber an hour later, a little breathless from her haste through the dark streets, she gave a gasp of wonder and delight.

Flowers filled every inch and corner of the chamber: sheafs of roselilies, tall queenflowers, snowbells with their delicate scent, branches of dark blue lilac, even bunches of the little red wild-flower called flame-of-the-ground. She bent her head to breathe deep of a timanth's clean wild fragrance; when she looked up at Fionnbarr, tears stood in her eyes.

''So beautiful—but you had no need.''

''Ah, but I did, so. Come and sit; I have a thing to say to you.'' He drew her over to a plush-cushioned bench set invitingly before the fire, and seating himself beside her, drew a deep steadying breath and took both her hands in both of his.

''Come with me when we leave Ganaster,'' he said, his eyes fixed on hers, ''and wed with me in Keltia. My kindred will embrace you, my people will adore you, and I will love you and keep to you forever.''

The face upturned to his was a study in tension of contrast: alight with her love for him, her happiness at his asking; yet pale with some unknown fear, and all overlaid with a sickening dull despair. The contrasts battled a moment in silence; then—

''It is not possible.''

''Is it because I am a prince, and heir to Keltia?'' he asked, not understanding that she had refused him, not knowing which side, if any, had won the battle he had seen in her face. ''Nay, *look* at me, Syvy—or is it that I am plain and simple a Kelt, and for all our joy these past nights you can still think of me only as an enemy?''

Her outcry was immediate and genuine. ''Nay! *Never* that! But—there is a reason.'' She was silent, and Fionnbarr waited for her to choose her words and her moment. "I knew that you would ask me this," said Basilea at last, defeated, as if all her strength had gone into the vehemence of her denial that his race was the cause of her refusal. "And I knew that when you did ask I must refuse; not for that I do not love you, Barraun, for by the gods of my people I shall love you all my life and after, but for that—other arrangements have been made for me by my family."

"You mean that you are already betrothed?"

She nodded miserably, not looking at him for fear of what she might see, or fail to see, in his face: love and tenderness changing to revulsion and distaste, even contempt. "Not by any choice or will of my own, and I do not love him; but a contract signed, sealed and settled all the same, and I must abide by its terms."

"Contracts are built to be broken," said Fionnbarr airily; he was recovering his poise and his wits, and knew that he must argue his case for himself as carefully as he had been arguing Keltia's case before Celarain. "I have never made practice of trading upon my rank, but if your kin were to be told that a prince—a Keltic one, but a prince nevertheless—had asked for your hand—"

He did not understand the desperate little choke of laughter, half sob, half mirth, that escaped her then, nor the violence with which she turned away from him.

"Nay, not even then, I fear! Oh, Barraun, if you love me, do not press me. I said on our first night that I sought neither promises nor pledges of you, that this would be enough—and it has been, and it is all there can be. Do not make it more painful than it must be; no more, I beg you."

Fionnbarr took her chin between his fingers and turned her head round to him again. "No more then, for now, but only this." Before she could pull her hand away, he had slipped a ring from his finger—a great amethyst set in dark heavy gold that he had worn since boyhood—and placed it on hers. She stared down at it disbelievingly, then began to weep: neither sobs nor sound, just a face held expressionless as cold marble, tears silently streaming down her cheeks.

Fionnbarr pulled her close against him. "Nay, Syvy-fach, there is naught to weep for . . . Only think on what I have said, and wear the ring so that you do not forget. We have yet some time before we return to Keltia—after all, the case has not yet been settled—and your folk will be here just as long; there is time.''

Basilea looked up at him, her face glittering with tears in the light from the fire. "Nay, that is one of the things we do *not* have. Let us waste no more of it.''

Her loving that night had an edge of desperation to it that it had not possessed before; Fionnbarr, a little astonished at the fierceness of her passion, was more astonished still when, wakening at dawn, he found her gone from the bed. Her clothing and cloak too were gone, so plainly she had left the inn, and as he himself dressed he pondered what her departure, with no word of farewell, might in fact bode.

When he returned to his own lodgings, he found what it might bode for him, now, at this moment: In his chamber, in a chair beside the windows, sat Queen Gwyneira, fully dressed and full awake, her face expectant of the explanation she clearly had no intention of forgoing.

"Well, Barraun,'' she said. "What is her name, and where from?''

"If you know so much, then, why do you trouble to *ask* me?'' cried Fionnbarr in despair; it was going on now for nine of the clock, and though as it was not a court day he had no need to be anywhere in especial, he would sooner be anywhere else in all the known universe than here in this room with his mother. For the past three hours, Gwyneira had harrowed him as only she knew how, and he was by this time a bundle of scraped and jangled nerves.

She will have it all out of me in the end—why do I even bother to try to hide it . . .

"I know that for the past fortnight you have not once slept in your own bed,'' said his mother calmly.

"You knew? Then—''

"So I made certain inquiries in certain quarters,'' said Gwyneira. "The inn-master in Fountain Street was most particularly helpful. The one thing he could not supply, however, was the lady's true name.''

"Well, do not look to *me* to give it you,'' said Fionnbarr bitterly. "I can scarcely believe it of you, madam, that all this time you knew and did not say. Have you told my father of this?''

''Nay, Barraun, I have told no one; and as for knowing and not saying, perhaps I failed you there . . . But think a little, Prince Fionnbarr; think of Keltia, if you will not think of yourself or of your father and me: She is a gallwyn, a foreigner; you have known her barely a fortnight! I have never presumed to pry overmuch into your loves, Barraun, whatever I may have thought of them in my heart, but this— There is of course no question of it, but could you even think of making such a one as this Queen of Keltia to follow me?''

''I have asked her,'' he said simply.

''You have *what*?''

''Oh, do not fear, she declined the asking; most definite and final.''

Well, that at least is something *to be said for her*, thought Gwyneira with deep relief. Plainly the girl had some sort of breeding after all, some sense of what was right and fitting, not to seek to wed a lovesick prince even though he would have her . . . Still, it was astounding all the same: Fionnbarr was the most sedate, the most restrained, the most conservative of all her children; that he should conduct himself in so uncharacteristic a manner—offering queenship to some galláin lightskirt that he scarcely knew—

''Will you tell my father?'' asked Fionnbarr again.

Gwyneira sighed. ''Nay; the King has graver matters on his mind just now—as should you—so I will say nothing of this to him. Only let you promise me faithfully, Barraun, to have no more to do with this—this lady.''

Fionnbarr gave her a look compounded of anger, inflexibility, and, strangely, sorrow. ''Nay, Majesty; that I will not.''

It was not until after she had left her son's room, balked and angry, that Gwyneira knew what had been different about him: Fionnbarr's ring, the big amethyst that she herself had given him on his seventeenth birthday, and that he never took off even to bathe or sleep, had been nowhere to be seen.

At very near the same hour that Gwyneira was missing the amethyst ring from her son's hand, Bres was noticing it on his betrothed's forefinger, and with an instinct both direct and cunning he sensed at once its message. But he had concealed his suspicions, merely asking with a casual indifferent curiosity where she had found such a fine jewel, that he himself should give her such trinkets; and without an eyelash's flicker Basilea had replied that she had purchased it from a goldsmith's stall in the marketplace—had even, rashly, named the shop. Rash enough, for Bres was making personal inquiries there before the morning was out, and learned to his chagrin that no such jewel as he described had even been offered there for sale, let alone sold the previous day to a Fomorian lady.

So all day long Bres had brooded, and now, at sunset, he received a certain message from those he had set to watch Basilea's comings and goings. When she slipped out of the palace by a side door into the gardens, muffled in a dark cloak, a half-mask over her face such as Ganastrian ladies wore when out after nightfall, he was waiting in the shadows, and, himself cloaked in concealment, he followed her at a distance through the streets, and saw her go in at the door of the inn in the Street of the Fountains.

He was there too when she left at dawn, saw her come out into the mist-drenched street and peer fearfully around her; saw her turn to the cloaked man who followed close behind her, saw his head bend down to hers and her hand lift lovingly to his cheek, before they parted.

And, as the man passed by a lighted window, Bres saw his face brief and unmistakable in the sweep of illumination, though even then he could scarcely believe it, and yet it seemed somehow so inevitable that he should have guessed it long since: Fionnbarr of Keltia.

There was a court session that next afternoon, and at last, after making her own deliberations and polling the legists on the merits of the case, Celarain would hand down her final judgment.

Bres seemed to have other matters on his mind, though, and despite some sharp words from his father did not join King Budic or the other members of the Fomori delegation in their speculating. Basilea too seemed preoccupied, and when she excused herself from attendance on the queen and left the palace, many noticed that Bres bestirred himself at once and went after her.

Keeping well back in the crowded streets—it was market day in Eribol, the narrow thoroughfares choked with people—Bres soon saw where she was headed: down to the river beyond the city gates, where there were many ornamental gardens and landscaped walks frequented by the city's inhabitants, on fine days or even foul ones; doubtless for a prearranged rendezvous with her lover, Bres thought, and fury rose up in him as he strained to keep sight of her slim hurrying back.

But before she reached the gate, a man emerged suddenly from a little side-lane, taking her arm and guiding her through the thinning crowds, and Bres could see her face profiled as she turned to look up at her companion.

That was more than enough for him; he increased stride, coming up behind the pair in only a minute or two, and reaching out he caught Basilea roughly by the arm. She cried out as he spun her to face him, and then Fionnbarr, for it was of course he, had turned also, and the two rivals stared long and hard into each other's eyes.

For that first brief instant of horror it seemed to Basilea that time had actually stopped; but for an instant only, and then it all seemed to be moving much too fast. She had in her darker moments wondered often how it might happen that her two princes might meet; and now the moment was at hand, and it was no moment that she had foreseen.

She began to move, to put herself between them, but Fionnbarr had already thrust a protective arm in front of her, and Bres glared down at her from across that barrier.

"Madam," he said looking not at her but at Fionnbarr, "I think it best if you return to the palace; Her Majesty my mother has been asking for you."

Fionnbarr felt Sovay—for as yet he still knew her by no other name—flinch a little against his arm, then with great dignity she stepped out of that shelter, bowed her head to him with that same air of formality, and vanished up the street. She was barely out of sight when Bres, who had been staring at Fionnbarr like some cur about to bare fang and fight, made as if to speak. But Fionnbarr was quicker.

"How comes it that the Prince of Fomor is sent out by his mother to recall a maid of honor playing truant from her duties?"

And is that truly what she told you . . . Though Fionnbarr's tone had been light it had been warning, and Bres looked savage. "How comes it," he said presently, "that the Prince of Keltia sees fit to tumble the future queen of Fomor like some common strumpet in a backstreet inn?"

It gave Bres some satisfaction to see the white shock on Fionnbarr's face. *I had not thought he knew—not even a Kelt could stoop so low as that a-purpose—but now I am sure of it.* She, *though; she knew* well *who he was, and for that, oh, by the gods, she shall pay* . . .

"She said her name was Sovay, that she was but maidservant to Queen Melaan your royal mother," Fionnbarr was saying in the voice of a sleeptalker, staring dazed up the empty street.

"Aye, she would! She would *not* have told you she is in fact the Lady Basilea of Rhanos, daughter to an ancient and noble family, and betrothed since the age of thirteen to the heir of Fomor."

"But you were not then—"

"Nay, I was *not* heir to Fomor, not then. That was my elder brother, Budic, Crown Prince until he was killed in a skirmish at Halistra—by the guns of your uncle Prince Elharn's warship."

"So you inherited his place as your father's heir, and his betrothed as well. Did Sov—did the Lady Basilea have aught to say in the matter? Or was she simply passed along from one brother of House Corserine to the next, like an outgrown tunic?"

To judge from the murder that leaped in Bres's eyes, only the fact that they stood in a public street, and were both of them unarmed, prevented him from drawing on Fionnbarr then and there; if there had been steel to hand Fionnbarr would surely have died where he stood. It took Bres the better part of a minute to control himself, but when he spoke again his voice was cold and courteous.

"I think it best, Prince of Keltia, if this matter between us be kept apart from the dispute we have come here to Ganaster to settle. But, go that decision this afternoon howsoever it may, after it is declared I offer you a trial of another sort." And drawing off his gauntlet he flung it full in the other's face.

Fionnbarr made no move to catch it, letting it strike him across the cheek; then, holding Bres's gaze, he bent to scoop it up, only his fingers clenched around the soft leather betraying his own anger.

"And I have the pleasure to accept," he said smiling. "May I take it that your friends will call on mine? Whom shall I tell them to expect?"

"The lords Resler, Thyle, and Corsin Letro. On whom shall I tell them to call?"

"Prince Faolan, the Master of Douglas; Sithney Countess of the Cathedine; and Master Resoghen Keresk," said Fionnbarr, naming the three close friends who had accompanied him from Keltia. "The terms may be agreed upon among the six of them."

"Well enough for my part," said Bres, standing aside to allow Fionnbarr to pass. "As for that other matter, *that* the High Justiciar shall settle."

He stared after Fionnbarr until he too had disappeared among the crowd, then himself began to walk aimlessly, until it was time for him to betake himself to the Houses of the Law.

Well—if there is no justice to be found here, he thought, *then at least I shall have the chance to make a little justice of my own; and we shall see then who will have the right of it.*

Chapter 5

When he arrived at the law-chamber, Fionnbarr saw that Bres was already there; saw too that Sovay—*Basilea!*, he corrected himself—was seated in her old place beside the Fomorian queen. But she would not look at him, and neither would she look at Bres, but kept her eyes fixed on her lap or on the tall white figure of the High Justiciar seated behind the marble judge's bench.

Celarain wasted no time, tapping the silver bell for silence herself and not waiting for her officer to do so; and using no notes, she began at once to give her verdict.

"The High Justice thanks the petitioners here before me, Fomor and Keltia, for electing to resolve their differences on this matter in peaceful fashion rather than bringing their two nations to *overt* war"—the slight emphasis plainly a slap at Bres for his raid on Lykken, and the first hint Celarain had given in all the course of the trial of how she was likely to judge.

"I thank Lykken here present for its forbearance and its facts," she continued, "and I thank the empanelled legists for their care in considering every aspect of this very interesting case. Now I give the verdict of the High Justice, which shall be binding upon you, Fomor, and you, Keltia, according to the terms of the Protocol of Banna you have both acknowledged: In this matter I find absolutely for Keltia." She waited a little for the tumult to die down; when it did not, the great wings mantled behind her head, and silence fell over the room like sudden snow. "The system of Lykken is declared a Keltic protectorate, as it has attested under oath that it so wishes to be. Fomor shall be levied against, in an amount and kind to be determined by this office on a date to be decided, and Fomor is ordered in addition to pay all court costs for this case.''

That was all; Bres began a heated protest, but Celarain, standing up at her seat, extended her wings in anger and warning, and the protest died unspoken. In a stunned silence, the protagonists of the case watched her glide from the chamber, the legists following after; though not without a knowing glance from Strephon at Bres and Fionnbarr alike.

In the crush of people thronging the outside corridors, Fionnbarr caught up with Basilea and, taking her by the arm, glancing round to make sure they were unobserved, drew her into a small anteroom adjoining the main chambers and shut the door behind them.

"Are you mad?" she cried, her voice shaking. "What if they find us in here?"

"It would suit me well enough if they do," replied Fionnbarr, seating himself upon the nearest desk. But she would not look at him, not even when he took her hand where she still wore the amethyst and raised it to his lips.

"Leave here and come with me. I will make you queen of Keltia."

"You will not," she said after a while. "And now I shall tell you why not: Because I am to be Queen of Fomor."

"Only if you choose to be, Basilea," he said quietly.

At that her head jerked up, eyes wide and startled as a fawn's who hears the hunter's step. "You *know*! But how could you?" Then understanding came, and the fawn fled.

"He told me himself," said Fionnbarr, and he did not need to speak the name of Bres, any more than she did need to hear it spoken.

"I would have told you myself, for my sake as well as yours," said Basilea tonelessly. "And soon, too—it could not have gone on much longer, that you did not know . . ."

Fionnbarr said nothing, but pulled her thin shoulders gently toward him. After a moment's resistance she let the stiffness go out of her, and crumpled against him with a sound—half sigh, half moan—that nearly tore him apart. He had not told her, nor would he, of the challenge and acceptance that had passed between him and Bres following that telling; only prayed that she would never come to hear of it, that Bres would never be fool enough, or cruel enough, to tell her.

Then she straightened her shoulders, and stood away from his side, and Fionnbarr knew from the sudden remove of her bearing that she was lost to him. "There will be a feast tomorrow night, I have heard," she said then. "King Budic and your father King Lasairían have agreed to it, and will announce it publicly in a few minutes, if they have not already done so. A feast of reconciliation, they are calling it"—for a moment her voice cracked on the word, or the thought—"and we must be there, you and I; and we must be there as strangers."

"If you accept my proffer, we might be there as living earnest of the bond of friendship between Fomor and Keltia."

"It cannot be!" Basilea's control shattered at last. "Why do you think I kept my very name from you as long as I did? Because I knew that from your love you would offer, and I knew too that from my love I must refuse. That you offered to Sovay, maid of honor to Queen Melaan, and not to Basilea of Rhanos, I shall treasure for the rest of my days. But those days shall be spent at Bres's side, not yours; because I must."

"You cannot."

"I can, and I will . . . Barraun, the time is not yet come, if indeed it ever does, when the heir of Keltia may wed a foreign woman, and a Fomori woman at that . . . I pretended I did not know you were the Prince until I could no longer pretend ignorance; I kept my name from you because I wanted you, wanted this fortnight we have had together to last me down all the years of duty. And now I have had it, and I will never let it go from me; but you I *must* let go, and you must do the same for me. I wish you better fortune in the lady you shall come to wed than I have found in my own lord. Surely you see it must be so."

"Surely I do not! Syvy—"

"Then you will have to learn." With one quick fluid move she twisted the amethyst ring off her finger and thrust it into his hands; then she was out of his reach and past him, flinging wide the door, and her running footsteps echoed down the hall until he could no longer hear them.

When Fionnbarr emerged on the wide marble steps leading up to the Houses of the Law from the square outside, he saw a strange thing: Below him in the open space, Budic and Lasairían were standing deep in apparently amicable conversation. Their queens stood a little apart, with their respective courtiers and ladies; neither Bres nor Basilea was to be seen, and Fionnbarr could think only the worst of that.

Coming up beside his mother, he gave her a questioning look, but she only shook her head, and he turned his attention to the two kings.

"So that Keltia may know Fomor to be no graceless loser," Budic was saying, and now he held out both hands to Lasairían, and the Keltic king clasped them unhesitatingly, "it is my pleasure to invite Your Majesties and all your folk to a banquet on the morrownight. The Justiciary has been gracious enough to offer the use of their grounds along the river, and all may see how, justice having prevailed, the case is settled in peace."

"And so that Fomor may know Keltia to be no gloating victor," replied Lasairían, "it is my pleasure to share the hosting of that feast with Your Graces of Fomor, so that all may see how that peace you spoke of may turn into friendship at the board."

And in that moment, seeing their honest faces and hearing their earnest words, some believed that perhaps it was even possible.

Prince Fionnbarr was not among them. Though the balance of that day, and many hours of the night also, was spent in minute rehashing of the trial, Fionnbarr, impatient of the endless what-ifs and self-satisfied pedantry of the brehons and jurisconsults, had left them to it as soon as he could safely do so, and had hurried through the now-familiar turnings that led to the inn on the square of the fountains.

But though the innkeeper, knowing now who his guest had been, greeted him with a combination of roguishness and awe, he had regretfully informed his royal visitor that the young lady he sought was not there.

"And great sorrow it is to have to tell you, lord; but there it is, a servant came to settle accounts with me for the room-rent, and told me that the chambers would no longer be required." He looked as if he would have said more, and more gladly still would have heard more, but a closer look at Fionnbarr convinced him otherwise, and he merely repeated his regrets—doubtless sincere ones, for the rooms had been far from inexpensive—and offered to send a servitor to escort the prince back to his own lodgings.

But Fionnbarr shook his head, not even hearing the man's bletherings, and went out alone into the dark street. *And is that all the farewell we are to have, then?* he wondered with bitterness. *That moment this afternoon—nay, it cannot be; any road, surely she will be at this feast my father and old Budic have concocted between them. It will go hard indeed if I cannot manage at least a few minutes with her; if only just to bid her a proper goodbye, and to wish her well for the future. Might we not have that last, before duty claims us both for the rest of our lives?*

But he had no answer to that, and as he walked slowly back to the Kelts' hired palace Fionnbarr did not even notice when the sound of the fountains faded behind him.

On the night following the giving of the verdict, pavilions were pitched on a wide greensward behind the House of the Law, a smooth, manicured lawn that sloped gently down to the tree-edged riverbank. Torches glowed softly in baskets atop silver standards thrust into the lush turf; bright pennants and lanterns were strung from tree to tree; a dancing-lawn was laid down, smooth and even as velvet, beneath the neatly pollarded branches of a circle of goldwillows. Within the great central pavilion, long tables were laden with precious plate set out upon brocade runners, and servitors stood waiting to bring in platters and decanters as soon as the guests, and most particularly the guests of honor, should arrive.

They arrived upon the same stroke of the hour, most carefully prompt so that neither king should appear to be host above the other; they met outside the gates, embraced as friends embrace, and then proceeded with their queens and entourages to the pavilions upon the lawn. Celarain was there, among other distinguished guests, in a robe of blue and silver, looking no less impressive in a social setting than she did in the seat of the High Justice; there were other legists—including Strephon of Alphor—and justiciars from every level of the Courts; civic dignitaries of Eribol, lords of commerce and envoys from many worlds.

"This is no feast of friendship, for any sake," remarked

Lasairían to Gwyneira as they paced, her hand upon his outstretched arm, between the rows of smiling and bowing guests, bowing and smiling themselves to left and right as they did so. "It is merely another form of warfare."

"Better to fight at the table than on the field," murmured his wife. "Though the tongue be sharper than the blade, yet the casualties are as a rule fewer. It will soon be over, Laisren, and then we may go home."

"Not soon enough." They had reached the doors of the golden pavilion, and now, with Budic and Melaan, they went inside, Lasairían escorting the Fomorian queen and Gwyneira on Budic's arm.

When the rulers reached their places—four high-backed golden chairs at the center of the great half-moon-shaped table—the queens decorously seated themselves, and then Lasairían leaned over and spoke in Budic's ear, and the Fomorian monarch nodded agreement.

Lasairían turned to face the assembled guests. "Insofar as Fomor and Keltia have agreed in peace together according to the judgment of Ganaster," he said, his voice filling the tent and carrying to the lawn where many guests still lingered, "so shall the princes who defended so ably agree in peace together. Bres, Fionnbarr: Come forward and be in friendship."

Fionnbarr, taken off guard—he had been staring at Basilea with desperate eyes, where she stood a few yards away—collected himself and came forward as his father bade him. Bres gave his own father a savage glare, but he dared do nothing but obey, and stalking across the space before the high seats he came face to face with Fionnbarr. There was a moment's electric pause, a silence like the stillness that goes between the lightning and the thunder, during which those in the pavilion seemed to hold their breath. Then, with the air of men forced to embrace a pillar of fire, Bres and Fionnbarr gave each other the embrace of peace. It lasted only a moment, then they pulled apart, to a storm of approving and relieved applause, and took their seats at the table. Across the board's curve, the two queens exchanged quick glances of perfect understanding.

But their sons too were well content: For when Fionnbarr and Bres had stood for all to see in their embrace of peace, Bres had muttered somewhat into the other's ear, and Fionnbarr had murmured back assent. What Bres had said was the time and place of their combat: dawn, out on the meadows to the north of the city; and what Fionnbarr had answered was his agreement.

The banquet went on for some hours, the guests taking their cue from their hosts, and those hosts exerting every ounce of their social talents to keep the mood of reconciliation in control.

Gwyneira had been watching her son closely, and it had not taken her long to notice the direction of most of his attention. Watching him, watching Basilea who sat along the curve of the table to the right, watching them struggle not to watch each other, Gwyneira suddenly knew the truth. *Well, perhaps I cannot blame him; and for certain I cannot blame her . . . But Bres's betrothed! Could Barraun find no other lass to please his fancy? Every eligible lady in Keltia, and plenty not so eligible, has pursued Barraun for years; small wonder that he would turn to one who need think of naught but love. Not title nor rank nor fortune would matter to this one, I think . . .* And that, she saw with respect both unfeigned and ungrudging, would have been just the same had Fionnbarr been no prince but in truth only the retainer he had claimed to be.

Against her will, Gwyneira smiled, and saw a wondering smile light Basilea's face in answer, and the dawning comprehension in the girl's eyes that the Keltic queen must know all the tale of herself and Fionnbarr. There was no shame there, nor defiance either; only honest gladness, and a kind of gratitude for Gwyneira's knowing. *A great pity*, thought Gwyneira, looking away at last. *This would have been one I could have loved and welcomed as daughter; a hard dán for her to bear, that she must take instead the lord to whom she has been promised . . .*

Fionnbarr too had noticed his mother's noticing, had sensed her sudden change of heart as well. But he was enough the prince that no lying hope rose up to cheat him: No matter how he himself did feel, or Basilea—the name came easier now—or Bres, this was the last time the three of them would ever be together all in the same place. *Unless we should meet years hence, on some state occasion, when she is Bres's queen and I have a queen of my own; and so it is farewell, my Syvy, here and now . . .*

As soon as the kings had dined, and had begun to mingle with their guests, Fionnbarr slipped from the pavilion and headed for the safety of the trees. Once shielded by their shadow, he waited a little, and presently other figures, moving as silently as he had done, came to join him: Faolan Douglas, bright-eyed but disapproving, his friend from boyhood; then Resoghen Keresk, another friend and a Fian medic; and last of all his uncle Elharn; and if Faolan's face had borne a look of disapproval for Fionnbarr's conduct, Elharn's bore it twenty times over. But he said no word just then to his nephew, and the three hastened downriver a mile or so, to where Sithney ní hAiseadha, senior second in this matter, awaited them with an aircar.

She greeted Fionnbarr with the same resigned willingness shown by the others—if he must do this, she had argued with the other seconds, when first Fionnbarr had approached them to act for him, and clearly he must, then at least they should make it as safe and as easy for him as might be, and in the end they had bowed to her—and exchanging a glance with Elharn, gestured them all into the small craft.

For all her doubts, Fionnbarr saw, Sithney had performed well her duties: In the main cabin were all his weapons, meticulously cleaned and laid out, and a change of garb—something more suited to combat than the festal garments in which he had attended the banquet; and, over against the padded blastbench, Keresk's healer's tools, in their case with the Fianna seal.

In silence they took their seats, and Sithney, with one final look from face to face, went forward to the command cabin; and a few moments later the aircar rose whispering out of the grove of trees.

Chapter 6

The sun had still not climbed above the line of distant hills when Fionnbarr stepped from the aircar, to stand on the edge of the misty meadow where in a very little time now he would face his rival.

He had spent the hours since leaving the banquet in such rest and reflection as might be managed, stretched out on a padded couch in the aircar's main cabin, for he had not dared return to his rooms in the palace lest he be seen and questioned—worse still, detained or even prevented from keeping this morning's tryst. Now, as he looked across the field to where another hovercar could just be discerned in the trees' long shadow, he wondered briefly if his opponent had spent as unrestful a night.

I hope so, he thought, *and on the whole I rather think he did . . .* Fionnbarr did not turn, though he smiled a greeting, as his seconds emerged from the aircar to stand, a little uncertainly, nearby. They had had as little sleep as Fionnbarr had enjoyed, and now in the cold dawnlight were even more unsure than ever of the rightness of their compliance with their friend's wishes; most particularly Elharn, who immediately fixed his brother's son with a dark reproving eye.

This is never *like him,* Elharn was thinking as he studied Fionnbarr's determinedly averted face. *Where now the caution and forethought he has never before been without? Never did he make a move without giving it twice its weight in thought; now he seems to act without having thought at all—without caring, even. And to my mind there is a little too much of my mother in that for any of us to be easy with . . .* He sighed. Perhaps that was the nub of it right there: that having been so long ruled by reason, Fionnbarr now chose to act for once according to his feelings, and those feelings, to everyone's profound discomfort and dismay, bore all the stamp of Aoife. *But what a time for him to choose to act so, and in such a matter—*

"Barraun, I ought by rights to forbid this," said Elharn aloud, following his nephew's gaze across the field, to where Bres, clearly recognizable in the growing light, now stood among his own seconds, testing the weight and balance of a succession of swords, donning the few pieces of light armor worn for such a contest. "You were not quite what we thought of in the Fianna as a natural swordsman."

Fionnbarr laughed and began to arm himself, securing the elasteel vambraces worn over the forearms, a hinged flap over the back of the hands leaving his fingers bare for better control; no gauntlet was worn.

"Uncle, you were ever a diplomatist . . . What you are too polite to say is that I was the worst Fian novice ever to lift a glaive."

"Not the worst," said Elharn after a moment, with a smile that seemed a little late in answering. "But Bres—"

"—is by no means renowned for his skill of fence. You have said so yourself."

"But still he may well prove more skilled than you, Barraun," said Sithney urgently. "And that is all he need be, today . . . Do not take a risk, for any sake. You are Tanist of Keltia, and you have better purpose to your life both now and later. Let one of us take up the challenge in your place. It is your right to do so; and it may well even be your duty."

Fionnbarr, moved by the plea and the feeling that had spoken it, put a hand on his friend's shoulder. "And it is his right to fight me, m'chara; to fight *me,* not you or Faolan or Keresk or Ironbrow. His right to seek my blood for his grievances as he does see them: for Lykken, and for the verdict, and most of all for Sovay. And is it not my duty to bide that challenge for all those reasons, and for that last reason most of all?"

"Ah, Barraun, we know all this," said Faolan; and indeed they did, for in the long sleepless hours before dawn Fionnbarr had at last confided in them the true reason for the challenge, and for Bres's mood of wrath. "And we understand, truly, only—"

"Then if you understand, let me go into it with no more heartscaldings and an undivided mind. That is what you must now do for me, if you love me—it is all you can do."

Throwing this last over his shoulder, and never glancing back to see where it did fall, Fionnbarr pulled tight the last strap on the vambrace and stepped out onto the open meadow. Bres was already advancing toward him across the short grass accompanied by his seconds, and Fionnbarr named them to himself as they had been named in the delivered challenge: Corsin Letro, chief among them, a baron of Fomor and close friend to Bres; Thyle, a law-lord who had assisted with the case before the Justiciary; and Resler, a military healer, who had had word only last week of the birth of his first child—Borvos, the boy was called, so Sov—*Basilea!*—had said.

The two groups halted perhaps thirty feet apart, Sithney and Corsin Letro, as senior seconds, coming forward to parley together as was custom. For lack of a neutral mediator, the which they had not dared to seek in Eribol—the merest whisper of a duel in the offing, here on the Justiciary's own planet, would have brought down upon them all that body's full wrath, and it might yet—these two would serve as co-judges of the bout, each to call the other's touches; on the always sound principle of one divides the cake, the other has first choice of portion, and so the calls would be honest ones.

While their seconds conferred, Bres and Fionnbarr stared at each other as if their gazes had locked and frozen. Yet each man knew very well that the other saw only what he himself was seeing: not his adversary, but the image of Basilea plain before his eyes.

Then at last Sithney and Corsin Letro beckoned, and they went to take up their positions. They responded to the usual formal questions—the ground of their quarrel, could it perhaps even now be settled by other means, and if not, would they both swear to seek no further satisfaction than first blooding—with the impatient courtesy of men whose minds had been long since made up, and who now wished only to get on with what they had determined should be.

Corsin spoke, in Englic as a neutral common tongue. "My lords, take your stands."

They moved into dueling distance, either side of the crossed and lowered swords of Sithney and Corsin. In the unison of automata, Bres and Fionnbarr saluted their seconds, saluted each other, and then fell into opening stance, their blades crossed and touching above the blades of their seconds.

The stance lasted an instant only, as the upward flash of steel—Corsin and Sithney withdrawing their weapons—freed them to begin, and barely were the seconds out of sword-range before Fionnbarr and Bres had engaged.

In the first few exchanges, it was Fionnbarr who won most often the right-of-way, but Bres managed to parry each lunge, though never quick enough or strong enough to win time and room for a lunge of his own. But gradually that began to change, and the cold formality of the contest began to warm to red rage, as heat from the earth's core will melt the ice-mantle on the frozen sides of a volcano.

"I like this not," muttered Elharn to Thyle, and the Fomori nodded agreement. But the fight could not now be stopped; not until blood had been drawn and honor satisfied, or until some infringement of the rules of the bout had been committed.

For all his friends' fearing pessimism, Fionnbarr was agreeably surprised to find that he could more than hold his own against his rival: Bres, thus far at any rate, was as usual too impetuous, lacking the coolheadedness that distinguishes the superior swordsman from the merely competent. Though Fionnbarr's own strategy was scarcely planned, tags from his time with the Fianna were coming back to him—fence with absence of body, fence with absence of blade—and he was employing the advice contained therein as the thoughts occurred; which made for little smoothness in style, but great advantage in surprise.

And Bres, for all his heedlessness, was at the same moment discovering that his anger was lending a certain cohesiveness to his swordplay, and his lines had a logic to them that his opponent had yet to overset or match. Yet still had neither of them drawn blood; which, to Bres, was all the reason for the fight. If he could not slay his enemy—though, with luck, even that was not impossible—at the very least he should have that enemy's blood upon his sword. And that would have to content him, for now; later, perhaps, there might come a chance for better satisfaction, and a greater vengeance. But he was growing weary, and impatient; even that poor satisfaction, if it was to be his, must come soon or not at all . . .

Fionnbarr's trained eye had seen his adversary's flagging arm, had marked it thankfully, knowing as he did that he too tired, and hoping as he did that the end of the bout was perhaps near. And, thinking and hoping so, he did not note the instant when another blade flashed in the light of the new-risen sun; an utterly unlawful blade, a blade so quickly there and gone again that Fionnbarr could never afterwards say in certainty that he had seen it.

But if he did not see it, he felt its presence and its passing, there along his left side where Bres had ripped it open from ribs to hip. Suddenly sick and faint, Fionnbarr let his guard fall away, and saw Bres's face contort with triumph as he leaped to take the advantage that his treachery had given him.

But Sithney and Corsin Letro had moved as one, were in between them now, knocking away their blades with their own; for both had seen Bres's illicit sleeve-knife, and both knew well what its use might signify: that the Kelts would be perfectly within their rights to demand immediate recompense for the violation—even to ordering Bres to stand unarmed against a blow from Fionnbarr's blade.

For a moment the Fomorians stood tense and still, carefully keeping their eyes from Bres where he stood, waiting for Sithney to pronounce as was her right under the law. But some message apparently passed between Fionnbarr and his seconds, for none of them spared even a glance for Bres, but instead, quickly and carefully, assisted their injured prince from the field to the waiting aircar, where Faolan Douglas was already at the controls.

Sithney did not let them off so easily. Tarrying a little, gathering up the weapons and other gear left behind by her friends in their haste to succor Fionnbarr, she lingered until her companions were out of earshot, then seized Corsin Letro by the arm, and he flinched less at the pain of her grip than at the fury in her face.

"My lord Fionnbarr may have chosen in his chivalry to give over the match, but I assure you none of the rest of us consider ourselves bound by a like noble thought. We are each—myself most particularly—very much at Prince Bres's service should he ever choose to renew this challenge, or to make news of this affair public knowledge. I am sure that His Fomorian Majesty would like but little to hear that his heir should have so compounded his already less than admirable behavior. Do I make myself clear, my lord?''

Corsin bowed, repressing the wish to rub his aching arm where her fingers had dug into it. ''Perfectly, Countess; and I can promise you''—here he threw a glance at Bres, who still stood where Fionnbarr had left him, still breathing hard from the exertions of the bout—''that neither you nor any of your companions here this day will ever need to trouble yourselves on that account.''

''That is well, then.'' Sithney let the full weight of her disgusted gaze rest briefly on Bres, then turned her back on the Fomorians, striding across the meadow to join the others in the waiting aircar.

And so she did not see the woman who had stood a fewscore yards away all through the match, deep in the shadows of the concealing trees, no more than Bres or Fionnbarr had seen her; nor did she see the desperation with which Basilea—for it was she—looked after their departing craft; nor the way she lifted her head at last, and drew herself erect, and walked out onto the meadow to meet her lord.

Bres was still in the grip of an astonishment so complete that he had not moved for a full two minutes. *Why did he not demand an open blow? In his boots by every god there is I had done as much, if not more . . .* By all the laws of combat, such a blow was the right of a wronged opponent, as compensation and penalty; and it had been no scratch, either, that Fionnbarr had taken from that sleeve-knife—which should have afforded Bres much satisfaction. But his pleasure was overshadowed by his puzzlement that the Keltic prince should have forgone his right of return blow and conceded the match to him.

He started at a light touch on his arm: Resler, standing beside him, nodded to where a slim figure in a gray cloak had come forward out of the shadow of the wood. All Bres's rage rose up again, as he saw Basilea staring not at him but at the bloody knife he still held clenched in his left hand. With an angry oath he flung the blade from him, so that it landed in the long grass near her feet, and took a step toward her, extending a peremptory hand.

"Now we will go home to Fomor."

If he had expected—or hoped for—tears, or repentance, or meek compliance, or even anger, he was doomed to disappointment. With a silent grace Basilea bent down—it looked almost as if she were curtsying, though not to him—and took the dagger up from the grass, cleaning the blade upon the hem of her silver scarf. With an expression on her delicate face that forbade Bres's speaking, she thrust the knife through her belt and let her cloak fall closed over it.

"Nay," she said, in a voice as quiet as her demeanor, and as cold, "*now* we will go home."

In the Keltic aircar, flown by Faolan in a circuitous route back to Eribol, things were neither cold nor quiet. Fionbarr, whose wound had been graver than any of them—including himself—had at first suspected, had collapsed once inside the craft, and now he was lying white-faced and silent upon one of the wallcouches. Resoghen Keresk, his healer's task completed, was packing away his tools and shaking his head in silence, while Sithney was rummaging the cabin cupboards to find some less betraying clothing for Fionnbarr to wear.

"Well, Barraun," she said at last, "there is only the feast gear you wore last night, and that will not do, save for the trews only. For the rest, you will have to borrow Faolan's tunic and my cloak. No one will be watching to see how *we* are clad, at least, and with luck we shall be able to get you past the guards and your parents alike."

From his seat across the cabin, Elharn scowled. "Even so, that is but where my concerns *begin* . . . Fionnbarr—"

His nephew groaned and sat up a little. "Nay, uncle, do not start! I know very well what you would say, and I have not the strength to hear it: that you feel you must in honor tell the King and Queen what I have done, and that you yourself helped me to do it; not so?"

"That will serve to begin with," Elharn told him. "You think then I should keep this from them?"

"Why trouble either of them with it? The thing is done now, and honor is satisfied all round, and I am not dead."

"Only just you are not!" That was Faolan, who had put the craft on autohelm and come into the cabin in time to hear this last. "And whose honor is this you speak of? Certainly not Fomori honor—"

"Honor is honor." Fionnbarr resettled himself more comfortably on the couch's cushions; Resoghen Keresk had used a dermasealer on the gash along his side, and now the only evidence of a wound was the deep dull muscle-ache that would disappear in a few days, and exhaustion, and a punishing headache; and of course the mute testimony of the blood-covered tunic and trews. He saw the disbelief on their faces, sat up again.

"Did all you think I was out there to *win*? Nay, *my* honor would have permitted no less than this by way of quittance"—he gestured toward the bloodied garments—"and if Bres had not taken his own way to it, however treacherous, I should have presently allowed him his blow unhindered. For me, and for Sovay: call it corp-dira, the price of *our* honor—not his."

In the storm of appalled protest that broke then, no one reproof could be heard above the rest, until Elharn flung his arm up commandingly for silence, and it was given him.

"Fionnbarr, do you tell us that you stood there and *allowed* that—"

"Nay," said his nephew honestly, "for I truly did not see the sleeve-knife. But aye, for that I would have permitted Bres the winning of the match, the drawing of first blood, whatever need required I give him. I had determined on it since first I accepted his challenge, when he flung down his glove before me in the street; winning the judgment of the High Justice only determined me upon it all the more."

Faolan exploded. "Do you say so! And how if 'need required' that he had cut you down? What then?"

"Then Orlaith my sister would be Keltia's new heir." Fionnbarr leaned back again on the cushions; reaction was beginning to set in, and he had no wish for his friends to see him shaking. "But I *am* here, and so she is not . . . Perhaps there may be another time, some time to come, when another Aoibhell may face Bres and nothing need then be held back, to strike at him where I could not, perhaps even to strike him down forever; but that's as it may be, or will be." He closed his eyes. "For now—do what you wish, uncle, or what you feel you must. I shall never see her again, and if ever I do she will be Queen of Fomor. Is that not punishment enough?''

''There is no talk of punishment,'' began Sithney hotly, but fell obediently silent at a look from Elharn, who was by no means yet decided that punishment was *not* in order; and for the remaining miles back to Eribol there was no talk of anything at all.

That evening, Bres was sitting alone in his chambers, still in a state of mood and mind he could put no name to. Though it had seemed enough that morning—even more than enough—now in this calmer hour the wounding of his rival and the winning of the duel—if winning he could even call it—were not enough, and Bres had neither joy nor peace of mind of the day's events.

Nay, I wish I had slain him, he thought passionately. *No matter what would have come after—for a personal duel on Ganaster, the penalty must be unimaginable—and it would surely have cost me Fomor, but just as surely it would have been well worth the price . . .*

His thought turned to Basilea, how she had looked that morning, his blade in her hands and Fionnbarr's blood on her scarf. She had not said a score of words to him on their way back to the city, and on arriving at the palace had gone straight to her chambers and to the best of his knowledge—his guards' knowledge, rather—had not emerged from them all day; her state of mind was only to be guessed at. *Well, we shall be returning to Fomor tomorrow—and none too soon for me—and once we have come home Sia's feelings, I fear, will no longer enter into it. It will all then be according to arrangement; and not the least of those arrangements will be the one I contrived before leaving Tory—the taking of a formal concubine, along with my wedded princess. Thona, my lovely one; too much to hope for, I think, that you and my future queen should be friends, but let you at least each try to keep from pouring poison into the other's cup . . .*

A knock came at the door, and Bres started violently, first with guilt, then with hope. *Sia, coming to make amends?* He called admittance to the one who had sought it; but it was not Basilea, or any other expected visitor, whom the servant now ushered in, but Strephon of Alphor, alone, in an intricately draped mantle of heavy silk and a half-mask that hid the lower part of his face.

"I do not intrude?" he asked politely, but drew off cloak and mask and gloves uninvited, as if certain, or careless, of the answer.

"Surely not," said Bres after a moment. He had risen mechanically for his guest's entrance, and now sank down slowly into his chair. "Wine?"

The Coranian prince accepted the proffered cup and drank deep and appreciatively before speaking again. "I take ship presently for Alphor," he said. "And I believe you do depart tomorrow for your own world. But I wish to speak with you first, if you will permit."

"On what matter?"

"The outcome of the trial, for one; and perhaps some other things as well." Strephon leaned back comfortably in his chair, putting his feet up on the padded fireguard; this world was a colder one than his own desert planet, and he had spent the last fortnight chilled to the bone.

"I am sorry it did not go as you had hoped," he added. "But for all your efforts—and you did some shrewd arguing in an indefensible place—you did not expect any other verdict?"

Bres looked at him for a long silent moment, suddenly wondering exactly how his visitor had in fact voted in the legists' conclave; then he began to laugh. *This is just what he wishes me to wonder, and I have not disappointed him . . .*

"By gods, but I did not! Still, it was a good try?"

"A very good try," said Strephon, with a small smile. "As was your earlier effort to make Lykken see reason; a very great pity *that* piece of persuasion did not work out to plan. And your dawn colloquy this very morning with Fionnbarr of Keltia—that was a good try also; and I think a rather more successful one as well—at least from your point of view?" He shook his head as Bres flushed darkly and began to rise from his chair. "No, no, do not be offended, nor study to look innocent either. I know all about it, though I doubt that more than a dozen others do; and all of us can hold our tongues."

Bres leaned back now, balancing on his spine, weighing his winecup in his hand. "I hope so."

"Oh yes . . . The High Justiciar Celarain and her colleagues would be swift to tell you the penalty for such activities as a duel—and one that resulted in bloodletting—here on Ganaster. It is neither a light nor a pleasant one."

All at once Bres gave a shout of laughter, though Strephon's own bland expression did not change. "I am very sure it is not! All the same, Alphor, it was worth it, and I'd do it again if—"

"—if circumstances demanded," finished Strephon smoothly. "I thought as much. But am I to take it, then, that the Lady Basilea—or should I say Sovay?—has recovered from her, ah, lapse?"

"Whether she has or no," replied Bres, not surprised in the least that the Coranian should know the grounds of the morning's duel, "she and I will wed on Fomor in due course, as our kindreds have arranged it."

"And I look forward to attending the ceremony; pray do not forget to invite me! Pity it is that you have no such custom on Fomor as our own of the damacho-andra: the co-wife. That way a man may wed for policy and wed for love, all at the same time. But then I am forgetting, it is she, not you, whose heart seems not to be given to this match."

Bres scowled a little. "It might be so—and we too have certain customs not unlike that one you speak of . . . But enough; I think you did not come here simply to discuss my marriage plans."

"No." Strephon refilled his cup, though his host had not invited him to do so. "Your father King Budic has made official peace with Keltia, and we shall see in time what that may mean; what of your own private peace?"

"With Keltia?" Bres gave him an incredulous stare. "Sooner will the galaxy collapse . . ."

"So I thought; but I do like to hear you say so."

The glint in Bres's eye grew brighter. "And is there a reason that you should wish to hear me say so?"

"Nothing definite for the moment." Strephon set down the cup with an emphasis that punctuated his words. "Just a matter of mutual assurance, that may well benefit us both in the years to come. In the time, let us say, when I am Emperor of the Cabiri, and you are King of Fomor and Archon of the Phalanx."

"Archon!" Bres's voice betrayed his doubt and surprise: The position of Archon—supreme lord of that uneasy confederation of star-systems known as the Phalanx—was coveted by many princes, and usually attained to by cunning and other less admirable means than mere strength.

"Why not?" returned Strephon mildly. "The kings of Fomor have enjoyed that distinction more often than not over the years of the Phalanx's rise to galactic power—why should it not come to you in your turn, once you yourself are king? You are as deserving as any, and better fit for it than most," He masked a grin as he saw the idea take root in the other's mind. *Ah, now you have taken my lure, Fomor,* he thought. *Let you have some time—years, decades even, there is no haste in it—for the hook to set firm in your jaw; and then when it is most advantageous for me to do so, I—or one I will set to it—will reel you in like the greedy brute fish you are . . .*

For his part, Bres's own thought was not so unlike: thoughts of how when Budic was dead, and he himself was lord over Fomor, and the Phalanx too was obedient to his rein, he might be able to use even the great Cabiri Imperium as he did please; and as for Keltia— He set aside with an effort the tantalizing images Strephon's words had conjured. *He lures me on, like the jackals of his own desert, but he shall not know I have seen through his feigning . . .*

"A pleasant prospect, if an uncertain one; and a long way off in any case . . . How *did* you vote in conclave?" he shot suddenly at his quest. "For Fionnbarr or for me?"

Strephon's amber eyes lighted with the first real smile of the visit. "Why, Fomor," he said, "how do you think? It is you I am drinking with tonight, not the Prince of Keltia—"

"That is not an answer."

"It is all the answer you will get, and all the answer I am at present prepared to give. *Think* a little: Should the voting become public knowledge, Celarain could make things—difficult for us all. Could, and would."

That was likely enough, Bres admitted. One never knew when the goodwill of Ganaster might be a thing one's people or planet or kingdom could stand in sore need of; small profit then in incurring the wrath of the High Justiciary merely to satisfy one's curiosity.

All the same, he thought, having bidden Strephon farewell and safe journey, and watching the Coranian cross the courtyard below the windows, *all the same I'd take no wagers as to the truth of your vote, Prince of Alphor; and I'll keep my own counsel—as will you—on this evening's talk as well.*

Bres raised his arm in a gesture half salute, half leavetaking, as Strephon's distant form vanished into the maze of dark streets. "Until our next partnership, then," he murmured. "May it be against Fionnbarr, and against Keltia, and may it be not long delayed."

But it was to be many decades before that prayer came to pass; and when at last it did so, it would prove to be—as were so many answered prayers—not entirely what the petitioner had had in mind.

Chapter 7

For some time after the return from Ganaster, far from rightly rejoicing in his triumph, Fionnbarr was moody and withdrawn; his temper could even be described as sullen, a thing never before seen with him no matter the provocation, and his people and his parents alike wondered at the cause. But none dared inquire; and those few who did have certain knowledge of the reasons for the Prince's humor offered no word of explanation.

"What you need," said Gwyneira after a few months of this, "is something of substance to occupy your time."

"And I doubt not, my mother, that you have somewhat to suggest."

"Indeed I have," said the Queen. "A princess for Keltia. It is high time you thought of marrying, Barraun, and giving the realm an heir. Think if you had been killed in that ridiculous brawl on Ganaster—oh aye, I know all about what your honor demanded! Your uncle Elharn thought that *his* honor demanded he tell me, though I have not yet decided whether *my* honor requires me to speak of it to the King, and I have forbidden Elharn to do so. Bad enough that you were injured; had you been slain—"

"Then Orlaith would be Tanista," said Fionnbarr, bored with the discussion. "Or Deian Tanist, if she declined the heirship, as she might well have done—she has ever been a selfish girl."

"That is not the point," said his mother with considerable sharpness. "I have never *seen* you so, Barraun; you have ever been as responsible and dutiful a prince as Keltia ever had, and I do not understand this new turn of mood you have been showing. Almost I think that you wish Bres *had* slain you, or at the very least given you some debilitating injury, to bar you from the throne under the brehon law, so that you would not have to be Ard-rígh.''

Fionnbarr spun round to stare at here, but Gwyneira's violet eyes were averted, as if she feared to see upon his face the confirmation of his words; but when he spoke, what she had not wished to see sounded in her ears, and she could not escape it any more than could he.

"How did you know that?" he whispered. "How could you— I have not spoken of that wish to anyone living; not even to—" He broke off, but both of them knew the name he had been about to speak.

Gwyneira let it pass, for she saw that her son was trembling as with cold, or with a sudden unbearable pain.

" 'Not to anyone living,' you say; then I think I know to whom—to Aoife your grandmother, or to the holy stones; it matters not. If the prospect of your sovereignty to come mislikes you so, amhic, you know you are permitted to remove yourself by fiant from the Tanistry and the succession. Others have stepped aside in time past, and the realm did not crash into ruin for that they did so.''

"Aye?" said Fionnbarr bitterly. "Shall I demand of my father that he release me—and destroy him by the asking? Nay, I am bound to it; by love and by birth, by duty and by dán. Hear me gods, that I would choose other wise if only I could; I think that even Lasairían Ard-rígh would have chosen another way for himself—and who knows how many other rulers of Keltia beside, had they been free to choose.''

"I say again, there have been before now heirs who declined their birthright.''

"Indeed. I have studied their lives afterward; small good it did them. Nay, duty alone would suffice to keep my hand to this task; but dán makes it certain, and it is only love—for my father, for my King and for my folk—that makes it bearable.''

"Then perhaps you may take comfort in a thing your grandmother Aoife did See before she died," said Gwyneira after a while, at a loss to know how to comfort him. But her voice was soft with compassion for what he had already lost to duty, and for what he was sure to lose in future. "She even spoke of it to you, do you remember? That there are greater things to come of your rule than your happiness, or even Keltia's.''

"Oh aye," said Fionnbarr drearily. "My own heir—this Aeron that is to be. Pity it is that Aoife did not See also who shall be her mother; such knowing might have saved me both time and trouble and some considerable pain—and not me alone . . . Well, if Aoife Saw her, then doubtless she will come, and as she will be my child, I shall love her when she does. But I think she is still a very long way away, and many things may happen in the years between.''

They spoke no more of it then, and never did they speak of Basilea; and if ever King Lasairían learned from his wife or his brother or anyone else of the twin follies his son had indulged in on Ganaster—heart-affair and sword-affair—he never taxed Fionnbarr with the knowledge.

Fionnbarr's evil mood passed in time, though it seemed that he was never to be free of some faint shadow of his sorrow, and with the heartfelt approval—and relief—of King and Council alike he took up once more his royal duties. Their approval was tempered somewhat when he chose to rejoin his old Fian detachment; but their objections were overridden, chiefly by the firm eloquence of Gwyneira and Elharn, and with a small attendant company of cousins and friends and the sons of other princes— his comrade Faolan Douglas among them—Fionnbarr went out-Wall with the Keltic starfleet.

He was to spend the next few years beyond the Pale in defense of Keltia's Protectorates—those systems, too poor or too weak or too scattered properly to defend themselves, that had begged for and been granted the shelter of the Keltic shield; for not all Keltia's outworld troubles had ended with the settling of the Lykken matter, and there was much still to be attended to by rather less peaceful means.

Many there were in Keltia, the King and Queen among them, who thought they saw in these martial out-Wall exploits—fierce, frequent, always where the fighting was most deadly—Fionnbarr's hope that he might once again encounter Bres of Fomor, and this time upon the field rather than before the bench, in the kind of combat where other, less refined codes of honor might hold. They were right to think so, though they never knew for true.

But the Fomorian prince stayed these days on his own home planet, never venturing out among the stars where Fionnbarr sought him; and Fomor itself, for the moment at least, kept well away from the arenas of interstellar contention. It would be long and long before their paths and their fates crossed again.

The wall Fionnbarr had built around himself shattered once and once only, and even that but briefly: when news came to the *Firedrake*, the great golden star-dragon that was the flagship of the Keltic fleet, upon which Fionnbarr spent most of his service, that the heir of Fomor had at last taken a wife.

"They say the couple had been betrothed since childhood," remarked Donlin O Talleron, "ever since Bres's elder brother, her first pledged lord, died in battle—with us, I think."

Lasairían's former First Lord of War, upon his retirement from the Ard-eis and active governing, had been granted by his old comrade-in-arms a longtime wish: the captaincy of *Firedrake*. O Talleron had accepted Lasairían's offer with joy; he had been in command of the dragon ship two years, and now he lounged with Fionnbarr and several others of his personal staff officers in a comfortable common-room, off-duty and over methers of ale.

"Though I have heard that Bres has been flaunting a concubine—a legally attached one—almost since that time on Ganaster," said Morna Arc'hantet; she was a Fian commander, and close friend to both Faolan and Fionnbarr. "But you must remember this new Princess of Fomor, Barraun," she continued, turning to her friend who sat by. "Was she not with Bres in Eribol?"

Morna had spoken out of idle curiosity, and so both she and the other officers were astounded all alike when Fionnbarr muttered something savage as to how the marriages of foreign princes were no concern of his, theirs, or any other Kelt's, and strode from the room without another word. But the matter, though certainly surprising, was forgotten within hours by those who had witnessed it, and the campaign continued.

And after that campaign, many others, on many worlds and in the star-space between; until it was thirteen full years since "that time on Ganaster," and at last Queen Gwyneira prevailed upon her husband to summon their son home for good. For she had a campaign of her own that had been long in the planning, and like any good general she had chosen her ground well, and likewise her time to strike.

"I sent for my son two hours since." Gwyneira spoke crisply, but hid her annoyance, for the fault was not with her equerry. "Where is he, then? The Prince of Leinster and his family are on their way even now to the Presence Chamber, to do homage to the Ard-rígh for the dúchas of Leinster, and I particularly wished the Tanist to attend me."

"The Tanist has asked me to inform the Queen his mother," said the unhappy aide, "that he is much occupied at present, and regrets that he cannot oblige her wish."

'Occupied'! The truth of it is that he is still sulking over being recalled from service—well, after this afternoon I think his sulks will lift . . .

Gwyneira stood up and smoothed her skirts. "Inform the Tanist," she said with an unreadable smile, "that no more is this the request of his mother but the command of Gwyneira the Queen."

Fionnbarr presented himself before his parents on the stroke of high twelve, as they sat in their high seats beneath the canopy of state in the Presence Chamber. Gwyneira, in her place at her husband's right, saw that behind her son's princely bearing and formal uniform he was in a fury at being summoned so. *Ah, that will change,* she thought with unregal delight, *and so soon now too . . .*

Fionnbarr scarcely looked up from where he stood beside his father's chair as Farrell O Kerrigan, Prince of Leinster, came forward, his Princess, Ahès, on his arm and his grown children coming after, to kneel before Lasairían and repeat the oath of homage due every three years from one of Keltia's Ruling Princes to the Ard-rígh. Keltic law, though punctilious in such matters, was also refreshingly brief and direct about them, and the exchange between sovereign and sub-king—for as such did that same law regard each of the nine planetary princes—was soon completed.

If Fionnbarr had thought he would now be free to leave, he was soon to learn otherwise, as his parents came down from their seats to greet the members of the House of Leinster as the old and dear friends they were. Gwyneira took her son's arm, precluding his escape, and led him over to the mother of Leinster's brood, where she stood with her daughters around her.

"I think, Barraun, that you will remember the Lady Ahès, Princess of Leinster and daughter to the Lord Brychan of Kermarien?" When Fionnbarr made no immediate response, Gwyneira casually tightened her hand on his arm, so that her fingernails dug through the cloth of his uniform sleeve, and he started, giving her a baleful look.

"Surely—welcome, Highness, to Turusachan." He kissed Ahès's outstretched hand, acknowledging her return pleasantries, then turned to go.

"And this is Tamhna," Gwyneira went on inexorably, dragging him along the row of chairs. "Eldest daughter of the house."

Again Fionnbarr bowed politely over the hand held out to him, giving its owner barely a glance; and again with her sister Keina, the middle daughter, just that year attained to her Domina rank as a Ban-draoi; and with Ríada, wife of Morlais, Leinster's heir.

"And this Emer, the youngest."

Moving along as his mother prompted, hopeful that there seemed to be no more daughters past this one, Fionnbarr found himself looking down into the prettiest face he had ever seen: a heart-shaped, delicate face, with a dusting of freckles over a thin-bridged nose, and eyes blue as flaxflowers, all framed by amber-gold hair that glinted with red in the light from the windows.

Stammering something, Fionnbarr suddenly became aware that he was still holding Emer's hand; blushing, he let it fall, and saw with amazement that she was blushing too, and marvelled at the color. He was aware now of his mother smiling beside him, as if in satisfaction, but he was far too flustered to seek for that satisfaction's cause. He heard himself speaking, though he was never to know for the rest of his days what in truth he had said, heard a clear young voice answering, though he understood not a word of that reply.

Then his mother's voice cut through his bemusement. "The Prince Farrell and his family shall be our guests for a month, Barraun, here in Turusachan; and then they will accompany us to

Nancarrow, when we go for the hunting. Is that not a thing to look forward to?''

Now there was a note of distinct triumph in Gwyneira's voice, though it seemed for some reason to escape the hearing of the men present, for Lasairían and Farrell barely stopped their own talk, save to nod absently in agreement to the Queen's words, and the Kerrigan sons Morlais and Estyn were deep in conversation with Faolan Douglas and young Prince Deian, and Fionnbarr himself seemed to have taken a faery-stroke, so still and dazed did he stand.

But Ahès heard the note, and met the Queen's smile with a matching one; and Tamhna heard it, and sighed; and Keina heard it, and laughed; and Emer heard it, and blushed again.

The month of guesting at the palace passed quicker than Fionnbarr could have thought possible. There were ceilis and banquets and other merriments to pass the time swiftly and pleasantly; and to the astonishment of the entire Court Fionnbarr did not absent himself from a one of them—what was more astonishing still, he appeared to be enjoying himself. And since such delight in social occasions had never before been seen with him, the speculation grew daily.

At the end of the month the Court moved to Nancarrow, the royal hunting lodge that lay in deep forest near the Avon Dia, in the wide valley of the Strath Mór some two days' ride from Caerdroia.

Nancarrow—the Valley of the Stag—was a place Fionnbarr had known and loved since his childhood: a maenor rather than a palace or a fortress, a large and comfortable country-house built of honey-colored stone quarried from the nearby Loom, with a family feeling about it that Turusachan, for all its grandeur and history and stateliness, could never hope to rival.

And in the warmth and ease of Nancarrow, away from whatever ghosts had walked so long with him and whatever necessities had pressed so hard upon him, Fionnbarr let down at last the walls he had so long defended, as perhaps he could not, or would not, have done in any other place.

At the end of the hunting season, as the Court was making ready to return to Caerdroia for the opening sessions of the

House of Peers, at which sessions Lasairían must preside and his heir must be in attendance, Fionnbarr came to his mother as she sat reading in her gríanan. He made small talk a few moments— very small, which was not usual with him—then, as was more his wont, came directly to his point.

"I wish to wed the Prince of Leinster's daughter."

Gwyneira hid her smile and turned a page of her book. "Tamhna is both clever and handsome," she murmured casually. "She will make you a fine queen. Or is it rather Keina? As a Ban-draoi Domina she will be of great and unusual help—"

"You know very well who," he said with some heat, "since very like it was you who devised our meeting. But if you would have the pleasure of hearing me say it, it is Emer."

And saying it, the fact that it was, indeed, Emer amazed Fionnbarr anew. Though there had been a respectable number of romances in his life—some serious, most less so—over the years since Ganaster, Fionnbarr had found no woman since Basilea to win his heart so surely and so swiftly. Not until he had taken Emer's hand in the Presence Chamber at Turusachan, and had known at once that here was his queen that would be. *As it was then with Sovay*, he thought, *this now with Emer is the grátintreach, the lightning-love, that strikes from nowhere and lights even the darkest corners* . . . The past two months had fairly blazed with its brilliance: He and Emer had spent as much time together as could be decently contrived without causing talk. Or so at least they had fondly supposed, for in truth they had seen nothing beyond themselves and never knew that all Nancarrow was delighted, and hopeful, privy to their idyll.

Not that it would have mattered to either of them if all Keltia had known: Having lost one love to duty's dictates, Fionnbarr had no intention of losing another; and Emer, whose name meant "granite" and who had no smallest thought of allowing herself to be lost, revealed for the first time the findruinna core beneath the lovely face that was her armor to the world.

Had they been any other pair of Keltic lovers than the heir to the Throne of Scone and the daughter of a planetary prince, the thing would have been simple. But they were who they were, and it was not simple, and so they agreed together that Fionnbarr should speak to his mother the Queen, and see what might be done.

Emer . . . Gwyneira closed her book and set it aside. "Emer is a lovely young woman, full fit to be my successor as queen-consort. But you know that she *is* young, perhaps overmuch so—in no case of an age to wed without consent, and I doubt that Farrell and Ahès would permit her to marry for some years yet."

"Aye, and even so, knowing full well what would happen, still you yourself brought us together," said Fionnbarr evenly. "Nor would it much surprise me to learn that Ahès—and maybe Keina?—abetted you in this . . . And that is why you must help us now."

" 'Us', is it? You have spoken to Emer, then?"

Fionnbarr flushed, but looked his mother straight in the eye. "I have so, and beyond all hope she shares my wish. And any road, it is not as if she is not of an age to marry—she turns twenty-one in a week's time. Many women in Keltia, and men also, have wed at so young an age."

"Not all that many, and certainly not many who were child to a Ruling Prince. I do not think you will obtain Farrell's consent for some years yet, and should you run off to wed in secret it will cause great trouble, Barraun, with your father—and more trouble still with hers. Such an elopement could even jeopardize your Tanistry; have you thought of that?"

He nodded soberly. "We have spoken of all these chances, and we are willing to risk the hazard. What is our choice else? To wait tamely six years for her to reach her final majority, when we might have had those years together? Besides," he added, "though she has still so carefully not confessed to it, I am much mistaken if I do not recognize the Queen's hand in this matter."

Gwyneira met his eyes steadily, and after an instant they both burst into laughter.

"And we both know that you are not! Ah, Barrachaun, I am more pleased than I can say—the Mother knows I have waited long enough for this. Ever since I saw Emer as a hoyden lass of twelve or so . . . She is a charming and accomplished young woman—did you know she has only just completed her Fian training?—and I shall be well pleased to welcome her as my daughter, and queen to follow me. But it will be no easy matter to get the two of you safely, and secretly, wedded."

"But it can be done?"

The Queen nodded slowly, one hand tapping thoughtfully upon her chin. "It *shall* be done. I have had a plan or two made ready, against the need. Here is what we must do—"

Drawing him down beside her chair, Gwyneira began to speak, quickly and confidently, and Fionnbarr nodded as the particulars of her plan began to unfold.

Chapter 8

"Let them approach."

Lasairían, robed in blue and wrapped in royalty, watched as his
son and new daughter entered the Council Chamber, halting at
the far end of the long granite table. Their faces were serene, if
not blithe or gay, as Emer gave the Ard-rígh a low curtsy,
Fionnbarr making the bent knee that was his due to his King.

That King let them stand there in silence for a long half-
minute, then nodded once.

"Sit."

They obeyed instantly, taking the places left for them along
the table's right-hand side, and under cover of the short cloak he
wore, Fionnbarr took Emer's hand to give her heart.

There were others also at that table—not a full Council quo-
rum, as for all its staggering import this was scarcely an ortho-
dox session—and those now present were here at Lasairían's
command, as advisors and friends and experts on the sort of
problems this hasty match was like to bring about.

None of them would look at Fionnbarr and Emer, not yet;
none save Gwyneira, who alone of those in the room seemed to
be enjoying herself. As for those others—Sighile of Ossory, still
Taoiseach though drawing near now to the close of her long
royal service; Dorn Arghans, now Home Lord, in charge of all
internal Keltic affairs; the Chief Brehon, Rohais Errocht; Sodor
Tannow, the Archdruid; Elharn, not much better pleased with
this exploit than he had been with his nephew's conduct on
Ganaster long since; Emer's parents and elder brother, Morlais,
her father's heir; Orlaith and Deian, Fionnbarr's own brother and
sister—as for all these, most of them were near as wroth with the

Queen for abetting her son's deed as they were with him for compassing it, though none as yet had dared tax her with it.

For the moment, none could charge any other with anything, for Lasairían still allowed the room to labor under enforced silence, grimly savoring the knowledge that no one could utter a word until he did. He could sense Fionnbarr growing angry and restive under protocol's artificial constraints, and was glad to see his protectiveness toward his new Princess, but he knew his son would obey convention; and if Fionnbarr obeyed, so too would the others.

Ah, gods, why do I draw this out . . . All at once Lasairían grew unspeakably weary of the whole coil. "Let the Chief Brehon read the charges against the law," he said, "and the ground of our discontent."

The air in the chamber thawed perceptibly, though to be sure those charges and that discontent were grave enough. In her place halfway down on the King's left, Rohais Errocht took a deep breath and began a neutral recital of the various offenses committed against the marriage laws and—far worse—the succession laws of Keltia, by the Tanist Fionnbarr Kieran Alun Diolach Aoibhell and the Princess Emer Daráine ní Kerrigan, with the connivance of Gwyneira Queen of Keltia.

Hearing it all read out so cold, Lasairían permitted himself an inner wordless shout of rage and disbelief. How had they *dared*; not so much their defiance of him as their betrayal of the laws that were the soul and armor of Keltia, those very laws they were all of them, as Keltic royalty, sworn to uphold and obey; and not a one of them was repentant of either deed or defiance, he could sense *that* through a stone wall . . .

Rohais, concluding the charges, turned as did everyone else in the room expectantly toward the High King. Lasairían was not ready for them, and passed a hand over his face before speaking; his voice, when he did speak, was oddly lighter and milder than his wont.

"What says the Tanist Fionnbarr in answer to these charges?"

Fionnbarr was on his feet before his father had finished speaking. "Much, Ard-rígh! First and chiefest, that all in this room consider the fact that I have found not only a queen for Keltia's future but a love for my heart. As to our offenses"—he glanced down swiftly at Emer beside him, saw her tiny nod—"we freely confess that we studied to break the laws, and it shall be our pleasure to furnish all due fines and honor-prices to those whom we have wronged.''

Lasairían raised his brows. "Indeed. And if I say you shall pay honor-price to Keltia itself, Prince Fionnbarr? And if that honor-price be the name and rank of Tanist, will you still be so pleased to pay?''

There was an angry flush on Fionnbarr's face, but his words came cold. "Aye, and aye again. Only name the price, Lord; as for my Princess and myself, we have neither of us shame or sorrow in this, save that we have displeased you and Leinster. It is all now at the Ard-rígh's pleasure.'' He seated himself again, and taking Emer's hand kissed it in full view of all, as defiance to them and apology to her.

Lasairían slanted a look sidewise down the table at his old friend Farrell of Leinster, and in spite of the worries of his heart, and those same worries he saw reflected on the face of his old friend, he smiled at warm memories. *Well, O Kerrigan, I see that you have passed down your impetuousness to at least one of your children, and true it is I have ever hoped you and I might be kin one day . . .* He sighed, and capitulated.

"Ah, Barraun, I have no pleasure in any of this, and any road it is now all a matter for the brehons to work out . . . Emer, my dearest child—'' He held out his arms, and Emer slipped gracefully from her chair and ran to him, curtsying and kissing his hand.

"Athra-cheile,'' she murmured, using the formal address— 'mate-father'—and not looking up until he bade her. When she did raise her eyes to his, Lasairían caught the full effect of the turquoise gaze, and laughed helplessly.

"You have vanquished *me*, alanna, and I doubt not you shall do the same to the rest of our folk! Nay,'' he added hastily, "no tears, I do not think I can bear it. There now''—kissing her brow—"go to your mother. All will be well.''

Ahès, who had dared not speak in her daughter's defense or even her own, gathered Emer to her, and over the girl's wheat-gold head spoke to Lasairían from her heart.

"My thanks and her father's, Lord, for your—'' She could not go on, for her fear for her child had been near to choking her, and the others looked courteously away, until she had mastered herself.

Across the table, Gwyneira smiled in sympathy, but rolled her eyes with impatience all the same. *I told the silly sow no harm would befall her pet; if she doubted my word, why did she allow me to proceed with the arrangements? Still, now it is settled, and we can all sit back and put our feet up and wait for an heir . . . and not before time, either.*

But now Sodor Tannow had risen to speak. "My preceptor on Erinna, whose Druid it was that wedded these two by the Queen's contrivance and in her presence, has taken oath to a robed brehon and to Rohais here present and to me that the rites were correctly performed, and so the match is lawful if allowed. Under ordinary circumstances, he would have to be disciplined for such a breach of law, but now—"

"Aye, aye," said Lasairían, waving his hand, "if these are not to be punished, then surely he should not be."

"Still, Lord," put in Dorn Arghans, "I think another ceremony would be well thought of. The letter of the law may have been met and honored, but great violence has been done to its spirit; and also there is no question but that some public ceremony will be needed to satisfy the folk."

"True enough," remarked Elharn, and his eyes sparkled as he looked at his brother. "I take it, Laisren, that you will not now shunt the Tanistry off on Orlaith or Deian?" He winked at his niece and nephew, who had turned horrified faces to him, not immediately aware that he but jested. Seeing it was so, they smiled, a little nervously; their elder brother, so long dull and dutiful in their eyes, had for once dazzled them utterly by the sheer dash of this runaway wedding, and the thought that he and Emer might be made to suffer for it had appalled them. But now, apparently, things were right again.

"Nay, nothing of the sort," said Lasairían impatiently, not for the first time taken aback by his younger brother's irreverence. "But let the public rites take place as soon as may be; I wish to put all this behind us, and begin afresh. Leinster, Ahès, you find this satisfactory?"

Farrell O Kerrigan, who like his wife had had no word to offer through the proceedings thus far, now looked his old friend in the face and nodded vigorously.

"Not my place, Ard-rígh, to object so long as *you* find it satisfactory; but since you do me the honor of asking, then aye, I do indeed approve, and I offer my regrets, for what they are worth, for my daughter's conduct. She was ever a headstrong lass, and the despair of her clannfolk; but glad am I, and her mother, to see her happy, and so well wed."

Emer smiled at her father, the smile of a daughter who knows just exactly to a hair's thickness how tightly her father is wound round her finger. And Farrell answered that smile as if he too knew the thickness of that hair, and it mattered not at all.

Seeing that the worst was over, Gwyneira let her glance fall upon her husband for the first time that night, where he sat two places away in his tall carved chair. He felt the glance at once, she could tell, though he refused to meet it, and she laughed inwardly, knowing his mind and the many horns of this dilemma that had been goring him for a fortnight past: He was pleased beyond measure at his heir's choice of bride, but every bit as furious at how that choice had been effected.

And furious with me as well, for that I intrigued behind his back on so vastly important a matter. But surely he sees too that that same importance is the very reason I did so. If I had spoken of it to Laisren, that Barraun and Emer should wed, he would have hesitated, and delayed, and postponed, and pondered, and perhaps even in the end have refused his consent to the match. And it is a fine and necessary match, perhaps the only one to ensure Keltia's future, and to fulfill Aoife's Seeing. She hesitated, then forced herself to frame the true reason, the deep reason that had lain hidden in her heart all this time. *And then too there was that other princess whom he loved—and that too was why: Having seen my son give up his heart's wish once before to duty, I would have done far more than this to ensure that he need not lose so much again. And if it costs me a tongue-lashing or two from Laisren—well, I daresay I can bear it.*

Gwyneira's thought was suddenly jolted back to the moment by the realization that the King had risen and the others with him. She stood up hurriedly, casting a guilty glance at her husband, but as before he gave no sign that he had noticed, either her prolonged abstraction or her tardy courtesy.

"I leave the jurisconsults now to their work," the King was

saying, "in full confidence that my brehons and Leinster's together, with Rohais's guidance, will reach a settlement of enech-
clann and tinnscra and all the rest of it that shall please everyone.
Only, let it be done quickly . . . And now, if the rest of you will
await us in the family gríanan, I have somewhat to speak of to
my Queen—alone. Lady," he added ominously, looking Gwyneira
in the face at last, "do you remain."

As the others thankfully fled the chamber, Lasairían seated
himself again in his chair, and Gwyneira, with a sense of growing unease that even her usual confidence could not dispel, heard
the doors close behind the Councillors with a dire boom.

Ah well, she thought, resigning herself to the inevitable, *I had
my own way, and now I must pay for it. What I did was done for
Keltia, and Laisren knows this; else had he taken me to task in
front of the others just now, or permitted the Council to pass
censure on me as Queen. And, aye, I admit, I too owe somewhat of an enech-clann to the Ard-rígh if not to the realm; if he
considers a scolding fair reparation, well enough. How bad can
it be?*

But as Gwyneira turned to face her husband, for all her fine
confident words she had a sinking certain feeling that it was
going to be very bad indeed.

When the news of the marriage was announced at last to
Keltia, and the rites publicly repeated at the royal nemeton of
Ni-maen a fortnight later, even Gwyneira could scarcely credit
the delight it caused among the people, though she of all the
principals had had most cause to foresee it. Greatly though the
folk of Keltia loved their Prince, it seemed that they were of but
a single mind on the double matter: that Fionnbarr should have
wed long since, and that his new Princess was their new darling.

And by the Mother Herself, it was *worth it,* thought Gwyneira,
as she watched Fionnbarr and Emer pledge each other before the
Archdruid and the Ban-draoi Magistra and the Chief Brehon at
the holy circle's central altar. *Worth every bit even of that flaying
I got from Laisren* . . . She laughed out loud at the recollection,
though it had been at the time by no means a matter for mirth,
and she still smarted from the sting of his words. Indulgent a
lord as Lasairían had been to her, still he was Ard-rígh, and it
had been as Ard-rígh that he had reprimanded his queen. *He*

does not show Aoife in him often, but when he does there is no doubt whose son he is . . .

Her attention was recalled to the moment by a none-too-subtle nudge from the Ard-rígh's elbow. Fionnbarr and Emer were leaving the circle, the rites having just now ended, and they had paused to make formal obeisance to their King and Queen; it was this that Lasairían had prodded his wife to acknowledge.

Gwyneira smiled at them, a mother's smile and not a monarch's, looking fondly after as the new-wed pair, now safely sealed in the sight of all Keltia, went with their bridal party down along the paved path leading back down the side of Mount Eagle to Turusachan, and taking Lasairían's arm, she followed after.

For all that, though, Emer did not conceive straightway, as most Kelts had expected and many more had hoped. When the months became years, and still no sign of any heir was toward, some began to grow apprehensive lest the direct succession fail to be properly secured, and almost all wondered at the seeming delay. Their Princess was young, she was healthy, she was plainly happy with her Prince, who just as plainly adored her: What then was the difficulty?

Those the matter most closely affected seemed not to share the widespread public worry: Fionnbarr and Emer themselves appeared untroubled, Gwyneira and Ahès showed no signs of matriarchal concern, and Lasairían said only, to those bold enough to dare inquire, that as Emer had been so very young when she and Fionnbarr had wed, so unacquainted with the true weight of the royal burden she had taken upon herself, this delay served a most useful purpose, buying time for her to grow into the task before her—that of being Keltia's next queen-consort. True, the producing of Keltia's next heir of line was the chiefest part of that task, as the siring of such heir would be the chiefest duty of any lord who wedded a Tanista; but more folk than the Ard-rígh alone deemed a hasty delivery not worth the sacrifice of Emer's health and well-being. She and Fionnbarr were contented and busy and deep in love; if they wished to wait on the birth of their offspring, well enough. Though the folk quite naturally longed for a new prince or princess, and it was to be hoped more than one, in the normal course of things Emer and Fionnbarr had many more decades ahead of them in which to provide one, and more than enough to occupy them in the meantime.

And if Emer ever daydreamed from time to time about her child to come, or if ever Fionnbarr pondered yet again the dying words of his grandmother Aoife as to that firstborn's name and life and dán, none but they themselves—and perhaps Aoife—ever knew.

Chapter 9

The years that followed upon the royal marriage were learning years for them all, the time full and never wasted. Emer plunged into her new responsibilities and kept up her own chosen pursuits— she had had a Fian training before her marriage, and now as wife to the Tanist she was patroness of the twelve Fian legions known as the Pillars of Tara—while Fionnbarr continued to learn from his father that which he would need to know in the time of his own kingship to come.

But the Prince stayed at Caerdroia now, for there was no question of his venturing out-Wall on the warrior's service at which he had so long labored: Until he had an heir of his body, and for safety's sake more than one, he was never again to be so employed, and in any case he had no wish to be apart from Emer.

Those were happy years also, so that when Fionnbarr looked back on them later from the throne itself, they seemed all lighted with a golden glow, and twenty years was to his longing backwards glance as but twenty months. Though politics filled the most of his days now, still there was time for friends, and his friends had become Emer's as well: Faolan Douglas, who was so soon to succeed his father as Prince of Scots, and Mared his wife, who had been brideswoman to Emer; Arawn ap Kenver, latest in the ancient line of Penarvon Princes of Gwynedd; old battle-comrades and companions in peace—Sithney ní hAiseadha, Countess of the Cathedine, his staunch second on Ganaster so long ago; Trystan Drummond, whose family had been courtiers to the Aoibhell monarchs since the days of the Ard-rígh Tigernach; and other friends both old and new, and so the years went by.

But though Fionnbarr had at present no hand in them, matters beyond the Pale, down those same years that passed so peacefully in Keltia, were by no means of a like tranquillity on the Curtain Wall's other side . . .

On Alphor, Strephon's daughter Helior had borne her lord Phano a son; called Jaun Akhera, the boy was thought by seasoned political observers, reading the signs, to be his grandfather's likely successor; indeed, they noted, his mother had already resigned her own heirship rights in the child's favor, to be the surer that the Eagle Throne of the Cabiri Emperors would one day come to her firstborn.

On Fomor, King Budic, he who had disputed with Aoife and with Lasairían and who had so nobly accepted in the end the Justiciary's ruling, died very old, and his son came now to reign as King of Fomor, and, as Strephon himself had once prophesied, as Archon of the Phalanx. His queen, Basilea, was at his side, but his concubine, Thona, was queen of his affections for all his world to see; for Bres had neither forgiven nor forgotten the long-ago indiscretion of the girl who had called herself Sovay, and who had loved her lord's rival and her kingdom's enemy.

Nor had he forgiven Fionnbarr her lover, or indeed Keltia itself. But to those whose business it was to mind such matters, it seemed that Bres's great feud had been for the time being set aside, or submerged as it were in more pressing concerns—such as Fomor's continuing struggles with the systems of the Phalanx, for though Bres was Archon it by no means followed that he was master. Or perhaps, some even thought, all that bitter enmity was truly ended, written off as an unpleasantness of the past best left buried in the past. But they were wrong indeed that thought so: If Fionnbarr had in his new happiness forgotten Bres and the ground of their disputation, or had at least put the memory aside, there was not a day—some days, not an hour—passed that Bres did not remember.

And, too, there was Earth itself; though many wondered, none in Keltia knew what might be happening on, or to, that planet once their home. And just exactly so did many more wish to keep it: *That* disagreement had been alight for three thousand years, born almost in the very moment of the launching of the first great immram from Earth led by St. Brendan himself, shifting back and forth like a restless tide over the millennia since, nay and aye and nay again forever.

There were good and gainful reasons to be set forth by either side: On the one hand, some argued, Keltia had grown to be a power in the galaxy in its own stead and by its own might; what harm now to reveal itself to the world from which it had sprung? But others said better it was to stay hidden, apart from the entangling alliances Terra would surely try to force upon them. Keltia stood in need of nothing Earth could offer; what profit to admit the ancient kinship?

Even the rulers of Keltia held no consensus on the matter: Lasairían opposed any trafficking with Terra, but Aoife his mother had been nowhere near so adamant; had indeed thought it by no means an ill thing if Keltia and Earth came to be allies and friends, under properly controlled circumstances—though she had left no doubt in anyone's mind as to whom she meant to do that controlling. Before her, the monarch's stance had swung back and forth with nearly each new reign: Líadan and Declan IX and Lassarina V had been for, Fionnbarr XIII and Jenóvefa IV and Brendan XXVIII against; before those, the civil wars begun by Lachlan and ended by Tigernach had precluded a firm foreign policy, or indeed any need for such, as Ard-rígh and Ard-rían in swift bloody succession fought for peace at home.

The opinion of the future Fionnbarr XIV was not yet known; it was believed that he inclined more to his father's mind than to his grandmother's, but as he did not yet rule, the official position remained unchallenged and unchanged. Keltia would continue to remain barred to its Terran cousins, isolate and unknown, and that was all there was to *that*.

But not quite all there was: In the spring of that year of Brendan 3475, twenty springs since they had wed, Emer told her husband that she was with child.

It had been a long labor for Emer, nearly seventeen hours. But as the sun rose over Caerdroia on a cold morning of early October, the red leaves flying on a northwest wind, Fionnbarr emerged from his wife's chambers carefully cradling a shawl-swathed bundle.

With Gwyneira, weary but radiant, close beside him, he ignored the jubilant friends and relatives and palace officers who had spent those hours waiting sleepless in the corridors of Turusachan, and going directly to his father where he stood with most of the Court behind him, Fionnbarr placed the bundle carefully into Lasairían's arms.

"May I present to the Ard-rígh Her Highness Aeron Lassarina Angharad, Princess of the Name and undoubted heir to the heir of Keltia."

The formula of presentation set off a most unregal volley of whoops and cheers among those who heard Fionnbarr's words, and Gwyneira, happy tears spilling over at last, turned back the shawl, that Lasairían might look upon the scrap of infant within the folds of gold-fringed white silk.

"Her hair is near as red as her face," he said, and chuckled as the baby's cloudy eyes opened, to give her grandfather what looked very like a disgusted stare. *Aeron Lassarina Angharad,* he thought. *Names for a future High Queen: Aeron as my mother so long ago commanded; Lassarina for me; and Angharad for that brave and lovely Ard-rían, Lachlan's only daughter, so long ago . . .* Lasairían brushed a gentle kiss on the infant's forehead, then with great care held her up for the Court to see. *My prayer for you, small one, is that what your great-grandmother Saw for you shall never come to pass; but if it must, and when it does, then may you have that which you shall need to meet it.*

Reclaiming Aeron quickly from her husband's long-unpracticed grasp, Gwyneira wrapped the child again in the shawl that had wrapped all three of her own children, with a gentle tickling touch on the dimpled chin until the baby opened her eyes once more, yawning tremendously.

"Not an hour old and already she is bored—blue eyes to go with that red hair, I think," said Lasairían, craning over his wife's shoulder. "*Your* hair, anwylyd"—he gave a loving tug to Gwyneira's still thick, still copper-gold plait, which had tumbled down unnoticed during her long vigil by the birth-bed—"and Emer's eyes."

"Nay," said Fionnbarr, suddenly sure. "Her eyes will be green as the skies over Erinna; green as Aoife's own."

He held out a finger, and the tiny hand closed on it with a strength and eagerness that astonished him. *Those green eyes of Aoife's Saw your coming long years ago, alanna,* thought Fionnbarr then, much as his father had done. *And such things she did See for you as I would spare you, if I could, or if our dáns allowed. But this I do promise: As I am permitted, so will I protect you—not too much, for you must learn; not too little, for you must grow. You will be Ard-rían in your turn, and that is your doom; mine is to empower you to face it, and to teach you that it is not by any measure the worst fate one might draw for one's own.*

All the same, in that joyous moment, in the midst of that delirious crowd, hearing the bells in the city below begin their long ecstatic peals, Fionnbarr felt a touch of sudden bleakness, like a cold breath of air sifting through a distant window.

For all the grace and glory of her life to come, his daughter had been born to a sentence as surely as to a scepter; even as had he, and his father before him, and every Aoibhell who ever had held the Silver Branch and worn the Copper Crown and sat upon the Throne of Scone. *Aye, and the Douglases before us, and the Penarvons before them, and all the other Keltic royal houses back to the sainted Brendan himself. My daughter's first inheritance from me is an éraic above all éraics: the royal ransom, the blood-price for Keltia, which is paid in life so that the realm might live. It is the Ard-rígh or Ard-rían whose life is coin for that buying, for that is the ruler's duty, and for eight hundred years the Aoibhells have gladly paid. And now this Aoibhell born this morning will be next to stand pledge for that reckoning . . .*

Fionnbarr became aware that his daughter was staring up at him, the wide veiled eyes fixed upon his face, as though she saw his sorrow or sensed his thought; and for all he knew that a child an hour old sees but light and shadow only, and maybe not even that, he felt oddly uncomfortable all the same under that strangely piercing gaze. *Come to it, who knows for sure what babes may have power to see—the coron-solais, even, or other things we grow blind to as we grow older.*

He took Aeron back again from Gwyneira, who was understandably reluctant to surrender even to the child's father her most eagerly awaited grandchild. But time it was now to return the baby to her mother: Aeron's birth had been witnessed and properly attested, her rank and heirship confirmed by the High King and the Taoiseach and the Councils. All who needed to had at least glimpsed her, and Emer would be fretting.

As he retraced his steps back to Emer's door, where her ladies kept vigil still, Fionnbarr felt the child settle close against his heart, and he tightened his hold on her. *A strange thought, my Aeron, for the hour of your coming into the world: Most fathers in Keltia would give their lives to know that their daughter would one day be High Queen. I think I would give my soul to know that you would not.*

"Great profusion of heirs just now," said Fionnbarr to his wife, one afternoon a week later.

Emer lay in her bed, propped up on pillows; though she had been on her feet again the very afternoon of Aeron's birth, she was still easily fatigued, and took advantage of time to rest whenever she might. Fionnbarr, who had no such excuse, was merely lounging beside her, idle and happy, both of them watching their daughter trying to hit herself in the eye with one small fist.

"Mared?" guessed Emer, her face lighting for her friend.

Fionnbarr nodded, not taking his gaze from the baby. "After all those lads, a daughter at last, born early this morning at Kinloch Arnoch. They have called her Morwen."

"A likely foster-sister for Aeron, when time comes that we need think of that."

"I thought you might say so. In fact I have already spoken of the matter to Faolan, and to Arawn of Gwynedd as well. Even though Gwynedd's daughter Arianeira is already five years old, it will make no differ later on."

"A useful connection, that with the Penarvons."

"Aye, and to Caledon as well, though when I spoke of heirs I was not thinking of the Douglases alone—but since you mention connections, this new Morwen will one day be Duchess of Lochcarron when her grandmother Raighne is gone, and that may be to Aeron's advantage when she is Queen . . . Nay, the heirs I had to mind were not Aeron's future friends but her enemies that will be: Jaun Akhera, Strephon's grandson, must be eight years of age by now, and Helior produced a second whelp—Sanchoniathon, they have called him, another barbarous name—only a sixmonth ago."

"Bres of Fomor too; has he not a brace of sons?"

"You very well know he has," said Fionnbarr quietly. "Elathan by his queen"—Emer's eyes flew to her husband's face, but there had been no break in his voice, the falter was all in her hearing—"and Talorcan by his longtime concubine—whom he seems to hold in higher regard than he does his own wife."

"Ah, Barraun, I did not mean to pain you." Emer took his hand and kissed it tenderly. "I am not the woman forever to be throwing lost loves in your face. I know you loved Basilea, and know why you were forced to give her up, and I know too that it has been long over. And even did I not know all this of my own kenning, and by knowing of your love for me, still had I your word on it all these years to take as troth. You lost her, but I neither expect nor demand that you forget her also. Have I not said so, many times?"

"Aye, you have, anwylyd, and I love you for so saying." He returned the kiss, pressing his lips to the back of her hand. "All the same, someday her son may be my daughter's enemy. That is something hard to face."

"And it is on the knees of the gods." Emer kissed her baby's silky hair, the fine soft wisps just beginning to show rich red-gold. "But howsoever it may go, I think this one here will be well able to deal with it."

At the advanced age of thirteen weeks, Aeron Aoibhell, Princess of the Name, made her first formal appearance in a life that would henceforth be ruled by such things. In the arms of her grandfather the High King, before most of the highest nobles of the realm, she was presented in the stone circle of Ni-maen for her saining, the first rite of the Keltic faith, by which a newborn child is consecrated before the gods, and returns thanks—or rather its parents do, on its behalf—for a safe rebirth into the world of Abred and for its time spent between the worlds since its latest life's ending.

Any saining is by nature a solemn event, for all its joy; but at a royal saining, signs and portents are more than usually minded, and guidance most particularly requested, though what signs and guidance may come are not always the most welcome of guests.

"A geis for the Princess," prompted Fionnbarr, as Teilo ap Bearach, the new Archdruid only a year in office, seemed about to end the rite.

Teilo fanned the nicksticks used for such divinatory purposes, then laid them on the bluestone altar in the pattern called peithenyn,

"Elucidator," and did not look at anyone who stood near: not Kesten Hannivec, the Ban-draoi Magistra, nor the Ard-rígh, nor the child's parents, nor even the infant Aeron herself.

What he saw in the pattern was perhaps not what he would like to have seen, for he said no word for long moments, and all round him the watchers grew uneasy.

"She is not to carry war out of Tara in the Wolf-moon," said Teilo at last. "And should anyone bid her stay her hand from her sword in Nia's name, she is bound to do so."

Emer, holding Aeron now, felt the baby give a little kick, and looked down in alarm. But the infant seeméd happy enough, giving her mother a gaping triangular smile and grabbing for the golden swans that bound the ends of Emer's golden plaits of hair. She raised her eyes, to meet Kesten Hannivec's unexpected dark gaze, and for no reason she could ken, then or later, Emer shivered a little, and wrapped a corner of her mantle round her child.

"That is not so bad a geis," offered Fionnbarr later. They were back in their chambers at Turusachan, where Emer was removing Aeron's ornate pearl-embroidered saining-robe and readying the infant for bed; the rite had taken place at sunset, as did all major Keltic ceremonies, and it was now long past Aeron's sleeptime.

"No monarch in right mind would lead an army on Tara in March," continued Fionnbarr, a little desperately, as if he were trying to convince and reassure himself rather than his wife. "And any road, what monarch has had need to lead one here? Not since the days of Lachlan has Tara, or any other world of Keltia, seen civil war."

"The words were 'take war *out of* Tara,' " Emer reminded him. "A rather different prospect."

"No matter, I say. It is a long way off, it may never come to be; many geisa go all unfilled, and their possessors none the worse."

Emer placed her sleeping daughter in the cradle—wicker, as was usual among the Kelts, but instead of withies the wickerwork here was all soft woven gold—and stood watching her a moment. *I am not overpleased with all this,* she thought then, careful to keep her doubts shielded from her husband. *All these warlike portents for my daughter . . . even her very name. It was not the name I'd have chosen, and none of this what I had in mind for her, when first I knew I was to bear Keltia's next High Queen. But if such must be her dán, then my prayer is this: That her three holy protectresses, in whose care we this night did place her, have each their full share of the watching and warding of her: Aeron for whom she was named, the battle-goddess of the Kymry; and Nia the Golden, mother of Brendan; and Dâna who is the foremother of the line of Aoibhell. She will have need of them all, I fear, before her life's task is done with; and if Aoife, who seems to have started this coil, could spare some attention for her great-granddaughter, I would not be at all unhappy to see it . . .*

And, thinking so, the thought that she might not live to see it never entered Emer's mind.

Interlude

Upstairs, in a crowded state bedroom of the palace of Turusachan, a king lay dying. Outdoors, in the chill of an autumn afternoon, a four-year-old princess was hiding in a wood.

Aeron had succeeded in eluding her nurse Nessa, her aunt Keina and her uncle Conor all three; no small achievement for a child just four. But it had been a confusing and unsettling afternoon; that even a young child could sense: Her parents and her grandmother, who as a rule could be counted upon for loving attention even at the busiest of times, were today somehow too taken up with other matters to have any time to spare for her. That all the melancholy murmurings had to do with her grandsir the King, she knew vaguely; the old man himself she knew scarcely at all, for he had been ill beyond the powers of the healers, or even the sorcerers, for much of her young life.

But earlier that day she had been taken into the dim bedroom, and her father had lifted her onto the big bed, so that her grandfather could kiss her on the forehead as he had used to do, and her small brother Rohan and baby sister Ríoghnach as well. He had seemed terribly tired, Aeron thought, and he had not even been able to join in the festivities for her birthday the week before; but today his face had been kindly as ever, and though she could see he had barely the strength to do so, he had ruffled her hair in the old affectionate way; and then he had spoken to the other people in the room. They had all gone very quiet while he spoke, but though Aeron had not understood his words, whatever he said had seemed to make them a little less somber, for most of them had smiled at her.

Then her favorite aunt Keina, at a murmured word from

Aeron's mother, had gathered her up and carried her away, and others had done the same with Rohan and Ríoghnach; but her father and mother and grandmother had remained beside the old King's bed, all looking very solemn. The babies had then been put to bed, but Aeron had been delivered into the care of her nurse, Nessa. Yielding to the child's entreaties, Nessa had put her favorite green cloak on her—the worn old one her mother despaired of, saying it made her look like a woodcutter's daughter, though Aeron loved it—and had taken her out into the palace gardens.

"Only for a little while, though, Aeron-fach; it is cold, and grows late, and you will be wanted again by your parents very soon now."

But Aeron could not imagine why, nor yet why Nessa seemed on the verge of tears every time she looked at her charge; and so she had slipped away while Nessa was deep in conversation with some of Aeron's mother's waiting-women. And now she was all the way up the hillside behind the palace, where she knew very well she was not permitted to go, in the small, sun-stippled pinewood she had longed to enter ever since she had first been forbidden to do so.

As she looked round in the clean-scented dimness, Aeron saw that she was not alone in the little clearing in which she stood, as she had thought herself to be. Across the width of the open space beneath the branches, lying so very still, half in and half out of the moving shadows, that she had not seen him straightway, lay a very large animal.

"You, Ruan?" she asked; her grandfather's giant deerhound was a familiar friend and guardian. But though the beast's feathery tail stirred the pine needles carpeting the clearing floor, it did not lift its nose from its paws, and it did not take its eyes from her face.

Not Ruan, then . . . Aeron walked forward without fear—never since her birth had she shown fear of any creature, had indeed a bond and rapport with beasts that was exceptional even among Kelts—and now she halted only a foot or so from the animal's great ruffed head. She put out her hand, eyes widening as the beast, slowly and lazily, stood up, stretching in every limb as it did so, and put its wet black nose to her hand to sniff it. She had not thought it was *so* big—now that it was standing, she could see that it was very much larger than Ruan: taller far, and thicker all round, with a rougher, shaggier coat and a white star upon its breast. Its head came well above her own, and she had to put her hand up as far as she could reach. But she could see its eyes strangely clearly in the forest gloom: green eyes, like her own, almost, with pretty gold flecks in them like that necklace of her mother's she so loved to play with. Then she felt the rasp of its tongue on her hand, astonishingly warm and rough and friendly.

She looked into its eyes again, and they seemed like a real person's, not an animal's at all; the dog, if dog it was, seemed almost to be laughing with her. There had not been much laughter all that solemn day, and Aeron was suddenly filled with love for the huge strange creature. Throwing her arms around the massive, rough-maned neck, as far and high and wide as she could reach, she felt the muscles shift as the beast put its head over her shoulder and snuffed at her hair, just as Ruan did.

Then all at once the muscles froze as the animal stiffened, and Aeron felt rather than heard the low warning growl that came from deep within its powerful chest, though she sensed that the growl was not meant for her. Turning round, she saw on the edge of the clearing Nessa and her aunt Keina, her uncle Conor just behind them. *Why, they look frightened,* she thought with surprise; then, *Nay, as if they are trying* not *to look frightened—but whyfor?*

The great hound draped one enormous padded paw possessively over Aeron's shoulder, and the three adults froze to immobility as it growled again, very softly. Then, startlingly, the beast licked her face, and when Aeron raised her arms to hug it again it was gone.

Before she could register her surprise, her uncle Conor had dashed forward to scoop her up in his arms, and her aunt was talking very quickly, and her nurse was weeping noisily, and all of them were asking her was she *all right*?

"I am not hurt, truly," said Aeron desperately, though she knew better than to try to escape from her uncle's grasp. "But why did you frighten my dog away?"

She had no answer from any of them to that question. Her uncle settled her more firmly in his arms and turned back to the palace, the two women close behind. Then, as they went down the hill, so fast that it seemed to Aeron that the grownups feared some strange pursuit, a sound went up behind them to freeze their blood.

It was the long high howl of a wolf, but like to no wolf's cry that Aeron had ever heard before. It rose and fell and died away, then mounted again; it seemed full of the most terrible sadness, yet also it carried overtones of salute, and triumph, and, strangest of all, satisfaction. Three times the cry rang out, until all the mountain side echoed with it, and it overspread the palace and throbbed in the air over the city below. And all that time Aeron's uncle only clutched her closer and quickened his pace.

Then they were back in the palace, and Aeron's father, serious and quiet, was kneeling in front of her, holding both her hands in both of his, explaining that her grandfather was dead, and that he was now the King, and that she herself would be Queen one day when she was grown. Stepping forward, her uncle Conor, gray-faced, told her father about the great dog she had been with in the wood, and of the lamenting howl they had all heard and recognized, even here in the hush of the palace. At that her father went quieter still, turning her chin so he could look full into her eyes.

"Aeron? Is this true? Tell me about the strange dog. You are sure it was not old Ruan?"

"Oh, not; it was bigger than Ruan, and different." And she told him, and when she was done telling, and the other grownups standing by were all as hushed and still as her father, her mother came forward and picked her up and carried her away to the nursery, without a word to anyone.

But when she was in her bed, and her father came in to kiss her goodnight, she asked to be told.

"Very well, alanna," said her father—the King! "Your mother thinks you too young to be told, that you cannot yet understand, and that it would only frighten you needlessly. But I think you can well understand what it is that I shall tell you, and without fear; else you would not have met—that which you did meet today in the wood."

The child looked up at him, eyes wide and shining. "It was not a dog like Ruan, was it, tasyk?"

"Nay, cariadol, it was not. When you are older, you will

know more of it, and deeper; but for now I will tell you that it was magic—you know what magic is, Aeron-fach?''

''Oh, *yes!*''

''Well then, it was magic, and it was a magic wolf you saw. A wolf that has been a special friend to our family since the first beginnings of Keltia, and maybe even longer than that. It helps us, and protects us, and when we are near to our passing it will give voice for us, as we heard today for your grandsir.''

''What is its name?''

''Doubtless it has one, or even many; but it has chosen so far not to tell us, and so we call it the Faol-mór, which is to say 'great wolf' in our Erinnach tongue.'' Fionnbarr smiled at the rapt look on the child's face. ''Perhaps it will be you, Aeron, who shall come to learn its truename.''

She was struggling to stay awake. ''Did you see it, tasyk, when you were a little boy?''

Fionnbarr brushed back the copper hair from his daughter's forehead. ''Nay, alanna, not so young as you today; though when I was older, I did so, once . . . It does not often show itself to us, though we know it is always near, and often we may feel its presence though we see it not. When you have need to see it again, Aeron, or when it thinks there is need, you will see it, so. Sleep now.''

After Aeron had finally relinquished her stubborn grasp on wakefulness, tumbling all at once into that total sleep of childhood that is as abrupt and complete as that of some young exhausted animal, Fionnbarr sat on beside her, holding her hand in his own. *What a weight for such small shoulders! I was into my twenties before the Tanistry came down upon my own, and I thought even that very hard . . .*

The door opened, and his wife came quietly into the chamber. ''Asleep?'' she whispered, and he nodded. ''The others as well,'' she said then. ''Though I think Rohan is still too young fully to understand, and surely Ríona does not . . .'' A look of relief was on Emer's face: It had been a demanding day all round, and she had been more concerned for her eldest child than she had allowed herself to admit; she was cheered now to see her safe from the press of events, at least for the brief hours till the morning. *And that morning will bring cares enough when it comes; no reason to race to meet them . . .*

She bent to kiss Aeron's damp brow, then drew her husband out of the room with her, for there were many matters that the new Ard-rígh of Keltia must attend to, and near as many for his Queen. Behind them, though they did not see, a Fian guard moved silently into her post before the nursery door.

Turusachan was strangely quiet for this time of early evening, yet both Fionnbarr and Emer felt the touch of that new, almost hungry attention which now followed them even in the eyes of those closest to them.

And that is how it will be from now on, thought Emer, her hand tightening on her husband's. *For the Ard-rígh Fionnbarr, and for the Queen Emer, and most particularly, now and always, for the Tanista Aeron.*

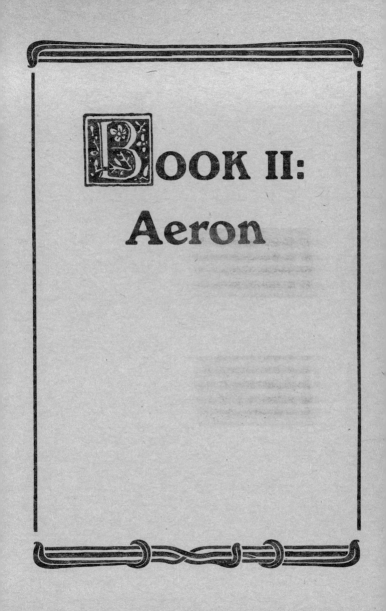

BOOK II:
Aeron

Chapter 10

However hard or heavy the new demands of the Crown may have weighed upon their parents, Aeron and her brother Rohan and sister Ríoghnach had just now but small sense of that weight, and of how it would come to fall upon each of them, and their siblings to be, in future; and if they had but little awareness that was all to the good, for they had then less concern.

They were handsome children, solemn for the most part and well-behaved, though Ríoghnach surpassed in obstreperousness both the others together when the mood was on her. Each a year apart in age, it seemed to all of them that never had there been a time when they had not been together, and each was already dimly aware, for all their parents tried to shield them, that somehow, for some reason, things were not for the three of them as things were for other children. There was much that their playmates, the sons and daughters of the other dwellers at Turusachan—Court officials and Fians of the Royal Guard and palace retainers and servitors—might do which they themselves were strictly forbidden; likewise there were things they must endure where their friends were free of duties.

Again unlike others, the royal children spent the greater part of their time in the company of their elders: nurses first of all, and the ever-present guards, always friendly, yet always watchful, whose vigilance's purpose their young wards as yet only vaguely understood. And from birth, shoals of kindred, from grandparents and great-uncles to first and second and even third cousins; also from birth, tutors, charged with instructing them in everything from letters to horsemanship to swimming.

And of course above all the rest there were their parents, who, far from being remote glittering figures glimpsed only at a distance, were warm and near and loving, as unhappy as the children if circumstances prevented as much time being spent together as any of them might like. Even Fionnbarr's assuming the High Kingship was not permitted to too much alter this: If anything, he and Emer were now more insistent than ever that the structure of their family should remain untroubled and untouched. They had waited too long for it, and enjoyed it too much now that it had come at last, to allow any of it to be lost to the insatiable maw of royal chores.

Too, as the King himself never tired of pointing out to any daring to tax him that he spent more time with his children than with his Councils, was not the proper rearing of royal heirs the utmost concern and task of any monarch; and if the Ard-rígh should involve himself so closely with the upbringing and instruction of those heirs, was that not a matter for thanks and rejoicing rather than blame? To which logic, of course, Fionnbarr's critics could make no reply at all; and life at Turusachan, for Aeron and Rohan and Ríoghnach at least, went on happily unchanged.

But when Aeron was five years old, barely a full twelve-month after her father had become King, life changed indeed, for now it was time that she should begin her years of fostering.

As was universal custom in Keltia, for the child of king and farmer both alike, her fostering had been decided upon, and documents drawn up to bind it in law, before Aeron had attained six weeks of age.

All Keltic children of royal or noble family were put at a very young age into compliance with an-altram, the ancient institution of fosterage; would leave their own families and all they knew and loved, and go to live as members of other clanns and kindreds, often in far-off places or on distant planets. The bonds forged thereby were as clear in law, and as binding in love, as the bonds a child was born to; and much thought was given by prospective parents to their baby's future guardians.

By mutual treaty, Aeron was to be fostered to two families as old and as royal as her own. A happy coincidence—the old queen Aoife would have smiled mockingly to hear it called such—had so arranged it that in both of these houses there were daughters of or near to Aeron's own age, though this was not invariably the case in fostering, or even always desirable; but it was in part why these particular princely kindreds had been chosen over many others equally eager for the honor.

For honor it was, even to such houses as these: The young Tanista would become foster-sister to Morwen Mariwin Douglas, six days her junior, eldest daughter of the Prince of Scots and herself heir to the duchy of Lochcarron; and to Arianeira, five years her senior, only daughter of Arawn Penarvon, Prince of Gwynedd, and twin sister to Gwydion, heir of the House of Dôn.

On Aeron's last night at home, having said her farewells to her brother and sister and playmates and others she loved, she had been put to bed by her nurse Nessa, who would be accompanying her to Caledon in the morning, to the home seat of the Douglas family at the castle of Kinloch Arnoch; and who had direly impressed her with the need to sleep well against the morning's demands.

Any other night she would have obeyed, but tonight was alive with change: Tomorrow she would be leaving everything and everyone she knew—her parents, her grandmother Gwyneira, her brother and sister, even the beautiful city that had been the only home she had ever known. It would be an adventure, of the sort she loved to have read to her, and to read for herself, out of the old books; but it would also be something to fear, and so, overexcited and consumed with imaginings and thumpingly hollow inside, Aeron had lain awake long after Nessa thought her safely sleeping, and now she slipped out of bed to stand, barefoot and irresolute, in the middle of the cold nursery floor.

Her first thought was to go and creep in for comfort with Rohan and Ríoghnach, as the three of them so often did in times of need, snuggling together like a nest of baby otters; but their nurses would surely catch her even if Nessa did not, and send her back to sleep alone. Then she thought of going to her mother, but that did not sound like it either, and mamaith would only chide her for being so late awake. Her grandmother Gwyneira would *not* chide, and would surely welcome her, but that too did not seem to be where she wanted to be.

Then, as Aeron stood considering whether it might not be best after all simply to do as she had been bidden and go obediently to sleep in her own familiar bed, the door to her room swung open so quietly that she did not notice; and, so quickly that she had not time even to stir, much less to leap guiltily back into bed, her father stepped inside. He seemed not at all angry to find her awake, not surprised even, for he only smiled, and put a finger to his lips, and then held out his arms to her, and Aeron ran to him without a word.

Lifting her up, feeling the sleep heavy in her battling the anticipation of the morning to come, Fionnbarr carried his daughter to the comfortable old longchair in which the nurse Nessa so often dozed, over next the fire, and settling Aeron on his lap he wrapped them both in one of the fur throws from the window-bench. The child leaned her head against her father's shoulder, and he put up his hand to stroke her hair, both of them watching the fire in perfect happy silence.

And that was how they found them in the morning, long since asleep, Fionnbarr's head resting on the pillowed wing of the chair, Aeron still curled neat as a palug-kitten under the fur blanket, and the fire cold gray ash upon the hearth.

Three hours later Aeron took ship from Tara—her first time off-planet—for Caledon in the Scotan system, and Kinloch Arnoch, home seat of the Douglases for five hundred years. As befitted a princess of Keltia, she went with a household of her own: Nessa her nurse; and Tryfan, the bard who had taught her her letters before she was yet a full year old; and Farrand and Desma, the two First-rank Fians whom Emer herself had appointed to be Aeron's guards from the day she was born; and Rochana, the tall Ban-draoi who was also Kin to the Dragon, given the charge by Gwyneira the Dowager Queen to defend her granddaughter from possible perils against which a sword alone might not suffice.

She was met at the castle gates by her new family. Faolan Douglas, Fionnbarr's longtime friend, was a cheerful, blond-bearded man, who kissed Aeron's hand with a formal bow and called her Tanista, then swooped her up on his left arm and his own daughter, Morwen, on his right. And there was Mared, his wife, a small woman, quiet and brown like a forest-hen, unlike Emer her own friend in all ways, whom Aeron instinctively loved on sight. And, standing off to one side, as if she were but an observer to these proceedings that in fact so closely concerned her, was a girl of ten in a black riding tunic and soft leather trews.

"This is Arianeira," said Mared, in the sweet low voice that had won Aeron to her so swiftly, drawing the other child forward. "Ari is daughter to the Prince of Gwynedd, and she will be sister to you both."

Aeron and Morwen looked down from the safe remove of Faolan's arms at a slight blond girl, not much taller than themselves, who after a moment raised a pair of astonishing blue-green eyes to them, and smiled.

"Glad am I to meet you, Aeron," she said in a soft, almost lisping voice. "I have always wanted a sister of my own, and now by fosterage I am given *two*. Though I am a few years older than you, in a few years more it will make but little differ; and when we are all women grown it will make no differ at all. Until then think of me as your elder sister, for I will look after you both as an elder sister would do." She held out a hand to each of them, a little imperiously, and Faolan set them down so that they might take it. "Come; I will show you where we are all to lodge."

As they went through the castle halls to their new domain, Aeron glanced surreptitiously upward at the self-possessed ten-year-old Kymri keeping so firm a hold of her hand. *Well, we are all princesses here,* she thought to comfort herself. Still, even to so young a child it was plain that Arianeira already made far more of that name than her two new sisters; or perhaps it was just that she was more of an age than the younger girls to understand the meaning of such rank.

For all her regal bearing, Arianeira was small of stature for her years—her twin brother, Gwydion, now away himself in fosterage to the princely house of Dalriada on Erinna, being trained for both master-Druid and master-bard, seemed to have garnered all the height that should have been shared out between the pair of them—and she was as fair as he was dark. Aeron covertly admired the other's assured prettiness: long hair of a gold so pale it seemed more like sun-kissed silver, fair skin with a few freckles, and those wonderful blue eyes.

Then from Arianeira's other side Aeron caught a look from eyes near as blue and a good deal warmer: Morwen, stealing a glance at the newcomer. Aeron ventured a smile, hoping that she had found a friend as well as a fostern, and felt a sudden happiness as Morwen shyly responded.

"Here now," said Arianeira, stopping before an open door. "These will be your rooms; yours there, Wenna, and that one yours, Aeron. My own is just beyond. They join all three on to a gríanan and garden, and a faha for exercise, and there is a schoolroom on the garden's other side. My parents have arranged for Kymric bards, than whom there are none finer, to instruct us, as my brothers and I were taught back on Gwynedd at my home."

"We have Scotic bards of our own here at Kinloch Arnoch," said Morwen, feeling the need to assert herself; for one who was after all only a guest here, Arianeira was making very free. "And Aeron brought with her a bard from Turusachan, a *king's* bard; he came from Seren Beirdd."

Arianeira smiled at the pride in the words. "I know, and they will continue to teach you; I meant no slight . . . Shall we look at your rooms, then? Do you like dogs, Aeron? I have my puppy here with me; he looks like a snow-lion, his name is Wynos—"

They were two years together at Kinloch Arnoch, the lovely old red sandstone castle at the head of the long blue loch; after that, they would go to Turusachan, and after two years more, to Caer Dathyl, Arianeira's home on Gwynedd. The order had been randomly chosen by lot; but every other detail of the children's fostering had been as carefully arranged by their parents as the initial choosing had been.

Some there had been who had thought that Aeron, as heir to the throne, would benefit more, and learn more, from a humbler environment than that to which she was accustomed; had pushed for her fostering to some family of no rank and little wealth: farmers perhaps, or craftsmen, with deep roots in everyday Keltic life and no connection to the Crown. But Fionnbarr, though very tempted by the idea, had in the end decided otherwise, to the relief of most of his advisors. Aeron's fosterns should be princesses; and of all Keltia's nine princely houses, only Gwynedd and Scots had daughters of suitable age, and were friends beside to the King and Queen.

Though it was more usually the custom in fosterage for the

children simply to be exchanged one for one, royal fostering was often otherwise, and it was Emer who had insisted on the present arrangement. "If the aim is to foster closer bonds between our three houses," she had told an unconvinced High Council, "let the lasses stay together. You will see; it will not be only with each other that they shall forge lasting bonds." And in the end Emer had had her way, as usual, and the girls had been sent into fostering as a threesome; though many would recall, after, the words the Queen had spoken.

But Aeron and Morwen and Arianeira, unaware of any of this, began their six years together happily enough. They were instructed much as were all young Kelts of their age and talents, in matters of the mind and skills of the hand. Aeron learned to ride like a bansha, like one of the Wild Hunt itself, though neither of the others was quite so fearless in the saddle; she learned the games any active child will learn, and the lore that would make a firm foundation for the other, harsher learning that was to come.

Emer's foresight was proved early on, for Aeron took her foster-kindred to her heart: Morwen's six older brothers and the four sisters who came later were to become as dear to her as her own; and Arianeira's two brothers as well, though she did not see as much of them. But above all the others in Aeron's child's heart was Roderick, Morwen's eldest brother.

Until that time, being herself the eldest, Aeron had never experienced that particular sort of hero-worship a young child may feel for an older sibling; and to her, Rhodri, the Master of Douglas, seemed almost godlike. There was nothing he could not do, and do better than anyone else, be it riding or fighting or singing or swearing; eight years Aeron's senior, he was being trained as a prince, for he would inherit from Faolan when the time came, but his real love was given to bardery, and already his gift for it was plain.

Morwen, who felt the other way that a child can feel about its elder sibling—vastly unimpressed by Rhodri's accomplishments—was disgusted by Aeron's adoration, and lost no opportunity to tease her unmercifully for it. Arianeira, who being five years closer in age to Rhodri than the younger girls might well be expected to feel differently, had as little use for him as he for her, and the two seldom exchanged more than the barest civilities.

But two years, though at first it might seem forever, will pass swift enough when one is young and those years are full and happy; long before any of them thought to look for it, it was time for the royal fosterns to move on to Turusachan, and the care of Fionnbarr and Emer.

Mared watched the children as they prepared to go aboard the craft of the Royal Flight that Fionnbarr had sent to carry them to Tara: no pleasure cruiser but a warship, its cúrsal escort waiting in orbit out beyond Ruchdi, Caledon's huge moon.

The martial formality pleased Faolan, she knew, but Mared could find little to please herself in this parting. *Two years may have seemed long to them—or perhaps not, children have so little sense of time passing—but to me it has seemed more like two months of high summer, bright and glad and so soon over. Mighty Mother, but I shall miss my babies; I know it is her fair turn, but I envy Emer that she shall have the next two years with them, years I shall not be sharing, save for special feasts and flying visits . . .*

In spite of the tears that threatened, Mared smiled: Babies they may have been when they came to her, but they were babies no longer. *True princesses, the lot of them . . .* She ran a quick maternal eye over them. Blond braids gleaming, neat and serious in her red cloak, Morwen to her mother's eye was eager for the adventure, but in her usual grave little way the most self-possessed of the three. Arianeira, overeager, was polite enough in her farewells, but her willingness—her haste, even—to shake the dust of Kinloch Arnoch from her boots was plain to the most casual onlooker.

And Aeron . . . As usual the untidiest of the three, hair and cloak and tunic already askew though she had begun the day as neatly turned out as the others, Aeron seemed just as plainly torn between joy that soon she would be in her own home with her own family, and reluctance to leave Caledon. Here Mared smiled a different sort of smile, for she thought she knew the reason that lay behind that reluctance, and the thought did much to dispel her present heaviness of heart.

I know it is very early days to think of such matters, she chided herself, as she watched Aeron take shy farewell of Rhodri, saw her son smile down from his superiority of years and height and ruffle the child's red-gold hair. *But from such small beginnings great things can sometimes be coaxed to grow . . .*

As Mared bent to hug the children one last time, she felt Aeron's thin arms tighten suddenly around her neck, and the resolve was made: to speak, not too soon but in good time, to Faolan her husband, and to Rhodri's own foster-parents, and to her friend Emer the Queen in especial, on what might prove to be a matter of great interest to Clann Douglas and House Aoibhell—and a matter of greatest import to all Keltia.

Chapter 11

"If Aeron is to be High Queen when she is grown," said Morwen one day, "what shall be, Ari, for us two?"

The three royal fosterns were in their grían, a spacious sun-drenched room atop a small tower on the palace's eastern side. They spent most of their time here during Caerdroia's long snowy winter, taking their lessons from the bards Fionnbarr had set to teach them. Just now they were enoying a rare free moment, and each had taken advantage of it in her own way: Aeron, as usual, had buried her nose in a book, Morwen was absorbed in her beloved mathematicals, and Arianeira was merely idling.

At the younger girl's question, though, the Gwyneddan princess's face clouded over, losing just a little of its facile brightness, and across the width of the grían the bard Tryfan paused in his work to hear her reply.

"Well, your mother's mother, Wenna, has left to you her dúchas," said Arianeira, well aware of Tryfan's attention. "So that you shall rule Lochcarron upon achieving your full age. And to be a ruling duchess is no small or easy task."

"And you?" persisted the future duchess.

The cloud deepened. "Oh, my brother Gwydion, when he is sovereign prince over Gwynedd, will find somewhat for me to do; it is only by twenty minutes or so that he is heir to Gwynedd and I am not, so it would seem he owes me some due—a dúchas or council position or rule-rank of my own. Or perhaps I shall wed some other prince or great lord, and share rule with him as his consort, as the man you shall marry, Wenna, will share Lochcarron with you, or as Aeron's chosen lord shall be King of

Keltia. Even maybe Aeron herself, when she is High Queen upon the Throne of Scone, with that same king-consort beside her, will bestow upon me some small thing, out of her royal favor.''

But even an eight-year-old could not miss the bitter sarcasm that seasoned that last, and Aeron looked up guiltily from her book, her cheeks crimsoning, not understanding entirely, but feeling that somehow she had wronged her foster-sister, and owed it to her to make some kind of amends.

"I shall give both of you whatever task or title you like, so that we may always be here together at Turusachan, if it will make you happy, Ari. When I am Ard-rían, then I may do as I please."

Arianeira threw a quick furtive glance across the room, but Tryfan had his eyes again on his music-copying, and appeared to be paying no heed whatever to the conversation of his charges. All the same, Arianeira chose her words this time with more care.

"As Ard-rían, Aeron, you will find that pleasing yourself must be the last thought in your mind. But aye, I too hope that we may continue to be together for as long as may be. Come now, I see that Master Tryfan has finished copying out that chaunt Rhodri wrote for Wenna's birthday. Shall we fetch our instruments, then, and learn it, to make a surprise for the King and Queen?"

To that Aeron and Morwen eagerly assented, and they ran to fetch their small telyns from the press where they were kept. Tryfan silently passed the music sheets to Arianeira, but he continued to study her even after the three had begun amid much giggling to play; there had been a note in her voice and manner that his bard's ear had caught and his deep instincts did not like. *Princess or no*, he thought, *that is a cold young bit of work there, not like the other two little bandits . . . whoever saw fit to name her 'Silversnow' was not far from the mark. There will be trouble with her later on, I think, for my lasses; pray gods, not too much trouble—but we shall see.*

"Now, my young madams," he said aloud, rising from his place and crossing the room, unslinging his own harp as he did so. "Though I say it as should not, you have a far better musicmaster than that untuneful row might bear witness to, and before I let you touch so much as one string before the King and Queen, there will be a deal more practice around here. Now, a little more care and less expression, if you please, to do justice to Prince Roderick's bardsmanship.''

As her two years at home passed steadily by, Aeron seemed more and more anxious to store up as much of her family as she could, as if to last her against a leaner time to come. She had two more brothers now, infant twins named Kieran and Declan, and she was enthralled by their baby antics; but her first comrades, Rohan and Ríoghnach, were themselves now away in fosterage, and sorely missed by their elder sister.

To compensate a little for this, and also because it was his delight to do so, Fionnbarr made as much time as he could to be with his daughter—and with her fosterns as well, though Morwen seemed to prefer Emer's company and Arianeira most often chose to be alone.

The two had gone riding over Miremoss, a wide stretch of peaty uplands and high meadows in the hills east of Caerdroia—a precious private time in a busy season—when Aeron asked a question that startled her father.

''Who is this Jaun Akhera?''

''Why do you ask, cariadol?''

''Oh, only for that I heard mamaith mention him to my uncle Ironbrow.'' Aeron looked up at her father, but he was staring straight ahead over his horse's pricked ears. ''She did not seem to like him much,'' she added hopefully.

Fionnbarr laughed. ''Nay, and with good reason! Well, Jaun Akhera is a prince of the Coranians; you have studied those folk, I think, with Tryfan? Most like they will have Jaun Akhera to be their next Emperor.''

Aeron urged her gray pony along, to keep pace beside her father's long-striding chestnut stallion. ''Emperor—that is like an Ard-rígh. He is only a boy?''

''Of I believe seventeen years, or nearabouts. His grandfather Strephon is Emperor now, and his mother is the Princess Helior.'' Fionnbarr paused a moment. ''Was it your mother spoke first of him to you, Aeron-fach?''

''Nay, Faolan-maeth. And said too that I must never forget

this Jaun, or lose sight of him—do you know, tasyk, why he spoke so?"

The King's face changed just a little, then changed back again, and he smiled down at her, though to Aeron it seemed that her father's smile was the one all her elders used when they wished to conceal their true feelings from the children, but at the same time wished not to alarm.

"It is nothing you need fret yourself about for a good many years yet, alanna, gods willing; though your foster-father was right to speak of it to you. Now then, shall we see who will be first across this field, Eirlys or Suran?"

Aeron, with a delighted squeal, dug her heels into the patient Eirlys's gray sides and raced off over the moor. Reining back the powerful chestnut so as not to overtake her, Fionnbarr gave rein instead, now his daughter could not see it, to all his own cares and fears. *Faolan did well to bring the Coranians to her attention, as I did bid him; and he must have done it artfully, else she had been more curious, and more alarmed—and that is not how I wish her to learn of these matters. Indeed, I could wish that she never need learn of them at all, but there it is, and I must mind me to speak again to Arawn, so that he may teach her in turn of the Fomori. Knowledge of them will best come from elsewhere; not Emer nor Faolan nor I would be as impartial as we must on that subject, and I would have Aeron learn of her future foes—and her father's past nemesis—from a more temperate teacher . . .*

But Aeron had reached the far side of the meadow, and was now waving triumphantly to him, a small excited figure in green atop the stolid garron. Fionnbarr waved back, bowing in his saddle to acknowledge her victory, but in truth he wanted to weep. 'Tasyk,' she had called him; the old baby-name, nursery-name, that of late she had very deliberately begun to correct herself of using, in her new dignity scorning to call him anything but the formal appellations—'athra,' 'syra'; even, sometimes, 'Ard-rígh.'

She is growing up, he thought with a fresh pang. *And that is of course the thing to be wished for; but sometimes she forgets, and that too is precious, for it will not last much longer . . .*

He looked past his daughter to where, unobtrusive and vigilant, her Dragon guard Rochana waited in the shadows of a small wood, and he knew too that his own guards rode not far off, fanned out on either side. Fionnbarr disliked the practice, as did most Keltic monarchs, but it was more a matter of long custom than real necessity. High-ranking Kelts seldom went anywhere unattended, and it had been long centuries since any ruler of Keltia had been dealt harm from a subject's hand—and on balance, unlikely to happen again any time soon.

Still, that too is part of it; and the sooner she learns not to chafe under such harness, the better for her. But I had liefer that she need never have to pull against so neck-bending a bit, nor yet against those harsher curbs that are still to come. Even though it were to deny dán itself, I wished it in the hour of her birth, and so could I wish it still, for my child.

Fionnbarr felt the stallion shift restlessly beneath the gilded saddle; all unthinking he had been reining Suran back all this time, and the horse was fretful. He patted the gleaming chestnut neck as his Fian guards rode up beside him.

"Go collect the Tanista," he said aloud, and one of the Fians spun his own horse on its haunches to obey, giving as he did so an arm-signal to Aeron's guard Rochana. "We are late in returning, and the Queen will be growing anxious."

About that same time, there came to pass an episode about which the Queen might well have been more anxious still, had she but known of it; but she was not at hand when it happened, and Fionnbarr did not tell her all the truth of it, not then, and not for some time after. And when at last he did, for it was a thing she must hear sometime, for all her distress that he had so long kept it from her, Emer was in her heart not entirely sure that he had been entirely wrong to do so; and wished a little, even, that he might have been able to spare her the knowing longer still, if not forever; but it could not be . . .

Of all gifts a hopeful parent might watch for in a growing child, the gift of magic was in Keltia far and away the most treasured. As a rule it was an obliging gift, showing itself early on in those whom it chose to favor; but though it was so eagerly looked for, so welcomed when it first appeared and so cherished when it was at last confirmed, its first stirrings were very often not easy ones, nor yet particularly pleasant; and oftener still, the

greater the power that would be, the more troublous its onset—
and not always to its possessor alone.

On the day of Alban Hefin, the summer solstice, that year that
Aeron was nine, Fionnbarr the High King stood in the center of
the great stone circle of Ni-maen, to conduct the rites according
to his duty.

Like its fellows across all the Keltic worlds, Ni-maen had
been raised upon a place of ancient power, a high narrow valley
known as Calon Eryri, tucked in among the three peaks of Eagle.
Its ring of bluestone trilithons, with the altar at its center and the
tall carved pillars at the eastern gateway, was little different from
thousands of others, and for most of the days of the seasons'
rounds there was no difference at all. In every weather and
mood and need, folk came up the Way of Souls that climbed the
mountain from the City below, to pray or petition or simply to sit
and think, to praise the gods or thank them or berate them, for
any reason and no reason. Many days there were that the stones
had no visitors at all, or at least no mortal ones, and those days
the circle fed itself on solitude, and thrived.

But on the eight hallowdays each year that were the chief
festivals of the Keltic faith, marking out the year's slow wheel
like eight great beacons of the Light and the Dark, Ni-maen
stood above all the rest, for here it was that the monarch of
Keltia, Ard-rían or Ard-rígh, led the services for the people.
Some sovereigns were devoted to this sacral function of their
ancient role, would indeed have chosen a life as Ban-draoi nun
or Druid monk over the wearing of the Copper Crown, had they
been free to choose; while others, and Fionnbarr was one of
these, were of more worldly mold, and performed their holy
duties only so far as the law did demand.

That year for the first time the King had brought his heir with
him to the ceremony. Queen Emer was away on progress to the
Kernish worlds, and had taken Rohan and Ríoghnach with her,
though the infant twins had been left behind; and Fionnbarr
thought it good that Aeron should take advantage of the time to
learn somewhat of her own future duties. To his mind she was
now of an age to begin to understand such things, and in any
case he simply wished for his daughter's company.

So Aeron stood now to one side at the circle's heart, yawning at being so early awakened, watching her father as he performed the intricate solstice rite, speaking incomprehensible words and being answered just as incomprehensibly by the solemn-faced Druid priests and Ban-draoi priestesses who assisted him. No one, not even her grandmother Gwyneira or her aunt Keina, both of whom stood by, seemed to have any attention to spare for her just now; and so after half an hour's impeccable obedience, finding herself for the moment unobserved, Aeron slipped quietly out of the circle and down over the sloping ground.

Luck held, and no one saw, to drag her protesting back—or perhaps luck had little to do with it: She possessed a knack for remaining unseen when she wished, much as some small animal might do for its own protection, and she had her goal clear in sight.

Some yards away from the nemeton's outer ring stood a stone apart from the others. Though she could not recall ever having been told, Aeron knew that this was the Helestone, one of the nemeton's points of sacred focus. Neither dressed nor carven as were the trilithons, but rough-hewn and crudely shapen, or perhaps not shaped at all, it stood precisely in alignment with the rising Midsummer sun, and was plainly not aligned so by chance. Aeron had felt strangely drawn by the great stone ever since her glance had first fallen upon it, and now, still unnoticed by any elder's eye, she dodged round its far side so that the stone's gray bulk shielded her from view.

Not so tall as were the pillars of the circle, still to a small child the Helestone loomed tremendously, and yet Aeron felt no fear. Crouching down in a little grassy hollow at the stone's foot, she reached out a hand to touch it, thinking to feel cold rock that had been all night in freezing shadow. But to her surprise the rough surface was warm to the touch, and it was not blank and gray but veined with subtle traceries of crystal and silver, tiny sparkling rivers in the stone.

Though it had been barely light when the royal procession had come to the stones, by now the sun had climbed to crest the line of the horizon, where it showed far and blue in the east between the gap in the mountain peaks. The chanting in the circle above now grew exultant, and as the flaming solar disk mounted swiftly to balance upon the point of the Helestone, Aeron lifted her face to the welcome warmth and stared straight into Grían's white blaze.

Something seemed to have happened to her sight, for her eyes were neither dazzled nor pained by the brightness, and a joy such as she had never felt before came with the light. A sudden surge of power—though she did not yet know to call it that, nor even that it *was* power—rose up from the earth beneath her feet, and instinctively Aeron put one hand to the stone to steady herself. The contact grounded her, and the joy and the power grew together, twining round each other in a shining spiral, and in this incredulous new state Aeron raised her other hand in salute to the sun. *Dance,* she thought to it, *oh, dance now so that I may see it! Dance for me!*

And it seemed then that the sun did dance: a grave measure at first, such as a star in its dignity might be expected to pace; then that changed, and Grían spun across the sky in such a reel as no mortal had yet beheld. It was changing color now as it danced, the white light broken up as if by some galactic prism—sapphire and emerald and garnet and amethyst and white-gold—the waves of successive color sweeping like the Solas Sidhe, the Faery Fire itself, over the land beneath, and across the upturned faces of those thousands who had gathered in Calon Eryri to witness the rites.

Now Aeron could hear their cries of fear and amazement filling the air, though she herself felt neither, only a delight in the dancing star, and most wondrous of all, the delight she felt it took in her. Then her father's voice cut clear and commanding across the tumult, the King's voice, calling her name, and for the first time in her life she did not run eagerly to the sound but stayed where she was, and stayed silent.

"Aeron? Aeron, for the love of gods, answer me—"

Fionnbarr, who had broken from the circle and come running down past the Helestone, stopped short at sight of his daughter. When the sun had first begun to spin in the heavens, his only thought had been for Aeron, lest she be frightened; and seeing her gone, though he knew she could come to no harm there in the sacred precincts, he had been concerned and a little angered, but not fearful. Yet now as he saw her standing glad and unafraid, one small hand on the great Helestone and the other lifted to

Grían, he felt in himself the terror he had thought to comfort in her.

She saw him then, and smiled. "Look, athra," she said excitedly. "The sun dances!"

Fionnbarr spoke from a suddenly dry throat. "Why does she dance, Aeron? Did you bid her do so?"

Aeron nodded, still watching the sun. "I was happy here with the stone, and I thought it would be a fine thing to see, that Grían danced; and I asked her and she did."

Softly, now; if you betray your own fear to her, she *will be afraid, now and perhaps for always* . . . "It *is* a fine thing, cariadol; but the folk do not know that you speak with Grían, and they are afraid. Can you bid the sun be still again, just so feat and quiet?"

The child considered. "I had liefer not, but no one must be feared—"

"Even so, alanna. Bid her stand."

Shouts of wonder and alarm still rent the valley air as Aeron, looking up one last time at the spinning star, lowered her arm, and took her hand from the stone, and thought stillness in her mind.

And Grían sailed again her path of old, and danced no more.

"She did not, of course, truly cause the sun to move," said Teilo ap Bearach carefully. "It was but an appearance of movement."

"An *'appearance'* that half the planet saw, Archdruid!" snapped a dark-haired man still robed in the black and purple he had worn for the rites: the Pendragon Corentyn, head of the Dragon Kinship. "Folk fainted from here to the Rhinns of Kells— It was well that today being Alban Hefin, the thing was held by most who witnessed it to be a holy sign, and so general panic was averted—though only just."

"And thus the panic we find ourselves in, here and now," remarked Fionnbarr from his seat at the table's head, and the others sighed agreement.

It was early evening of that same Midsummer Day. Still shaken by the morning's events—a state he shared with most of his subjects—the Ard-rígh had upon his return to Turusachan summoned the chiefs of Keltia's magical orders, to discuss among themselves the Tanista's remarkable feat. Aeron herself, after a brief questioning by her aunt Keina and the Ban-draoi Magistra Kesten Hannivec, had been sent early to bed; though she had answered her inquisitors cheerfully enough, she had been strangely subdued all day, and had made not even her usual token protest at the enforced removal.

"I have summoned you here because you know among you far more of such matters than do I," added Fionnbarr. "What I wish to know is this: How did it happen, and why, and will it happen again? Magistra?" he asked, turning to his right.

Kesten Hannivec smoothed her sleeves down over the backs of her hands, and shrugged.

"The short answer, Lord, is that it happened because of the power of the place, and the power of the day, and the power in Aeron herself that the day and the place brought out. As to whether it will happen again—is this the first magic she has managed?"

"The first of note," said Fionnbarr. "Up until now she has been guilty only of the usual children's tricks: earthfasting folk, small conjuries and pishogues like cloudshaping or calling up the tinna-galach . . . naught to compare with this."

"Yet she does not know what in truth she did," said Keina. "I read it in her mind when Kesten and I kenned her earlier; there was no intent in it at all, and it was much as she herself did tell you. She was happy, and to her the sun too seemed happy, and she thought it would be a fine thing to see it dance. Many children might have thought so."

"But not many would have made it happen!" shouted Fionnbarr. "And fewer still would have managed to terrify half their homeworld in the process . . ." He took a deep calming breath, carefully folding his hands together. "My sorrow to shout, I am overwrought—but, my friends, I think it might be best if the folk not be told just yet it was Aeron did this thing. If any were harmed by her action, I will of course make proper reparations on her behalf, but I would not have her named or blamed for it. If, as seems to be, she has the gift for sorcery, they will learn of it soon enough."

"And what of the Queen?" asked Corentyn. "Surely she must be told?"

"In time; and I myself shall decide when that time has come.

Emer is as you all know no great friend to magic, and this will be to her no welcome news.''

Kersten looked exasperated. ''Emer will have no choice in the matter; no more will Aeron or you yourself. Not only that, but all three of your daughters, Lord, will be that way gifted, so that you and the Queen would do well to make up your minds to it with as good a grace as you can.''

'' 'All *three*'? But—'' Fionnbarr broke off in some confusion, and the smiles round the table were kindly ones. ''Well,'' he said after a while, ''that's as the Mother will have it to be. The problem now is Aeron only.''

''Then there *is* no problem,'' put in Teilo smoothly. ''You have only to think now in terms of a Ban-draoi Ard-rían to follow you.'' He laughed outright at the look on the King's face. ''Barraun, it is no bad thing! Let Kesten tell you—''

''Aeron will be a Ban-draoi, right enough,'' said the Magistra of that order. ''And, I think, such a one as we have not seen for many years; certainly not for many reigns . . . Also I think that Corentyn will not give me the lie when I say that most like she will be Kin to the Dragon one day also?''

The Pendragon's nod confirmed her judgment; but Fionnbarr needed an answer to a question he had been dreading all that day, and turning now to his personal Druid, who had taken no part in the discussion as yet, he forced himself to ask it.

''What if she had not obeyed me—if I had not been able to cause her to cease? Would she have done a thing perhaps more harmful—not from malice, but from unknowing—*could* she do such a thing in future?''

The Druid Laoghaire Grannan shook his head. ''Not to my mind, Lord,'' he said firmly, and his certainty was echoed all round the table. ''Her sense of rightness—aye, even in one so young and untaught—would not have allowed it; and that will be her great safeguard in time to come as well, to keep her from the misuse of her powers. Let you think of this as a warning as well as a showing: For she *will* have powers, and she must go to Scartanore to learn to control them. In the meantime, give her such teachers as are themselves gifted in magic, and in the perceiving of magic in others. The ground must be prepared.''

Fionnbarr looked from one to another of the sorcerers, reading the same truth on each face, and all at once he gave up the struggle.

"Then to Scartanore she shall go, when she is of an age for it. But how I am going to explain all this to her mother, I have not the smallest idea."

So the matter was explained away to the folk as a favored vision for the Midsummer feast; and, later, was explained to Emer, though Fionnbarr alone knew how. The Crown made discreet reparation in such claims as were made, none of them grave ones; and in time the event was half-forgotten, passing and being overtaken by the march of other matters.

So did Aeron's time at Turusachan pass, and her last two years as a fostern in care were spent uneventfully enough at Caer Dathyl, the great gray fortress that had served the Princes of Gwynedd as home and stronghold and seat of government since Keltia's early days.

By now Aeron and Morwen were far closer of heart than either was with Arianeira; perhaps the age difference was to blame, perhaps it was some other reason. But their closeness would mean more to them now than formerly, now that Arianeira was once more in her own home place, and almost from the day of their arrival she spent as little time with the two younger girls as she might without incurring her parents' wrath.

But if Arianeira felt freer now to ignore her fosterns than she had been in their homes, her brother Elved and her parents Arawn and Gwenedour more than made up for her lack, with a warm reception and unstinting affection, and both Aeron and Morwen soon felt entirely at home. But there was another son of the house—

All through her years of fosterage, Aeron had seen little, though she had heard much, of Arianeira's twin brother: Gwydion, heir of Gwynedd, eldest of the children of Arawn and Gwenedour. He had himself been away as fostern to the Dalriadic court, and from there had been sent to Seren Beirdd, Star of the Bards, in Turusachan, and to Dinas Affaraon for Druidic instruction. His presence on Tara, and Aeron's on his own home planet, had not previously coincided, and though on occasion they had met each other at some feast or function, she had by no means seen anywhere near as much of him as she had of Rhodri Douglas.

The summer before Aeron's thirteenth birthday, she was once more at Caer Dathyl. Though she had been out of fosterage for two years now, having spent that time—much to her profit— with the bards in Turusachan, she was making a round of visits to her kin and foster-kin before going to Erinna to begin her schooling with the Ban-draoi, as Fionnbarr so long ago had resolved.

That summer Gwydion too was at Caer Dathyl, home himself on a visit before his departure for Caer Artos, in the vale of Arvon, where he would take instruction as a Fian. He was just eighteen years old, already taller than his father, with dark hair and the gray eyes of his mother's family, already skilled at magic and at music.

Aeron had glimpsed him but seldom those weeks of high summer: every now and again, a tall figure clad in bardic blue, walking in the palace halls, or riding out under the gate on his favorite hunter, or at swordplay in the faha with one of his father's officers, already showing promise of the warrior he would become. She had even seen him walking in the gardens with various young ladies of his mother's court; but no flicker of prescience had troubled her heart, nor did it seem that he saw her as aught other than the Tanista Aeron, his sister's fostern. There had been no foreshadowing of what they would in future be to each other, no revelation of othersight, no an-da-shalla of the heart to tell them of what was to come.

So it came as a surprise to them both when it did come; both would remember, years after, that first sight each had had of the other—or so it seemed to them the first, the first true seeing, for certainly they had seen each other often enough in the years of their earlier lives.

It was in the peony-garden, a great overgrown alley of ancient trees planted by a princess of Gwynedd dead now three hundred years. Aeron, who would be departing Caer Dathyl on the morrow, to spend her last few days of freedom with her own family at home, had been all at once afflicted with the dubhachas, that savage black melancholy that so often possesses Kelts of sensitive nature. To combat it, for she refused to yield to it and resolved too that it should not leap like some soul-contagion from her to others, she had gone to walk alone in the gardens.

But the gaiety and lightness of the thousands of rioting summer blooms had done little to chase her mood, and now Aeron found her steps leading unerringly to the cool dark depths of the peony walk. The time of flowering was over that year for those great trees, but under their deep-green, glossy leaves, Aeron sensed a mood of completion, a feeling of impending autumn, and far off, past the well-earned sleep of winter, another spring when there would be other blossoms, and a satisfaction for it; and the trees' mood seemed to march with her own.

As she passed a kilvach to one side of the path beneath the trees—a little alcove-garden, bordered with low thick hedge, within whose precincts stood several stone benches and a marble summerhouse—Aeron saw that she had not been the only one that day to seek the solitude of the peony alley. She stopped short, constrained by shyness and good manners, still in the protecting shadow of the vast dark trunks, and then had of force to remain, for she did not know how to withdraw unseen.

Two there were in the kilvach, and one of them seemed very angry indeed. Though Aeron had not noted their presence with her conscious mind, she must have heard their voices from a distance, and it was that which had caused her to halt.

She knew the one only slightly: Merinda, daughter of the lord of Seil; one of the Princess Gwenedour's younger ladies. Even to Aeron's child's mind Merinda was a spoilt, pretty, painted court darling; but she was not pretty just now. The little kitten-face was flushed and pinched with anger, the rosy mouth spitting words that Aeron did not know but whose sense she could not mistake. But her companion, whose back was to Aeron and whose face she had not yet seen—

Gwydion's whole frame seemed to convey only boredom, the courtly patience bred into the bone of a prince of the blood; indeed, it seemed that the hotter burned Merinda's anger, the more coolly polite he became. Aeron, still the unwilling spectator, was by now all too uncomfortably aware that she had blundered into a small drama of advances made and advances spurned: the advances having plainly been Merinda's, that the heir of Gwynedd had just as plainly found unwelcome, and for which she was now berating him; so much was plain even to a thirteen-year-old.

Then, with a last flung viciousness, Merinda was gone, and

Gwydion did not even look after her as she went, but sighed and stretched and took a deep breath of the summer air, as if in breathing it he could be cleansed of the past minutes.

Aeron had seen in the moment her own chance of escape, but she had left it just that one instant too long, and now Gwydion had turned—as if Merinda, like some annoying buzzfly, had distracted him from noticing aught else, and her going had cleared his senses—and was staring straight at Aeron.

His expression did not change; or if it did, grew only into greater and genuine courtesy, and he bowed to her, as was due from his rank to hers. Though embarrassment flamed in Aeron's cheeks to rival her hair's redness, she lifted her chin and met him glance for glance in silence.

Some sense came to them then that had been hidden before, some dim hint of the future that would be and what they would in that future be each to the other; but still they could not, or would not, give it a name—at least Aeron could not, she was still perhaps too young for it, and if his own Sight showed him clearer he gave no sign.

The moment lengthened unendurably; then Aeron, suddenly recollecting that even an heir to a princely house could not in courtesy withdraw from the presence of the heir to Keltia, however much he might wish in his own embarrassment to do so, gave him a small quick nod, and fled back the way that she had come.

The next morning she left Gwynedd and returned to Tara; she did not see Gwydion again before her departure, and it was to be nearly seven years before they would set eyes upon each other again.

Chapter 12

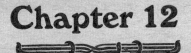

The chief training-school of the Ban-draoi order, Scartanore—the Thicket of Gold—had its pleasant seat on the summit of a great flat-topped green hill, the sides of which were clothed with the tall goldenbirches that had given the place its name. For nearly two thousand years there had been a convent-college on this site: Young women from every part of Keltia, of every rank and station and every degree of magical talent, had come here as students and had left as sorceresses.

But not since the reign of Declan IX, who had sent his daughter Líadan, had a female heir of Keltia come to Scartanore to take the full Ban-draoi training: four years—from thirteen to seventeen, childhood to young womanhood—to make a priestess; one year more, usually taken later, to attain the rank of Domina, a High Priestess of the order.

That Aeron was to be schooled here was due to an unusual combination of circumstances: her own talents and inclinations, already so memorably demonstrated; her father's wisdom, and, not least, her great-grandmother Aoife's prophecy.

Though Aoife was no sorceress herself, thought Kesten Hannivec, standing in the archway of the school's main gatetower, watching Aeron's party approach from the landing-field across the valley where their ship had touched down. *She may not have been a Sister of ours, but still the Old Queen proved she had a Sight on her when there was need for Seeing clear and far. . . .*

Kesten touched the silver collar of office she wore, smoothed the folds of the black robe, very much aware of the mood of her senior preceptresses who stood in rows behind her. *Wondering what like will be this new recruit to the Sisterhood; wondering*

*too how their Abbess-mother and Magistra will rise to so great
and lasting a challenge: a royal heir to train. Well, let them
wonder. I am wondering too: Save for her saining, I have only
ever seen this young Aeron but the once, and that was long
ago—though I daresay the memory of that episode will not soon
fade . . . For the moment, she is but another new pupil; as to
later, we shall see.*

A voice of drawling amusement came from behind. "Just
another new pupil, eh? And so common or garden a pupil that of
course you are here—in formal robe and collar, too—to greet her
in person? Or is it that the Magistra now welcomes all new girls
so?"

Kesten knew the teasing voice well, and did not look round,
though she permitted a matching amusement to show on her
face.

"Oh aye—the same way *you* have prised yourself out of
Lundavra, like some winkle off its favorite old rock, to come
here and see her for yourself. And you too would do as much for
any new student?"

Tybie ferch Eilir laughed out loud, ignoring the sidelong
glances cast her way by certain of the other preceptresses standing by.

"You have me there, Magistra . . . She will not see me, but I
would see *her*, Kesi. Later, when she may come to need me, she
will herself seek me out, and I will be there for her."

"As you have ever been for me." Kesten threw a look over
her black-clad shoulder at her old friend—a long look, full of
years and affection—and the look was returned full measure.

Kesten no more wondered, as she had done for longer than she
cared to recall, why Tybie Vedryns ferch Eilir, a duchess's
daughter, brightest of her year and closest friend Kesten had
ever been blessed with, had chosen in the midst of a brilliant
career to retreat into a lonely stone llan in a remote valley, there
to lead the contemplative life of an anchoress.

What a waste that choice had seemed then to Kesten, and to
all who had known that Tybie. *She might have easily have been
Magistra,* thought Kesten, *could even have been Taoiseach, had
she set her mind and heart to it . . .*

But Tybie's mind and heart both had chosen otherwise, and
though her friend's choice had troubled Kesten for years, simply,

suddenly, one day long past now it had all seemed so right that Kesten had wondered then why she had ever wondered at all. Though she had no more inkling now than then, of where it might lead and whyfor, she felt again the rightness of Tybie's choice, and was again contented.

And as Tybie has been for me, so too will she be for this new one who will have need of her wisdom . . . this one who will someday be Queen.

"But look," said the Magistra aloud. "She is here."

Aeron never forgot in after years her first sight of Scartanore. Though it was to become to her a place as loved and familiar as her own home, though she had seen it many times in books and on the farviewers, that first real beholding seemed to her at once both beginning and completion, as if only to see the Thicket of Gold were to receive all it had to give.

The ship of the Royal Flight that had brought her from Caerdroia had taken a northerly course up the valley, and so on her way in Aeron had had no glimpse of the convent that had trained so many Ban-draoi down the centuries, and that was to be her home for the next four years. *Always given,* she reminded herself, *that I may meet its standards . . .* For many did not, and the Sisters spared neither time nor tact in sending them away.

As the small party set their horses to the road that climbed the hill, Aeron looked up to see the great weathered buildings strong against the sky: a fortress, but a place of peace and power also, its ramparts of oyster-colored stone rising sheer out of the spring grass, the bright flags of the birches all round and Erinna's extraordinary sky behind, tourmaline-green at the high zenith, shading to pure clear blue at the horizon's curve.

But there, in the shadows beneath the huge masonry gate . . .

"That is the Abbess-mother, the Magistra Kesten Hannivec, there in the black robe," said Keina, who rode at Aeron's side. Emer's sister, herself a Ban-draoi Domina of long standing and high repute, was serving as her favorite niece's sponsor to the order. It was long tradition in Keltia that a woman should raise her sister's daughter to magic, or a man his brother's son; and Keina delighted to do so now for Aeron. "She has been Magistra for near thirty years; she was my first preceptress when I studied here, before she took office, and now she will be yours."

As they halted in the faha before the gate, Aeron could not take her eyes from the face of the Magistra. Although she knew that Kesten was of an age almost to be her great-grandmother, Aeron saw that the face beneath the silver fillet and black wimple was ageless. No maiden's cheek could be fresher, yet the dark eyes that were watching Aeron so steadily from out of that unlined countenance seemed to have looked upon not a mere hundred years and threescore, but millennia.

Beyond Kesten's shoulder, there seemed to be someone else in the darkness under the arch, someone Aeron could not see clearly; indeed scarce could see at all, for whoever stood there had chosen to veil herself in the ceo-draoichta, the druids' fog, as well as in mundane shadow. Still—

Unthinkingly Aeron put forth that new power which of late had been making itself felt more and more. Untried it was and chancy, and by no means reliable—that was why she was come here, to learn to be its master, so that it would no longer be hers—but all at once she felt it leap out strong and sure, like a questing glance or a reaching arm. And under the momentary touch of that sureness and strength, as under a strong light or blaze of the sun, the ceo-draoichta shimmered and faded, enough to let Aeron see the woman who had masked herself with its magic.

An instant only: a quick impression of a tall figure, a smiling face, surprised and approving. Then the ceo-draoichta swirled round again, easily as a cloak might be drawn and wrapped close, and the woman was gone; and Aeron slid from her saddle to greet her new teachers.

Later that day, alone in her newly assigned chamber—Keina had returned to Tara, after a long private conversation with the Magistra and a last loving interview with her niece—Aeron sat staring at the stone-flagged floor.

This was the first time in all her life that she had been truly left to her own resources. Though she had been fostered away from home since the age of five, those to whom she had been entrusted had still been family—intimate friends to her parents, known to her almost since birth—and so the strangeness there had bean nearly nil. But here at Scartanore there would be neither kin nor friend to sustain her; Fionnbarr had so decreed, and on that point he had been adamant—with Keina and Gwyneira to back him when Emer had protested.

Already she missed them all: Morwen, Ari, her brothers and sisters and cousins. *Well then, if I am not to be allowed old friends, I shall make shift to find myself some new ones* . . . She laughed suddenly, remembering: When Morwen had learned that Aeron was to be sent to Scartanore, she had tried every tune she could think of to get her own parents to send her too. She had been very persuasive; but the broken reed to *that* pipe was that Morwen had less aptitude for magic than perhaps anyone ever born into Clann Douglas in all the years of Keltia. So for all her eloquent pleadings, Faolan and Mared had not been swayed and she had not been sent. But that same eloquence, ironically enough—or perhaps not, if one factored dán into it, and one was generally unwise not to—had managed only to get Morwen admitted as novice to the Hill of Laws, the brehon school on Arvor in the Brytaned system, where she had been student for two years now, and where she would remain for four more.

She complains of it bitterly, I know, but I also know she loves it, thought Aeron with a smile for the memory of her friend's lamentings. *It is as suited to her mind and talents as I hope this place will be to mine; and it will be an excellent thing for us both later on, when I am Ard-rían and shall have need of a brehon-trained advisor who is also a longtime friend. All the same, for now it is hard to be apart, and it does not make me glad* . . .

Aeron looked up as the door opened, and Arianeira entered the room. So stunned was Aeron to see her there that for a moment she believed the newcomer to be no creature of flesh and blood, but that she herself had for the second time that day tapped unthinkingly into unthought powers—and untaught powers—and conjured up a taish . . .

"Ari? Ari, is it you?"

Arianeira laughed and came forward to take Aeron by the hands and kiss her cheek.

"Well, who else, to give fitting welcome to my fostern on her coming to Scartanore? —Nay, Aeron, it *is* I, truly! Why do you look so confounded?"

"For that I am! My father told me most pointedly that I should have here for my comfort no one known to me; and now, apart from the Magistra Kesten's, and—and another's, yours is the first face I see.''

Arianeira slipped her arm through Aeron's—a gesture not habitual with her, though the younger girl was grateful for the touch, and had no thought of the calculation behind it—and drew her out into the corridor, down a wide stone staircase to the convent's Great Hall.

''Your father may be Ard-rígh, but here Kesten Magistra is the only sovereign; she it was who summoned me here from Errigal, where I had been serving my prenticeship to the Abbess Roewyn. I do not know what put it into her mind to call for me, but I am very glad she did! To come to Scartanore is a thing every Ban-draoi hopes for herself, and not all are so invited. Oh, surely I was glad too for that I knew you would be here, and no doubt that is why the Magistra did summon me . . . You know I did not take my own training here, but at Marazanvos on Kernow; a worthy school, though scarcely Scartanore.''

All this was news indeed to Aeron, who wondered briefly for whose true benefit Arianeira had been summoned: Aeron's or Ari's own. But they had come by then to the Great Hall, where the nightmeal was awaiting them, and merging into the stream of others, clad for the most part like Aeron herself in the plain dark gray of learners, they went in at the students' entrance.

So did Aeron's schooling in magic begin, there at the Thicket of Gold. She was taught first of all how to learn, and for that she had to unlearn much that she had thought she knew, before the true teaching could begin; and even then for much of the time she would teach herself.

Then the spells began, all manner of spells: the little spells, for souring milk and sweetening butter, for curing and for cursing; the spell of the Spancel, and the words to break its bands; the spell to lift the faery-stroke, the one given by the queen of the liss and the worse one dealt by the Fool of the Forth; the spell of the corp-creidh and that of the glas-ghairm; spells to raise a bridge from a hair of the head, a brier-hedge from a comb; to raise an iron-fence from a hair-pin or a wave from the contents of a flask.

And then the greater spells, the spells to bless or to blast, to send or to bind. Spells too there were that none should teach, and that none should ever seek to learn. But since to forbid knowledge was contrary to wisdom, there was no bar even to these, for a determined student to get the mastery . . . and some did.

But most of this learning lay yet in the future. For now, Aeron was still a novice, however talented, at present struggling to prove herself in the eyes of her teachers; struggling likewise to prove herself to her own classmates, that she was here by merit and not for her royal blood. Too, as she met and mastered one lesson after another, she had to prove that she was no togmall, no pet lamb or glozer to curry favor with the preceptresses; for these her classmates were after all scarce out of childhood, even as Aeron herself, with all childhood's uncertainties still strong in them as in her, and there was bound to be envy: envy of her brilliance in her studies, as well as envy of that rank they affected to disdain.

So for all her resolve, Aeron made no new friend for some months. It seemed that all those with whom she would be friends had each of them some cause for turning that friendship aside: Either they were students more advanced than she in their training, and had neither time nor inclination to befriend a novice; or they had sufficient of friends and wished for no more; or they were simply fearful or resentful of Aeron herself—of that aura of power already around her which was growing daily more pronounced, or of her royal rank, though she never flaunted it or even spoke of it, or, more likely, of the sharp tongue she was coming of force to depend upon for her chief and instinctive defense.

Whatever, as the weeks passed Aeron found herself increasingly alone, save for Arianeira; but even Ari could not always spare time for Aeron from her own studies and duties, and indeed was not always inclined to do so. And however much Aeron tried to console herself with the thought that "alone" was a useful and necessary thing for Keltia's next Ard-rían to learn well, for a girl not yet fourteen it was hard and harsh, the coldest of comfort, and it had brought her more than once to tears.

Matters arranged themselves, though, one afternoon of late summer. True it was that Aeron, to cheer herself up, had been showing off just a little; true also that she had been called upon it by another novice: one Duvessa, dark-haired, sallow-skinned,

short and stocky and—or so at least went the general opinion—
not overly talented. But if she was not gifted much beyond the
common run in magic, Duvessa Cantelon had a kind of mean
perception that could pierce her victims' defenses, to wound
where wounding would pain the sorest and surest, and this she
now employed to insult Aeron to her face, and a small crowd
quickly gathered to enjoy it.

Any other time Aeron would have given back as good as she
was getting, or better, for in these months out of her need her
tongue had grown sharp and facile. But all at once the freight of
those months came down hard upon her, all the loneliness and
petty snubbings and nameless sorrows, all the pinpricks that had
festered like bitterthorns, all the woes that weigh so heavy at
such an age, and it seemed to her more than she could bear even
to listen to her tormentor, much less to strike back. So though
she flushed under Duvessa's words, she spoke none to defend
herself, and she was turning away to hide her unhappiness when
out of nowhere she found herself possessed of a champion.

Aeron had noticed before today the girl who now spoke
out—a young Erinnachín, with brown-gold hair and warm brown
eyes, a novice like herself; had noticed her to be both talented
and industrious, not one to court favor or friendship, but to be
her own woman only, holding herself apart from the petty factions and rivalries that were rife among so many of her fellows.

Indeed, she had seemed as much a lone-walker as Aeron
herself, though perhaps for rather different reasons, and so it was
with surprise redoubled that Aeron heard her now stand out in
Aeron's defense against Duvessa, with a tongue that dripped
poisoned honey, so smooth and artful that though Duvessa could
take no exception to the words she could not but at the same time
take their sting.

Nor did the others miss the wasp in those words: Swift and
heartless to change sides to the stronger, they were laughing
openly now at Aeron's discomfited attacker, and soon dispersed,
Duvessa among them in a fury, until only Aeron and the brown-
haired girl remained in the courtyard by the fountain.

Aeron turned to the stranger with gratitude in her eyes, and a
certain diffidence also. "My thanks, mistress," she said then.
"That was nicely done of you, though no doubt they will now
accuse you of coming to my defense merely to court my favor."

The other shrugged, though plainly pleased at Aeron's words. "Small care to me; that pack of snipelings concerns me not at all, and still less should they matter to you." A grin flashed then, merry and malicious. "And as for that muck-mouthed little streppoch Cantelon, I'll pin her ears back for her in earnest if she tries *that* again any time soon . . . But it is no matter for praise, Tanista; anyone with any decent upbringing would have done the same, no matter if the victim were princess or pig-girl."

"Then those others here just now can have had *no* decent upbringing, for they did nothing where you did much—and risked much."

"I risked naught but their contempt! That is less than naught."

"I say otherwise," persisted Aeron, for it was suddenly important to her that this girl should accept her words and her thanks. "And I say too that I hope we may come to be friends, you and I, for I should dearly like a friend such as you in this place—or in any other place."

Her companion looked astonished, as indeed she was. "The heir of Keltia must be neck-deep in friends and would-be friends, and surely would not need to ask for comradeship."

Aeron gave her a strange smile. "If everyone thinks so, then small wonder the heir of Keltia has no friend to her side; but such a friend as you have just proved yourself is never easily come by, for pig-girl or princess. Maybe more easily for a pig-girl than for a princess . . . And any road, I am not 'Tanista' to those friends but 'Aeron'."

Each of them felt the spark of friendship born in that moment, and each of them put away their defenses between them forever.

"Sabia ní Dálaigh," said the brown-haired girl, holding out both hands, and Aeron eagerly clasped arms with her in the traditional gesture. "My family are horse-breeders, we have a farm on the Timpaun—"

As they walked away together, deep in talk, high above them in the south tower Kesten Hannivec let fall the curtain across the window from which she had been watching, and smiled with satisfaction.

Chapter 13

Though there was peace and to spare at Scartanore, Aeron soon found that she had need of more, or other; and in the first months of her residence at the school she had taken advantage of every spare moment to ride out into the hills and woods surrounding: with Sabia, once their friendship began, or with Ari on rarer occasions, but generally alone, and generally in unsettled frame of mind. It seemed to her that she sought something, though she had no smallest idea of what, or of where she might go to find it.

But for all her seeking, it was not until the next spring that she found Lundavra, and Tybie, and the white stone llan beside the Roaringwater.

She had ridden out that morning in what felt to be a mood more evil than any she had ever known. There was no reason for it either bad or good: Her studies had been going well as ever; she had had no quarrel with friend or enemy; no preceptress had reprimanded her with or without cause—the day itself was surpassing fine, cool and sunny, with high white clouds and a strong wind, the kind of day she best loved.

But her life's present brightness seemed only to make her mood the blacker, and when all at once, after half a morning's ride, she came over the breast of a ridge and looked down into the broad valley of the Roaringwater, Aeron was near as weary and fretful as her horse, and just as happy to halt.

She had never come that way before. For the past hour they had been crossing a region of upland valleys, wide and lonely, lying across their path like folds pinched into the green fabric of the land, even and regular as waves in a rising sea; and in all those miles she had seen no more than a scant handful of farmsteads, or even the maenors of gentry, and in her dark mood she had taken care to pass by them at a distance.

But now as she looked along the valley's length, her gaze fell upon a white stone structure on the near slope, no more than a mile or so distant. It was a llan, a retreat-house for some religious—Druid or Ban-draoi or Dragon Kin—who had chosen to live a life apart from what most of the rest of Keltia would call living. Built into the side of the hill, beside a leaping waterfall that helped to swell the infant Roaringwater, the llan was sheltered by ancient elms and beeches whose leaves were just now turning spring's bright shouting green. Peace lay upon that place like a visible veil, and the water that foamed and fell only yards away from the white walls, though distant as she was Aeron could not yet hear its music, seemed only to underscore that peace with its very chatter.

And as she looked upon the llan, Aeron felt her black mood lift and take wing, and in its place came a sudden desperate need to speak with someone—with *that* someone, with that very one who lived in that llan and no other, to learn who it was that dwelt in so lonely a place, and whyfor, and since what time, and did that someone have aught to say to her.

So it was with a sense of some vast unposed question about to be answered that Aeron touched her horse's neck; and the tired beast, sensing her goal, and food and rest for itself, carried her gladly over the lip of the hill.

No sooner had she slipped from her saddle, to stand in the grassy faha before the llan's gated walls, than the dark weathered wooden door in that high wall swung open.

Turning her head at the sound, Aeron saw a woman in gray, a Ban-draoi plainly, of great age and greater serenity. Her immediate thought was of Kesten, though the two women did not physically resemble each other in the slightest: Kesten's face was cool and chiselled, a scholar's face, and this face was strong and square, broad of brow and cheekbone, with the complexion of one who spent much time out of doors. But there was the same bearing, the same smile, and above all the same light in the eyes . . . She caught herself staring; it seemed somehow—though she knew it was not possible, never would she have forgotten such a face as this—that she had seen this woman before, and her puzzlement showed.

The woman's smile warmed, as if she knew perfectly well the girl's thought and understood her puzzlement; as perhaps she did. She stood aside now, holding open the gate in the wall, and gestured Aeron to enter.

"Come in, Aeron," said Tybie Vedryns ferch Eilir. "I have been expecting you; you must be near famished by now, and your horse as well."

If the face had not been so friendly, or so strangely, maddeningly familiar, or the eyes less warm or less plainly perceptive, Aeron might well have been alarmed, to hear her name spoken so; might have had thoughts of old tales, that told how the folk of the dúns, the Shining Ones, were wont to lure unwary mortals into their hollow hills, with smiles and fair speech and the promise of refreshment and rest.

But as it was, she felt welcomed, as if her spirit knew better than her mind, as if she were no stranger here but had been a guest in this place many times before, and would be again.

With sudden decision, Aeron untacked her horse to allow him to graze in comfort, saw that there was water for him near at hand, in a little pool continually replenished by the waterfall itself, and, murmuring the ritual formula courtesy and custom demanded of one on entering another's home for the first time, went in at the wooden gate.

"But an anchoress!" Aeron, sitting very much at her ease in a heap of cushions, looked up at Tybie both envious and appalled.

The two had spent the greater part of that day in the llan's main room—its only room, apart from a small cookplace, the requisite annat or place of contemplation, reached from the llan by a short cloister, and a pool-room off the cookplace, through whose flagged floor coursed the waters of the little cataract. The main chamber itself, a combination of gríanan and library and sleeping-room, was rich in its very plainness: stone walls and floors, a small telyn of excellent make hanging from a peg, several alcoves lined with books, a tall pointed window that opened into the beech-grove like a gate into summer. Privation, bodily or mental, formed no part of the Keltic contemplative way: Those who practiced that way knew well that discomfort was as great a distraction from the higher life as was indulgence, and avoided either extreme in their disciplines.

"To be shut away so fast from the stream of the world—" Aeron was still mourning Tybie's isolation, and was startled when the anchoress's laugh pealed out, brightening all that chamber.

"Who is shut away the faster, child, you or I? Nay, Aeron, I'll tell you a thing: When first I came to this place, I thought much the same as you think now; or at least my fears did think so. Then, over the months that went to years and now to decades, I came to see that this place, far from being too small, is in truth far too vast for me. There are worlds in here, galaxies, universes even—far larger within than without, just as it must be with one's own soul. There are more worlds and more possibilities here within these walls than you or I or all the Ban-draoi who ever lived could dream of encompassing even in the span of limitless lifetimes. It was to *this* that I was called; for I was called, you know, I did not run away. It is I who am free of the worlds, not shut out from them." Tybie smiled at the expression on her young listener's face. "You do not understand me, I know," she said; a statement, neither question nor accusation. "But you will. Even now you understand better than you know."

But Aeron, chin still in hands as she had listened, shook her head slowly.

"I do not know if that shall ever come to be, mistress. But I do now know one thing: that I envy you; and I think I shall envy you all the more when I sit upon the Throne of Scone itself."

It was long past nightfall when Aeron, having taken affectionate farewell of Tybie, promising to return soon and often, arrived again at Scartanore. The gatewardress on duty had been told by Kesten herself to expect the truant after curfew, though how the Magistra had known *that*, only she herself could tell . . . But there Aeron was, leading her horse, for the beast had fallen lame two miles beyond the gates.

She glanced up at Kesten's windows a little fearfully, for the truancy was a real one, and under usual circumstances she could expect to be punished. But there was no sign there of the Magistra, and no message demanding Aeron's presence, when, having cared for her exhausted horse, she went at last to her own rooms.

Aeron had bathed and performed her usual devotions, and was lying upon her bed contemplating the day's events, when there came a soft knock at the door. Before she could rise or respond, Kesten came inside unattended; in her hands she carried a tray, which she set down carefully on the low chest beside the bed.

"Nay, Aeron, as you are . . . No pupil of mine goes to bed without her supper," she explained smiling, nodding toward the tray. "Well, not unless it suits my purpose that she should do so—but you do not merit punishment, I think, for how you spent this day. I have a fair idea you must be half-starved; I warrant you and Tybie both talked so hard you forgot entirely to eat."

Aeron, who at the sight of supper had suddenly realized how hungry she was—for Kesten had the right of it, neither Aeron nor Tybie had halted their discourse for a matter so mundane as food—turned her eyes from the tray with an effort, to stare up at her Abbess-mother.

"With respect, Magistra, but how is it that you know? Did Tybie—"

All at once Kesten was no longer Magistra; curling up comfortably in the room's one guestchair, she seemed just another student, of Aeron's own age.

"Tybie and I are friends from of old, alanna," she said then, her face warm with firelight and memory. "There is very little one of us knows that the other does not . . . But she was herself here to see you, you know, the day that first you came to us; do you now remember?"

It seemed to Aeron at those words that a veil had been ripped from her othersight, or else that that sight came fully focused at last, and she sat up, pulling her bedgown around her, all hunger and weariness forgotten.

"In the gate, standing behind you—it was *she* I saw! But I could not see her, not completely, not until I—"

"—not until you put forth your power. Aye, and you did extremely well, being an untutored child, to see her at all; you succeeded in surprising her, as she has not been surprised for many years. I prepared that food with my own hands, Aeron," added Kesten with a touch of exasperation. "Do me the grace of eating it before it grows too cold to do you any good."

Aeron began obediently, and willingly, to apply herself to her supper: thick slices of beef in a rich gravy, well-roasted framachs, applecake and hot bread and new salt butter.

"But even so—" she began with her mouth full.

"Even so, why did she not tell you herself?"

"Nay," said Aeron with a grin, "even so, for a Magistra of the Ban-draoi of Keltia, you are a more than passable cook."

Kesten laughed. "My thanks; if ever I think to seek new employment, you may look for me in the palace kitchens. But to answer that question you did not ask: I think it was in Tybie's mind to let you remember for yourself—and you would have done, before very long. You know it was but the third time in all her years of enclosure that she did leave Lundavra."

"Only to see *me*?" Aeron found herself shocked at the idea, even somehow guilty: that so small a matter as her coming to Scartanore should bring a holy anchoress out of her chosen solitude.

"She came to see not Aeron but the next Ard-rían," said Kesten, watching the play of thought across her pupil's face. "To see for herself what stuff was here, out of which to make a queen . . . You could not have known, and I doubt she did tell you, but Tybie ferch Eilir, heir to the Duchess of Lanihorn, was once much in the stream of high politics at Turusachan. She knew your grandfather Lasairían well, helped him in many matters; she even served your great-grandmother the High Queen Aoife—to Aoife's satisfaction, I might add, and be sure there were not many who managed *that* . . . Very like, Tybie could have been Taoiseach had she chosen to seek the post; surely she could have been Magistra in my place. I will be training you, Aeron, but it is Tybie shall judge you most surely, when the time comes for it; shall judge of you, and shall judge of my training as well. And she will help you, as she helped Lasairían and Aoife, in ways that I cannot."

"Cannot? Or will not?"

"May not," said Kesten honestly, though she was faintly surprised at the royal snap behind the question; surprised, and not displeased. "Certain things there are which even the Magistra must stand away from, however much she may be otherwise inclined. But that is another trouble for another time." She rose, and Aeron scrambled respectfully to her own bare feet. "I am more pleased than I can say, or you can know, that things have fallen out so. Now for my sake and the Mother's, finish your supper and go to your bed; the rest of the house is long since asleep, and you have had a tiring day.'' She laid a hand on Aeron's head in brief benediction, and was gone.

Aeron, who had been struggling heroically to suppress her yawns these last five minutes, was now paradoxically wide awake, and munching absently on the remnants of her supper, she sank back into the chair Kesten had vacated, her mind running on what the Magistra had said.

Small wonder I should think I had seen Tybie before; all the same, though, it is in my mind that there is more at work here than even the Magistra knows—or Tybie either . . . Though such a thought was no doubt a heretical one, and was surely no comforting one: She had poured out her soul to Tybie that afternoon, as she had never done before to any living person; and the idea that dán already had its hand over her was no idea that Aeron, who still clung somewhat to her childhood faith that she and she alone would determine of her life's course, could find either easy or pleasant.

But be that as it might, or must, there was at the heart of what she now felt a kind of perverse satisfaction, in the certainty that, whatever was in truth at work, it was as far beyond Tybie and Kesten as it was beyond Aeron herself.

Chapter 14

"It moves!" said Aeron, delighted, staring down at the cup she had just lifted, by power of mind and will alone, from the tabletop. "Hard work to make it do so, but by gods it moves!"

"Certainly it moves," replied Kesten, no less pleased than her star pupil. They were in the Magistra's private study, a pleasant, book-crammed room in the south tower, where for the past year now Aeron had been coming three afternoons a week, to take at Kesten's hand special training and tutelage in the ways of the Ban-draoi that her classmates did not share.

In the two years Aeron had been at Scartanore, she had progressed further and faster than even Kesten had thought possible. Or, perhaps, desirable; and the Magistra was not alone in her feeling that, left to shift for herself in the routine of normal classwork, Aeron would only so outpace her classmates as to cause dissension and difficulty, for herself as well as for them.

For whether it was at Scartanore or the smallest hedge-school run by a journeyman bard, there were few more pervasive influences in a schoolroom than a bored gifted student. Mischief was sure to be made, not out of malice but out of inadvertent tensions: Such students, though they generally could not be bothered with such petty pursuits as the stirring up of deliberate turmoil, had genuinely not the smallest idea of the impact their talents had on others, or the havoc that impact could wreak. And where magic was involved, the impact—and the havoc—grew dangerous indeed.

So the consensus among the preceptresses was that Aeron should now begin to receive such private instruction as would best serve her and her fellows; and the consensus too was that the Magistra was the best choice for the job. Much to Kesten's relief, there had been little note taken of the matter among the other students, and, perhaps not so surprisingly, no scrap of envy or ill-feeling or resentment of such privilege could be detected among the novices. In part, this was due to the effect of two years' training in the Ban-draoi way; but even Duvessa, Aeron's perpetual nemesis, forebore to grumble, so plain had Aeron's pre-eminence by now become—and no doubt also the thought that Aeron would of necessity be more frequently removed from Duvessa's path was not without its appeal. In any event, the tutelage had gone smoothly, and was proving most fruitful—as Aeron had just now shown.

Kesten drew her attention back to the hovering cup, and her pupil's glowing face.

"If we can learn to do this—" began Aeron.

"—why need we lift a finger ever again?" finished her teacher, with a sigh, and taking control set the cup down firmly again on the table. "I have had no pupil yet who failed to ask that question."

Aeron looked a little chagrined, but asked doggedly, "Well, *why* trouble to do so?"

"Because by the time a Ban-draoi arrives at the place where such a thing—very hard work, as you just now admitted—*is* no more difficult a matter than lifting a finger, she is also at a place where she sees that the energy expended so is far better spent or saved for graver matters. So by the time you, Aeron, learn to do it at ease and at will—"

"I shall no longer be wanting to do it."

"Exactly." Kesten smiled at her crestfallen student. "You lose your labor, Aeron-fach. Such tricks have their uses, I do not say you shall never have need to employ them; but by the time you are their master you shall be wanting to do far greater things; and those, I promise you, you will be well able to do."

Aeron looked out the window at the goldenbirches, now in full summer leaf under a hot sky that presaged storm.

"Sometimes I feel as if I shall never be able to perform even the tiniest pishogue," she confessed. "Things I could do as a child, without training, without thinking even, have suddenly left me. I have not managed to work the least littlest rann for almost a sixmonth now; and as for greater magics—"

"Nay, that is a common thing," said Kesten reassuringly. "And a thing that everyone who sets a hand to magic must face, soon or late. Usually sooner . . . It is because your mind is adjusting to its new knowledge on many levels, most of those sub- or superconscious. And until all this inflow of information is properly sorted and stored, your abilities tend to shut down for their own protection—and yours. In truth, the greater the potential powers shall be in the end, the earlier and the more firmly do they lock themselves away. I have seen it over and over; I promise you there is no cause for concern. You are learning and working sorcery, Aeron, even when you think that you are not: waking or sleeping, when you ride or read or sing or dream or do any other thing that seems to have no link to magic. It is all magic."

"Then if that be so, how shall I know when I have come to my power, if my power cannot be wakened by will?"

"When you are ready to begin to use your power—and your power, not you, will make that determination—it will come to your hand all of a piece, and all at once. You may think of it as a mill, where the shuts have been raised so that the water-force of the stream may build up behind them; when the work is ready to be done, and the gathered force sufficient for the job, the gates drop and the stream pours through upon the mill-wheel. Only here it is not the miller decides when those shuts shall be opened, but the mill itself."

At the beginning of Aeron's third year at Scartanore, the smooth routine of her days was troubled when Arianeira, who had been at the convent since Aeron's own arrival, was suddenly sent away.

"Home to Gwynedd," she told Aeron, who was helping her pack up her belongings. "I would have been leaving at the end of this year in any case, Aeron, you know that."

"Aye, but why now? There is not some problem at home you have not told me of?"

"Not that my parents have told *me* of; and both my brothers seem well enough . . . Besides," she added, with a tight little smile, "you have gone far beyond my help in sorcery; if ever help I gave you."

"Ari, you know you have done so—"

"Well, be that as it might, you do not need me now; and this order comes from Kesten Magistra herself. *She* need not tell anyone of her reasons—or lack of reasons—ask howsoever you might."

But when Aeron, a little cast down, did ask, for once she received from her teacher a sharper response than she had looked for.

"Who stays or goes in this place is my concern, Aeron, and I will not be questioned on it; not even by you. I will say only that Arianeira had no further need that would have been served by her remaining here, and so she has gone. No more."

Though Aeron moped for a time following her foster-sister's departure, there was too much else to fill her days for her long to brood over Ari's absence. Though she and Sabia remained close as ever, Aeron had other friends now, and all of them good friends together; there were days spent at Lundavra with Tybie, still special enough in Aeron's mind to need a reason to justify her going, though Tybie only laughed at her diffidence; there were even visits, off-planet and on—home to Tara twice a year; shorter stays with Sabia at her home on the Timpaun, clear on the other side of the planet from Scartanore; one treasured visit to Morwen on Arvor, and one time just as happy that Morwen had come to Erinna.

Later that same summer, Aeron's sister Ríoghnach arrived at Scartanore, to begin her own studies as a Ban-draoi. Though Aeron was by now so advanced in her training as to be studying matters more usually left to a Ban-draoi's Domina year, she found both joy and profit in giving her sister what help she was permitted, and her third year at the Thicket of Gold drew swiftly to a happy close.

It was the custom at the end of a student's third term at Scartanore, or any other Ban-draoi school, for the Abbess resident to summon her for evaluation, to inform her whether she would be permitted to enter her final year of study and seek initiation—the goal to which all training was directed—or if it would not be better for all concerned that she should find herself another calling. The training itself was never wasted: Even for those who chose or were counseled to take themselves elsewhere, three years of a Ban-draoi education provided the groundwork for almost any other pursuit one might care to follow.

When Aeron found herself so summoned, to that private study of the Magistra's where she had been accustomed to spend so many hours of such hard work, for all her confidence in her skills she could not help but feel the same quakings of inner uncertainty that she presumed all the others must feel. Though she herself had no real doubts, who could tell what flaw or failure the othersight of the Magistra might not have detected, and upon which she was now preparing to act?

But in the end there was no cause to have feared. Aeron heard as if from a few lightyears' distance the voice of Kesten across the cluttered desk, telling her how very pleased was the Magistra, and all the other preceptresses as well, with Aeron's achievements; no question but that she should continue, and take her initiation at the usual time with those others of her year who had qualified.

Relief so great that she collapsed into the depths of her chair came over Aeron—who till that moment had held her back stiffly away from the cushioned back of the seat, a legacy from Emer— and she raised grateful eyes to Kesten.

"When I first came here," she began, a little tentatively, "I did by no means expect—or dare to imagine, even—that the Magistra should concern herself so nearly with my training. Has that been for policy's sake, for that I am heir to my father, and will be Ard-rían in my turn, if the Mother allows?"

Kesten permitted herself a smile. "She not only will allow, Aeron, but She approves; as She has already revealed to me— and, I doubt not, as She will one day reveal to you as well. But to answer your question: Nay, not because you are daughter to the High King—though I admit that for such reason alone I should have closely followed your progress through the schools, as I shall follow that of your sister Ríoghnach, and likewise that of little Fionnuala, when she comes to us in her turn. Nay, it has been rather because of your talent, your Gift: its nature and scope and depth and potential. We have not had an Ard-rían who was also a Ban-draoi Domina, as you will be, for a very long time; and have not had one of such promise of power for longer that. And a Ban-draoi Ard-rían will exert many subtle influences— and perhaps less subtle ones as well—on the folk and the realm alike that a non-sorcerous monarch would not, and could not. This is what all we who have trained you here have striven to keep in mind, and if naught else, it shall not be recorded of Kesten Magistra that she sent Aeron Ard-rían into her reign as a half-schooled puppy. You have spoken to me often enough, Aeron, of your liking and aptitude for the craft, but I tell you now it is far more than that. And as to power—I think you have already felt more significant stirrings of it than merely moving winecups might indicate?"

Aeron lowered her eyes before the keen dark gaze, nodded. "I thought it at first merely the Aoibhell traha," she said artlessly, "striking early and unlooked-for. But then one day it came upon me, just as you did say it would: So small and simple a beginning—I was but raising a riomhall, as I do every night, to sleep in; and yet I knew all at once that I had such power to my hand as could build or blast a world, merely by the willing of it."

"And how did that knowing cause you to feel?"

"Terrified. Exhilarated. And, my sorrow to say, extremely pleased with myself."

Kesten gave over being Magistra and judge, became once more Aeron's friend and loving tutor.

"How *usual* of you, Aeron-fach," she said smiling. "But those are classic normal reactions, I promise you; no more than that—and also no less."

"Then I shall have no difficulty?"

"Ah, now I did not promise *that*! There will be difficulties, certainly; but you will have whatever you will need to deal with them, and that too I promise."

When Aeron left the Magistra's study a little while later, she was aware only of an exploding elation, a dizzying joy and pride such as she had never thought, or hoped, to feel. *What shall I do with myself!* she thought, hands hugging her elbows in delight. *I am too overwrought to get any work done, and it would be churlish in the extreme to inflict my happiness on my friends when their own fates are not yet decided. Even Sabia, though of course she would rejoice with me, and there is no doubt of her own success . . . Nay, the best I can do for them is to keep apart awhile, until all have seen Kesten; and the best I can do for myself is—what?* She considered going to visit Tybie, to share her triumph with her mentor and friend, but Lundavra was too long a ride for so late in the day. *And any road, it is in my mind that she knows already . . .* But all at once Aeron knew where she both wanted and needed to be just then, and turning on her heel outside Kesten's study she headed purposefully for the north stair.

If Scartanore was the heart of the Ban-draoi order, then the annat in the great north tower was the soul of Scartanore.

Of the many centers of worship in Keltia, chief among them were the nemetons, the awesome bluestone circles built in the earliest days by the first settlers from Earth, who laid out these great shrines according to the ancient patterns along the tântads— the Dragon Paths, the lines of power in the earth itself that mark the tides in the land. It was at the nemetons that the Kelts observed the holiest rituals of change in their long life-times: the saining of newborns, the dedication of youths and maids, the handfasting of couples, the blessing of new-made parents, the speeding of the dead.

But the annats—personal places of worship included in or attached to dwellings, serving as family shrines, private sanctu-aries of contemplation and devotion—were warm and welcoming and scaled for humans, in a way that the majestic nemetons could never be; and, in truth, had not been built to be.

So it was to the school's annat that Aeron now went: a chamber of vast and lovely proportions, large enough to hold not only the hundredscore or so who dwelt at Scartanore—Sisters and students and lay retainers—but all those who came up to the Thicket of Gold from the nearby villages and maenors and farmsteads as well, at the times of the great feasts of Samhain and Beltain, Lughnasa and Brighnasa, to celebrate with the Sisters the quarterings of the year.

Grand as was the annat, as befitted the mother-house of the Order—all marble and polished precious stone, jasper and chrys-oprase and jade and chalcedony—there was a place within it that Aeron loved best of all: a humbler place than the great main vault, a small fane or alcove in the eastern wall, separated from the nave by a pierced screen of pure wrought silver.

Others of these alcoves ran like a chain of bright beads around the annat's outer wall, each sacred to a particular divinity of the Keltic pantheon, but this one had been Aeron's own especial refuge since her first unhappy days at Scartanore. Those days were long done with, but the peace and protection Aeron had found in this small hidden sanctuary had never once failed her in adversity, and she knew that it would welcome her now in joy.

She entered quietly, making a deep reverence at the door, and crossed the floor to seat herself in the fane's one chair, a great high-backed throne carved of gold-veined lapis that was set facing the only other thing in that place: before a fair jewel-colored window, a white marble statue of a tall woman, robed and cloaked, her unbound hair rippling to her heels.

After a while Aeron lifted her eyes to the statue before her, seeing for the thousandth time the serene countenance, the carven curve of cheek, the broad brow where hung the chain of stars: St. Nia, mother of Brendan and founder of the Ban-draoi order.

Not for the first time, Aeron felt her eyes fill with tears as she stared at the calm marble face, and the tears seemed but part of the joy she had come here to give thanks for. She raised her hands in the attitude of prayer, beginning silently to chant the beautiful Litany to the Goddess that some said Nia herself had composed, or that had been brought long centuries ago out of the Danaans' vanished first home.

Breastplate of the Gael, hear my prayer; Queen of the Danaans, hear my prayer; Tear of the Sun, hear my prayer; Hawk of Morning, hear my prayer . . . Usually this was chanted in the hour of rising by all the assembled Sisters, priestesses and novices alike, their voices clear and glad in the dawn; but now Aeron chanted it in silence and alone, verse and response alike all within her own heart. All the lost and lovely names: *Sword of Perception, hear my prayer; Shield of Silver, hear my prayer; Dancer in the Moon, hear my prayer; Fire of Roses* . . . *Oak of Morven* . . . *Water of Vision* . . . *Wind out of Betelgeuse* . . . *Light of the Perfection of Gwynfyd* . . .

She stood up, caught now in the web of words, carried upon the power of the prayer like a leaf upon the torrent; and yet not so, for the leaf is borne helplessly along, whether it will or nill, and she moved strong in the torrent as she did please to, wrapped in the joy that had brought her here, and did not even know that now she spoke aloud.

"O Thou who weavest the world in the mountain of mystery; Thou who went as a banner before Alexandros; Thou who knowest the names of the stars, from East to North, by South and West thrice round again . . ."

And it seemed to Aeron then that the face of the statue changed before her eyes, changed to the face of a living woman, the white marble suffused to the warm tints of living flesh. *Nay, no mere woman this; not even thee, blessed Nia* . . . The face was filled with ancient wisdom, the brow blazed with glory to outshine the chain of stars, and the eyes, oh, the eyes of her— Aeron dared not look, dared not look away; and then slowly, still glance for glance with the revealed divinity, went to her knee before the goddess.

Nay, kneel not to me, Aeron, came the clear strong voice in her mind, *thou that art a daughter of my line. Come, speak and do not fear. Rise. Face me.*

Lifting her head from where it had been bowed against her skirts, rising as she had been bidden, Aeron sought for the inner speech as she had been taught.

Then, Thou art not—

I am not, said the Lady, this time with a shimmer of amusement in her mind-voice, *and so you need not 'thee-and-thou' me; though many down the years have so confused us—you will know Her when you see Her, without a doubt! Dâna am I, the mother of your house; I am Nia's foremother, and Morgan's, and I am likewise yours.*

Name me not with such as they! Aeron's protest came quick and heartfelt. *Even the Aoibhell traha, though I confess I have as great a share of it as any, would be slow to claim a place beside those, or even to dream of so aspiring.*

The amusement shone out this time strong and warm, like a sudden shaft of sunlight lancing through the jewelled window.

That's as it is. It lies in other hands than mine, and you and I must wait alike the truth of it. For now, I am come only to hearten. You will not remember this meeting, not with your waking mind; but I say now we shall meet again, and more than once, and it may be that you will be given to remember then what cannot be allowed for now. Even so, you will know in a deeper place that Dâna came to bless your Path, and the strength of that knowing will be enough to serve. And not Dâna's bless-

ing only, but that of all my kin upon you. Though our Houses, some of them, have dwindled and faded, others of them stand strong, and the hidden blood of even those fallen houses still runs among the Kelts. For the Kelts are ours forever, and they will be yours, for you too are ours, and of our own blood.

Awe had fallen anew upon Aeron at the mention of that highest kindred: the true Danaans, those most ancient gods and goddesses who stood nearest the Keltic people, between them and the High Powers who stood nearest the One—Brân and Fionn and Lír and Mâth, Lugh and Arawn and Midir; Síon and Gwener, Morna and Brigit, Malen and Dôn—and Dâna who was queen above them all.

But at that queen's double reminder, of both their ancient kinship and Aeron's rule to come, the girl took courage again to speak.

Is there nothing I shall recall of this, then? I will make my immram, my voyage of initiation, in a little time; the Magistra has just now told me. Will you not give me a word for that journey?

The light began to grow in the little fane, as Dâna seemed to draw it in around her, as prologue to farewell; so bright had her countenance now become that Aeron could not gaze directly upon it.

My word to you is that you will need no word. But one thing I will tell you: Your ship shall touch sand at the journey's end, and you will be empty-handed; yet those empty hands shall hold the world's will, and you will have brought more away with you from your immram than you bore when you went forth. Child of mine, 's ê do bheatha.

The light that had been steadily growing suddenly dazzled, as if the sun beat upon the vast blue shield of the sea, turning it to flame; and when her sight cleared of the radiance, Aeron was alone in the fane, the white marble statue before her once again cold stone.

She looked around, frowning slightly, as one who has lost something, or forgotten something, but cannot recall just exactly what. Whatever it might have been, it was gone now, though some fleeting trace of its presence had been left behind, like some mighty footprint set upon the air. With all the power she had brought to Scartanore and all the skill she had been taught there, Aeron cast after it; but it was not to be caught. The memory of the vision, and the vision itself, had faded like the light.

Yet the joy that had led her to the annat still remained, and after a while Aeron seated herself once more in the lapis chair, still unsure of what had passed but strangely contented, knowing only that something tremendous had been and gone.

Chapter 15

In the weeks before her initiation, Aeron was strictly enjoined, as were all the other novices, to spend neither valuable time nor precious energy taxing herself with speculation on what was to come. And indeed, there was no mystery in the knowledge of the actual events: The Ban-draoi preceptresses had begun drilling the novices in rehearsals directly after the celebration of the Brighnasa feast, and the outward form of the ceremonies was by now well known to them all. It was the inner reality that would be brought about by execution of that form, upon which that form and all else for the past four years was grounded, that was so troubling to the priestesses-to-be.

Aeron, for all her excellence—or perhaps because of it—seemed more troubled than most, and had withdrawn into herself further even than was usual. Even her visits to Tybie at Lundavra had been curtailed for the moment, for which she felt both guilt and remorse, though Tybie well understood.

It was not that she had any real doubts of her abilities: From the first, she had taken to the training like a young seal to its home oceans; at times, during this year just past in especial, it had seemed to her teachers that they were not instructing this particular student, but only reminding her of lessons she had learned long since in some former life—as most like she had.

Likewise she had long since defied the order not to think overmuch on this impending initiation, at least in her conscious mind. But far below her everyday awareness, or perhaps above it, initiation's changeful tidal process was already well advanced.

*   *   *

"So in this dream you met three beings," said Kesten. She was seated in her chair behind the desk in her study; facing her, in the blue-cushioned chair she knew so well, that was so usually dreaded by those summoned to occupy it, was Aeron.

She looked however neither dreading nor fearful of being there; had in fact herself been the one to seek this interview of the Magistra, for the troubling dreams Tybie and others had foreseen for her had now begun.

For one on the threshold of initiation into any magical discipline, such dreams—dreams of prescience, of retrocognition, of othertime or otherwhere—were by no means unusual, and Aeron had been well prepared as to their likely occurrence. Tybie had been first to warn her, for the anchoress had herself been given some knowledge of their coming and content; as had Kesten, though both women kept carefully to themselves any misgivings that knowledge may have caused them.

"Three beings?" repeated Kesten, sharpening her tone to reach Aeron through the reverie that seemed to have seized her.

Aeron started a little. "Aye—aye, three."

Kesten grimaced. "Well? Must I drag this from you like a stump from a swamp? Men, women, sea-pigs? What manner of beings?"

"One was a woman," conceded Aeron. "The one in the midst of the three— She said her name was . . . well, she said her name. The one on her right was a man—a youth, rather—very young, and fair enough for a maid. He carried a telyn of a shape I have never before seen. He did not offer his name, but he greeted me by mine."

"So." Kesten joined her fingertips together, tapped them twice. "And what of the third?"

Aeron shook her head slowly. "I know not. He—she—was cloaked and hooded, and silent as well. I could not call that one either woman or man; perhaps it was both, or neither. I think it did not matter."

"Nay, very likely not. What place was it where they came to you—or was it you who came to them?"

"Somewhat of both; the place seemed a tryst arranged. It was out upon the edge of space; far enough out so that Banbha was a star and not a sun." That was said confidently, from the knowledge of one trained as a star-pilot. "Yet it seemed the other stars were strangely different, so that I could not tell in truth where in space we were; and though I was spoken to at length, save what I have just now told you I cannot recall one word of what was said."

"No matter." Kesten's smile held warmth and deep affection. "Always in each class there is one girl at least who insists on wandering about upon the astral. I might have known it would be you."

"But my dream?"

"A welcome, I would say. I myself had a very similar encounter as a young novice, and, I would bet, so too our friend Tybie. Go and tell her, if you need more assurance. Go and tell her anyway."

Again Kesten's study, a week later. "And the dream this time?"

"The City destroyed." Aeron's face was white and taut with the strain of remembering. "Yet it was *not* the City, not Caerdroia, for it had no walls, only high thin towers, all blasted, and was built upon no mountain but girdled round by a broad river. A river near its mouth, I think, because of the light; there were sea-birds flying, and a ruined temple or fane upon a little island. A bridge crossed the river, but the bridge was in ruins even as the towers; and over that ruined bridge I was leading twelve times twelve people out of the dead city. I had no word of guidance, no map or lithfaen; only the command laid most hard upon me—I cannot even say by whom—that I must lead these folk north to a place of safety." She drew a deep breath, for this dream and its present recalling had shaken her to her soul's roots. "There were many score other parties led by others charged even as I; thousands and thousands and all heading north. What does it speak of?"

"Another life, another task; this life, another where; a different now and a might-have-been; the future and a never-to-be. The place might be anywhere in the galaxy, or in any other galaxy; Earth, even, perhaps, and the city Lirias of Atland, our long-ago home—or it might be some other. Or it might be a task you will be charged with between your lives, to lead souls by what your own soul has learned in life. I cannot say—but you will know."

And yet a third time: "And this?"

"A castle, seen from a distance; I am in a pass between two peaks, and the castle is below me across a valley's width. I think there is the sea beyond. It is no castle I have ever seen in waking life: It sits upon a high black rock, and the road runs down from the pass where I stand, through the valley and up again to the castle's gates. There is much mist and cloud, and no folk are about, and no other dwelling that I can see."

"And then?"

"And then it seems to me that I am within the castle, in a high bare chamber that overlooks I know not what, for I cannot pass the door. There is a tall pointed window with a seat built into the stone beneath, all hung with tattered curtains of dark green velvet. A fourposted bed is in one corner of the room, with hangings and a coverlet of the same perished velvet, but the featherbed in the frame is long gone. Everything seems old and long deserted, bare and poor and unused, and the afternoon sunlight falls in upon the dust, for the roof is broken and the chamber stands open to the air."

"Has this castle any name?"

"Argetros," said Aeron automatically, then looked up sharply at her teacher with what was almost a gasp. "I did not know that name before! In my dream I heard no name; but I knew that I had been in that chamber many times before, and I knew also that the chamber is—somehow—mine."

When Aeron had gone at last, with the Magistra's words of reasoned comfort strong in her ear, Kesten walked over to the windows, to look out upon the well-loved view over the convent's home fields and down the length of the valley. But at that moment she saw not so much as one inch of it.

Three dreams, three different glimpses of a soul's reality . . . One's initiation dreams, though often so abstruse as to be near impenetrable, opaque though one probed them to the end of one's life, all the same often conveyed a burden too deep or too dramatic for more usual methods of transmittal. Given, of course, that they even came at all: For many candidates they never did;

and though those so unfavored were no less Ban-draoi for such a lack, still there was something incomplete about them, some stamp upon their souls that was somehow absent. *As if the Mighty Ones who rule such matters saw fit to withhold their sanction and blessing, though the Order did not. And that is not to be wondered at,* thought Kesten, *that some Ban-draoi should be more truly Ban-draoi than others . . . For so it is with every kind of binding one can make by choice: For some the choice, or the oath, or the promise, will ever be more real than for others, whether that choice be a vow to love or to magic, or the coronation oath of a ruler. And for those whose oath is of the soul, their pledges will ever be redeemed full measure.*

Still, a half-hearted commitment was scarcely the problem here; if anything, too much the opposite . . . These three dreams of a young Ban-draoi who would be Keltia's next Ard-rían—it stood to reason there would be more to the dreams of such a one than to another's—and too that they should be more than usually proof against overglib interpretation.

We are making a High Queen here, thought Kesten again, as so many others had thought before her, and would again after. *That itself—a Domina High Queen—is a glory and a pride; but a pity also, that I have had so little to go on for my own guidance, that I might have guided her better . . .* And then too, Aeron's brilliance as a pupil had further compounded matters, though of course brilliance of itself was hardly to be deplored. *If she had been free to pursue magic only, no other demands on brain or body, who can say to what she might not have attained? Even as it is, I think she could well approach the greatest among us by the time she grows to her full stature; how was I to teach such a one?*

But clearly it was the dreams that were the key to her student's future. It seemed to Kesten that, for all her genuine puzzlement, Aeron well understood them, though in a place so remote from her everyday awareness as to be effectively inaccessible. Yet those deep dreams would shape Aeron's actions for the rest of her days, and into her next lives; would mold her reality as she would in time mold Keltia's. *And she will never be able to say for true how she is being shaped, and upon what Wheel, and by Whose hand, to what End . . .*

Kesten thought back, immense satisfaction her prevailing emotion, over the past four years. She and every one of Aeron's other teachers could in honesty swear before the Goddess that they had done their proper jobs, had given her the best of their minds and hearts and spirits. And with that given knowledge, all the usual prohibitions had been instilled as well; though Kesten was nowhere near so sure that they had taken, or if they had, whether they would hold when put to the test.

Still, the Order would have one more chance to make sure of this new Sister: when Aeron returned to take her final initiation as Domina, in three or four years' time, following her stint with the Fianna. *And that will be our last chance, to train her to the fullest, for my heart tells me she will have great need of every ounce of that training in time to come.*

For Kesten too had had dreams: dreams of the lost Treasures of Keltia, those thirteen hallows, strong and ancient, that had been lost to the world with Arthur of Arvon, or perhaps not lost, none now could say; dreams of a Keltic princess whose face she could not see—though she had had strong presentiment, and so Arianeira had been sent away—a princess who would betray her own Queen; dreams of an out-Wall stranger, a man such as no Kelt had ever before beheld, a man with skin the color of honey-butter and dark slanted eyes, an air of command and humor both upon him; dreams of yet another stranger, a Coranian with golden eyes and a golden collar at his throat, a tall prince clad all in white, magic and betrayal both to his hand.

And Kesten's dreams, like Aeron's, gave the dreamer no comfort at all.

Though they had for the most part taken their training all together, each of the new Ban-draoi candidates would undergo her initiation alone, among certain of the senior Sisters. Alone save for one chosen companion, the Guide of Souls, who would escort the candidate through the rite and receive her at the end of the immram—the voyage of initiation.

In the ordinary way, the candidate's choice always prevailed, for obvious reasons; but for Aeron this had become somewhat of a problem. She and Sabia had of course wished to choose each other for guide; this not being possible, Aeron had then asked formally for Arianeira. But Kesten had let it be known that she looked with disfavor upon this choice, though she gave no reason for her disapproval—nor, as Magistra, did she need to give one.

So Aeron, half in baffled anger, half in challenge, had then requested none less a personage than Tybie herself.

If she had sought to rattle her Magistra, she succeeded beyond her wildest expectations: Kesten stared at her astounded, unable for an instant even to respond. Then:

"*Tybie!* You would so trouble her peace?"

"Your Reverence's refusal of Ari has troubled mine," said Aeron stonily.

Kesten studied her pupil's mutinous face. She knew as well as did Aeron that if for any reason a candidate's first choice for Guide of Souls is rejected, that candidate's second naming must be accepted without demurral. *Oh, she does this to test me, the tiresome little bonnive! Still . . .*

"Very well so. If you can gain an acceptance from Tybie, she may so serve. Now go."

When Kesten told her friend that evening of Aeron's stratagem, Tybie laughed long and loud.

"I see no cause for mirth," said Kesten sourly. "She only does it to plague me, and you will only encourage her if you accept. You will *not* accept, of course."

"And why would I not? Certainly I shall accept, and honored to be chosen. It is after all *her* choice, Magistra—and I think you will not tell me why you saw fit to refuse her her first choice? —Nay, well, I thought not. Still, Kesi, she's stymied you fair and final. Admit it with a good grace, and let her win the round."

"Though I am forced to allow this choice," said Kesten stiffly, ignoring Tybie's renewed merriment, "*you* are not so bound. As an anchoress—"

"Oh aye, I know, right enough. But I think this will be one making I would not miss for worlds."

Chapter 16

Though at Scartanore the annat was of all that holy place the crown, yet there was one more place that was more sacred still.

Behind the high altar in the nave, wrought findruinna gates guarded the mouth of a narrow passageway, where, lit only by small sconces and the crystals set therein, a flight of secret steps led down into darkness, their worn white marble treads bespeaking the passage of the bare feet of countless Ban-draoi down the centuries.

The steps ended in a low wide tunnel that ran arrow-straight back into the heart of the hill upon whose breast lay Scartanore; two sharp-angled turns, one to sunwise, one to antisunwise, and the tunnel debouched unexpectedly into a huge hollow cavern, cut by nature and by human purpose from out of the granite guts of the hill. Its domed ceiling, some thirty feet above the smooth slate floor, was incised with cryptic symbols, symbols whose ancient meaning had long been lost to the rest of Keltia, here not only remembered but reverenced: devices that resembled shapely mirrors and curving combs and spiral-backed shieldbosses. Animals too there were upon that roof: stags and sun-sharks, wingwide eagles and rampant bulls; and stranger beasts beside—piasts, hippocamps, nameless grinning creatures with tufted head-knobs and long drooping snouts. But chiefest among all those patterns was the holy mark of the Ban-draoi order, given to them at their founding by Nia, to be their sign and sigil for all time: the crescent bisected by the V-rod—some plain, some richly ornamented, but all carved into the vaulted ceiling with the same loving attention and the same sacred purpose.

Below that rioting dome, the chamber was bare and austere.

Four huge pillars of carven crystal marked the four Watchtowers, the Airts—the sacred directions of East and South and West and North; an inlaid gold roundel, a yard wide and near sixty feet across, delineated the precincts of the magical circle; and a low bench of black basalt stood on a three-stepped dais in the circle's north.

No more than that; and no more needed, for this was Broinn-na-draoichta, Magic's Womb, the place where Ban-draoi were born to their art and to themselves and to their Sisters; and Magic's Tomb it was also, Laba-draoichta, where if by any means possible each Magistra, and each Domina of Scartanore, was brought to die, to pass beyond with ease and grace, out upon the Path to her next life and lives. Every Ban-draoi school and convent had such a place, to serve its own daughters; but this at Scartanore was the oldest and the holiest, and here it was that Aeron and her fellows would face their last test.

When the hood was removed from her eyes, Aeron, blinking a little in the sudden brightness, saw after a moment that she stood on the eastern edge of the circle.

Tybie was at her left elbow, had been the one to hood her and take her arm and lead her down the steps and through the tunnel's length to where they now stood. The sacred chamber was softly lighted with the white glow from the crystal pillars, and Aeron knew from that that the Circle had been cast for her coming. By that light she could see also that the chamber was near filled with figures robed and hooded in black, one of which—the one standing on the lowest step of the dais, perhaps—was certainly Kesten.

But she would not come to that dais for some little time yet, for three figures faced her across the circle's golden boundary, and in the hands of one was a naked sword to bar her way.

The voice that came from the depths of the swordbearer's hood was harsh and clear, like an eagle's cry, and the swordpoint advanced to touch Aeron's breast.

"Why have you come?"

Aeron forced the response from a suddenly dry mouth. "To make my immram."

"Where would you go?"

"Where the Road may take me."

"You cannot travel upon the Road until you have yourself become the Road."

"What Road must I become?"

"The Road that is the Heroes' Way," said the one in red to the swordbearer's right. "Spear-straight and edged with flame."

"The Road that is the Tântad," said the blue-clad one who stood to the left. "That Path by which the Dragon comes."

"The Road that is the Way of the White Cow," said the swordbearer again, "of cold and starry death. Knowing this, will you walk it still?"

Aeron drew a deep calming breath. "I will walk it."

The green-hooded head bent once in acknowledgment. The sword fell away, and the voice spoke now in the cadences of the High Gaeloch, grave and sonorous and somehow terrible. "Be it so. Who shall pledge thy conduct?"

Tybie spoke up, clear and firm. "I will pledge it."

"Who art thou, to speak here?"

"Kevarwedhor, the Guide of Souls."

"How offer in pledge?"

"An éraic m'anama." *In ransom for my soul*—

"The pledge is acceptable." Again now to Aeron: "Begin thou."

"Nay, thou," responded Aeron as she had been taught.

"Halve it, and begin."

"Let the rock beyond the billow—"

"—be set in order at the dawn," came the countersign. And those were the words that the Danaans spoke when first they came to Earth; that Amergin spoke when first the Milesians came to Ireland; that Brendan spoke when first the Kelts came to Tara.

Aeron felt Tybie take her arm and begin to lead her around the circle's perimeter. Then the hood was over her head again, and she could see nothing. For some reason it was suddenly strangely difficult to take a step; all seemed slowed to the pace of half-time or dream-time, and though she herself felt light as air, she could sense the effort Tybie must make to move her, hands spread clawlike over Aeron's shoulder and back, almost pushing. *The resistance is not in me,* she thought, *but in the air itself; physical reality is itself altered here.*

Then came a challenge, cried across the circle's width.

"You who would walk this Road, come first to the Wind!"

Aeron felt Tybie's hand tighten on her shoulder, halting her, and knew she must stand now before the great crystal pillar in the East. All at once a strong fresh wind out of that Quarter came to her, so that her robe streamed out behind her, and her head bent backward with the force of it.

"What will you ask of the Wind?" said the voice that had cried the challenge.

Aeron spoke with difficulty against the blast, as it blew the cloth of her hood against her mouth.

"Fill my sails."

"Be it so, and pass south." Though Aeron could not see, she knew that the guardian bowed to her and to her guide, and Tybie turned her sunwise to the right.

Another cry: "You who have been to the Wind, come now to the Fire!"

Sun blazed at midnight: Aeron felt that she stood in a strong light that fell on her from a place just above her head, felt the heat of it, the brilliance that dazzled even through the masking hood.

"What will you ask of the Fire?"

"Light my way."

"Be it so, and pass west."

As they turned again to deosil, Aeron felt the resistance redouble before her. *It is not that I am unwelcome here, but so the thing may be not too easily won. But the real test, the immram, is yet to come. All this is but prelude.*

"You who have been to the Wind and the Fire," they cried to her then, "come now to the Water!"

But it seemed instead to Aeron that the water came to her: a great glassy wall of wave, green and roaring and footed in foam, that hung motionless in one place and did not break; she could smell its cold salt exhalation.

"What will you ask of the Water?"

"Lift my craft."

"Be it so, and pass north."

One last turn; Tybie's hands were trembling now with the effort it cost both of them to move—Aeron's shoulders would show for days the blue bruises left by the anchoress's fingers. But she could not have stirred otherwise.

"You who have been to the Wind and the Fire and the Water, come now to the Earth at the last!"

And a coldness and a darkness crept down out of the North; the bite of winter air was all around them, the smell of leaf-mold and frozen grass strong and clean in their nostrils.

"What will you ask of the Earth?"

"Bear me up."

"Be it so, and it is done."

Then all resistance vanished before them; Aeron could move freely, and the hood was pulled from her face. She saw that she stood now in the circle's north quarter, though in an unexpected orientation: The dais with the low bench was before her, and Kesten, one hand held out to her, stood at its foot.

"What is offered to the Airts in true offering," she said to the silent chamber, "the Airts repay a thousandfold: Gaoth, Tân, Dwr, Daearawr. Come then to thy immram."

Without hesitation Aeron took the Magistra's hand, and ascending the steps of the dais stretched out upon the bench. All her will to move was suddenly taken away; and when Kesten and Tybie, one on either side of her, had folded her hands upon her breast and laid each in turn a gentle hand upon her forehead in blessing, she knew the time had come to turn inward for her journey. The immram-trance, deepest of all—far deeper than the marana, deeper even than taghairm or imbas-forosnai—came upon her without mystery, and the last thing Aeron saw was Tybie's hands drawing the hood forward over her eyes; then it was only darkness.

Darkness a long time, it seemed, though Aeron was not much alarmed that it should be, and indeed could imagine no other condition in which to be; then it drew back before her like clouds after rain. She was in a boat, a small light craft like to a pinnace or masted curragh: a dainty craft, trim and high-riding, gray-hulled with sails of red leather. She could feel the swells passing beneath her, could hear the slap of water against the boat's timbers; and yet she knew also that her body lay upon a stone bench in Broinn-na-draoichta, with Kesten and Tybie standing watch beside it. *If I come not back from this immram, they will destroy that body, lest it be inhabited by some malign being, some banacha or bonacha that looks to take over human shapes, what way a tenant-crab will move into any empty shell that offers. And for all that, it is the least of my risks; which my father knew well would be before he did send me . . .* But the thought caused her no distress, and Aeron turned her attention now to the sea that stretched before her.

No earthly sea, surely: Over all that featureless watery waste hung a sky like dull gold, and there was a metallic taste in the air that breathed from the bronze clouds massed upon the horizon. No birds stitched their flight-lines across that sky, and no fish leaped above the crests of the little waves: Aeron knew that in truth she was creator and only beholder of all that world. She had made it of herself, for herself, by herself alone; she would find within it only that which she would find within herself, and that she had brought with her to this journey.

What passes here is for me and none other, in time or out of it. Get on with it, then . . . Loosing the tiller from the twist of leather that had held it, Aeron closed her hand over the smooth-grained ash, and steered toward the only land that she could see.

The Island of the Stone Door

As her curragh drew near, Aeron saw the first of the islands of her immram: a great, high, bare rock of an island, one huge gray stone that rounded itself like a whaleback above the waves. In its side was a small door strapped and studded with black iron, opening directly into the sea, so that one landing by boat could step through with ease.

Making fast the little curragh to a ring beside the door-frame, Aeron entered boldly, to find herself in a spacious chamber of what seemed a rich and pleasant dwelling.

Yet an empty one . . . are there no folk here, then? But a fire burned merrily on the tiled hearth, and a wide couch hung with silken curtains stood waiting, and food and drink filled dishes of gold and cups of silver upon the table near the fire. Aeron hesitated a moment—*Fine it would be to eat and drink and rest awhile, but I am on a voyage where there is no time for such; and even if there were, still I think it is better not*—and fighting down the relentless hunger and weariness that had seized her, she turned from the chamber, and loosing her boat from the iron ring sailed swiftly away.

Looking once behind her, Aeron saw the island of stone sink into the waves, as if it had never been.

The Island of Apples

Now all that region seemed thick with islands, so many and so various that Aeron could not choose which of them to steer toward, and she guided her craft now more by instinct than by thought or design.

A short sail from the stone island, she came upon another, this one tall and wide, cliffed round by precipices of clear green glass. From the top of the glass cliffs, the laden branches of apple trees hung down almost to touch the sea.

As her boat moved past those shining cliffs, Aeron reached up to snap off a green twig from one of the bending boughs. Though she sailed round that island for an hour or more, she could find no entrance to the land within; but three golden apples grew from the twig she held in her hand, and those she kept close by her.

The Island of the Silver Pillar

Once she had left those waters behind her and was again upon the open sea, Aeron saw the next wonder from a long way off: a colossal silver column, foursquare, rising straight and shining from the bottom of the sea. Not a sod of earth nor grain of sand was round its sides but ocean only, and its top was lost in the bronze clouds.

From that unseen summit, a huge net of silver, wide-meshed, each knotted strand of it thicker than her body, was flung far out into the sea; thrown by what fisher, to catch what behemoth, Aeron did not know and dared not think. Sailing through the glittering meshes, she was filled with a longing to cut a piece of the silver seine; but, as in the chamber of the isle of stone, she knew that she must not, and putting down the wish by will she headed once more out to sea.

As she did so, she heard a voice from the summit of the pillar, slow, clear, glad, mighty: a voice like a great bell to summon all creation. But she knew not the tongue it used, nor the words it uttered.

The Island of the Glass Bridge

Beyond the silver pillar, the sea grew empty again, and Aeron sailed on for some hours, as it seemed, before another island raised itself up out of the gray waves: low and green, rising to wooded hills in its center, with a fine fringe of gold sand beaches.

Now by this time Aeron was cramped and restless from her long lonely hours in the curragh, and as soon as her gaze fell on those green machairs bordering the shore, she felt a desperate wish to walk upon them. *Not for long; surely it cannot harm, and I will see what may be seen.*

Not five minutes ashore, Aeron spied a fortress across the machair, atop a small hill; it had a door of bright brass, and a glass bridge led up to it, and on the instant she turned her steps that way.

Coming to the palace, she sought entry; but though she tried again and again, she could gain no footing on the bridge's smooth glass surface, and this went on until she grew peevish and weary, and the soles of her feet bled in her boots.

She was sitting disconsolate by the end of the bridge when the brass door opened without a warning or a sound, and a young man emerged from within. Crossing the bridge of glass with no difficulty whatever, he passed so close by Aeron that the wind of his cloak stirred her hair. Going to the foot of the castle hill, he drew water from a fountain into a silver ewer and returned with it to the palace, and all that time he paid no heed to Aeron at all.

Thrice this happened; then Aeron, remembering on a sudden the golden apples, drew one from the folds of her cloak and tossed it at the youth as he passed.

"Well for you, Aeron, had you thought of that sooner," he said laughing, and placed the apple in the breast of his black tunic. "Better for you to have me with you than against you, and best of all for you that your hands are empty when your immram ends."

I have heard those words somewhere before . . . Aeron made as if to speak, but the young lord raised the silver ewer and poured out the water he had drawn from the fountain, and Aeron was transfixed by the glittering stream. When she looked up again, she found herself back in her curragh; not the youth, nor the glass bridge, nor the palace, nor the island itself, were to be seen, and soberly she sailed away.

The Island of the Eagle

She was growing tired in good earnest now; the strangeness and the spaces and the silence were beginning to wear her down. *Now I see why the form of this journey is the form of an immram, why Nia in her holy wisdom made it so; now, now at last it all comes so clear . . .*

Looking up at what seemed a sudden shadow across the sun, though sun there was none over those waters, Aeron saw a cloud coming swiftly out of the northwest, dark and thick with thunder. *There is a storm in the belly of that one and no mistake; and nowhere I may shelter from it . . .* A kind of calm despair came over her, and she smiled a little as she made fast the leather sails to take the wind now rushing toward her. *I will ride it out if it can be ridden; though if the curragh oversets I am lost indeed. But is that not the risk in any voyage?*

Then as it was all but upon her, she saw that it was no cloud but a tremendous eagle, so vast that the wind of its wingstrokes flattened the tops of the waves. It took no note of her, seemingly, but giving one harsh cry altered its course for an island Aeron had not seen until that moment: a dark and somber island with beaches of stone, its slopes all forested in oak and yew.

Sailing after, and leaving the curragh on the rocky shore, she followed the great bird as it flew heavily into the island's heart, and coming through the dark trees she found herself on the edge of a reed-fringed lochan, its deep waters still and cold.

As she stood there, the eagle came circling down to hover above the little lake, and it seemed not so huge as it had done before. Aeron could see now that it was old—very old—its fierce golden gaze dimmed, all its once-bright plumage dull and molting.

"There is hunger on me," it said to her then, and Aeron pitying it reached into her cloak for the second of the golden apples.

"I have naught but this to give you," she said, and flung the bright apple out over the lochan, so that the eagle caught it in its talons. "There is another, and you are welcome to that as well; though I fear neither will be enough."

"One is enough, and more than enough," replied the creature, and folding its wings plunged deep into the waters of the lake. The little waves ran up the foreshore to break in ripples at Aeron's feet, and all was very still; then with a great rush of air and sparkling spray the eagle burst up from the lochan, and now it was young and strong and beautiful, all its life and power renewed, every feather clean and sharp as a sgian, and its voice as it cried to her was fierce and glad.

"Though your hands are emptier than before, Aeron, still are they not empty entirely. But for that you have given me to eat, I shall give you a wind."

It took to the air, gaining back all its tremendous size as it did so, rising so high above the island that it seemed barely of the bigness of a wren. As Aeron hastened back to her curragh, and pushed off from the shore, far above her the eagle closed its great wings to stoop with a sound like thunder, and passing powerfully overhead beat clean wind into the red leather sails.

Under that wind, Aeron in her boat sped southeastwards, and as night began to turn the bronze clouds to leaden-gray, she saw one last island lying like a fallen flag across her path through the waters.

The Island of the Homecoming

In that low light it looked to her very like to the sea-lands about Caerdroia—rough wooded mountains running back from towering cliffs, white beaches where a broad river came down to find its mouth stopped with salt—and Aeron was seized by a sudden ferocious longing for her home. *Not yet; not yet may I turn for home—there is one thing more must first be done.*

The curragh ran ashore of itself, unguided this time by her hand or her mind, to touch sand where it—or someone—chose to set her ashore, and Aeron stepped out onto the pebbled shingle in what was now full dark.

Not far from the tidemark, there was a dún set among the sandhills, and as she approached it, she heard folk talking as they sat at table within.

One said, "Glad would I be, to see Aeron now."

"She will never come tonight," said another.

"Perhaps it is she shall shake you from sleep," laughed a third.

"Yet if she should come," said the first voice again, "what must we do for it?"

"Not hard," said one who had not spoken before, and at the sound of that voice Aeron felt as if a great tide of warmth and love lapped her round like a mantle. "She shall have great welcome if she were to come, for she has been a long time on a hard voyage, and we here her own kin."

Then Aeron, who had been hesitating on the threshold in the cold and lonely dark, took heart, and lifted a hand to knock upon the door.

"Who comes?" they asked.

She answered, "Aeron."

"Then enter, and be welcome."

The door swung wide for her, though no hand had been set to it, and Aeron found herself in a fair hall, lighted by sconces of silver and hung round with rich tapestries. Down the hall's length ran a wide banqueting-board of polished waxwood, its darkly shining surface all set thick with gold plate and silver methers.

Nor was that board a mean or bare one: Already the knife was in the meat and the ale in the cup, the bread served out with the salt. Though she knew well that the feast was not meant for her to partake of, or at any rate not yet, all the same Aeron liked not to bring nothing to the board; and stepping forward to the empty place at the table's foot she set down as guest-gift the third and last of the golden apples.

Only then did she look up at the faces of the company that sat there, and her mind rang like a struck sword at the sight.

From the high seat at the table's head, Dâna smiled on her with love and pride; and upon the countenances of those others as well there was honor and approval, as for a test well stood.

And those others . . . Aeron's gaze running swift and shy along the table fell upon one after the next, and knew them all: Mâth the ancient, Brân the blessed, somber Arawn; deft-handed Lugh, Lír the unbounded, tall Midir; on the women's side fair-faced Gwener and Morna the valorous, Brigit of the Fire and Síon of the Storms and Malen who was queen of love and war.

In the place nearest the door, scarce an arm's-length from Aeron where she stood, Fionn smiled and saluted her, and he was the young lord in black she had met beside the bridge of glass, and he tossed from hand to hand the first golden apple. Across the table's width from him, Dôn's calm lovely face was bright with approbation; her eyes were the eyes of an eagle, and her long white fingers curved like talons round the gleaming peel of the second apple of gold.

"Did I not say, Aeron," came Dâna's voice down the table's length, and at the sound of that voice Aeron's memory was freed, and she remembered all that had taken place in the annat at Scartanore, "did I not say that you should succeed in your immram only if you came away from it empty-handed? And now it is proved, and you have won. Go home now, use what you have learned; there will be great need of it soon. We will be waiting here for you, when it is time for you to come again."

As she gazed upon the face of Dâna, hoping that this time she might be permitted to remember, as she had not been before, Aeron felt the dún begin to vibrate around her. Before she could stir, or even cry out in protest, or farewell, there was a blurring, a short sharp jolt, and—

—she saw the faces of Kesten and Tybie looking down at her, felt their hands helping her to sit up, supporting her, holding a cup of water to her parched lips. For her part, Aeron clung to them both, as a runner who has victoriously crossed the finish line will collapse into the arms of the trainers.

"There now," said Kesten soothingly, gently disengaging Aeron's clutching fingers from the fabric of her robe and guiding her to a seat in an alcove just beyond the circle. "Nay, do not try to speak just yet—take your time to come back fully. You have been a long way away, and a long time gone. Drink now, slowly"—then, as Aeron grew more solid in her own body again—"aye, that is better. But you are shivering still, it was cold and far in that place . . ."

Before Kesten could command it, one of the other priestesses had thrust a clean robe, furred inside for warmth, into her hands, and Tybie was already stripping Aeron of the soaked gúna she had been wearing. Together they wrapped the newest Sister of the Ban-draoi in the fresh garment, and Aeron pulled it close about her, for she was stiff and sore and near frozen with her long ordeal. Someone else was trying to make her drink from a cup of warmed ale; she locked her fingers around the heated metal to get all benefit of its much-needed warmth, and though her hands shook uncontrollably she sipped with care at the cup's contents.

After only a few swallows, Aeron felt restored enough to look up at her two mentors with some degree of composure. She opened her mouth to speak, but no words came, and she gave a small helpless choke of laughter, shaking her head in apology and disbelief.

"Nay, no words needed; we know very well what you would tell us," said Kesten smiling, and Aeron felt rather than saw Tybie's wordless echo of the Magistra's thought. "As for the specifics, they can wait till morning; or when you waken, rather, for it is already dawn outside. Go now and rest without fear."

Aeron hardly knew it as two of the junior Sisters—now her fellow-priestesses—guided her back to her own chamber, and helped her to bed, and covered the windows against the growing light.

Chapter 17

Aeron's initiation was neither the first crop nor the last of that year's harvest: By the end of that month, all those who still remained as candidates after the final winnowing had been brought to their own immrama; though it did not follow that all had been equally successful at the test.

One of those last was Duvessa Cantelon, who when it came to the facing of the sword in Broinn-na-draoichta had backed away shrieking in terror, unable to bring herself even to endure the questioning, and Kesten had immediately terminated the rite, inhibiting the girl's ability to speak of it.

But the knowledge Duvessa had acquired over the past four years could not be similarly bound; and with the fact of her own failure as a hot iron in her hand, the success of the others— Sabia and Aeron in especial—grew monstrous unfair in her eyes, and the spitefulness she had long borne Aeron now rose up more virulent than ever . . .

It was on the day of her departure from Scartanore that Aeron, making for sentiment's sake a farewell round of the place that had been her home for four years, entered the annat and came all at once face to face with Duvessa.

She had not seen the other girl since the weeks of testing the previous month, though of course she knew that Duvessa had not succeeded. All the same, she was surprised to see her still at the convent, and her usual tact failed her enough to let her say so.

"Aye, well, it was the Magistra herself gave me permission to stay on until term-end," said Duvessa. "Perhaps I shall even try again to make my immram . . . But I have not congratulated you,

Aeron, on your own achievement. I have heard your initiation was replete with Presences—but of course what else were we to expect, from so exceptional a one?''

Aeron let it pass, held out a hand to Duvessa. "No matter, that. I shall be returning to my home today; will you not come with me to share silence before we say farewell?"

To Aeron's surprise, though the offer had been genuinely meant, Duvessa accepted at once, and together they went into the main nave of the annat. They were by no means alone in that place, for more than a few of the departing new-made Ban-draoi had had the same thought, and were scattered through that vast hall, alone or in small groups, with friends or with the kinfolk who had come to collect them, all wrapped alike in prayers for the future or memories of the past.

Sabia among them, Aeron saw. She inquired of Duvessa with a lifted brow, and when her companion made no objection, turned their steps toward Sabia where she sat near the high altar-stone. Sabia smiled at her friend, hiding the surprise and distaste she felt at seeing Duvessa—more, at seeing Duvessa with Aeron—but she said no word, and, seated together in apparent amity, the three turned their focus inward.

Presently Aeron, who had been absorbed in her own contemplations, felt Duvessa stir and stand beside her, and looking up curiously, she felt the smile fade from her face, for Duvessa's eyes were blazing with hatred.

"As in all the tales of old, Aeron, your triumph would not be complete did you not have a geis laid upon you." Duvessa's voice was high and tight, like the buzz of the evil biting cleggans that fly round one's head in summer. "Since none else has seen the need, plainly it is on me to fill this; we cannot have Keltia's future Ard-rían to labor under such a lack."

Sabia lunged forward, hands clearly destined for Duvessa's throat despite the sanctity of the surroundings; but Aeron caught her by the arm in an iron grip, and shook her head in warning.

"Do not—but let her speak it out. If it be true geis for me, you know as well as I that it cannot be gainsaid; and if it be but malice, it will only rebound on the one who gives way to it." She looked again at Duvessa. "Say on."

"Though the Mighty Ones saw fit to deny me my immram,"

said Duvessa, staring at Aeron with a kind of jealous triumph, "they have put it in my heart to pronounce for you."

"They have not, then!" snapped Sabia. "And as for denying you the immram—" She fell silent at a look from Aeron.

"These be your geisa," continued Duvessa, ignoring Sabia's outburst, eyes still fixed on her rival. "That you shall not eat of the meat of the red stag, nor shall you refuse any dish that is offered you at a feast."

Aeron smiled, considerably relieved, for geisa had been known to be far more onerous—impossible, even—than these. "Those seem not over-hard to keep to; my thanks that you should lay them so light upon me."

Now it was Duvessa who smiled, and the smile was not a merry one; but before she could say more, if more she had in mind to say, Sabria angrily interposed again, all her loyalty ablaze.

"I have no geis to set," she said, "so I give a warning instead. Aeron stoops not to your level, Duvessa of the Cantelons, but I am happy to say that I myself have no such scruples where you are concerned. You have ever been an evil star and an ill wind and iniquity's own slut; and if any harm befalls Aeron for what you have just now pronounced, be it true geis or but your own lying malice, I take oath I will kill you with my own hand."

But Duvessa had recovered from her first surprise at Sabia's unexpected virulence, and now gave her only a scornful look; another satisfied smirk at Aeron, and she was gone.

Aeron sighed, feeling as if a certain uncleanliness had been removed from her presence, and pitying Duvessa all the same.

"I am grateful for your loyalty as ever, my friend," she said to Sabia, "but all the same, you should not have demeaned yourself by taking such an oath against such a one, and in such a place as this."

But Sabia was still fuming. "I care naught for that! But does it not trouble you, that she bears such hatred to you and feels so free to flaunt it?"

Aeron shrugged, and taking her friend's arm drew her toward the annat's north door. "I regret that she seems to *need* to hate me so, and that she should express her malice openly in so holy a place—thus causing my true friend to take oath where she should not have . . . As to whether it be geis or spite, that the future shall show. As to whether it troubles me— My father says a king's best armor is a duck's-back; to let the mouthings of such folk—and there are many Duvessas in the world—run off like the rainwater. I admit it is a hard thing to learn," she added after a while, glancing a little shamefaced at her friend. "What is it?"

Sabia blushed. "The way you speak of the Ard-rígh; as if he were just—your father."

"But he is," laughed Aeron.

"Well, I know! It is only that sometimes I forget—not who you are, for you are my friend, but what you will be—for that is my Ard-rían."

"And gods, but I am glad that you do forget . . ." Aeron sobered, said so quietly that Sabia could scarcely hear her, "Would that I could as well."

But however much she might wish to, Aeron was not like to forget; and there were two people in Kesten's chambers that very moment who would not be slow to remind her, if ever it chanced that she should.

Kesten, coming into the gríanan from duties that had demanded her presence elsewhere, found Fionnbarr and Emer waiting for her, sitting there like dutiful children, their backs very straight and their hands folded in their laps. Accompanied by Emer's sister Keina, they had come to take Aeron home to Turusachan, though as yet their presence was unknown to their daughter, and a secret to all but the few who had seen them arrive.

"Nay, no state here, Magistra," said Fionnbarr with a smile, as he rose with his queen to greet Kesten, who, besides being Abbess of Scartanore, and his heir's chief teacher, was also a minister of his own government, sitting upon his High Council. "We have seen but little of you at Turusachan these last months; has all been well with your newest Sisters?"

Kesten returned the smile, hearing the real question the Ard-rígh had asked her—*How is it with my daughter?*—and with a nod to Keina, who as a Domina of the order was due a salute from her Magistra, and a deeper bow to Emer, she took her seat beside them near the windows.

"There is naught amiss with Aeron, Lord, for so I perceive

you are asking; in truth, very much the contrary." Kesten sat back, steepling her fingers in her habitual way. "You know I have been Ban-draoi Magistra for near forty years now; I have served upon your High Council, and upon the King your father's. Soon it will be time for me to step up and out upon the Path, and another will stand in my stead to the Sisters. But before that time comes, there is still much to do, and Aeron is very much a part of it."

"Aeron?" said Emer, wondering. "But—"

Kesten made a small gesture. "Once or twice in every teacher's life, it is given her to have to her hand a perfect pupil. Oh, not some biddable milk-and-water idiot who makes no trouble and does all she is told; quite the opposite—the best ones cost always the greatest pains, for themselves as well as for their teachers. And Aeron your daughter is for me that one: She is beyond question the most brilliant student I have ever been privileged to train up in the ways of Nia, and I would say as much to her parents were she the child of the humblest house in Keltia. Indeed, if it be not sacrilege to say so, I doubt even St. Morgan herself, blessed be her holy name, was much Aeron's better in her youth."

Fionnbarr let out a long breath and drew a hand over his beard, glancing at Emer in what might at first have been relief but then changed to something quite different; as if, having steeled himself to hear a thing both unpleasant and unwelcome, that which he had just heard had given him more pause than would the other have done.

"I think you know how well these words fall upon our ears, Magistra," he said. "But I think also that you have more cause for saying them than simply to gratify proud parents. What is it you would warn us of?"

Kesten shook her head. "For all you deny your own gift for magic, Barraun, plain to see where Aeron comes by at least some of hers . . . Well, as to what I would tell you, I am not entirely certain. Perhaps only this: Though Aeron is surely greatly gifted, very often with such talents go other things that are not near so welcome—things such as lack of moderation, intemperance, a sense of proportion not so finely tuned as it might be, or must be. To put it plainly, Aeron is headstrong, and I think dangerously so; though she is swift and sure off the mark, she often bends her bow before her target is fairly seen, and uses a boar-bow to shoot where a bow strung for rabbits would suffice. And *gods* but she is stubborn, so set upon her own road already that only the best-reasoned arguments have force to turn her aside; and she is impulsive, will leap first and think later—if at all. In a future Ard-rían, none of this will serve; but I think too that I tell you no new thing."

"Nay, she comes by much of that through me, my sorrow to say," observed Emer, giving her husband a rueful smile. "I had it in full from my father, and he from his mother, Fíona of Aros, who was not called Tarenna for naught."

Fionnbarr chuckled, thinking of some of the exploits that had earned Fíona the name of Thunder-striker. "Truly she was not; but my own father's mother has her share of fame, or blame, for Aeron's inheritance of temper . . . But Kesten, what do you suggest? Aeron shall as you say be Ard-rían, and such leanings must be curbed long before that day comes."

"And may that day be longer yet in coming . . . Well, only go on as you have planned with her training. She goes from here to the Fians; they will break that stubbornness, if anyone can."

Across the room, Keina stirred from her silence. "Yet all the same, I would not have my niece broken of it too far."

Fionnbarr turned in surprise to look at his sister-in-law; Keina was seldom cryptic except to very precise purpose. "What is it you say, Keindrych?"

"Aeron will need that quality too when she is Ard-rían. The stone easiest carved is easiest crumbled; it is the stone hardest to shape that lasts the longest—especially in the streams of the world."

On an evening some weeks later, Aeron entered the small, low-ceilinged chamber that was to be hers for this next season of her life: the cell of a Fian candidate, in the dorter-wing of the great training-school of Caer Artos, in the Vale of Arvon on the planet Gwynedd.

She took off her cloak and looked critically around. *A pleasant enough room, not all that unlike to my quarters at Scartanore* . . . Walls of white stone, with thick woven hangings to be put up against the winter cold—in a place designed to toughen both body and mind, overheated rooms were not to be indulged in; the furnishings of plain dark wood. There was a bedstead with a sheepskin coverlet and small flat pillow and hard mattress, comfortable enough, though not the traditional ''three beddings'' used by the Fianna of old Ireland—green branches, green rushes and soft springy moss.

A chest stood at the bed's foot for weapons and gear, and another larger one against the wall; there was a tall wardrobe for clothing, and sheepskin rugs strewn over the stone floor. No luxuries in concession to her rank: The room was no different in its particulars from any of the other rooms allotted to any other candidate. She would be treated here as but another potential Fian, as her father and grandfather and great-grandmother had been before her, and theirs before them, all the way back to Brendan Mór Aoibhell himself; and as her own heirs would be treated after her, when they would come to Caer Artos in their turn.

Aeron went over to the small window set in the thickness of the outer wall. The view was to the south and east, over the immense sloping fields used for drill and exercise. Beyond those, she could see carefully groomed ovals, cut like facets from the green slopes, for chariot and horsemanship training. On the other side of the dorter wings, she knew, there were stables and weapons halls, classrooms, swimming-baths and libraries and dining halls; across the valley lay the spaceport and the centers for starflight instruction.

Though all Kelts, man and woman alike, were liable for military service from the age of eighteen onward, and remained so, in time of war or national emergency, until well past a hundred, only those thought to be of officer caliber were sent here to Caer Artos, or to one of the other war colleges, to train for Fians. Rank played no part in such selection, nor in ultimate success: Aeron as Tanista was as free to fail as any merchant's son or soldier's daughter. She would undergo the training like any other novice; as Queen, she would have command of all Keltia's considerable military might, and so would be required to know intimately and immediately every aspect of it: from horse and foot soldiery through the sea-forces to the system space-navies and the main starfleet itself. She would of course in that time have the services of commanders and councillors alike to call upon, but she would need to know first-hand how best to employ these forces: what they were capable of, how they could be used to best advantage for Keltia and for those who sheltered beneath Keltia's shield. And the only sure way to come by that knowledge was to learn it the hard way.

Aeron felt a sudden colossal doubt of her own abilities to do so. Even though she had already proven herself as a Ban-draoi, what would be demanded of her here was of an altogether different order of effort. And not only that, but for the past dozen years or so she had been hearing stories of the Fian prowess of ones near and dear to her: Rhodri and Gwydion; her cousins Desmond and Slaine, Kerensa and Trystan; and now the turn had come to her.

But at least this time I am not alone, she thought to comfort herself. *Sabia is here, and my old playmate Deio Drummond, and best of all there will be Wenna . . .* For Morwen had finished her studies at the Hill of Laws, and as recompense for her daughterly obedience had immediately demanded of her parents that they send her to Caer Artos; and Faolan and Mared, battered not only by Morwen's eloquence—now brehon-trained! —but by Rhodri's approval, had given in.

That thought brought others: Stories of Gwydion and Rhodri came now clear to Aeron's memory, tales told over the table by fond foster-parents: their martial skills and friendly rivalry, and their matchless friendship; though neither prince had stayed on to become a First-rank Fian, as had Aeron's cousin Desmond and his father Elharn before him. *I should like to stay, if I am allowed, and if I am adjudged fit to. But it is early days to think of that: I have only just arrived here, and it may well prove that I have no aptitude for war whatever. And whoever in all Keltic history ever heard of an Ard-rían unfit for the field . . . and they shall not hear of one now, if I have aught to say in the matter.*

Still, there was more than weapon-mastery to the making of a Fian; and in that other learning Aeron had already a good grounding. Thanks to the efforts of the bards and the Ban-draoi, she could speak, besides all seven Keltic tongues and most of their many dialects, Greek, Latin, Englic, the Imperial Hastaic and the Fomorian Lakhaz, and other alien speech as well. Tongues had come easily to her, almost without need of study, far easier than such other learnings as the detested mathematicals, for one; but the course of study required by the Fianna covered all those and much more beside. It was said with truth that, outside the bards and not always even then, a good Fian was the best-educated Kelt there was. And for that alone, and the promise of high employment once their active serving days were done, the flower of Keltia fought so hard to enter the Fianna's ranks, and suffered so much once enrolled there.

Aeron laughed, and began laying away her possessions in the wardrobe and chests. *I need not worry even there; my future—one way or another, and Fian or no—is already assured . . .* She could not define the mood that had taken her; if asked, she would have denied even having one. It was not homesickness: Though she was like most Kelts deeply attached to her family, she had been living away from them since the age of five, and was well used to finding herself on her own in new places. Nor was it loneliness: Morwen was even now settling in over in the neighboring wing, Deio and Sabia were nearer still, and so was a cousin or two, and there were in this class of Fian candidates many others that Aeron both knew and liked.

So, not that either; what then? Perhaps only the uncertainty; the real chance that here for once was a thing at which she might well fail. *And would not* that *be a new thing . . . Though Scartanore was challenge enough, never once through all the pains of it did I doubt my right to be there. Though I might have died on my immram, or killed myself through some sorcerous stupidity, there was never any real uncertainty that I was fitted for what I had chosen to do. Here—here I am not anywhere near so sure. And so we all shall see.*

All unbidden, the thought of her great-grandmother Aoife came again upon her, and Aeron's smile this time was ironical. *I know not, dama-wyn, if it was in this place that the findruinna went into your soul; but if it were so, pray you have left a little of it for me.*

Chapter 18

The leaves had scarce been tinged with red and yellow when Aeron and her classmates began as Fians; it was winter now at Caer Artos, the great December storms sweeping down out of the north, scorning to halt at the barrier ranges that cut Arvon off from the rest of the main Gwyneddan continent. For the long months of hard cold, most of the training would be conducted within walls; and though the exercise of the body was by no means neglected, it was rather the exercise of the mind that traditionally took up most of these weeks of winter.

For all their newfound discipline, or perhaps because of it, the Fian novices were the ones who chafed the most at the enforced indoor activity, and sighed for spring, when they could be out and doing again in the open air, pitting their bodies against the strict Fian curriculum, training in the muddy fields. Their instructors, for their part, were glad of the relative respite.

Those fields the novices yearned for were under deep snow now. From her window Aeron could look out over untrodden white expanses leading up to the foothills, miles away, though in the clear cold air they looked near enough to touch, of the Grain Valley Range, westernmost of the mountain chains that ran five hundred miles north and south along Arvon's borders.

Those who dwelt in Arvon considered themselves a breed apart even among the Kymry, though gods knew the Kymry thought themselves set apart from the rest of Keltia as it was; an attitude in which this splendid isolation was doubtless a factor. *And they might well be right to think it,* reflected Aeron. *Arthur himself came from a valley not fifty lai from here; if this land could breed such ones as he and his sister, small wonder the Arvoniaid carry themselves so . . .*

A few miles down the open strath, a yellow spark shone warm, high on the dark side of the hills; a farmstead most like, tucked away in some remote valley, perhaps belonging to one of the local families employed by Caer Artos as retainers, to perform such chores as growing food or tending beasts or mending and making weapons.

Pushing the casement open, Aeron took a deep breath of the snow-filled air, clean and bitter cold. There was a tang of woodsmoke upon it, maybe drifting downwind from that very farmstead at whose lights she now so hungrily stared.

Aeron was seized with a sudden piercing envy of those unknown folk behind that distant window: what were their names and who their kindred; what were they doing at that moment and what did they do at leisure; what dreams did they have, and what burdens; were they contented, or would they trade their lives if given the chance . . .

She spoke of it a little later to Sabia, when they went out cloaked and booted for a walk before retiring; spoke of it half shamefaced, as if expecting her friend to laugh to scorn such romantic folly, and prepared to understand if so she did. But Sabia only smiled.

"That is the kind of wondering everyone has had, one time or another."

"Even you?"

Sabia's smile grew to a grin, and she gave Aeron a look from around the edge of her hood.

"Do you know what *I* used to wonder, on such nights as this, back on Erinna on my family's farm, when my life was much the same as theirs over yonder whom you seem to envy so desperately? What *your* life was like; I knew we were of an age, you and I, and I wondered what it must be to know yourself Tanista, the High King's daughter; to grow up knowing that you would one day rule Keltia yourself, to have anything in any world that you could wish for—"

Now it was Aeron's smile that quirked strangely, and within the depths of her own hood she shook her head.

"It was not like that at all! I was sat upon so hard, from so early an age—no special privileges, no deference paid and none to be looked for. As for having things, I was given so much to spend each quarter-day, and when that was gone there was no more forthcoming.'' She named the sum, and Sabia gave a disbelieving giggle, so unprincely was the amount. ''Truly! The palace servitors' children had more pouch-money than did I; if I wanted something special, whether for myself or as gift, I must earn the crossics for it if I had not sufficient saved. If I spoke roughly to anyone who could not answer as roughly back, I must apologize publicly, and was thrashed for it beside. And all the time there was the knowledge that folk were watching: watching me, watching my parents and my brothers and my sisters and my fosterns and my friends; knowing that never would there be a time, save by careful contrivance, when I might be private in public—might walk unnoticed, say, through the streets of my own city, as the least citizen of Keltia might do.'' Aeron gestured out to where the yellow light still shone in the dark folds of the hills. ''Certainly never to have a life like theirs—or like yours, back with your family on the Timpaun.''

''And that troubled you.'' *And, plainly, still does . . .*

Aeron shrugged under the stiff frieze-wool of her Fian-issue cloak. ''As much as it might; for the most part it was not allowed to—my parents and foster-parents saw to that. But I was shy as a small girl; lived mostly in my own head, was wary of strangers, wished to know no one new—'' She broke off, inhaled the cold air, still edged with woodsmoke over the bite of frost. ''No air smells so wonderful as that air off new snow, when the night is very cold with only a little wind . . . And all this woe came upon me tonight because there was woodsmoke on the wind, and it smelled to me like something I could never have, something I was so hungry for: something small and most unroyal, something infinitely ordinary. And it seemed too that I had never wanted anything so much.''

''Not even to be Ard-rían?''

''Ah, that. Now that is not a thing I can say I have ever truly wished for; it is dán, a thing as much unchosen as the color of my hair or the shape of my hands. I am sentenced to it; but I will make the best of it, and the most of it. And I doubt not I shall come to love it in time: the power and the scope, the ability to order things to my own will and desires, to right such wrongs as I may. I know my father has found it so . . . It may even compensate me for never having such a thing as that," she added, pointing down the valley. But the light at the farmstead had gone out, and now there was only darkness and the snow-wind blowing across the hills. "Though I think not . . . but the snow is getting into my boots now, and probably yours as well. Let us go back indoors before we are both nithered altogether."

Just before they reached the door of the hall, Aeron spoke again, hesitantly, but with real conviction.

"I have never yet said, I think, how glad I am that your family permitted you to come here with me after Scartanore. Good to have the face, and the ear, of a friend. I shall have great need of both in time to come—and of the heart of a friend, still greater."

And that simple speech—for Sabia heard plain in Aeron's voice what it cost her to utter it, to bring it out past all her natural shyness and reserve—meant more to Sabia than all that had gone before; and she forgot her own troubles, and her frozen feet, and they went back in to lights and warmth and company.

"No candidate is acceptable to the Fianna who has not mastered the Twelve Books," droned Aeron dutifully. "And these be those twelve: poetry, prose, heraldry, history, religion, science, husbandry, geography, astrography, tongues, medicine and law."

Across the library table, Morwen stifled a yawn, and looked longingly out the windows; it was a cool bright morning of early June, and she did not relish being indoors.

"And how is the Fian's life to be ruled?" she asked then, not troubling herself even to glance at the notes that lay open before her.

"A Fian is not to reserve to himself aught which another shall stand in need of," answered Sabia, taking up the drill when Aeron feigned a sudden doze. "A Fian in the field shall live by one meal a day, and that at evening; and this he shall not take until he has bathed, and combed out his hair, and arrayed himself in clean clothing, the best that his means may supply. And none of this shall he do until he has cared for his horse, and his hound, and his hawk, and any other who may rely upon him for care and keeping."

"And in war? —Aeron, you are the one said you needed this drill . . ."

Aeron groaned but sat up again. "A Fian shall stand to all odds, so far as nine to one armed, six to one unarmed."

"And in fealty?"

"The Fianna is sworn to uphold the rule of the Ard-rígh or Ard-rían of Keltia"—Aeron's voice did not change on the titles—"but the Fian's first oath, as feinnid of the true Fianna, is to his own captain." She leaned back in her chair again, blowing her breath out in an explosive sigh. "Whence came all these *rules?* I thought we came here to learn war."

Sabia closed the drill book and collapsed forward over it, resting her pointed chin upon its leather covers.

"We have had training in fighting already begun."

"Oh aye, little piffling combats with wicker shields and ash staves. But *I* was speaking of cold iron."

"Well, in a few fortnights then. You know the training sequence as well as the rest of us." Morwen stretched languidly. "There is yet an hour or so till the midmeal; let us go for a run."

To that the others agreed with alacrity, and ten minutes later they were pacing each other around the smaller training oval, one lai from start to finish.

They ran awhile in silence, then Aeron spoke: "Wenna and I have little to say in our own choice of future, but what shall *you* do, Sabhait, when your time here is done?"

"I had not really considered," admitted Sabia. "My services are not required on the home farm—my elder sisters and my brother will carry on from my parents—so I am mostly free to do as I will. There is always the starfleet, or one of the system navies; but I think I should prefer to serve in the ground forces, the cavalry by choice. I might take a command in one of the catha; maybe even the Pillars of Tara, if I am deemed fit and one is offered."

Aeron said no more for a furlong or so, and only the rhythmic sound of their footfalls on the gritstone track broke the stillness. Then:

"Would you think, perhaps, of coming to Caerdroia with me? As Tanista, and later, when I am Ard-rían, I shall need friends I can trust beside me; and a friend who is both Ban-draoi and Fian, who has shared my own training—" She broke off uncertainly, for Sabia had come to a dead halt and was staring at her. "If the idea is not to your liking, only say so. I shall not be offended. It is asking much, I know; life at Turusachan can be dull at even the busiest of seasons, and the—"

Sabia had regained her powers of speech. "To come with *you?* In your service? To *Turusachan?* Oh Aeron, could you even think I would not dearly wish to do so! It is what I have been so hoping you would ask—surely I shall come."

Aeron gave her a quick shy smile. "I had not dared to hope you would . . . After I leave here, I have still some education left to endure: a year with the brehons, for my father insists, and I shall need to know something more of the law than I do, if only to give fair judgment when I sit in hearing-court—I shall have Wenna to help me with the rest of it. And too, I would go back to the Ban-draoi to take my initiation as Domina. After that—"

"There is *more?*" Sabia looked dismayed.

"There is always more! My military service to perform; but you two will have that to fulfill as well, and I daresay three years of active duty shall pass quickly enough for us all. *Then* I shall be free to return to Turusachan."

Morwen laughed, not without sympathy. "But not to put your feet up for a quiet time."

"Scarcely that . . . By then I shall be rising twenty-seven; and that is the usual age at which Keltic heirs are formally invested with the Tanistry—though the Silver Branch itself will not be given me to wield until much later in my life. But when I *am* named Tanista I shall be expected to form a court and household of my own, one I hope will be with me for all my reign, and I would have the two of you to be among those at its heart."

They had turned off the track now and were walking back to the main hall; the bell for the midmeal had sounded a few minutes since.

"And what of a consort?" asked Sabia slyly. "If we talk of hearts—have you any in mind for that office?"

Aeron blushed; beside her, Morwen chuckled knowingly. "I might have," she admitted. "One or two, in any case . . . and, Wenna, do not you *dare* to make merry over this— But so also do my parents, and our minds do not entirely meet on the matter. Any road, I shall not do as my father did, and wait so long to share the throne. To rule alone is effective for a time, and captures the folk's fancy, but I think that after a while I shall start talking to myself . . . But look, there is Turlough, and Vevin with him; let us see what they have to say for themselves about yesterday's disgraceful showing at the spear-toss.''

"No rings on your sword-hand."

Aeron, about to take a sword from the weapons rack on the wall of the fencing-hall, looked up guiltily at her teacher.

"Again, athro?"

Struan Cameron, senior swordmaster to the Fianna when Aeron was still in fosterage, took both her hands in his own firm callused ones, turning them over critically, back and front, before releasing them.

"Not the best hands for it, but not too ill either: good long fingers, hollow palms . . . Aye, well, it is the first rule of the Fianna for swordery. Your fingers will need to flex and give and shift—sometimes greatly, sometimes less so—on the hilts of your weapons; we want no stones and metal to bind or pinch them as they do so."

"Ah. Well, as you see, my hands are bare."

"They will not always be so," Struan reminded her. "When their time comes to wear the Great Seal of Keltia and the Unicorn Seal of the Aoibhells—"

"A long way off, please gods; and by then there shall be others to do my fighting for me—indeed it will be their duty to do so."

"True; but if naught else there is always the fíor-comlainn: *your* duty to do so, if you are challenged to it—as much your duty to the Crown as the lowliest galloglass's duty to you as Ard-rían. And it is my mind that you will be one of those monarchs who choose to champion themselves in such a fight; therefore it is *my* duty to see that you will be able to do so without getting killed for your pains."

"And shall I?" asked Aeron, a little taken aback. "Shall I be able to?"

"By gods but you will, or I'll know why not . . ." Struan grinned, nodding toward the gleaming rows of weapons. "That is what we have come here to begin to learn. So, no rings, now or later. But choose one of those, and we shall see if it suits your arm, and your heart."

*   *   *

Though Aeron had been pining to begin swordwork ever since first arriving at Caer Artos, now that the longed-for schooling had at last begun she was suddenly terrified of proving inept. All at once, instead of the preliminary basic instruction that had been given her, in guise of game or play or mock-battle, since the age of six, her head was filled with daunting images of the skill of others: her cousin Desmond and his intimidating sister Slaine, who had completed their own Fian training in a blaze of honor, a few years back; Morna Arc'hantet, the tall commander of Fionnbarr's personal guard, who had given the child Aeron her first real fencing lessons, and who was reputed able to parry faster than the eye could follow. *Not to mention Rhodri and Gwydion,* she thought, *whom perhaps I had better not mention* . . . Emer too had been by no means unhandy with a blade, and had given all her children their introduction to the fighting arts, with wooden weapons and half-size toys.

But this was no longer a child's game nor play-practice; and though she could afterwards recall but little of that strenuous hour under Struan's cold critical eye, at the end of it Aeron lifted the last of the longswords to the salute, then collapsed onto the training mats at her teacher's feet.

"Well?"

He grinned down at her, his face inverted to her sight as he stood behind her. "Well. That was—not too poor a showing." Struan laughed as Aeron's arm swept round to catch him in the ankle. "Show your old athro some respect; come now, get up—" At the stricken look on Aeron's face, he relented. "If I were to tell you that you are one of the best natural swordsmen ever to come to my hand; that you seem not to learn but to remember; that you have perhaps the quickest right-hand parry I have ever encountered— I do not say all this is so, mind, but if I were to tell you—"

"If you were to tell me all that," said Aeron, rising to her feet and re-pinning her loosened braid, "I should be extremely embarrassed, and believe not a word of it, and despair of my chances. Or else I should believe *all* of it, and grow smug and lazy, and ruin my chances likewise with complacency. So tell me not anything, and we will go on so." But her delighted expression gave the cool words the lie, and she spoiled what was left of the pretense at disinterest by adding, "I like it *well*, though; the purposeful movement, and the way it is my arm seems to move before my brain can tell it."

"Indeed," said Struan crushingly. "Let us therefore hope that it will be only in such matters that your arm and not your brain will do your thinking . . . But you have not so many bad habits to unlearn as I had feared; Morna taught you well, and Emer too, more strength to their arms. And if you manage to sustain your aptitude for it, and to turn it into something more—the which I doubt—your arm will learn to think better and better as you do go on. But if you do not find some discipline from somewhere, and sooner rather than later, all the liking and aptitude in all the worlds will make no whit of differ."

After Struan had left the hall, Aeron remained motionless in the middle of the practice floor, replaying over and over in her mind the movements her teacher had demonstrated, feeling down her arm the shifts of the muscles as she moved her weapon in her mind.

Struan is right to tax me with undiscipline, she thought, gathering up the mats and rolling them against the wall. *And to warn me from being overeager; but he cannot damp what I do feel . . . Two things in my life have I longed to excel at, magic and swordplay; and I have been willing to work hard at both. The magic I have been given to master; now let us see about this.*

Chapter 19

Four years to make a sorceress, but three only to make a warrior:
Aeron had speculated once, at Scartanore, on the discrepancy,
but the shrewd old Ban-draoi preceptress of whom she had
inquired had only given a disparaging sniff.

"One thing the Fianna has not yet managed to learn," she had
said, "is that the power will never be in the sword if it is not in
the arm that wields it—and I do not speak of sinew-strength
alone. It goes as much for the slat-draoichta as for the claymore—if
it takes a bit longer to put it there, what of it?"

To Aeron's surprise, when she quoted this to Struan Cameron,
the swordmaster only chuckled.

"By gods, now that sounds a Ban-draoi thing and no mistake
. . . But your old teacher is not so far off a Fian truth as well,
Aeron, though plainly she thinks such subtlety beyond us: It is
the same principle whether your weapon be a rann or a glaive;
that it must be you, and not your weapon, that does the true
fighting. Admittedly"—and here he made comic pretense of
secrecy—"the moods of steel do take a little less time to master
than those of magic, but if you tell Kesten I said so I shall deny
ever having spoken. Now, again."

"What have I told you, a hundred times if once!"

As she had done perhaps as many times in the last weeks,
Aeron dropped her head, and sword-arm with it, and sighed.

" 'Watch the chest. Not blade nor arm nor face nor foot, but
the chest.' "

"So," said Struan, folding his arms across his own chest.
"And if you can repeat this so word-perfect, how is it you

cannot seem to make your eyes obey it? *Why* do I bid you watch the chest?''

"It is the body's center," recited Aeron as if by rote, "and betrays all movement, and so my sidesight will catch the smallest motion quicker and surer than if I did watch otherwhere.''

Struan flung back his head in despair. "Then *if* you know it, why do you not *do* it!''

"With respect, athro," said Aeron a little sullenly, "mostly I do.''

"Mostly!" Struan's voice was laced with scorn. "Mostly will not help you much when some Coranian pig-dog comes at you in battle and you are giving languishing looks over his shoulder. You will be spitted like a snipe, and you will well deserve it. Now again, and if you keep not your eyes where they belong I will blade you until you cannot sit for a week.''

"But.''

"What but now?''

"Again, with respect, but others have been instructed other wise, even here at Caer Artos." Aeron was choosing her words with care, not daring to look at her teacher's face. "As to such things as where to watch, what counters to make, how best to take the blade or overbear a parry. And all differing to that which you have been teaching me. Now Sabia and Deio—''

"That's as may be," said Struan with a grin. "And well enough for Sabia and young Drummond, of both whom I have had passable report. But each pupil here is different when it comes to swordery, and each master; and how your friends are being instructed has naught to do with you. You are *my* student, given over to me by mac Avera himself—or do you gainsay even the Captain-General? Nay, I thought not. Well, as I was taught, and as I see fit, so do I teach you; and by the gods you will learn, Aeron, or I'll know the reason why not. And even then you will still learn, all the same.''

But war was not the only skill Aeron came to learn that summer . . . By now the year had come round again to Lughnasa, Lugh's Night, when all over Keltia the great Teltown feasts were held, celebrations of summer and of summer's harvest bounty— and, for those young Kelts who had that year completed eighteen summers, their celebration of coming-of-age, when, under the goddess Tailltiu's auspices at the holy feasts, they would lie with another for the first time.

At sunset that day Aeron stood in her room, staring into the small stone-framed mirror that hung over the clothes-chest. Outside, the sounds of Lugh's Night—music, laughter, shouts of merriment—came clear on the summer air; the festival had begun, and she must soon go out to it.

She felt no fear; or only a little, for strangeness's sake. Almost all young Kelts took their first lovers at Teltown, and neither shame nor seriousness attached to it, for this of Lugh's Night was ancient custom, dating from the Kelts' time on Terra. To them the matter was a natural one, to be dealt with in a natural way, with none of the heavy judgments and implications attached to it in other societies. Custom too that one should choose a stranger for one's first partner, so that the one-night's-union should hold no sway over future life and loves. Not even sweethearts were encouraged to lie down together at Tailltiu's feast.

A simple thing, then, for a folk who were frank in such matters; a conventional experience that happened to nearly everyone. For Aeron, it was much the same that night as it was for any youth or maid of her year; indeed, as she stood in her chamber, so too in their own rooms did Morwen and Dafydd Drummond and Sabia and Turlough and Vevin and all the others of their company, unless it was that they were already out among the celebrants. And yet it was not entirely the same, for she was who—and what—she was; and so she had considered a while, and in the end had chosen to use those new skills to put a sorcerous mask upon her—a fith-fath, a shapechange. No one had even hinted that she should do so; it was not the practice for even royalty to wear such a guise on such a night, and neither her parents nor her grandparents, nor any other of her kin, had thought to do so at their own Teltowns.

But with that sense of what was right for herself which she had been coming more and more to count upon of late, Aeron had known that this was how she wished this night to be for her: neither to be refused by any youth whom she herself might fancy, for awe or shyness or fear of her rank, nor to be herself sought out and chosen for that she was after all Tanista, so that afterwards her partner might pride himself, or even boast to others, that he had found favor in Aeron's eyes. She would surely have other lovers in her life—more than a few, most like—before it came time to choose herself a lord; perhaps there would be more than one lord, even, before she took that one who would be king-consort to her High Queen; and to none of those would she dream of masking either her face or her honest desire.

Still, for all its weight of honored custom, and lighthearted aspect, tonight *was* different, and so now a stranger looked back at Aeron from the glass: a honey-haired, blue-eyed Scotan; a pretty girl, though not overly so, small-breasted and slight of build, different in all outward ways from the one who had created her. There was little time for Aeron to contemplate her handiwork. Her illusion was well crafted, and would last long enough for her purpose, but outside the feast was now in full spate, and if she tarried from it very much longer her choice of partner would be a scant one.

He was tall and dark, with darker eyes—a Kymro of Gwent or Powys, she guessed, or perhaps one of the black Erinnach who cropped out so often in the westlands of that world—and plainly innocent of druidry, for he saw no fith-fath but only a lass as taken with him as he with her, and laughing they broke away from the Long Dance hand in hand.

No word spoken: In the shadows of a fern-feathered hollow, out of sight and sound of the feast, not even another courting couple by, they fell together into the ferns. He was as inexperienced as she, but if neither of them had any skill, their youth and eagerness made up the lack, and Tailltiu was with them, and it was sweet for them both and soon over.

But that brief night's span was all there was to be of pleasure for that time, for now the Fian novices were entering the most demanding phase of their middle training.

For all Struan's professed pessimism, he was more than pleased with Aeron's progress on the dueling-floor—though he would not have dreamed of telling her—and with that of her fellow students as well. By Fionnasa, the novices had advanced sufficiently for their instructors to allow them to practice with, or on, each other; though it often made for harrowing sessions, the experience it provided would prove invaluable in time to come.

"Counter! Counter! Now! Again! *Now! Again!* Take the blade, you lazy wench, take the *blade!*"

Through the rasp of her own breathing in her ears, Aeron heard Struan's impatient shouts—*Easy enough for him to say, he stands well out of it*—but making a tremendous effort, brought her claymore around and down the blade of her opponent, who that afternoon chanced to be none other than her friend Vevin ní Talleron—grandniece of Donlin, Lasairían's onetime First Lord of War.

The metal screamed with the strain, for Aeron's parry had been, to say the least, unorthodox; then the parry's perpetrator disengaged abruptly and pulled up short. A sharp pain had run searing along her thigh; looking down, Aeron saw with dumb astonishment the neat slit in the fabric of her practice trews, blood just beginning to bead through where she had been caught by the counterstroke of Vevin's riposte.

Struan came forward, shaking his head. "Enough. Vevin, well fought; the fault is not yours. Use the rest of the day as you wish."

The girl saluted both instructor and opponent almost automatically—habit already even for the novices—then hesitated.

"Aeron, I am sorry, I did not mean—"

Aeron began to speak, but Struan cut her off. "That is understood. Go now." When Vevin, biting her lip to keep back tears, had left the floor, Struan turned on his other pupil. "Now I say that was careless work! I'd not have thought to see the like of it from you. Out of my sight, go; they will tend to your scratch in the healers' rooms."

Again Aeron started to speak, but thinking better of it, instead saluted Struan coldly and correctly; and with a straight-backed stride—for she would not have him see her limp if she went lame for it the rest of her days—she went from the hall.

It was her first training wound. Though shallow, it was surprisingly bloody, and stingingly painful in the manner of a cut from a paper-edge; her leg muscles had begun almost at once to stiffen. But by the time she had made her slow and halting way to the healers' wing, Aeron was far more pained by her own carelessness than by the wound's smart.

The healer Cormac, as he dressed the injury with professional quickness and applied the laser suturer to its clean edges, seemed much of her own opinion.

"From what Struan told me just now," he remarked, nodding toward the transcom, "you know what you did to merit it. And I have no doubt but that you will earn yourself a few more, before you learn better."

All Aeron's chagrin and anger with herself leaped out at him, like some furious small animal.

"Before I learn *better!* Keep in mind, O Sirideain, to whom you speak!"

"I shall keep it rather more in mind than do you, Aeron," he answered, patiently readjusting her leg in the restraint frame where she had moved it. "Was it not that you forgot, that earned you this scratch?"

The breath went out of her as if she had been punched; and after a tense moment Aeron nodded unwillingly, eyes on his deft completion of his healing work.

"Aye, master, it was . . . I will surely, as you say, take a cut or two more before I leave here, and surely some after as well, but I will not forget again."

"Good; then you have learned a thing today. Now let us see you stand. It feels well enough?"

Aeron nodded, flexing her leg at knee and hip. The pain was gone, only a soreness in the muscle, as that from a deep bruise, still remaining; that, and a fine white line across the skin where the dermasealer had worked.

"The scar can be removed as well," said Cormac, noticing her attention to it and reaching for another tool. "Two minutes more—"

But Aeron shook her head, and refastened the strap of her trews. "Let it stay. I can use all the reminders there may be—so that I do *not* forget."

Cormac laughed, but put his tools away, and she sensed his surprised approval. "Oh aye? What of that old law I have heard the brehons speak of, as to how the rulers of Keltia are not permitted bodily imperfections?"

"On the order of lost hands or missing ears," she said, smiling at last. "As you very well know . . . I cannot name a ruler of Keltia whose body bore no mark of the sword, and I would by no means be the first."

*   *   *

Leaving the healing-halls, Aeron went a little gingerly back to her own chambers in the dorter-wing, pausing for a moment in the connecting cloister to look out over the fields toward the woods. The cloister's arches were glassed in already against winter, which came early to this part of the Arvon vale. Opening a pane, Aeron felt the afternoon air cool on her flushed face. Already autumn's hand lay upon that country: the monochrome of a northern forest well down toward winter, gold leaves on silver-stemmed birches, short grass a frosty pewter green, the sky very low now, pale and milky.

Just outside the door of her rooms she met Vevin, who had plainly been loitering about in hopes of just such an encounter.

"Aeron, how is it with you? I did not mean to hurt you, but your parry was such a strange one, it could never hold—"

"And well I know it," said Aeron dryly. "Any road, Cormac has mended me; though I had him leave the scar. Now you may tell your grandchildren's children it was your sword gave the Ard-rían Aeron her first blooding."

Seeing the look on the other's face, Aeron was instantly contrite at her own levity.

"Nay, Vevinnach, I am *jesting!* Look—truly, the leg is fine now."

"I might have injured you far worse than that, perhaps even beyond Cormac's ability to repair."

"Aye; or I you, had the parry gone the other way, and who knows but that next time it might not? As Struan is forever telling me, better a Kelt to draw my blood in practice than a Gall to do so in war. It is a cheap price, even so, for such a lessoning; and in any case it is my own fault entirely. Come, let us sit for a while, and then go in to supper. It will make a tale for the others of our friends to laugh at."

Back in the fencing-hall, as he was putting away the weapons and gear used in the day's sessions, Struan Cameron looked up to see the Captain-General himself come in at the door. Though he spoke no word to his longtime friend, Donal mac Avera's face as he came up to Struan was grave and questioning.

"I see ill news travels as fast as ever," observed Struan. "Well, she was not badly hurt, and for that she has herself to thank. As she has herself to blame, for that she was hurt in the first place.''

Mac Avera sighed and leaned back against a row of spearshafts. "You have been very hard on her of late," he remarked after a while. "Or so I have been told."

"And you have been told aright," his swordmaster agreed grimly. "Twice as hard as I would be on any other, and not half so hard as I should be. For if I am not so now, think how hard the Coranians—and her own folk—will be on her later."

"She is not an apt pupil, then? I would have thought—"

"Apt!" The swords clattered as Struan flung them against the wall. "She is past apt; though I would never tell her as much, she is as talented as Gwydion Penarvon or Morna Arc'hantet or Duach Ruthven, and they were perhaps the finest students you and I have ever taught. Certainly she will be the best swordsman to sit upon the Throne of Scone for many reigns."

"Then where is the difficulty?"

Struan swung the findruinna gate closed across the entrance to the weapons room and activated the guard-field. "You have seen it often enough yourself: She does not spare time to think before she acts. The folk already have a by-name for her, did you know? They call her Aeron Anfa."

And 'Anfa' means 'storm' . . . Mac Avera frowned, but said nothing, and Struan was continuing, almost eagerly now, as if this were a thing of which he had for some time wished to deliver himself.

"When it comes to a choice, she will follow feelings over judgment every time. Not that feelings have no place—intuition and othersight are as necessary as a keen eye and a quick hand and a disciplined mind—but the idea, and the ideal, is to balance all. With her it seems ever to be 'neck or naught.' "

"And we both know well where that comes from." Mac Avera felt Struan's quick startled glance, but did not meet it. "So you too have thought of Aoife," he continued, "and you are right to think of her—though Fionnbarr himself has proved as unpredictable in his time—but with Aeron it is somewhat different, and indeed the Magistra Kesten warned me of this before the lass came here. So it is a known thing, and it is known that it cannot continue. Not if we are to make a true Fian of her; and that, after all, Cameron, is what Barraun and Emer are trusting us to do.''

"Aye," said Struan gloomily. "But a small thing by comparison to their own task, thank gods. We have only to train her up to a Fian. Barraun must train her into a High Queen.''

At Aeron's muffled shout of invitation, Sabia entered her friend's chamber. She found her rootling through her belongings, impatiently rejecting one gúna after another, tossing jewels through the air onto the bed as one ornament after the next apparently proved unsatisfactory. Though like all her classmates Aeron had not been permitted to bring overmuch gear with her, to judge by the depth of the debris in the room, most if not all of that gear was now in a heap on the floor.

Sabia shook her head in slightly awed disbelief. "It looks as if the goats had got in! Aeron, you are surely the untidiest person that ever I have known, or heard of, even.''

Aeron, rummaging through a hitherto unpillaged chest, looked up at her friend with a grin. "Would you rather I took a leaf in neatness from Wenna's book? Do you know, she has all her tunics arranged in order of hue, from the lightest to the darkest, and all so neat aligned you could flip through them like a pack of cards.''

Sabia laughed, knowing Morwen's passion for order all too well. "Nay," she agreed, "that would drive me directly out of my wits, though I cannot say that this through-other is far to the fore of it. But what is it you look for?''

"A respectable gúna, and some suitable jewels to wear with it; I have been summoned to sit at the high table for tomorrow's nightmeal, for what reason I *cannot* imagine.''

"Oh aye?" Sabia's interest was caught, and clearing away some of the rubble she sat cross-legged on the narrow bed. "Perhaps the Ard-rígh or the Queen come on a visit? Or your brother Prince Rohan?''

"Nay, they would have warned me, and Rohan does not come until the new term begins, when he too will be a student. But the last time I did speak with my mother—" Aeron broke off, muttering something under her breath, and pulled a few more things from the depths of the chest. "Well, in short, now that I have passed my Teltown and found such matters much to my liking, she would have me think of taking a consort.''

Sabia stared. ''So soon? But you are not of age to wed yet, even did the Ard-rígh give consent to it and you agreed.''

''Truly; but the talk is not of wedding but of pledging to wed . . . I fear that in my family these things are considered early on, and debated openly. Now my father wed very late for one of our kindred, and even when he came to it he thought it was he who did the choosing; but in point of fact my grandmother the Queen-Dowager, bless her meddling ways, engineered the thing to suit herself; though in the end it suited all.''

''I thought arranged matches were not so many, not these days.''

''No more are they,'' acknowledged Aeron. ''Save where there is more to be brought to the match than hearts alone; and that is often the case. It would surprise you, I would bet, to learn just how much arranging—some brazen, some more subtle—goes on in Keltia.''

Sabia held up a necklet of garnets and gold—one of the many that had been found wanting—and tried it against her throat.

''I can see where royal marriages, and those of the high nobility, might be brought about for political purpose, or to suit the best interests of the clanns involved; but families such as my own, say—''

''A cousin of yours, Sabia—aye, yours—was wed not many years ago to the daughter of an adversary neighbor, merely to resolve a grazing-rights dispute. True, the match did not last—we have long had enlightened means to end marriages found unfit or grown insupportable—but it served its purpose. So you see, it is not the rank of those the matter concerns, but very often sheer expedience; and I do not like it much.'' Aeron let fall the lid of the chest and looked round with some satisfaction at the room's disorder. ''I shall wear that one on the floor, there, and not a single jewel with it; the occasion deserves no better.''

Sabia fished the indicated garment, a little the worse for its sojourn underfoot, from where Aeron had pitched it, and then light broke.

''You think your parents are sending some candidate here! Hence mac Avera's invitation—''

''The thought had crossed my mind,'' agreed Aeron grimly.

"Well, whoever it may be, I think a trampled gúna and a bare neck will be more than fine enough for him."

But Aeron did not permit the thought of the evening to come to cast any cloud over her day, and next morning she went about her training as if nothing more unusual awaited her that night than the familiar routine of supper and study and sleep.

Coming back from the chariot ovals that afternoon, sweated and covered with dust, longing only for a good hot soak in the pool-room, Aeron and Sabia saw the spectators rimming the outdoor sword-ring, like a fringe of diamonds round a gemstone, and they turned aside as one to see what went on.

In the center of the tanbark ring, two tall warriors clad only in saffron fighting-kilts were deep in a bout with claymores, the huge double-handed swords favored by Scotan fighters. They seemed to make but little of the weapons' heft; in their hands the menacing silver blades, near as long as the pair who wielded them were tall, whirled and clashed almost as swiftly as lightswords would have done, and as the warriors moved in their martial patterns the muscles of their chests and backs and shoulders shone under a skin of sweat.

Seeing Vevin leaning on the rail, the two new arrivals detoured round to join her; their friend smiled a greeting, but did not take her attention from the fighters. *And no wonder,* thought Aeron, *for they are very good, and very fast, and by no means hard on the eyes, either* . . . Then, as she got her first clear look at their faces, she felt a sharp slap of surprise, and a strangely unpleasant one: *Rhodri and Gwydion* . . .

Most of the other watchers were apparently unaware of the princes' identities, for Aeron, as with preternaturally heightened senses, could overhear admiring comments on all sides, and— even as her own undeniable reaction had been—the admiration was not for their swordsmanship alone. *Even Sabia*—

"If not Brân, then his brother!" Sabia rested her chin on the railing, frankly staring, unabashedly appreciative of the sight.

"Which one?" asked Aeron, and for all her life could not fight down a certain possessive twinge.

"Both—or either! Who are they, do you know?"

"Oh aye, I know right enough . . . Well, the dark-haired one is Gwydion Penarvon, heir to the Prince of Gwynedd. The other is Wenna's eldest brother, Rhodri—Roderick, rather; the Master of Douglas.'' Their names sounded strangely in her ear, as if she had thoughtlessly told some secret she had not known she wished to keep.

Sabia cast a seeming artless glance in Aeron's direction. ''Friends of yours, no doubt.''

Aeron's smile was a little forced. ''No doubt.''

Chapter 20

That evening for the nightmeal in hall, Aeron dined as she had been invited, and, for the first and last time as a student in Caer Artos, as her rank required: at the high table with mac Avera and his chief officers and the two royal guests.

Morwen and Sabia had bullied her into wearing rather more elegant attire than she had originally planned, and Aeron sat now upon mac Avera's right clad in a brown velvet gúna, jewels of opal and silver at her neck and threaded through the shining copper hair. Gwydion was on mac Avera's other side, and Rhodri sat at Aeron's own right.

But so far she had barely glanced at either of them, and for all the pleasure she appeared to be having of any of it, she might have been taking a meal of rusks and water in the scullery. Indeed her unwillingness to be anywhere near the scene was so plain and so pronounced—it was the sulky expression gave it away—that all the hall wondered.

With the license of long acquaintance, and the freedom conferred by greater years and senior rank, Rhodri did not wonder but asked straight out.

"What is on you tonight?" he inquired quietly, after the first two courses had come and gone in sullen silence. "You look as if you had bitten a thistle."

Aeron forced the words past her savage humor. "Did my parents send you two here?"

Rhodri gave her a look usually reserved for kinfolk in their dotage. "And if they did—which I may say they did *not;* Gwydion and I came as we do every year, at the invitation of mac Avera and the Camerons, as old students and friends, to observe the tests—if they did, Aeron, what of it?"

"What of it! Do not the future Princes of Gwynedd and of Scots somewhat resent being paraded before the future Ard-rían, like promising colts in front of a likely filly? If they do not, then she most surely does . . ."

Her companion hid his grin behind his goblet. "Is that what you think it truly is, Tanista," he asked gravely, "or what you would like to think your mother is up to?"

She would not smile. "I would not put it past the Queen, certainly," she said bitterly. "Ever since my Teltown, she and old Trehere have been thicker than thieves plotting the succession— and the lord that the Queen and the Taoiseach would like to see ensure it. Do you know, she even invited Pryderi of Dyved to Court the last time I had leave for a home visit, in hopes I might fancy a match with him. Pryderi! Than whom a more pestilential prospect surely never breathed— I told my mother to put it out of her mind entirely."

"Oh, Pryderi is not so bad," offered Rhodri. "He was a good friend to Gwydion and to me when we were all three of us here for our own training."

"Maybe, but I'd sooner kiss a piast." Aeron halted in her tirade long enough to drink off her cup of wine; students at Caer Artos were allowed only ale with their meals, so wine was not to be wasted no matter the distastefulness of the occasion that had provided it.

"She and my father *press* me so," she continued after a while. "I have told them over and over that it is very early days to think of my taking a lord—no matter her own history, the which she throws up to me at every turn—but she does not listen. My father is more understanding, but even he loses no chance to remind me of my duty; though he most conveniently forgets how late he himself did leave his own."

Aeron stared down at her plate as if the food upon it were some prodigy she had never seen before, then began to eat, quickly and neatly, as though the supper held no savor.

"We have known each other a good few years now," said Rhodri after a while, "though of late we have not often met, having each to meet demands of duty and training—but would it surprise you so much if I should tell you that it has been spoken of, that you and I should one day wed?''

Only long discipline prevented Aeron from dropping her cup. ''*You* know this too?. But how?''

''Oh, Aeron, your mother and my mother have been haggling it over for years now, like two tigresses with a cherished old bone for their cubs; did you think I truly did not suspect?''

''Nay, well, *that* would have been too much to hope for . . . But I did hope that, perhaps, you did not know. What I love least about it is that we have ourselves not been consulted in the matter. It has seemingly not occurred to any of them that you and I might have other plans and wishes.''

''And do you?''

''How can I *tell!*'' said Aeron wildly; a shade too wildly perhaps, for covert glances were cast her way by those near that end of the high table, and she spoke now in softer tones. ''I love you dearly, Rhodri, that has never been a secret''—a glint of humor flashed in the green eyes—''since I first took a fancy to you at the age of five years. But now—'' In spite of her best resolve, her gaze wandered past mac Avera to Gwydion, who seemed cheerfully oblivious to any of this, making small talk with Fedelma ní Garra, an infantry commander recently promoted to Fianna general staff, and Struan Cameron's brother, Denzil.

''But now there is Gwydion,'' said Rhodri, not at all surprised; nor much distressed either. ''Whose own parents are raging to have him wed Delyth the heir of Sinadon. I myself, if pressed, might admit to a fancy of my own for two or three, or perhaps four, others—''

''Oh aye?'' she asked, interested and distracted. ''Who?''

''No matter who. Listen to me now: This is a matter will be a long few years in the making, and I for one would not have it wreck the friendship we three have made among ourselves. Let us not think too much on it just now, but let it resolve itself; it will in any case . . . Now, if you are done not eating, Aeron, I think mac Avera is waiting on you to call the tune for dancing.''

Sitting with Morwen and Dafydd Drummond and others of her friends in a corner of the hall, Aeron put her chin in her hands and relinquished her sour mood to the wash of the music over her. After quitting the high table for the lower benches and the music and dancing that invariably followed festival suppers, she and the others had been joined for a while by Gwydion and Rhodri—the one out of pure courtesy, Aeron was sure, though Roderick at least had the excuse that he had not seen his sister for some months—but the two princes had disappeared some time since, and none had any thought as to where they had gone.

But the beat of the borraun and the syncopated stutter of the bones were irresistible, and then the fidil soaring in above took her away, and she thought no more of her troubles. After a while, there was a pause in the music and some shifting among the players; and then another piece began, textured and intricate, beginning slowly but picking up speed and complexity as it did so, led by pipes and harp. Aeron's ear for music, ever a keen one, was caught at once by the difference: This new harper and piper, whoever they might be, stood out in skill from the other players like pines above goosegorse . . .

She craned her neck a little to see who they were, but the crowd was too dense; then the dancers in front of her parted for a moment, and she saw in the midst of the musicians Gwydion and Rhodri. *Well, no surprise there,* she thought; both of them were bard-trained, after all—as skilled with telyn and chanter as they were with sword or spear, and Roderick was more even than that.

The other musicmakers seemed to have drawn away from them a little, framing them out an arena in which to play to, or against, each other. Gwydion's fingers upon the telyn were a blur, and the sound coming off the dancing metal strings was a crystal storm; but Rhodri on the pipes seemed never to draw breath, and together they moved each other on to greater harmony and still greater speed.

It is like a dance, thought Aeron, caught up in it, *or a duel—they play together much as they fought together this afternoon; as if they can read each other's mind and moves; the most open of communicating, and that is not to be wondered at between two such friends . . .*

It came to an end, not trailing off as most such pieces did, but all at once, like hitting a wall, and in a sudden silence Aeron felt as if she had been dropped from a great height by a singing wind that had carried her far aloft, and had to catch her breath before she could think to cheer. The tumult of approval in the hall was like thunder, and shouts flew fast and thick for the arís, the follow-piece traditionally played by bards on such demand. But though Rhodri gracefully acceded to the clamor, Gwydion as gracefully declined, and slinging his harp over his shoulder headed toward the doors.

If he did not wish to play, plainly he had some other wish; and after a moment Aeron left her friends and followed after. Emerging from the hall into bright moonlight, she paused a moment as her nightsight adjusted to the striped and shadowed landscape; then she saw him not far away, alone, the harp lying beside him atop a wide stone wall and his arms folded under his cloak.

She hesitated then, not wishing to intrude upon his solitude if that was what he had come out in search of; but then he beckoned her to join him, and even through the dark she sensed his smile.

"I had need of air and silence," he offered, when they had sat a minute or two without speaking, side by side upon the stone wall, and Aeron wondered suddenly why he had not spoken to her all day; had, indeed, almost seemed to be avoiding her presence. Certainly he seemed glad enough of her company just now . . . "But you," he said then. "Since last I saw you, you have learned to be still even in the throng's heart. That is a great thing to have mastered." The approval in his voice was warm and unexpected, and Aeron found herself blushing a little, thankful that the darkness cloaked her face.

"Praise from a fellow adept is praise indeed," she said, and he in turn could hear the note of true-praise in her voice. "My uncle Corlann has told me how well you yourself have done, at Dinas Affaraon, and he being Pheryllt knows whereof he speaks. He tells me too that you have become Kin to the Dragon."

"Very newly Kin; a great honor, and one that will not be overlong in coming to you as well, I think. But Corlann gives me too much credit; he was a gifted teacher, and stood to me much as Kesten Hannivec did stand to you. But how is it with you here? You are happy? Your Fianship goes well?" he added hurriedly, and swore to himself at the babbling awkwardness of his own demeanor. He was as near her equal in rank as was possible in Keltia; her elder in years and in polish; her senior officer, come to that, as a Fian—why then this sudden green shyness that had seized him?

If Aeron noticed his unease, she made nothing of it, her own manner as easy and unconstrained as his had become unnatural.

"Well enough—though not to hear Struan tell it! Those Camerons are hard taskmasters . . . I have spent much time this past fortnight watching the tests, since I will be facing my own only a year from now." *And I wonder will you and Rhodri come to Caer Artos to observe those tests as you observe these—to observe me . . .*

As she spoke, Gwydion's composure had returned to him, and now he wondered only at the utter commonplace of her own manner; her light social tone suggested that any strain the moment may have carried belonged solely to him, that the Tanista Aeron could converse just so easily with any acquaintance or stranger, even, met by chance in unlikely places. For a moment he doubted even his own othersight, his own newly acquired powers: *Can it be she truly does not sense it, or, worse, does not share it even if she does? As soon as I saw her, there at the ringside while Rhodri and I fought this afternoon, I was sure of it; otherwise the bout had not ended in a draw . . .* And yet it had come as no surprise either: Gwydion had been, even so, sufficiently shaken by this new knowledge that all day he had not dared to approach her, much less have speech with her, lest his feeling pass all unbidden from his mind to hers. All his senses, sharpened by Druid and Dragon precepts alike, had seemed to tell him that she shared that feeling; yet here she was, apparently indifferent—could he have in truth be so much in error, and she did not know after all?

But then Aeron lifted her head to look at him, and he saw that she did know, and did share, and he bent to kiss her, one hand curving gently round her neck beneath the straight fall of hair. A gentle kiss and a brief one, for their first; then that changed, and their mouths met a second time in passion. He was first to break away, and both of them were trembling.

"My sorrow, Tanista," he said formally. "I meant no liberty."

"And took none," answered Aeron, her voice steadier just then than any other part of her.

And since there was nothing more either of them could say,

and nothing else they could do, Gwydion bowed, and offering her his arm led her back to the hall.

That year saw Aeron begin her royal duties as her father's official representative; though the Silver Branch was not yet hers to bear, she was thought by King and Council alike old enough to embark upon what would be for her a lifelong round of progresses and presidings and chairings and congresses, all in the name of duty and the service of the realm; and she was still young enough, and new enough to it, to think it a pleasant diversion.

In the early summer holiday at Caer Artos, Aeron bade a temporary farewell to Sabia, who was going home to her family's horse-farm back on Erinna, and to Morwen, who would be returning to Caledon, and herself headed for the other side of Gwynedd, to Caer Dathyl the seat of the planet's rulers, where she was to accept in Fionnbarr's name the homage of that world's Prince. The fact that the Prince was also her own foster-father gave a warmer feel to the duty than it might otherwise have had; but before the visit was done, Aeron would be bound to Gwynedd with links stronger far than either fealty or fosterage.

"It is ever a pleasure to have you with us at Caer Dathyl, alanna," said Arawn Penarvon, raising his voice so that Aeron might hear him through the voices and music coming from the great state chamber. "When you come as the Ard-rígh's surrogate, even doing fealty for Gwynedd becomes a pleasure. But this"—he gestured toward the crowded ballroom—"is more my idea of merrymaking."

Aeron smiled and took her foster-father's proffered arm. "Mine too," she said. "At the ceremony this afternoon, I was so nerve-ridden I as near as possible dropped the scepter on my foot. Well that you had a firmer grasp on it than did I . . . But I am afraid there soon shall be many more such chores for me. My father thinks it high time I should be performing as many official duties as I can manage—or as he can shirk."

"Ah, what else are our heirs for, if not to do gauran's burden when we would rather lighten our load? That son of mine, for one, says he has better things to do than play politics—not that I am not proud of him beyond all measure," he added hastily. "Your father has of course more and graver calls upon him than do I; still, that is not to underestimate the import of these go-abouts. You meet the folk in a way that you cannot, all tucked up close in Caerdroia. More to the point, they meet *you*—and begin to learn what like is their future Ard-rían. After all, they will be living with you for a century and more to come."

"And I with them! That sgian, Arawn-maeth, cuts both ways . . . But look who is here."

The Princess Gwenedour had come out to meet them at the entrance to the Great Hall, her court and guests arrayed in ranks behind her, and now greeted Aeron as formally and correctly as if she had not been her own foster-daughter.

"Welcome, Tanista, to the poor hospitality of Caer Dathyl."

Aeron embraced her. "And how, methryn, can I be welcomed to my own home, for so Caer Dathyl ever is to me." She spoke now to be heard by the assembled guests. "My thanks for the welcome of Their Highnesses of Gwynedd, and I convey to all here the good wishes and blessings of Fionnbarr Ard-rígh and Emer Queen of Keltia. The good wishes of Aeron you have ever had."

Gwenedour's lovely face—so like what her daughter Arianeira's would be in a few decades' time—flashed with a smile.

"Then let the dancing begin."

As custom decreed, Aeron danced the first stately strathspey with Arawn, alone on the floor, all the rest looking on until the first set of figures had been completed and protocol permitted them to join in. Clad in a gown the color of spun steel, bright as findruinna but soft as swanskin to the touch, Aeron shone like Aranrhod herself, the Silver-wheel Goddess, gleaming like a tailstar against the warm vivid colors of the Gwyneddan court.

She had been secretly relieved to hear, on her arrival that morning, that Arianeira was away from home just then on a round of visits. *Though there is no reason to feel so*, thought Aeron, with a fresh pang of guilt; still, there had been an uncomfortable coolness between them the last time they had met, though Aeron knew no cause, and she was glad now to be spared her fostern's presence.

Though she tried to conceal it, Aerön's eyes had been scan-
ning the room looking for one in particular. And of him she had
caught only brief glimpses all day long: at the welcoming ceremony at Caer Dathyl's spaceport, where he had stood behind his
father; at the brief ceremony of fealty, when he and his brother
Elved had accompanied their parents into the Great Hall, and had
watched Aeron receive the oaths due to the Ard-rígh of Keltia
from the rulers of Gwynedd. And just now, as he had partnered
his mother for the strathspey—but those few glimpses had been
enough to make her bones shake within her.

Now Gwydion presented himself before her, unsmiling, giving
the bow that was due to the Tanista and no more. Aeron responded with a curtsy that was but a dip of knee and flick of
skirt, puzzled a little at his seeming distance, and took her place
beside him in the long row of dancers for the reel.

Threading her way through the intricate figures, passing from
hand to hand of eager partners, Aeron was more than ever struck
by her own partner's apparent indifference. Did he not remember
the last time they two had stood so near—it was not so very long
ago—and neither of them had been indifferent *that* night—or
was it that he now regretted his actions then; or, gods forbid, had
some other in the time between taken his fancy more strongly
and surely? Rhodri had mentioned Delyth of Sinadon— For the
first time in her life, Aeron felt the green bite of jealousy: Delyth
might be stupid as a widgeon, as was well known, but she was also
equally well-known as a beauty, of such surpassing fairness as
might well attract a reluctant prince.

She herself was not always even pretty, Aeron knew—she
would not grow into her full beauty for years yet, though this she
did not know, and it would last her all her days when finally she
came to it—but she was also sure that this night she looked
exceptionally nice, hair softly done and shining, a collar of silver
sapphires setting off the silver gown. And so her young vanity
was a little pricked by Gwydion's outward coolness, so at odds
with what her intuition told her and her othersight confirmed.
The strong-boned handsome face remained courteous and correct, the gray eyes distantly polite, the clasp of his fingers round
hers only what the dance required.

Aeron could not say at what moment the knowledge finally
came to her. At numerous times over the course of the evening,

she had looked up suddenly to catch Gwydion watching her, and times there had been near as many when she herself had been the covert watcher, and he the one to be secretly stared at, to catch her in turn.

But it came to her all at once when at last it came, that what had happened three months since outside the hall at Caer Artos was by no means the end of it: that he felt even as did she, *his* bones too had turned to water, there was the same shaking in *his* chest. And as she looked on him now, and he on her, no word spoken and yet all words said, it came to Aeron more clearly still what must, and should, be.

The ceili had ended some time since; the palace was dark now, all the court retired, all the guests gone to their beds or to their own homes. Outside in the formal gardens, it was dark and very still, warm for the time of year. Beneath the peony-trees in the long alley, the scent of blooms hung heavy in the sea-touched air, and the thick-leaved boughs cut off the sky.

Aeron turned at his step behind her; she had for some moments known of his approach, though he made no sound as he had come along the long, dark row of trees, and made none now. He reached out to touch her cheek, but both of them shied a little at the touch, so that his fingertips ended half in her hair and half upon the line of her neck, above the sapphire collar.

Oh, do not ask me, she thought, and knew that he heard her as clearly as if she had spoken aloud. *Between us there is neither giving nor taking, but only what is, and what must be . . .*

Gwydion spread his cloak upon the soft turf beneath the trees in the little kilvach and pulled her down with him. Her own cloak fell around them to cover them, her hair as he drew out the silver pins veiling even their faces from sight, if any had been by to see. Then they themselves, even, saw nothing.

It was not as it had been for Aeron at her Teltown the summer past; that had been sweet in its hesitancy, its very ephemerousness. Here there was no hesitancy: They claimed each other as if by right, with a violence and a fierce perfection of certainty that made their loving as much a combat as a coupling, and each knew that the other rejoiced to have it so.

After, they lay quiet for a time, even their thoughts stilled,

Gwydion lying back upon the deep cushiony grasses, Aeron stretched beside him, held in the curve of his arm.

"They will try to keep us apart," she said presently, almost as afterthought; it seemed that all was known between them, no need of explanation or elaboration. They had only to think, and the thought was shared.

"They will surely try," he agreed. "And for a while they will seem to succeed. This is not for now, Aeronwy, what has happened here. Long and long it will be before we can be together openly. You and I have known, I think, since the last time we were together in this place—and you a brat of thirteen, all braids and bones, oh aye, I remember well—how it must be for us in the end. That is a thing no one may alter, for it is dán." He laughed suddenly. "Do you think you are the only royal heir whose parents know how to push? Yours are urging Rhodri; mine would have me wed Delyth of Sinadon."

Aeron was in a mood to be generous. "A sweet and pretty lady of excellent birth."

"A dull girl," said Gwydion unenthusiastically.

"Her family is both older and wealthier than mine," said Aeron straightfaced. "I can see where your mother would wish you to wed for advancement."

Gwydion laughed again and sat up, lifting her with him, to lean comfortably against the trunk of the tree whose boughs had sheltered them.

"No fear," he said with fervor. "Delyth has made her feelings on the matter quite plain: It seems she is not one for magic, and a sorcerer mate, however princely, is not her idea of what is fitting."

"Ah, then she is wise as well as lovely! Now who would have thought it— Still, that is well for her, for I had scratched her eyes out else . . ."

"Nay, that you would not; but if we speak of scratches—" He had drawn her hair away from her neck. The jeweled collar had cut into her throat where his mouth had pressed against it, and now tiny beads of blood gleamed like another necklace, of fine small rubies, amid the glittering stones. There was a cut too in the corner of his mouth, below the drooping crimbeul.

"How will you explain that to my mother?"

"I shall not have to." Aeron sat up, unfastening the necklace and a sudden stillness enfolded her. Gwydion watched with interest as, closing her eyes, she traced the line of tiny cuts with two fingers of her right hand, and the scratches healed up beneath her touch. Then she brushed her fingers gently over the corner of his mouth, and that wound too was gone, and he kissed her fingers.

"Ah, these Ban-draoi witches," he said smiling, the offending collar dangling from his hand like a string of snowstones, catching what light there was. "You will be putting the healers out of their trade."

"I will be doing no such thing," she answered. "Nor any of my Sisterhood, as you, being Druid, very well know. That is as grave a wound as we might mend, unless of course one chances to be a proper healer also. But I have not that gift."

"In the old days of the Danaans on Earth," he said in a different voice, settling her more comfortably across his lap and pulling her cloak around them both, "there were magical pools called crochans, that St. Nia taught Brendan her son to build, from lore that had come down to her from among her own people. Now these pools could heal any wound however grave; even—or so at least it was said—death itself, so long as the spinal cord had not been severed and the brain and bone-marrow remained intact."

"A faery-story surely, such as you learn among the bards. How could such a thing be? Only the Pair Dadeni itself, the Cauldron of Rebirth that has been lost these thousand years, has power to heal, and power over death."

"I know not," admitted Gwydion cheerfully. "Perhaps I shall learn more from the Pheryllt, when I go to Dinas Affaraon to finish my training for master-Druid. It might be a thing worth knowing, for a future need."

"It might at that." Aeron's smile vanished then, and when she looked up at him her face was troubled. "Gwydion, this that has been here tonight—"

"—is but a beginning." He kissed the top of her head. "You are trembling, cariad; surely you cannot fear it?"

"I think I must," said Aeron, and now the shiver had got into her voice. "You yourself said that it will be years yet before we may be together for all to see—I do not know if I can *bear* it . . ."

"You must," he said lightly, "and so must I, and that is why we have done as we did. This was a pledge to that future, Aeronwy, not a tumble in the gardens. But it *is* true dán, that too is certain; and I was as frightened by it at first as you are now, therefore I did not speak of it sooner. For my part, you shall have whatever time you need: to be afraid, to be with others, to obey your parents as Tanista, even to wed Rhodri if that is what dán demands and your obedience requires."

"And you shall not mind?"

Gwydion laughed. "Surely I shall *mind!* I am no perfected master, to accept all haps with calm untroubled . . . But I know we will not be kept apart for always; know too that just now you fear your own feeling, wish almost to run from it. And that is the real reason why you fear: because you cannot run from it forever."

A wild-doe look had come into Aeron's eyes as he spoke, and now in one swift flurried move she pulled away from him and rose to her feet, wrapping her cloak about her to hide her dishevelment and the ruin of her gown.

"That may be so, and doubtless it is; but, Prince of Gwynedd, I can run from it well enough now."

She was fleeing down the peony-alley almost before she had finished speaking, gone like a ghost into the soft dark, even the silver gleam of her gúna extinguished under the shadow of the trees. After a while, when he was certain she must have reached the palace and gone inside, Gwydion stood up, catching up his cloak from where they had lain upon it in the damp grass, still printed with their bodies' weight.

Had any seen him now, his face must have looked to them as does the summer sky when clouds race across it; deep emotions, conflicting and harmonious both together, chasing each other across his countenance swift and shadowy as any cloud: his love for Aeron, and joy that she loved him, wonder at what they had shared, and pain that it seemed to cause her such pain . . .

Bending down, Gwydion picked up from the grass a peony she had broken from its branch in her flight. Something glittered beside his foot, and bending again he scooped into his hand Aeron's jeweled collar that she had let fall or forgotten, so panicked had she been to escape. He smiled suddenly, then wrapping the sapphire strand around the flower's stem, he breathed deep of the cool fragrance of the huge puffy bloom, and went back to the palace alone.

Chapter 21

The next morning Aeron was gone from Caer Dathyl before most of the palace had risen. She had sent hasty and apologetic farewell to Arawn and Gwenedour—some unconvincing brabble of an excuse, an urgent summons from her father, that she return at once to Caerdroia—and by the time Gwydion awoke she was well off-planet. But the peony blossom, her sapphire necklace still wrapped round its stem, that a servitor had brought to her chamber that morning, was gone with her.

Though Emer was highly suspicious at her daughter's abrupt return, and more suspicious still when she came to discuss the matter with her friend Gwenedour, she was to learn nothing whatever from Aeron. And even those suspicions became suspect in their turn when Aeron began within a few months to flaunt a romance with Dafydd, the Master of Drummond, heir to a family close to the Crown for many reigns and himself a palace playfellow of Aeron's and Rohan's and Ríoghnach's since the age of three.

"It was so plain, Barraun, past all disputing," complained Emer to her husband. "Well, so at least it seemed to Gwenedour and to me . . . There was Aeron at Caer Dathyl, and there was Gwydion—Gwenedour told me herself that they were desperately ignoring each other at the ceili, and you know what *that* must mean. Then she is not three months back at Caer Artos, where she should be thinking only of training for her tests, and what does she do but take up with Deio Drummond for all the worlds to see!"

"A solid and worthy young man; I have always been very fond of him," remarked Fionnbarr placidly.

Emer flung back her golden head in exasperation. "Deio! Only too much so—and that is just my point, Barraun. He is the pleasantest, most easygoing, amiable lad . . . in brief, he is the least likely candidate for Aeron's affections I should have thought to find in all Keltia. Oh, mistake me not, he is perfectly suitable, and if she must choose some companion I am glad she has chosen so discreetly. But I think his chief attraction is that he is *safe*, and for some reason that seems to matter most with her just now. Whatever she wishes will suit him perfectly; nothing will be too troublous a burden for him; he will shield her as she wishes to be shielded, above all he will make no demands on her . . . She is fond of him, I am sure, but I am just as sure that she has taken up with him not out of passion or love but for protection."

"Well, where is the wrong there?" asked Fionnbarr, somewhat defensively. "Things can come down very hard on a young heir; I myself would have been grateful for some caring protection when I was her age."

"And if that were all there was to it, I should not mind quite so much," answered Emer. "Nay, she is employing strategy here as would have been worthy of Aoife herself. She is concealing something, and it is to do with Gwydion, and by the Mother I shall know what it is or I am not *her* mother."

"That you most surely are, my heart," said Fionnbarr soothingly, though in truth he was still bewildered by his wife's vehemence. "But since she is also your daughter, I would not care to take any wagers on who will have the greater success in her efforts."

If time were sole judge of those efforts, Aeron must surely have been counted victor, for her affair with Dafydd Drummond continued off and on for near two years, and there were several others after that: lighthearted romances for the most part, naught of weight on either side, with young men of good family and suitable discretion; romances that sufficed to hold Aeron apart—or protected—from other entanglements. And in all that time not once would she see, and have but little word of, Gwydion Prince of Gwynedd.

Heart-matters aside, there were more important things at stake just now: Little more than a sixmonth after that time at Caer

Dathyl, Aeron and her fellow students came to complete their three years' course at Fians, and, all too soon as it seemed to them, time was on them that they must face their tests.

The tests that alone could make a Fian candidate into a Fian warrior—the legendary triail-triarach—were among the most ancient institutions in Keltia, brought from Earth by the first Danaan starfarers, among whom had been the last of that first Fianna, the final heirs to the legacies of Oisín and Oscar, Caoilte and Conanmaol and Fionn the son of Cumhal.

Three tests there were, each designed to make trial of a different range of the candidate's abilities and suitabilities; each was hard, and all were fair, and the three of them together gave an accurate assessment indeed. For the mastery of them, the candidate must draw upon all that had been taught and learned in three years of tutelage; for some, even that would not suffice. Though failure to qualify for Fianship was keen disappointment and more beside, so fearsome was the triail-triarach that to fail in one or more of its parts was by no means the disgrace another failure might have been. Few there were in Keltia could not, or would not, commiserate with a defeated candidate, nor wonder how they themselves might have fared in like case.

First of the tests came the test of knowledge. From dawn to sunset, only the briefest of pauses allowed for a bolted daymeal, the test went on, spanning the Fianna's Twelve Books of Knowledge: heraldry to military science, poetry to astrodynamic theory; from how to jury-rig a crippled starship to how to mend a broken chariot-wheel; from how to weld a broken bone to how to parse an Englic sentence.

By dint of their own efforts and their tutors' drilling, all those in Aeron's year passed, most of them with ease; and that was usual. If a candidate were like to fail, more often that failure would befall in one of the two other trials, the test of combat or the test of soul; and both of these were yet to come.

Once the first test was done with, it lay within the purview of the trialmaster as to which ordeal each candidate would next face. For some, the test of soul came next, with all its strange terrors; for others, that test was reserved for last, and after doing battle with scholarship, they must then take up arms in good earnest for the test of combat; and in that part of the triple trial there were more passages than one.

That spring it was Denzil Cameron's lot to serve as trialmaster. Struan's brother, junior by some twenty years, Denzil had served as instructor at several Fian academies before coming to Caer Artos, and had been named only that year to the post of trialmaster. *Diceltair*, it was called by the Fianna, in the ancient bardic usage meaning the shaft of a war-spear before the point is riveted upon it. As Denzil explained to his charges, they themselves would be the head to that weapon—if they passed the threefold challenge.

For Aeron, the trial of combat was by Denzil's order to be her next to face; not an unusual sequence by any means, and that year it would be so not only for her but for Sabia, and for Vevin ní Talleron, and for very many others of their classmates. No one ever knew the reasons that the Diceltair should dispose as he did; all one could do was bow to his decision, and stand to one's tests however they did come.

"You are ready?"

Aeron nodded answer to Denzil's question, smoothing back nonexistent strands of hair from her flushed face. It was a nervous reflex gesture: Every scrap of red hair was already pulled smooth and tightly braided in the basketweave pattern used for this most ancient part of the test of combat: the Cúrsa-nan-coillta, the Running of the Woods.

"You will be given the start of a single tree in thick woods," continued Cameron, using the old words as they had come down unchanged over the centuries. He pointed down the rolling forested glen below them; from where they stood upon the hillside, it seemed empty, but Aeron knew well that all that glen held hidden watchers, though where they lay she could not tell.

"In there—" she breathed, dancing a little in her eagerness to be gone, nodding at the wood below.

"In there," agreed Denzil. His voice took on a ritual rhythm. "Not a single strand of your hair may be snagged by a branch; not a twig may snap under your foot nor a leaf tremble to betray your passing. You must pass without pause over branches the height of your eyes, and under others the height of your knee, and those branches may not shake when you have passed by.

And lastly you must take up a thorn in your foot without flinching and remove it without breaking stride. All this to be done while eluding the pursuers who will be running hard upon your track. If you put one foot wrong, you fail; if you pull up short, you fail; if your pursuers catch you, you fail. Do you understand?"

Aeron nodded again, face now taut with eagerness. The Cúrsa was the very heart of the triail-triarach, the most legendary of all the Fianna tests, devised by Fionn himself, maybe; she and the others had spent the past month training solely for this one ordeal. She looked down the hill to where the trees began: Ground mist, drifting knee-high up the short-grassed slope, gave way to cooler air; above their heads the sky was very high that day.

"Take your mark." Denzil stepped back. "When you are your full and lawful distance under the trees, the pursuit will begin. They are waiting, down below; you cannot see them, but know that they are there, and an officer to observe that you are given the full start to which you are entitled. There will be other watchers in the wood itself, and you will not see them either." He paused, a small smile gleaming deep in his beard; Aeron, eyes fixed on the gap in the trees where she had decided to enter, did not see. "Then begin."

She was away like a deer, the ground mist swaying where she broke through it. In ten seconds she had covered the open distance downslope and was into the trees. In the sudden dimness Aeron heard the barked command of the Fian officer that unleashed her pursuers, then heard nothing more; not the pursuit, not her own passage, the soft soles of the thonged slippers she wore making no more sound than a fox's pads on the forest floor.

They were hunting her by sight, and there was no compulsion upon her to stay unseen. All she need do was stay ahead of them, while still obeying the other rules of the chase, and she was seized by a sudden exhilaration as she flickered into and out of shafts of sunlight, where the leaves overhead had thinned in the spring storms.

Almost without thinking Aeron gathered herself to vault a branch "the height of the runner's eyes," and landed softly. Then another bough, this one at knee level; she rolled beneath it and was on her feet and running before she knew it had even been there. She dared a quick glance over her shoulder; three figures after her, but she had a comfortable lead.

The marked trail bent sharply to the left, and she saw no more than a score of strides ahead of her a patch of gold sand; in the center of it was set upright a row of thorns. The test required her deliberately to take one of the sharp draigheans in the sole of her foot, through the slipper's thin leather sole, and to remove it without breaking stride. It was a maneuver requiring dexterity, split-second timing and nerve, for the thorns were long, and needle-sharp.

Approaching the row of thorns, Aeron shortened her stride, gauging her steps so that her right foot would be the one to pick up the draighean. Two strides on soft sand, then a sharp lancing pain went up her instep; the thorn was in, and in the next instant it was gone again, as her hand reached down in a sweeping arc to pull the thorn out as her foot came up behind her. Except for the urgency of knowing the pursuit so close upon her heels, it was just as she had practiced it all those weeks, carefully timing the cadence of her speed and stride, enduring all those jabbing punctures to her feet.

Then she was running clear again through open forest, over pine-needles whose fragrance filled her lungs as she fought to inhale. *Not far now* . . . Another set of branches to pass over and under; seen almost too late, a carpet of twigs laid in her path. She half-ran, half-leaped over them, in a panic lest her foot come down too hard, but she heard no betraying snap.

And then Aeron was out into bright sunlight, Denzil and his officers not ten yards away, all of them smiling hugely. She slowed to walking pace, realizing that it was over, for good or ill. Denzil pointed behind her; she turned to see her grinning pursuers emerge from the wood, fists raised high above their heads in sign of her victory.

"Not a leaf trembled, not a branch brushed against, not a twig broken." Denzil ran a hand over Aeron's braids. "And not a strand out of place." He cuffed her lightly and affectionately, and she dropped the draighean into his palm with a grin. "Well run; Fionn himself could have done no better. Go now and eat your breakfast; you have the rest of the day at liberty, and you well deserve it."

Aeron saluted him with great correctness, then turned away to plod up the side of the hill. All at once she felt as if she had run fifty lai, not five; the overwound anticipation, and the terrific stresses of the run itself, had combined to leave her muscles like water, barely able to carry her up the hill and over the fields to the halls.

And now I think of water . . . I could drink dry the Avon Dia.

Sitting in the refectory—hunger subordinate for the moment to her thirst—Aeron drank impartially from a mether of light ale and a mether of cold spring water, watching with interest as others came in from their own tests, trying to gauge from their demeanor how they had fared in the Cúrsa.

"All that ale could float a birlinn! You had better eat something, Aeron, to ballast yourself; I am not sure we could summon the strength to carry you to your rooms."

With a wide happy grin, Sabia dropped down beside her, and Morwen appeared at that moment with Dafydd Drummond at the hall door; Aeron waved them over, giving each of them, as she had given Sabia, a quick affectionate hug.

"I heard Denzil Cameron telling his brother how well you did, Aeron," offered Dafydd, reaching for the ale keeve.

"Then let him pass it on to her himself," said Struan Cameron, coming up behind them and waving them all to keep seated. "You all did well, as my brother has indeed told me. Set a good pace for your pursuit to keep to, went lightly and neatly through the run, took out the draigheans quick and smooth. Oh aye, you did well today."

Sabia smiled with delight and triumph. "It was—I know not how to say how it was! I did not think to enjoy myself so at it. But it was grand, not so, Aeron?"

Her friend nodded, obediently stuffing a pastai from the platter in the center of the table. "Truly; I thought so even while I was running it. How did the rest of the company fare, athro?"

Struan shrugged. "Most passed; I did not suffer so with you lot merely to lose my labor and see you fail—at least not so early on," he added darkly. "The remaining tests will perhaps be not so pleasant."

But they laughed at him, and boasted a little, and refused to be quashed.

"Well," said Aeron through the last mouthful of the last pastai, "glad am I to know that we did not disgrace our tutor." She gave Struan a little bow, and he grinned at her and bowed back. "But I think I will have that rest now."

"You will need it," said Struan.

The next parts of the test of combat were almost anticlimactical by comparison, or so at least they seemed to Aeron. But they were hardly to be called routine exercises: In one, almost as old an ordeal as the Cúrsa, the candidate was buried to the waist in a sand-pit, given a stout hazel staff with which to defend himself, and then nine warriors flung spears at him from a set distance for a set timespan. If one spear touched earth behind the candidate's guard, he failed; if a spear struck him however lightly, he failed; if he tired in defense, he failed. And there were other tests as well; but the chiefest component of the trial by combat, the one most eagerly anticipated by the candidates, was the personal duel itself.

Even to this phase there were two parts: an unarmed combat, and a combat with weapons. Aeron, who had been triumphant in her unarmed fight the day previous, now stood at the entrance to the dueling ring, where she would face whatever champion Struan and Denzil and mac Avera had taken it into their heads to send against her.

For a while she had entertained the mad notion that they would pit her against one she knew; had feared, indeed, lest it be Rhodri or Gwydion or even one of her Fian cousins. But her reason had prevailed, and now she was calmly preparing herself for the bout. But still she would not look just yet at the opponent who awaited her across the ring, busying herself instead with minute, and wholly unnecessary, inspections of her gear. The swords were clean and oiled and gleaming; as well they should be, for only First-rank Fians were permitted to prepare the candidates' weapons for the tests.

At last Aeron took a deep calming breath and looked at her opponent. There was respect and careful judgment in her look, for this adversary must be assessed accurately indeed. His tunic badge proclaimed him a Vanxman, and Aeron guessed him to be in her early prime—mid-sixties, perhaps; whip-wiry, not so tall as she herself, clad as she was clad in the brown form-fitting unisuit worn for the challenge. But she was not deceived by his lack of bulk or inches: Too obvious to have matched her for this trial against someone the size of, say, her cousins Alasdair or Macsen—more than seven feet tall, massing over three hundred-weight apiece, who could fell a horse with one hand if so they chose.

Still, this Fian across the ring looked quick as a waterdog and dangerous as a nathair; it would be a real fight, and candidates had before now been injured, even slain, in Fian trials.

I, however, will not be . . . Aeron took her sword from the hands of her second, brought it to the salute, and stepped forward; seeing her ready, her opponent did the same.

In his judge's seat at the center perimeter, Struan Cameron folded his arms and leaned forward over the railing. He knew what was about to befall the Vanxman—a First-rank Fian for thirty years, and one of his finest swordmasters—though Aeron as yet did not, and he was eager to see it.

It was over almost before it could be fairly seen: The Vanxman's first mistake, indeed his only mistake, was to allow Aeron the opening blow, for from then on the thing was decided. Aeron had learned much under Struan's goad that year past, was by no means the same swordswoman who had allowed herself to be nicked by a fellow student in a practice bout. She had vowed then that such carelessness should never be seen in her again, and from that day to this it had not been, nor would ever be. Along with the new vigilance had come blinding speed, and uncanny precision, and a talent for predicting an opponent's strategy of stroke that had astonished even Struan.

Nor was he the only master to be so impressed: In his own chair facing Struan on the other side of the ring, Donal mac Avera watched as if he could not accept even the clear evidence of his own eyes, his jaw dropping lower with every exchange of parry and thrust. *Cameron told me she had come to her promise, but never did he suggest the like of this . . . She is stroke for stroke the equal of the best that have come out of this school, and who could have expected it?*

Even as mac Avera thought so and marvelled, the Vanxman held up his sword in token of surrender, from the corner of the ring where Aeron had backed him; victor and vanquished then presented themselves before the Captain-General.

Mac Avera rose in his place as did Struan across the ring, and returned Aeron's bow, with the traditional words that closed every successful trial of combat.

"Well stood, ban-laoch. What do you ask of us?"

"To be feinnid of the true Fianna," answered Aeron, "and to do you service as did my fathers and mothers before me, be it peace or be it war."

"May it prove so," responded mac Avera, "and strength to your arm."

Aeron bowed to him, and to her opponent, in thanks that he should have been the means by which her test was passed, and to Struan, in thanks for the teaching that had enabled her to do so; and all this was according to custom. Leaving the ring then, she was pounced upon by a knot of her friends, all of them in towering spirits, for they had passed their own combats that same day or the day previous, and had only been waiting for Aeron's victory to make their triumph complete.

For a little while she joined in their rejoicing, then made smiling excuse to them all and walked a little way up the fellside, to stand looking down across the valley ridges to the wood where, only a sevennight since, she had run the Cúrsa.

Seven nights! Already it seems years behind me. Two parts the triail-triarach won now, and I two-thirds a Fian—how if I lose at the last? Small profit in being two-thirds feinnid . . . Aeron sat down cross-legged in the wiry grass. She had prayed once, when first she had come to Caer Artos, that she might be allowed this second great wish of hers: to be a Fian, as her first wish had been to be a Ban-draoi. She had wished, and she had prayed, and then she had worked; and the first wish had been granted her, and now it looked as if the second was in a fair way to being won as well. Yet somehow the thought of the impending trial daunted her, as no test yet had done. *And why that should be so . . . Denzil Cameron had decreed that the test of soul should be for me the final test; surely he must have had his reasons for that decision. What did he see, that I have yet to have sight of?*

But for once no answer came, and she knew that there would be none, not until the trial of soul itself should be in two days' time both question and answer, puzzle and decipherment both together.

Aeron rose then, retracing slow steps back to the hall where her friends would be expecting her. *I have made an immram,* she thought, hugging that fact to her, a poor rag of comfort against the howling storm of the unknown. *It was far from here in Broinn-na-draoichta, and it took me farther still; this to come cannot be so very different after all.* She hesitated, then sighed and went on down the hill, more quickly now, eager to be once again among people. *But still and all, I am none so sure.*

They were waiting for her, their faces masked, one on each side of the narrow opening that was the only entrance or egress to the clochan, the beehive-shaped stone structure that stood on the side of the hill. There were other clochans in the country round Caer Artos, some in the high hills, some on the foreshore of the nearby sea, some in the deeps of the woods. But it was to this one that Aeron had been commanded by the Diceltair; she stood before it now, summoning the courage to step inside.

No haste, she told herself. *I may choose my own time to enter; though to delay overlong is as gross a failing as to enter overhastily.* She studied the structure: Built of dressed gray granite, the clochan rose to a height of perhaps twenty feet; a leather curtain covered the doorway, and from around its edges seeped blue smoke.

A puff of wind carried the smoke to Aeron then, and her throat constricted at the acrid smell of it: heavy incense mixed with certain herb powders of known properties—athair-talam, dubh-cosac, archmain, aquilegia, thale; all the mind-altering drugs of the Fianna pharmacopeia, to be used in today's test, the test of soul, that there might be induced in her what visions should come.

Gathering herself together, Aeron stepped forward to the doorway—low of lintel, she must bend her neck to enter—and unbuckled her cloak. One of the doorwards took it from her; beneath, she was clad in a straight-cut plain red robe, her feet bare. *Red, the color of death, for this is a little-death here; the death of my novice self, my rebirth as a true Fian, if I am found worthy* . . . She shivered a little, recalling another initiation, another little-death. *Only then I was robed in black, and it was Tybie led me to it. Today, I must lead myself* . . .

With a deep breath she ducked her head to enter the clochan; the warders caught back the leather curtain for her, then closed it behind her, and Aeron was alone inside the stone bell. She glanced upward, to the small high opening through which came the only light and air; then her eyes went farther, to the neat joined ceiling, not a dab of mortar in it—the stones had been fitted together solely in the shaping, so tightly that even rainwater could find no way inside.

She started at a sound from behind: Outside, the doorwards were lacing a wicker shield over the entrance; at the test's end, should she succeed, she would cut her way back out to daylight with the sword that lay in a niche of the rear wall.

Aoife's weapon, though I do not yet have the right to touch it . . . Aeron looked reverently upon the gleaming findruinna blade, the black hilt, the pommel tipped with a single huge red gem. That had been a surprise from Struan, a gift for luck and confidence from master to pupil: He had obtained permission from mac Avera that Aeron should use her great-grandmother's sword, and had then himself begged the weapon of Fionnbarr, arguing that it was only fitting for Keltia's next Ard-rían to use in her test the blade that had belonged to the latest, and the King had agreed.

In front of the niche that held the sword was a small bronze tripod censer filled with smoldering incense, and before that again stood a light wicker bier, of the sort used for Fian funeral rites in time of war: low, six-legged, its joints whipped round with leather.

Aeron stared at the bier, suddenly glad that neither Gwydion nor Roderick had kept to their usual custom and come to Caer Artos to watch the tests. *It would have been too much for me, and for Wenna too; we would not have been strengthened by their presence, only distracted—thank gods they seem to have realized that, or perhaps Denzil or mac Avera did warn them away. Whatever, it is best they are not here . . .*

But the drugs in the smoke were beginning to work upon her, and she knew she had not much time. Gathering the red robe around her, Aeron lay down upon the wicker bier and commanded herself to calmness. Directly above her, the sacred smoke curled and eddied and then closed like a ghostly hand round her throat. Looking up to the ceiling, she could see the tiny window being covered over from outside; then the smoke took her to another place.

* * *

Her Ban-draoi instruction, and her immram especially, had given Aeron good grounding in soul-travel; though the techniques used here were different, and the planes attained to also unlike, for the first stages it felt comfortingly familiar, and she let herself run out upon the spiral in the way she knew so well.

Some, the Fian instructors had warned, had not survived this test: Their bodies could not marshal the drugs properly, or their minds could not withstand the visions that were revealed in the marbh-aisling, the dreaming-death. But such tragedies were comparatively rare: If the candidate were destined not to succeed, it generally happened that he or she would simply fall asleep in trance and wake up a day or so later little the worse for it—save of course that the test had been failed.

But if the test of soul carried then the most danger, it carried also the most mystery, the true meaning of Fianship; and, pass or fail, no candidate had been known to speak of it after. Not even to the Fian instructors, nor the Diceltair, nor the Captain-General himself; what happened in the stone clochans was forever after a matter between the Fian aspirant and the gods who guided the test. *Fionn himself, it might be,* thought Aeron muzzily, *and of him at least I have no fear; or others of his companions, Coll or Diarmid or Caoilte. For a woman, Morna or Turenn, or maybe Sorcha or Saive . . .* She reached out with her spirit; a calling that was more than prayer: *Macha Ruadh, you who are the Red War-crow; Nia the Golden, you who are my foremother; Aeron whose name means Goddess of Slaughter, you whose namesake I am, hear and help.*

She could not feel her body any longer, could not smell the incense nor see the inside walls of the clochan. She seemed to be suspended in some vast hollow blackness, wide and deep as the mouth of a giant bell, and the slightest touch of thought set the bell to whispering. Though Aeron strove to still her mind as she knew she must, the faint chiming grew to a roar, and when it had filled all her head, and all the clochan, and all the world beside, suddenly it stopped; and in the giant booming silence it left in its wake, Aeron was there again.

But no longer alone: One sat now just within the door, sat very still indeed for Aeron not to have noticed before now. Or perhaps there had been no one, not until this moment; perhaps there was still no one, and the form she thought she saw was but hallucination. She could not think clear for the sick spinning in her brain; all her inner defenses, even her strongest Ban-draoi shields, seemed open to this one who sat so still and said no word. *Perhaps he—or she—has no need to ask; perhaps at this very moment I am somehow saying all that needs to be heard . . .*

Aeron forced her mouth and tongue to shape the words. "Who is there?"

The answer came at once, low and unemphatic. "I am the Red Listener."

"What do you hope to hear?"

"I listen for your choice: victory or destruction."

"No choice there."

"There is also the choice of the coward: the choice of refusing to choose."

The words struck Aeron with a sense of inevitable rightness she knew she would never be able to explain—or recall, even—with her everyday consciousness; knew too that this Red Listener—man or woman, god or mortal or creation of her own deep soul—was the Inquisitioner promised in the test. She and the other candidates had always assumed that their Inquisitioner would be a sorcerer, some Druid or Ban-draoi or Dragon Kin—at least a fellow mortal; but perhaps they had been wrong in those assumptions. And suddenly Aeron knew why no candidate had been known to speak of this moment once the moment was gone. *It may not be the same for each of us; what I am given to see and hear does surely differ from that which the others are shown; but howsoever it may choose to clothe itself, surely this truth is the same for us all.* And this truth of Aeron's would observe her in her trial, would without a question asked have of Aeron all the answers required, and would be the one in whom Aeron would see for herself, as in the most clear and perfect of mirrors, how she was made and how she would fare at the test.

"Then," said Aeron, and knew she spoke aloud, "then hear what I do choose—"

Standing impassive and unwearied to their posts, as they had done for near seven hours, the doorwards were not surprised to hear behind them a sound as of sudden fire, a rippling brittle snap as the wicker shield was cut away from within, the shining blade of Aoife's sword cleaving through willowwork and leather lacings alike; then they were free to assist gladly, pulling away the remnants of shield, tearing down the leather curtain that hung now in tatters over the entrance.

Aeron stood in the doorway, her great-grandmother's sword in her hand; and perhaps a little of her great-grandmother's look in her face, for the two Fians who had kept the door against her stepped back now and were silent.

Then mac Avera himself was there, with Denzil and Struan a little behind him. The Captain-General and his newest Fian looked long at each other; both were apparently satisfied with what they saw, for a smile broke over mac Avera's face, and a matching one lighted Aeron's, and he gave her then the words she had fought three years to hear.

"If armed service be thy design, thou hast won it. Be welcome among us, thou of the tribe of Fionn."

Chapter 22

Though the case was otherwise for most of her classmates, as she had so long ago lamented, the winning of Fianship by no means signalled the end of Aeron's education. So after the celebrating was done, when the others departed Caer Artos to embark upon their active military service, Aeron went instead to the brehons, those revered lawgivers out of the most ancient Keltic past, to study with them for a year's time at the Hill of Laws on Arvor: a year that she for her part found more demanding by far than the whole of the past three had been, as the energies that had been turned to winning the victory in combat were turned now to winning battles of a different sort.

"Still, it is not so bad as I had thought to find it," admitted Aeron to Morwen, one day late in the term when her friend had come on a visit to the place where she herself had spent so many years. "And by no means so bad as you, Wenna Douglas, did give me cause to think—I must mind me never again to give such heed to your complainings."

Morwen was unabashed. "Oh aye, easy enough for you to say, Aeron; you have only to spend a twelvemonth here, and most of that already gone. But *I* was here six long years together, and must yet return for another two. It is a thing I am resigned to, but not a thing I take much pleasure in."

"You will be pleased enough when it brings you to enrobement as a brehon, and brings us two together again at Turusachan," remarked Aeron, unmoved by her friend's display. "As chief advisor to the Tanista, when my household is assembled—well, I know *I* shall be glad of it."

"And so shall I," conceded Morwen, giving over the mock

annoyance. "It is just that it seems so far away— But if we speak of those who will join your household, what of our own fostern? What do you hear of Arianeira all this time?"

Aeron frowned. "Very little. I myself have not been the best of correspondents, but Ari has answered not one in ten of the messages I did send her."

"And what do you hear of her brother?"

Aeron shot a sharp glance at her friend, but Morwen's face was as studiedly innocent as her tone had been bland. Instead, Aeron startled them both with her answer, a question in its turn.

"How is Rhodri these days? He sent me no song for my birthday, and that is the first time he has failed to do so since all of us were together at Kinloch Arnoch. I do not know whether to be cross at his forgetting or worried that something is amiss with him."

"Naught amiss; but I fear that birthday remembrances—even yours—are not to the fore of his mind just now," said Morwen. Her blue eyes lifted involuntarily to the sky, as if to seek out her brother's current whereabouts; but it was midafternoon, and no stars were to be seen. She sighed a little. "He has full command of a star-squadron—as I hear so also does Gwydion—and both of them have been in the thick of heavy action against the Phalanx, in the Protectorate sector of Lavellan. He does well as commander, I am told."

"And why should he not? He excelled at Caer Artos—as also did Gwydion."

"So he did." Morwen put aside her reluctance to inquire into matters her friend did not choose to speak of. "I make no special pleading for Roderick, Aeron, my brother though he be; his deeds and virtues speak for themselves. But it has been long thought of, and accepted by many, that you and he should come to reign together. We have never spoken of it, he and I, so I do not know what he himself may think or feel or wish; and you and I ourselves have never spoken of it save in jest—"

"And you wish to speak of it now in good earnest." Aeron in her turn looked up at the cloudless blue above them. "Fair enough . . . What I feel for Rhodri," she began slowly, as if she herself had not yet fully fathomed the thing out, "is by no means the same as that which I feel for Gwydion. They are both so infinitely worthy, and so infinitely different—almost it seems, if such a thing were possible, that I do love them both.'' She gave Morwen a glance that could have been defiance, or apology, or guilt, or all three together, but her friend did not see.

''Well, clearly it is possible,'' said Morwen then with her usual logic, ''since you are in fact so doing . . But though one may well love two men at one time, I think it would not be possible to love those two in the same way, or for the same reasons. Reasons there are for you to love Gwydion, and reasons to love my brother, and those reasons are not the same reasons, and will never be so. As to which of them would make the better king for Keltia, I cannot say; though either would be admirable. As to who should be the meeter mate for Aeron, I can say still less. But both choices are yours to make.''

''Well, not yet they are!'' said Aeron with some heat. ''There are a good few other matters I must attend to first—but when I am finished here, as I shall be within the next few months, I am to be allowed an adventure indeed.''

''Oh aye? Where away?''

''My father wishes me to go on a short progress beyond the Curtain Wall, to represent him to the courts of Protectorate worlds and affirm certain formalities of our arrangement with those systems.'' The green eyes sparkled. ''I have never before been out-Wall, save for some training forays with the Fianna, and those brief ones, not far beyond the Pale.''

''I too have been on such raids, but who knows when I may again be out of the Bawn,'' said Morwen a little enviously. ''Where will you go to first?''

''A place I have long wished to see: our trading-planet of Clero.''

''What does your father tell you of Fomor?'' asked Emer the Queen. ''Do you speak of such, with him?''

Aeron, sitting on the floor sorting through a pigpile of her belongings, gave her mother a considering upward glance. They were in her own chambers—a new suite of rooms in the Western Tower overlooking the sea—to which Aeron had recently relocated from the palace's family wing, as prelude to the establishment of her own independent household as Tanista. In one of the adjoining chambers, Aeron's old nurse Nessa—gray-haired now, but fierce and loving as ever—and a few of the Queen's ladies were making final additions and adjustments to Aeron's gear and garb, which Aeron from where she sat was just as swiftly undoing, preparatory to the departure for Clero and the other worlds of the progress.

Fomor! Why does she ask this of me now . . . Though, as Aeron well knew, her mother was of course interested in politics insofar as they affected her husband, and only secondarily in how they might bear upon her position as Queen, she was not usually one to concern herself with the affairs of the galláin, and her question at this time made Aeron wonder.

"Well, surely we speak of Fomor," replied Aeron at last. "It is a thing of which I can ill afford to be ignorant. I must deal with it one day, as my father deals with it now—or rather does not deal—and as did his father before him."

"He has told you, then, of those past dealings?"

"Often," said Aeron, warming a little to the subject despite her puzzlement; she and her mother did not often have a chance for intimate conversation, and still less chance for political discussion. "For one, he has told me often of his journey to Ganaster, what time he was defender for Keltia before the High Justiciar against Crown Prince Bres of Fomor, as he was then."

"What does he say of Bres?"

"What does he not! Though little enough that is not commonly known: He speaks more of Bres's heir, Elathan, who most like will be my own particular punishment—he and that one on Alphor, Jaun Akhera, Strephon's daughter's son. My father thinks that Strephon will name him Imperial Heir some time soon, now that Phano, his father, has been executed for plotting treason."

"Like enough," said Emer, uninterested. "But about Bres? Or"—she paused almost imperceptibly—"Bres's queen?"

"Basilea?" Aeron was more surprised still. "Never to my recall has he spoken of *her* . . . I think she plays but little part in Fomorian or Phalanx affairs of state—unlike other queens I might name," she added with a smile, and Emer laughed.

"Indeed you might, but see you do not; it is largely by this Queen's grace that you are going on this jaunt to Clero at all. The Councils thought it by no means worth the risk, to send you on so routine a progress."

Aeron nodded. "I know; my uncle Elharn spoke to me of the

dangers, should the Coranians or the Fomori learn that the heir of Keltia is outside the Curtain Wall, and but small force with her. The risk is real enough.''

''And?''

''I am a Fian; I have been trained to risks . . . Besides, the advantages to be gained by my going far outweigh the chances of my coming to harm. And even did they not, still would I go; for it is a thing for the Tanista to do, and I will do it.''

Emer made no reply, folding away a favorite gúna of Aeron's and watching her daughter pack a few small personal tokens—a book or two; some bits of jewelry; miniature portraits, framed in gold and pearls, of family and friends—for the journey.

For all I think I know her well, as a mother ought, still she is forever surprising me . . . Emer and Aeron had never been wholly at ease with each other; down the years, their roles as mother and daughter, queen and princess, had precluded true closeness—they had shared familial battle aplenty, but little else. It had been the fault of neither, but the price of royal duty. *So much has been sacrificed on* that *fane,* thought Emer now; *I never permitted myself to regret it while she was growing up— while any of my children were growing up, for that matter, not Aeron only—but I am sorry now we could not have been closer, or at least seen more of each other over the years. All that time she has spent away from us . . . and now she is bound out-Wall on this sleeveless errand that I myself fought the Councils to send her on . . .*

Emer forced herself, as she had never before done, to an impartial judging of her eldest child. Quick of mind and quicker of tongue, Aeron often lost patience with those whose minds were less swift to follow her own; she would grow out of that in time, it was true, but it was also true that it was something she had in full measure, undiluted, straight from the High Queen Aoife—who had, as was well known in Keltia and far beyond, *never* grown out of it. Yet, however snappish she might be with anyone who could snap back, Aeron was unfailingly courteous with any who for whatever reason could not; nor had she, so far as her mother knew, ever maliciously caused anyone pain, nor misused her great gifts of spell or sword. For one so young, she displayed an astonishing grasp of detail, which would stand her in excellent stead as Ard-rían; yet at the same time she often fell prey to the larger picture, could not as it were see the trees for the forest.

On balance, we have done extremely well with her, Barraun and I, thought Emer, and now she was a queen making a judgment, not a mother doting upon a child. *With the others too; we were wise to wait upon their coming as long as we did, though for a time there I think all of Keltia was of the opinion they would never come at all, and that after the haste and scandal of our elopement.* A sudden chill touched her, some wind from the future shivering her soul. *Yet Mighty Mother, how I do not like this venture beyond the Pale . . . It is almost as if she will be rashly daring some great malign attention to focus upon her, some droch-shuil that if she stayed at home would never be turned her way. Fomor is in it for certain, I can feel it; though I say I shall not have raised my daughter to see her fall to any son of Bres, or whelp of Alphor either. Goddess forbid it, Dôn and Dâna; and, Aoife, if you have any say where now you are—and I have not the smallest doubt but that you do—look after this successor of yours who bears the name you Saw to give her. It seems the least you can do for her; what shall become of Barraun and myself matters not, but if you fail in this you will answer to me . . .*

A light touch on her arm. "Mother?" said Aeron again, and Emer came back to herself, to see her daughter's green eyes peering anxiously up at her.

"Is anything wrong? You look so strangely—"

"Nay," said Emer, and patted her hand in reassurance, or for reassurance. "I was but thinking of what else you might stand in need of, once you are beyond the Wall. Let us look over what Nessa has packed for the journey."

As soon as she could see her chance, Aeron had slipped away from her Fian escort—it had been shamefully easy—and vanished into the crowds in the vast market-square. Making sure she had not been followed, she doubled back on her own steps a few times more and then relaxed into the day's festive mood. It was feast-day and market-day and high-day here on Clero, in the capital and chief trade-port of Lissnagall, and her own presence on the planet heightened still more the air of festival.

Which is very fine and well for them, she thought enviously.

But where is the holiday in it for me? Even the strictest duty allows for some leave; but so far it is not to be found . . . So she had had to escape; to contrive for herself some respite, however brief, from the intolerable ceremonial and protocol that of necessity attended on the visit of the Keltic heir to Clero. It had seemed that of all the folk on the planet, Aeron alone was not permitted to enjoy herself, and that had seemed hardly fair. So she had run away; and though they would find her soon enough and drag her back to her royal chores, for a while at least she would be free, and that would have to be enough to content her.

Once she was certain that she had in truth eluded pursuit, Aeron allowed herself to relax and look round at the bustle of the market. It was hard not to stare. *This place is like the galaxy in small—never have I seen so many galláin all in one place, or folk of so many other races all together* . . . Her secret hopeful wish was that she should meet, or at least see, a Terran, one of the Kelts' cousins from of old, but she knew that wish for the sheer spun fancy it was: The Terrans' path had not yet re-crossed that of the Kelts who had fled Earth three millennia since, and maybe would not do so for another three thousand years. Called though it was the Fort of the Foreigners, Lissnagall this day would harbor no folk from Earth.

Aeron wished she could be as confident that certain other out-Wall races were not present, but that too she knew for fancy. Open as it was to all who came to trade—and to those who only seemed to—Lissnagall, and the rest of Clero, was sure to be thick with Coranians and Fomori both; either members of the two hated races themselves—spies passing as nationals of better-liked kingdoms—or their agents, bought or bound by other covenants. In either case Aeron could find herself in real and sudden peril should she be recognized during her stroll by less than friendly eyes; but senses that Kesten had awakened and Struan had honed to high perfection told there was at present no danger anywhere nearby. She felt herself walking in some bubble of protection, an aura or force-field, almost, that moved with her as she went.

All the same, she thought, and it was the Fian who thought it, *this place is far too open for my liking; if open to infiltration, then surely open to plain attack—and both have happened before. There is little I can do about it just now, save to warn those who came with me and to stay sharp myself; but when I come home, I think I shall speak of it to my father and some of his Council. We must maintain such a place as this for trade, but that is no reason to allow enemies to come and go as they do please . . .*

But for all these grim thoughts, there was much to see that was of distinctly pleasanter stamp, and Aeron found herself watching the throbbing crowd with wonderment, even while noticing that she herself was being studied just as intently, though more covertly. Still none had seemed to recognize her, which was a great relief; in the haste of her unplanned escape she had had no time to put a disguising fith-fath upon herself, as she might otherwise have done, but had simply seized the moment when it came. But though she might not have been known for Aeron, she was surely known for a Kelt, for she heard herself being greeted more often in the Gaeloch—with varying accents and degrees of fluency—than in any other tongue, and she took a strange delight in both the Gaeloch and her own seeming invisibility. It was not Aeron, Tanista of Keltia, that these merchants were hailing, but merely another prospective buyer, a well-dressed young woman like many others here in the square, of obviously good birth and deep pockets. Though her lack of escort was a mark against her: Even galláin traders knew that no Kelt of decent family would be out in such a place without a "tail" of at least three persons.

Aeron felt a pang of guilt at the thought of that escort, who must even now be scouring the square in grim desperation, for if anything untoward befell their royal charge, the blame—rightly or wrongly—would be theirs and not her own, and that was not a thing she would wish on any. *Still, it is their own fault,* she thought, defiance struggling to color the guilt, *for had I not been smothered with duties but permitted a little time to myself, I should not have felt the need to flee . . .*

"So there you are, you wicked girl! How dare you run away!"

She whirled round, cheeks already crimsoning, but it was only a worried young father scooping up his strayed daughter, a giggling blond mite of no more than five. Aeron smiled at the sight, and peering shyly over her father's shoulder, the little girl smiled back at her in perfect understanding, as if they shared a secret, had each of them run away for the same reasons and knew the other knew it.

Cheered by the incident, Aeron continued her leisurely stroll through the maze of stalls. Vast though this marketplace was— easily five times the size of the huge market square at Caerdroia—it was the least important, if most colorful, of the business-arenas here on Clero. There were great elegant brughs on wide streets, Aeron knew, where sober-clothed merchants from every corner of the galaxy arranged trade contracts worth billions of crossics to Keltia; she herself would be shown off by the planetary officials to not a few of those traders, at the many official ceilis and audiences and receptions that comprised the chief part of her duties here.

She let her thought range over the sheer uniqueness of the place. Clero was Keltia's only ground of full and free contact with the out-Wall worlds it had so long stood aloof from, an outpost of commerce where Kelts and galláin could meet and mingle as they did in no other place. The only other Keltic holding beyond the Pale was Inishgall, the quarantine planet used to house, very temporarily, those few permitted into Keltia itself as ambassadors or guests; and that place was rigidly controlled. Here, matters were indeed more open, as she had already noticed: Anyone with legitimate commerce to transact was permitted to land and remain for as long as that business required— there were even permanent trading envoys in residence here in Lissnagall. But for all the easy interchange, the free trade and trafficking, Aeron knew very well how these same merchants who now chaffed her so casually would conduct themselves were they suddenly made aware of her identity.

For Fionnbarr Aoibhell was Ard-rígh here too; and to the people of the Keltic protectorates, many of whom did business and resided on this world, he was Imperator also, Emperor of the West—the proud and ancient title restored by Arthur himself and borne by every Keltic sovereign since. These folk would defer to her as daughter to the Imperator, herself one day to be Aeron Imperatrix among them, and never then would she be able to do as she was doing now.

All the more reason, then, to enjoy myself while I may . . . A stall caught her eye, and she paused to examine some of the beautifully crafted wares displayed for sale therein: elegantly embroidered long coats such as the Kutheran ladies favored, all gold and silver and furred brocade; barbaric jewels of jade and ivory, set in copper or the pale water-gold from Yjenar; puff-sleeved doublets that only great lords would wear, the dags and slashings bound round with silk and trimmed with river-pearls.

If she were to come by here as Aeron, she knew, the crafts-men would be only too delighted to load her down with any or all of these as gifts: gifts calculated in hopes of future trade, true enough, but still it seemed unfair, and she reached for the pouch at her belt . . . Doublets for her father and brothers; curved foreign daggers for Rhodri and Gwydion; jewels for her mother and grandmother and sisters; Kutheran coats for Morwen and Sabia: It was a happy and expensive hour before her escort at last came pouncing hard upon her. Though they came discreetly enough, and, to Aeron's mind, in good time to carry her pur-chases back to their palace lodgings—seeing the results of her marketing, she had been a little dismayed at the thought of conveying them herself—they were implacable in their insistence that Aeron must come along, and her escape was over.

She was not, however, to escape a scolding, and later in her rooms on the palace's east front she stood unflinching, if unre-pentant, to take the angry tongue-lashing being dealt her by the commander of the escort: none other than her own Rochana, Aeron's personal guard since the day she was born, and her friend for all that time.

"Have you naught to say for yourself, then, Aeron?" asked Rochana at last, having worn herself out with sheer solicitous wrath, while her charge seemed apparently untroubled. "Your father, if I may say it, would never have dreamed of slipping away so to alarm us."

At that Aeron sighed, though for the sake of old times shared her voice was gentle. "But I am *not* my father. Will all you never learn?"

Others there were that day beyond the Curtain Wall who spoke the name of Fionnbarr, though they spoke it with neither friend-ship nor love . . .

In the tall-storied graystone palace overlooking the city of Tory, on the planet of Fomor, Bres the king was staring, angry and baffled and neither of those for the first time, at his son and heir.

What in all the hells is *it with him?* he wondered privately. *I have just told him the most intriguing piece of news heard here for long—that Fionnbarr Aoibhell's daughter has ventured out from behind the Curtain Wall at last, is even now on their tradeworld Clero for a state visit—and for all the interest he shows, he might be on some other planet himself. Now Talorcan, when I told* him *the same news—*

But then there was little, if any, point in ever comparing Elathan with Talorcan, and Bres put the thought aside, for that thought these days too often led to others best not thought at all: chief among them the half-resentful, half-regretful wish—passionate desire, rather—that Talorcan the concubine's child were his legal heir and true successor, not Elathan the son of Basilea the Queen.

In the years since Ganaster, Bres had had such thoughts many times; since the birth of his two eldest children the thoughts had become more frequent still. When his Queen had informed him that she would bear him his heir, and all Fomor had rejoiced, Talorcan was already a year old, and since that time Bres had been so flagrantly faithful to Talorcan's mother that all Fomor had whispered—if that was the word—that in truth it was Thona who was queen, and the Queen but Bres's sidethought.

For a man so set on having his own way in all things, to be thwarted in, or by, his heir, was near intolerable; for a King, how much more so. And since what way he wished could never be, better it was not even to think it. *Yet he* drives *me to think it, so often . . .*

"I said—" began Bres again in a high sharp voice, but now Elathan, flushing a little, was looking him in the eye.

"Your pardon, lord; my mind was— You did say?"

Bres could not keep back a snort of annoyance. "I said nothing of any great import, Prince of Fomor; not beside that thought of yours." He paused, evidently expecting further contrition, but Elathan merely regarded him with cool politeness, and at length, in face of that amazing detachment, Bres capitulated and continued. "Well. The Keltic king's heir is tonight within striking distance of our forces on Bellator—should we choose to strike."

Elathan's undivided attention was suddenly fixed on his father. He was a young man of near Aeron's own age, tall and well-made, and of a great personal beauty, though of this last he himself seemed unaware: hair of a rare dark-gold color, clear brown eyes that now looked upon Bres with alarm and an indefinable distaste—which last Bres was only too well accustomed to see there, and it pleased him now no better than ever it did.

"Do you say then—" began Elathan.

"I say only that it is somewhat for us to consider." Bres's usual truculence seemed oddly compounded, as if there were more to this than he was prepared at present to admit, or would care to. "Think a little! Your own path, as King of Fomor and Archon of the Phalanx to follow me, would be much the smoother if this one were removed from it now, before she becomes Queen of Kelts to trouble you. I have heard much of her—"

"I too have heard." Elathan was silent, calling to mind what in fact he had heard: Aeron Aoibhell—there had been much reluctantly impressed report of her brilliance and beauty, of her great temper and greater talents, in magic and in war. His interest quickened: *She might well be someone I would wish to know, someone who might even be a friend to me and to Fomor, or more than friend* . . .

Bres spoke to scotch that thought half-born. "Then you must surely see that she will make a redoubtable enemy, and a great trial for you when you are King. She is much of an age with you and with Jaun Akhera of Alphor, so that it will fall to the three of you to carry on the quarrel when Fionnbarr and Strephon and myself have gone."

But Elathan was still caught up in his dream of friendship, and unwisely spoke it aloud. "Or to make peace among the three of us—"

"Do not say it even in jest!" The look Bres bent upon his son would have turned anyone else to frozen stone. "Should you as King attempt such a thing as *that*, your reign would be without a doubt the briefest in all the history of Fomor, and rightly so. I would come back from my tomb myself to turn you out."

"But Keltia—and Aeron?"

His father looked as if the very names dripped slow poison in his ear. "The time is not yet right," he said at last, reluctantly but firmly. "Even I can see that—much as I might wish it otherwise. It is tempting to think of this Aeron neatly dispatched before she can cause us the trouble she will surely one day cause, but I shall wait and hope for a better chance. The gods will give it us, and so I shall pray."

When the King had gone, the Prince sat on awhile alone. *If we persist in such unholy prayers, certainly there will never be any peace for any of us. But if—somehow—Aeron could be persuaded to join with me, and Jaun Akhera to join us both, and if we could then lead our realms to follow us, Phalanx and Cabiri Imperium and Keltia and her protectorates all after us like pigs on a string—would that not be a greater glory to our worlds than any war that ever was . . .*

He sighed and shifted in his chair. They would never allow it: not his father, nor the Council, nor the Phalanx lords, nor his half-brother Talorcan. Even his own mother, Queen Basilea, seemed to have some sort of private war with Keltia, though what could be the cause for that he had not the least idea, and in any case it seemed more a sorrow than a grudge.

I wish I knew more, he thought suddenly. *So ancient an enmity, and so little real knowledge of its roots or reasons . . .* He thought again of Aeron of Keltia, of the few facts he knew of her; what he had heard of those closest to her—the princes Gwydion Penarvon and Roderick Douglas, either of whom bid fair to be her future consort, and therefore King of Keltia to Aeron's High Queen, and both of whom were even at that moment ravaging Phalanx interests in several galactic sectors; her foster-sister Morwen Douglas and close friend Sabia ní Dálaigh (who would have been shocked to the marrow to learn that a foreign prince knew all about her); her seemingly innumerable siblings and cousins and fostern relations.

And that thought led inexorably to a familiar and bleak reflection of his own life as a prince of Fomor: the few friends he could count on; the strained relationships that afflicted House Corserine and the family of Magerus, not least among those last the long bitter estrangement of Bres and Basilea, and the liaison, longer still, between the King and the royal concubine, Lady Thona.

Even Elathan's own siblings seemed not entirely to be trusted: his hoyden sister, blond Rauni, Bres's pet; their young brother,

Tharic, barely out of the nursery; and of course Talorcan, the elder half-brother, demiroyal by Bres's own decree and full heir—after his three half-sibs—in the Fomorian succession.

The thorn pierced sharper still: Talorcan, not Elathan, had ever been the favored son of their father, and both of them had ever known it. The resentment, or disapproval, or whatever it might be, that Bres displayed to his heir before all of Fomor had inevitably influenced the younger children, so that Elathan had never been able to come as close to Rauni and Tharic as he, or they, might have liked. Aeron Aoibhell had been by all reports luckier far: Her family was well-known to be a close and loving one, a rare thing among royal kindreds. She had grown up among all their warmth and support, had never known a moment's doubt of her kin, never known what it was like to mistrust a brother, to suspect a friend, to be rebuffed by a parent—

Though that could be a bad weakness right there, reflected Elathan cynically, knowing even as he thought it that it was the kind of thought his father might have, and of which he certainly would approve. *Never having had cause to fear betrayal near at hand might result in a certain blindness, and a total devastation when such a betrayal came at last; and either of those might prove useful tools indeed to an enemy's hand . . .*

Suddenly revolted, Elathan shook himself and stood up. No thought of that for Aeron, at least not that he could see. As for himself—well, things were not so dark as sometimes in his despair they did seem. Though he might have no brother as did Aeron who would stand back to back with him, he did have one to stand beside him, one who was worth any number of brothers—Camissa of Broighter, his chosen betrothed, still scarcely more than a child herself—and he might even yet have a friend to stand to his other side. Whether that friend would be Aeron Aoibhell, as he hoped, or Jaun Akhera of Alphor, as his father hoped, Elathan would not know for years yet to come.

Though I know even now that it can never be both of them; if one is friend, then the other must as surely be enemy. Which one shall be which—in the end, that choice shall change all, for good or for ill; and there will be no going back from it, ever, for any of us.

Chapter 23

When Aeron came again to Scartanore, it was as if she had never been away. As the aircar that had brought her from the orbiting destroyer touched down outside the great gates, she looked up eagerly to where the windows of Kesten's chambers stood open to the summer day. But no one looked down from those tall oriel bays, and Aeron felt a twinge. *Does my teacher not even think enough of my returning to greet me with a welcome-back . . .* Then it came to her where she must go for her welcome. *But I shall not ride this time; their patience, great though it be, would scarce stand for it.*

With a smile, she ordered the craft airborne again, and dismissing the Fian pilot who had flown it took her place at the controls, heading south by west, for the valley of the Roaringwater.

"We thought you would surely come here first," explained Tybie, pouring out for her guest another mether of ale.

"I was something slow of thinking today," admitted Aeron, recognizing with delight the beautiful old carved mether, made of dark fine-grained wood, that she had so often drunk from on past afternoons very much like this. "No doubt overwrought by the fact of my return—"

Kesten laughed indulgently from across the chamber's width, where she had arranged herself in comfort on a pile of furs and pillows to await with Tybie their star pupil's arrival. *Though she is in truth a pupil no more,* she thought. *All the same—*

"How many times must I remind you, Aeron-fach—"

"—that feeling will be my death," recited Aeron dutifully, "if I learn not to temper it with thought. But I *have* done so, somewhat: I am sure that Struan Cameron, or Donal mac Avera, or Tirechan who was my chief tutor at the Hill of Laws, will have sent you instructive reports over the past four years."

Kesten nodded. "Oh aye . . . and I read them all, and was not displeased with any. Not *greatly* displeased . . . You did well at the triail-triarach."

"Well enough." Aeron found that, much as she wished to do so, she could not speak of what had happened in the stone clochan; it was as if a remembered hand had closed round her throat in warning—a hand whose spectral grip would tighten should she try to force her words past.

"It is not for us to hear," said Tybie, divining at once the truth of it. "But tell us instead what you may rightly speak of—for a Sister of the order, you have been a lamentable correspondent."

But she was laughing as she said it, and Aeron blushed and laughed too, and the afternoon passed quickly by, so that it was time for Kesten and Aeron to return to Scartanore.

Tybie accompanied them outside, where the aircar and its bored pilot had waited on their departing, but crossing the faha Aeron turned suddenly away, and strode purposefully over the sloping ground to where the waterfall, before it flowed down to join the Roaringwater, foamed and writhed above its little pool.

She stood there for so long, staring down into the stream's clear bubbling depths, that Kesten frowned in concern; but Tybie lifted a hand and shook her head, and went to Aeron herself.

"What is it?" she asked after a while, when Aeron still showed no apparent intent to speak. "All is well at home—with the Ard-rígh and the Queen?"

Aeron nodded. "It was well enough when last I did see them . . . Nay, this coil is mine alone: a matter I must decide for myself."

"But, I think, not a matter which must bear upon you alone."

The girl gave a laugh that was a little harsh, a little despairing. "How could it! I am Tanista; whatever I do works upon Keltia, as Keltia must work upon me. I must myself be judge of what is right and best, for Keltia and for me."

"But?"

"But—only tell me, ban-leginn, how shall I be judged in turn?"

'*Ban-leginn*,' thought Tybie. '*Woman of learning*'—that title given by a student to a teacher, usually one only in a lifetime of study, who has had the deepest and broadest and widest effect on that student's life and mind. Tears veiled her vision; though she feigned it was but mist from the cataract, both of them knew that it was not.

"The judges of this world matter but little, Aeron-fach," said Tybie presently, recovering herself. "When it comes to the greater judgment, the one that you yourself must pass upon yourself when your next turn upon the Wheel is the stake, the brehon in your soul will not let you escape strict justice. That judging is the same for each of us, whether we have been in life daer-fudir or perfected saint. Besides, and this you know as well as I, we are judged then by the highest in ourselves, not by the lowest: The noblest and finest thought or deed of which we have proved capable in life shall determine our dán in death. Here in the body, we see not so clearly, and so we torture ourselves through all our lives by our failings and fallings and what we or others call our sins. But when we are free the standard is other wise, and that is by grace of the Shepherd of Heaven; not by Kelu alone but by all gods together; not by them alone but by our own high selves. We are made to see those lowest not as sins but as errors; not to be punished for them but to learn from them; and we are judged not by the depths to which we may have fallen but by the heights to which we have climbed. Those heights will be different as our souls are different, and, aye, some higher than others; for a time, for a time only. Some will take longer to learn to climb, while others will reach the heights in only one leap or two. But in the end, Aeron, all will reach them; this is the promise of the Mother to all Her children."

Aeron's face, that had been clouded still, had cleared as her teacher had spoken, and now lighted from within.

"And if sometimes a child of Hers forgets, no matter; the promise stands the same. But let us go back to Kesten; I think I have kept the Magistra waiting on my forgetfulness long enough."

Aeron's Domina year passed swiftly and smoothly, interrupted now and again for state duties that Fionnbarr could not, or would not, spare her. But those were neither many nor onerous, and for the most part her year was undisturbed by outside demands.

That year was consecrated to magic and to contemplation; a thing she would have welcomed in any circumstances, being by nature that way inclined, but Aeron, knowing as she did that these days were the last when she should have freedom and the luxury of time to study as she pleased, cherished the months all the more, and made good use of them.

It was different from her earlier instruction at Scartanore, though she laughed at her own initial surprise that it should be so. Beyond a few training sessions under the guidance of senior preceptresses, in certain techniques of sorcery that were strictly reserved to a Ban-draoi's Domina year—her own sister Ríoghnach was even her tutor for a class or two, having come as Kesten had once foreseen into the early flowering of her genius for pure magical theory, and was in such matters already far above even Kesten herself—and of course the old tutorials with the Magistra, there were no formal classes and no set pattern of study. Aeron taught herself now, and it seemed to those who discreetly invigilated that her progress—and her power—grew visibly from day to day.

But the year's wheel spun the same whether that was so or no, and soon it was coming on again for Samhain, holiest night of the year for Kelts, and the night on which, amid the solemn celebrations of the New Year, the Sisters of the Ban-draoi were accustomed to raise their own from priestess to High Priestess.

When Aeron entered Kesten's study this time, there was about her none of the diffidence or uncertainty that had plagued her in previous interviews; she was no more either the shy novice she had been at thirteen or the hopeful candidate she had been four years later, desperate to be found acceptable as a Ban-draoi, terrified that the Magistra would find her flawed. Now she came in confidence, sure of herself and her powers, and as she came into the old familiar room that confidence seemed to enfold her like a shining mantle.

Kesten watched her come. *Holy Mother,* she thought behind deep shields to hide her delight *but was I not right about this one! That first day I saw her as a child—and what a day* that *was, when she made the sun dance over half Tara, and she barely nine years old—I knew then, though I dared not burden Fionnbarr with it, what she would in time become. She has mastered herself well for the most part, and her power with it; now we can only wait, all of us, to see how she will use them both.*

"I know I need not tell you," said Kesten aloud. "But allow an old woman a few poor satisfactions. Be seated."

Aeron laughed and took her usual chair. "It seems I have spent years and lives here," she remarked, running her hands over the smooth wood of the curved arms. "A seat more to my liking, maybe, than ever the Throne of Scone shall be—but that is part of what we shall speak of now, not so?"

"Very much so." Kesten touched her fingers to the silver collar of office at her throat, as she so often did in a reflex gesture she could somehow not break herself from, as if she sought reassurance in the metal's chill splendor. "Well. In years to come, it may be that you and I will not be given another chance to speak fully and frankly; you will soon be confirmed as Tanista and take up full duties as your father's successor, to bear the Silver Branch. I am a member of the High Council, as I have been these forty years past; I have served Lasairían, and Fionnbarr, and though I will serve you as heir it is in my heart that I will not come to serve you as Queen." She waved away Aeron's protest. "Nay, come, we know better than that . . . In a fortnight's time you will be made Domina, a high priestess of the order of the Ban-draoi, and there has not been a High Queen of Keltia who was also Domina since the time of Líadan Ard-rían."

"My great-great-great-grandmother—"

"A gifted sorceress, but—I speak plainly now—she had not *your* gifts." A sudden smile warmed the wintry face. "Nor yet the gifts your sister Ríoghnach has been granted—she is a keen thinker now, but she will be a far more formidable theorist in time, and many things will change because of the work she will accomplish. But I speak now of Aeron only."

"I think I know what you would say, Mathra'chtaran." *Reverend Mother:* an ancient title of the Ban-draoi Magistras, seldom used in these latter days. Aeron used it now, deliberately and with love, and the sound and sense of it brought tears to Kesten's fine eyes.

"So this is how you do—you make Tybie weep when you arrive to begin your year, and you make your Magistra weep when you come to complete it."

Aeron took the mock chiding for what it was. "Ah, to my very great sorrow, I think those tears are by no means the first you both have shed on my account: tears of rage, and frustration, and despair too, most like. I know I have been no easy pupil."

"That you have not been! But as I told your parents and your aunt Keina that day they came to fetch you home, the biddable ones never amount to much in the end, and so Tybie and I grudged neither the labor nor the tears . . ." Returning to her topic: "I know you already know what I shall say, but I will say it all the same. You are Tanista, soon to be Domina, later to be Ard-rían. Great powers will be at your command as High Queen; but greater ones are yours even now—to be confirmed, only, in two weeks' time, not conferred. Fionnbarr and Emer and many others have trained you in your duties as Ard-rían, and I have no fears at all for you there."

Aeron's gaze, clear and steady, lifted a little. "But it was you and Tybie did most of my real training as Ban-draoi and Domina, do you then have fears for me *there*?"

"It is only the fool never fears . . . I know we have taught you to the best of our bent, and I know you have learned to the best of yours. There will ever be doubts—I doubt myself at times, so must all if they are truly wise—and we have spoken before now of the ground of my chief misgiving for you."

"In that I act from feeling," said Aeron, not at all vexed to hear her teacher speak so, for it was pure truth, "and not from thought. No one has considered this more often or more carefully than I; but I think it is less true now than it has been formerly." She leaned forward, and, covering the Magistra's strong thin hand with her own, placed her other hand over her heart, as all Keltic oaths were sworn. "I cannot promise I shall always act from the right," she said quietly, "or that I shall be always wise in my exercise of power. But I *can* swear, and do so to your presence, that I will never act from power without true cause."

"That is what I have waited to hear you say. It is enough." Kesten's hand tightened on Aeron's for an instant, then gently disengaged, and the younger woman rose, knowing the interview was ended and its purpose accomplished.

"One thing more," added Kesten casually, as Aeron reached out for the door-latch. "In the rite that will make you Domina, you will choose—doubtless have already chosen—certain influences to guide and guard you in your magical undertakings. You are under no compulsion to reveal these beforehand, even to the Magistra, but—''

''—but you in your unworthy and very human curiosity would know the choices I have made,'' said Aeron with a grin, delighted to see Kesten's cheeks color a little as she gave an unapologetic nod. ''The Magistra has only to ask.''

''And you do love to make me—who shall you take, then, for patron?''

''At my saining I was placed in the patronage of my foremother Dâna, as a certain Magistra who assisted in the rite will no doubt recall. It comes to me, I know not why, that it is a link I would reaffirm and strengthen.''

''And for protector?''

''The Faol-mór, the fetch of the Aoibhells. He is an old friend, that wolf of ours, and I think will be a better friend yet.''

''And for dewin-arwydd?'' That was to say magical emblem, the totemic symbol chosen by every sorcerer in Keltia to stand for the soul of one's magic. The choice was different for each, as different as were each's various magics: It could be beast or bird, tree or flower, sea or stone, field or mountain or any other power of nature—any spirit of the natural world, to be as balance to those other influences that were of worlds beyond nature. The dewin-arwydd gave form and direction, as the protector gave strength and the patron conferred blessing.

Like any sorcerer, Aeron had given much thought to all these choices, since they would rule her magic for all her life to come; as for this last choice, she had made it long since, and spoke it now without hesitation.

''Saille,'' she said. ''The willow tree, that grows tall in peaceful summers and yet can bend to endure the blast.''

The door closed behind her then, and still Kesten did not stir. *Those are all three of them fine and far-seeing choices*, she thought after a while. *But that last one—that last may prove to be the most far-sighted Seeing of all.*

The Magistra Kesten thought nearer to the mark than she could ever know. For Aeron was not the only royal heir who came that year to full stature as sorcerer: On the desert world of Alphor, seat of the Cabiri Emperor Strephon, another magician was being made—one that Aeron, and Keltia with her, would come to know in future years better than they liked, and in ways other than they would have chosen.

But just now it was a clear cloudless day out in the sandy wastes beyond the gates of Escal-dun his capital, where Strephon, flanked by members of his family and court, stood in the cool morning stillness before the feet of a stone colossus. He was silent, as were all the rest of them, and his eyes were fixed even as were theirs on the double doors let into the base of the stone edifice.

His daughter Helior stood beside him. She had, much to Strephon's interest, put off at last the blue mourning garments she had so pointedly worn for the past months, ever since the day her father the Emperor had executed for treason the husband he himself had chosen for her.

And that was one of the poorest choosings I ever made, thought Strephon. *I freely admit it; but also I think that Phano's passing was perhaps not entirely a grief to his wife and sons; certainly Helya seemed more concerned that the taint of his treason—and I admit too it was a bold and clever plot—should not cling to those sons; and chiefly anxious that of the two of those sons it should not touch Jaun Akhera the eldest.*

He shifted his stance a little, and all around him he felt their attention shift in response, as a pool will ripple where a casual stone has been tossed in. *Well, she knows I dote on Akhi; have I not reared him to become Prince of Alphor, accepted her resignation of succession rights in his favor, put him through this . . . Does she still think I could set him aside after all that? All the same, perhaps it is better that she should not be entirely sure; uncertainty is a sharper goad, and a firmer surety of conduct, than complacence . . .*

He broke off his musings as a sound of stone moving in sand-gritted grooves came from the belly of the towering monument before him. Part eagle, part lion, part rough nightmare beast, the colossus crouched in the drifted sand like some great watchful stone monster. It was the Maitagarri, the place of initiation for those would become adepts of the Cabiri, the order of priest-sorcerers who had given their name to this empire; who had, many thousands of years since, given victory by their magic to the Telchine race, back in the last days of Atlantis; those

Telchines who had become the root-race of the Coranians, as their defeated adversaries the Danaans had become the progenitors of the detested Kelts.

But that seemed to Strephon scarcely to be thought of now, as he watched the darkness gape in the beast's stone belly, where at any moment now the new Cabiri adepts would emerge, and by the favor of Auset Jaun Akhera would be among them. The candidates, all young men of Alphor of good family and more than average talent for magic, had been shut in the deep places of the Maitagarri for the past three days and nights, for twelve of those hours sealed up in stone tombs—that for some became their tombs in sad earnest. Strephon, recalling his own initiation so many decades ago, felt his bones ache at the memory of those hours stretched out in utter blackness upon the unforgiving stone, and then there came a flutter of movement within the darkness just past the doors.

A small cadre of young men stepped blinking into the growing dawnlight, their orange silk robes, newly and proudly donned, glowing like flame against the sand. Strephon, searching their ranks for the face he longed so desperately to see, heard Helior exclaim in delight and relief, and followed her gaze to where the Imperial Heir walked among his fellow priests.

He has filled out much in the past year, in body as well as in spirit—tall he is, and well-grown, and pleasant to look upon . . . "He will make a fine Cabiri, and a fine Emperor to follow me," Strephon heard himself saying. "Glad am I that I have such an etcheko-primu—" *Though of course he has not been officially named so just yet . . .* He scarcely heard the chorus of sycophantic agreement that rose around him, as his eyes met his grandson's; and, not breaking his measured stride among his comrades, Jaun Akhera withdrew his hands from the depths of his wide sleeves and raised them to his grandsire in formal greeting.

Oh yes, thought Strephon, returning the courtesy, *this one will surely be the one that is wanted. I said long ago that I should one day have need of someone to reel in for me such wily fish as Bres of Fomor; to send out in harder hunts against still cleverer foes—Keltia itself, maybe even. I think my need is met.*

*   *   *

It was about that time when dán struck suddenly, in a manner none of those it most closely concerned had foreseen; or would have easily accepted if they had.

Upon completing her Ban-draoi studies, having received at Kesten's hands the rank of Domina, the silver collar and the blessing of the Magistra that went with it, Aeron had begun her service with the Fianna. She served as her father and his Council saw fit to send her: Already she had put in time as cavalry and chariotry adjutant to the great commanders Maravaun of Cashel and Hollin Macdonald and Tegau Rhanddir; as aide to her great-uncle Elharn aboard the flagship *Firedrake,* wonder of the Keltic starfleet; and as ensign to Ranait of Ulidia, a princess like herself, who was Ship-lord of the Scotan sea-navies.

She had seen combat, too, far beyond the Curtain Wall; even those who were hardest on her—out of love or out of envy, it made no differ—were forced to admit that she acquitted herself well and bravely. That came as no surprise to her own folk; the surprise was all belonging to the galláin, astounded anew that the Kelts should permit—encourage, rather—their royal heirs to engage in deadly war so far from home, in a cause arguably not even theirs. Which only proved anew that they did not know their enemy, and had learned but little from the conflicts of the past: Keltia held sacred indeed her obligations to defend her Protectorates against those who sought to annex them, either by open force or stealthy attack—more sacred, certainly, than those same would-be conquerors held their own attempts, for seldom did it take more than a few sharp exchanges before the aggressors fled before the sting of the Keltic lash.

Aeron was far from unique or alone in her martial exploits beyond the Pale: At times it seemed that half the flower of Keltic youth was out there with her. Morwen, and Deio Drummond, and Sabia, and Rohan, her Kerrigan cousins Solais and Trystan and her Aoibhell cousins Slaine and Desmond: All came and went as Aeron did under orders. Rhodri and Gwydion too continued their military careers; though by now both had covered themselves with glory, having risen to the rank of full captain of the Fianna, cath-milid, and so were rather removed from the orbit of mere lieutenants such as Aeron. But they were ever to be found where the fight was fiercest; she had encountered them both, more than once—even come under their orders from time to time—in the course of her own service.

That week of high summer, Gwydion was at Caerdroia, on a flying visit to report to Donal mac Avera at the Fian Commandery, which stood across the Great Square from the palace of Turusachan; and by happy coincidence Aeron was home just then on brief leave. Neither of them had much leisure, for Gwydion had just received from his Captain-General the command of a full sector squadron—a great achievement for one of his years—and Aeron herself had recently qualified as starship captain and been given a small destroyer to command; the continuing out-Wall hostilities could spare neither of them for very long.

But they had contrived to spend some happy hours together, and now on this last day before his departure Gwydion was waiting for her to come to him from the morning audiences to which she accompanied her father. Though he would indeed be leaving Caerdroia that day, it would not now be as had been planned: There had been news for him an hour ago, from Gwynedd, and Aeron would have to be told, if she did not already know of it; for it would in the end affect her near as much as it had already affected him.

Aeron came laughing into the room—*nay*, he thought, *clearly she does not yet know, and that is well, for I would rather she hear this from me*—but seeing the look on his face, she let the laughter fade out of hers.

"What is it?" She put out a hand to him, and reached out with her mind, almost impatiently, to know his thought.

But for perhaps the first time ever the gray eyes would not meet hers, and in his mind was a rigid barrier, strong as findruinna and just as impenetrable. *What is he holding back?* she wondered with rising terror. *It must be something fearful, never have I seen him look so . . .*

"My father is dead," said Gwydion presently. "A hunting accident. My mother has just spoken to me—told me— His horse fell at a stone wall; he broke his neck and died instantly. The horse died too," he added inconsequentially, and looked up at her at last.

Seeing those eyes Aeron ran to him and put her arms around the bowed shoulders. "Ah, my heart, do not!" They stayed so for a moment, her arms about him and her head bent to his; then, ever so slightly Gwydion's shoulders straightened, and she drew away at once.

"My sorrow for my foster-father," said Aeron softly, not in the least offended by his characteristic retreat into himself. "I loved Arawn-maeth as dearly as my own father . . . Now, if he will allow it, I shall accompany the Prince of Gwynedd to Caer Dathyl for the funeral rites."

Though she had spoken so softly that scarce did he hear her with his ears, the title she had chosen to use exploded like sudden thunder in his mind. *'Prince of Gwynedd'* . . . *the first time I am called so; gods, I did not even think to think it* . . .

Aeron could see that he had not, that the realization of his own new sovereignty was a naked shock to him; no consolation but only a bitter ironic compounding of his loss. *Salt in his wounds,* she thought, watching him battle with it. *Is that what it must be like for me, when I come to my own heirship's end, my own accession? A terrible policy, that makes one's parent perish before one's lifework can begin* . . .

"I shall miss Arawn," she whispered, and felt him tremble; she brushed the tears from his cheek with gentle fingertips and never noticed as she did so that her own face was streaming. "Come, let us go to the King. He will want to speak to his friend's son of the passing of his friend."

At Caer Dathyl a week later, once the solemn business had been concluded of setting the dead Prince upon his last road with fitting ceremony and confirming the new Prince in his reign— Gwydion had put his foot resolutely down on any talk of a coronation, doing only what was mandated by the brehon law to seal his accession to his father's title, though a formal crowning would have to be held at some future time—things were slowly settling down again after the vast dislocation caused by Arawn's utterly unexpected death.

It had been as great a shock to the folk of Gwynedd and the other Kymric systems, indeed to all the Keltic worlds, as it was to the Penarvon family and their connected kindreds. But for all their stunned sorrow, they felt at the same time a certain uncertainty concerning the new lord of their planet.

Though few of his folk had dared to think, and none had dared suggest, that Gwydion might not be equal to the task of planetary command, the feeling was there all the same, a vague disquiet. He was young for it, they murmured among themselves; he had only just turned thirty; he had other calls upon him; he was more inclined to sorcery and battle than to the demands of daily politics and governance . . . There was no breath of criticism, nor smallest intimation that he lacked strength of mind or will or arm to prove an effective ruler for Gwynedd; only a notion, or perception perhaps, that he might be better contented elsewhere; or that, having so much else upon his shoulders, he himself might welcome a regency, at least a limited one, to spare him some labors, though he was of course of full age by three years to rule in his own right.

Those who thought so would have been surprised indeed to learn that Gwydion himself, at one dark hour or another over the past week, had entertained every last one of those very same doubts—had confessed them aloud, even, to Aeron, and to Gwenedour his mother, and to Fionnbarr, who with Emer had come to bid their last farewells to their friend Arawn. But though he had weighed most finely all their reasons and reassurances— and of all those it was the High King's which had counted most with the new Prince; they had talked for hours together, gravely and alone—in the end the decision to accept entirely the coronet that had fallen to him was very much Gwydion's own; and once that decision had been made as plain to his people as it now was to himself, there was no further thought either of abdication or of regency.

One alone there had been who had done more than think of it: Powell Prince of Dyved, Arawn's foster-brother, who was now by Keltic law closest male kin to Arawn's three children, had gone so far as to press his own fitness for regency—and his company—upon the widowed Princess Gwenedour.

Powell's hopes had been short-lived by any measure: Gwydion, with Aeron—and, by implication, Turusachan itself—standing behind him, had responded curtly and coldly to Powell's suggestions; Elved and Arianeira, though their brother had not attempted to influence them in any way, had done the same, and Powell had withdrawn in embarrassment and fury.

None ever knew what Gwenedour had said to her husband's fostern—Gwydion himself did not learn of Powell's unwelcome advances until years later, in vastly altered circumstances—but the effect was seen to be the same. Powell took ship with almost indecent haste for his home planet of Dyved, and the family, in their sorrow and distraction, put it out of their minds. But Gwydion, for one, did wrong to forget his rejection and his foster-uncle's response to that rejection, for surely Powell did not forget . . .

But all that was yet to come: For the moment, it was the moment that must be endured. To that end, Aeron remained at Caer Dathyl a while longer, with her father's reluctant permission and very much against her mother's will—Fionnbarr and Emer had returned to Tara, taking young Elved with them, once the rites for Arawn were accomplished—but entirely in accordance with her own wishes.

She walked with Gwydion now under the peony-trees in the palace gardens. It was winter on Gwynedd, and the branches that had once bent with blossom to shelter them as they lay beneath were bare now, and sheathed in black ice from the previous night's storm.

"I have thought much of the future this past fortnight," she said without preamble. "For good or for ill, I would speak now, lest there be no time to speak later; I am sorry for it, for the matter I would speak of bears on you, and you have had to bear overmuch already . . . You know my parents wish me to wed Rhodri Douglas one day; in truth, they have done all but command me to do so, and I have no doubt but that such command will come." She did not look at him as she spoke, but stared straight ahead down the line of trees, and her voice was low and unstressed. "I would tell you now that it is not the choice I would make had I alone the choosing; if it must be, it will be by no means a permanent choice—and there will be a very different choice to be made afterward, if . . . well, if."

"And for all that," he said, "it is no ill fate." Gwydion stopped under the black canopy of branches and turned her to face him. "Aeronwy, you need not fear for me, now or later; and you need not fear for us ever. I have told you so before, and I tell you now again. Things will not change between you and me, or between Rhodri and me, or between Rhodri and you. There is no problem here, unless you insist on creating one."

There came a clatter from overhead, as the ice-coated trees moved together in a sudden wind. "You know this?" breathed Aeron at last, not daring to look at him. "Can it be? I have thought—"

"Aye, and aye again. I know what you have thought and hoped for, for I have thought and hoped the same. Even my father believed you and I should be together in the end; though we never spoke openly of it . . . This is but one step of all the steps you must take upon a long and difficult path; but it is *your* path. Some of those steps you must take with others—with Rhodri, if that is to be your dán and his—and not with me; not yet with me. You and I shall have our time to walk together, doubt it not."

"I do not doubt," she said after a while. "But it is that first step that costs."

"Aye," he answered at once. "But the last step that counts."

But that night when Gwydion returned to his own chambers after the day's many labors, long past owl-time, cold and sad and weary, a shadow stirred in the corner just past the dying fire. Before his warrior's instincts could bid him draw blade, other, deeper, instincts had told him there was no need to, and before his tired brain could puzzle it out in words he was holding out a hand to her, all his cares and griefs and troubles falling away.

Aeron came forward into the firelight, cloaked in a black mantle over the fall of her unbound hair, white skin gleaming through the red-gold strands. "I wanted you, and I did not want you to be alone this night, and I am here," she said, and let the mantle slip to the cold floor.

Chapter 24

"The Ard-rígh did summon me?"

Called by her father to the Presence Chamber, Aeron had not expected to find what she had just found there: Fionnbarr, still of bearing and grave of face, seated in his gilded chair beneath the canopy of state, the queen's chair empty beside him, and all the chamber empty as well.

If I am called for reprimand, best that it be dealt in private; but if I am to take a scolding, this is a strange place for my father to choose to give it me . . . But Fionnbarr made no answer—indeed Aeron's question had been tantamount to demanding an explanation of her father, and in any case she should not have spoken first—and with a sigh Aeron drew herself up and came forward to stand before the dais. She gave him the salute of the Fianna but made no other obeisance and spoke no other word, standing straight, waiting for the Ard-rígh to address her.

And still Fionnbarr said nothing, studying his daughter's face and mien and manner as if he had never seen her before. *As perhaps I have not,* he thought with a pang. *She has been long apart from us who love her; it had to be so, but I wish it might have been other wise* . . . But those years the King regretted had produced a true princess: Aeron stood before him now tall and straight and unafraid, her green eyes gazing levelly into his hazel ones. *She is grown lovely too; she has her mother to thank for that—though true enough the hair comes through me—and will be lovelier still when she has more years on her . . But this is not what I have called her here to tell her.*

"Ironbrow gives me excellent report of your latest tour of duty," he said at last.

"So my great-uncle the Prince Elharn has told me, Ard-rígh."

Fionnbarr hid a smile. *She cloaks her doubt and fear in formality; I myself did just so at her age . . .* "And you will be twenty-seven years of age in a month's time."

The smile her father had hidden flickered now at Aeron's mouth. "So my mother the Queen of Keltia has told me, Ard-rígh."

At that her father laughed out loud and unbent. "Well, no more suspense then: I have put it to my Councils that I wish you to be invested formally as Tanista on the day you turn twenty-seven, and entrusted with the bearing of the Silver Branch, and to this they have most willingly agreed." He raised a brow at the look on Aeron's face. "Surely this had occurred to you as a likely thing? You have been called Tanista since the hour I became King, but the Tanistry is not yours—nor any other heir's—until it is lawfully bestowed in full court ceremony. It is as you know most frequently conferred at the age of general majority, which is twenty-seven—though in law you could not hold the Throne unregented for six years more, should it come to that."

Aeron instinctively made a warding gesture, to fend off evil mischance. "Aye so, but the Silver Branch does not of necessity go with it. Most heirs do not receive the scepter from the monarch's hand until they have further proved themselves, and their worthiness to bear it."

"Well," said Fionnbarr, "you have proved yourself quite worthy enough for me. Your deeds in combat this past year alone have confirmed that; else neither Elharn nor mac Avera had sponsored you to take valor as a knight of Keltia, as they did and as I was proud to bestow . . . But it is the monarch alone who determines as to when his heir shall receive the Silver Branch. I had it from my father at thirty-three, what time I reached full age to rule unregented if my own dán had ordered it so. But, you know, your grandfather Lasairían had to wait for it almost to the very year that Aoife his mother died."

Aeron smiled, though again she made the small warding gesture she had made earlier. "I would be happy to wait longer still for it, so that it meant my father lived as long before he gave it me."

"Ah, cariadol, I know that! But that is just the great irony of monarchy: A king or queen spends time and pains in the rearing of an heir, then must die before seeing what manner of monarch has been in truth trained up. That is kingship's flaw and failing. I shall never see you High Queen, that is the way of it: unless I should fall ill enough to resign the Copper Crown to you, or the folk should vote to depose me for cause. But if you take up the Silver Branch as soon as lawfully you may, then at least I shall have that to content me. And—selfishly, I admit—I shall have you to assist me as well; for you will have many official duties once you are formally Tanista and hold the Branch that you have managed thus far to escape.''

Aeron made an amused despairing face. "Oh aye, I know well what *that* shall mean! Progresses, and court sessions, and—''

"—*and* Council chairings, *and* presiding in the House of Peers, and anything else I can think to get out of by passing it over to you.'' Fionnbarr smiled. "Does it please you, then?''

"And if it did not,'' said Aeron with a laugh, "there would always be Rohan to pass it off on in my turn! Nay,'' she said, suddenly grave, "it pleases me very well, so that the King of Kelts is pleased.''

"Done, then.'' Fionnbarr stood up, satisfied, and descending the steps of the dais put his arm around his daughter's shoulders, startled anew to realize she was but an inch or two less tall than he himself. "Now let us go and tell your mother our news.''

The day of Aeron's investiture dawned cool and bright: the sixth of October, her twenty-seventh birthday. When faithful old Nessa came in to draw back the heavy curtains, as she had done every morning here at Turusachan since Aeron was a babe, for the first time ever she found her charge not only awake, but bathed and fully clad.

"I should have done all this for you,'' she grumbled, setting to rights Aeron's shimmering formal apparel: the stiff silk gown of royal green, the heavy jewels of gold and pearl and emerald, the purple mantle, trailing in a thirty-foot train, embroidered in gold and silver thread with the armorial bearings of the heir to the Throne of Scone. "Not fitting, that the Tanista should be her own tiring-woman on the day of her investing—''

Aeron dropped a kiss on the top of the old woman's head.

"Still less fitting, that you should have to do so for her; I think the Tanista is well able, after all this time, to dress herself."

"Ah, sweeting, that is not the point—" began Nessa with a broad smile, tears of pride and love in the still-keen blue eyes. "But sit now; at the least I will arrange your hair for the day. You must wear it loose, you know."

"Be sure to brush it straight out, Nessa, else this will not sit evenly upon her head." Emer had come in, and was watching with a smile from the doorway. In the Queen's hands was something wrapped in purple velvet, the fabric's rich pile thin and bare with age, and it was this she now held out to her daughter.

Aeron took it a little hesitantly, for she knew well what the velvet enfolded, and turned back the worn stuff with careful fingers. Hearing Nessa's gasp of wonder, she smiled and held up to the light the thing the cloth had shrouded: a fillet of silver, a browband, its knotwork panels deeply incised and inlaid with black enamel, set at intervals with round studs of water-clear rock crystal. There was an air of many years upon it, yet no sign of age: no chip in any stone, no nick in the heavy silver, no fleck of enamel missing from its bed in the softly glowing metal.

"The cathbarr of Nia the Golden," said Emer. "It has not been worn since the time of Aoife Ard-rían. For some reason your father and grandfather did not feel enough at ease with it to set it upon their heads; there was no cause for them to feel so, though perhaps it does sit easier upon a woman's brow—or, to say it the other way, perhaps a woman has greater strength to match its own. But man and woman alike have worn it down the years—Nia gave it to her son Brendan, and *he* wore it often, and passed it on in turn to his own son, and that son to his daughter, and on, and now it comes to you. I spoke of it to your father, when first we discussed the plans for this day, and we agreed that you should wear it. Put it on."

Aeron lifted the cathbarr to eye level and looked into the clean clear brilliance of the center stone, set into the frontlet piece: square-cut, bigger than the other gems—over an inch across— and more elaborately faceted in a more antique style. She caught something from the stone then, some sense of doom or history, or of dán perhaps yet to come. *This one is different from the others; a sacred stone of Eruinn—ancient Ireland—or of Atland itself, even; or older still, from the Danaans' first home . . .*

A gleam came of color and movement in the crystal's depths: Aeron unfocused her gaze quickly and as quickly focused her othersight, to "look-past" in the Ban-draoi way to see what might be seen. But the visions locked within the jewel, if visions there were, veiled themselves from her, and with a little inward reverence to the stone and its secrets Aeron held out the fillet to her mother.

"Nay," she said, "I would ask the Queen to place it upon my head, if she would do me such grace; and I would beg my mother's blessing as she does so."

Emer, much moved at the request, fitted the silver band around her daughter's forehead, murmuring the traditional blessing, and then stepped back, smiling at the surprise plain on Aeron's face.

As the metal had settled chill and close around her temples, Aeron had raised her hands to touch it, to adjust its fit, and now she looked at Emer in amazement.

"It is as if the smith did have my very measure! It fits to perfection—yet you said just now Brendan and other kings did wear it, and surely their brows were broader round than mine."

"He who wrought it had the measure of all who would ever come to wear it," said Emer. "And he did his work excellent well: his smithwork, and his—other work. Be glad it sits so light upon you. But now," she said, moving to the door, "no more delay. The Ard-rígh waits upon the Queen to go with him to the Hall of Heroes; and all Keltia waits upon the Tanista to follow."

"Well," said Aeron lightly, to put as bold a face as she might upon it, though her heart was suddenly hammering and her blood was ice down to her toes, "they cannot begin without me."

It was Aeron's first full-dress court ceremony; or at any rate the first in which she had herself to be the chief actor. Though there had been endless instruction over the past fortnight, from her mother and grandmother and the various court and household officers charged with the smooth running of such events, and endless rehearsals to boot, still she was numb with apprehension; and now, as she stood alone outside the great beaten-copper doors of the Hall of Heroes—all her attendants had left her, had arranged her train and her cloak and smoothed out her hair and had gone—she felt a wave of nervousness wash over her to swamp all her confidence.

I would rather face battle ten thousand times over—I feel like the greenest actor who ever set foot on stage, or some new-made bard about to chant in company for the first time . . . this is foolishness. But fight them how she might, the fears kept returning to lap round her in little cold wavelets, rising higher and higher. *Foolishness perhaps; but it is also Inadacht-na-laithe, the path to the kingship, and I must step out upon it.*

Moved by instinct, or perhaps it was some other cause, Aeron lifted a hand to her forehead, to touch the great crystal that blazed there, and a feeling came over her then of strength and continuity, of sharing union with all those souls before her, and some of them mighty ones, who had themselves borne Nia's cathbarr upon their own brows, and with all the ones who would do so in time to come.

Then the doors opened for her, silently swinging inwards, and Aeron straightened her shoulders under the heavy silk mantle, and lifting her chin stepped forward to face what lay within.

The interminable rehearsals profited her almost at once, for in concentrating upon the form of the ceremony—she had even been instructed how to walk!—Aeron forgot her fears entirely. The measured pacing took her between the endless rows of seated guests: They filled all that vast hall, lords and commons alike, and not a one of them bowed or rose for her as she passed by. For not until she was invested Tanista, and the Silver Branch given into her hands, would Aeron be in law and truth her father's surrogate, due all the royal courtesies paid to the Ard-rígh himself.

Ahead of her, at the end of the long, long aisle, the High King sat upon the Throne of Scone, the high-backed ancient chair of cloud-white granite. Every inch of that royal seat was carved with glyphs even the most learned among bards and sorcerers could no longer interpret: the same weird beasts and runes of mystery that were cut into the ceiling of Broinn-na-draoichta far away, here side by side with more familiar symbols from Keltia's everyday heraldry—the wolfhound gorged with a crown that was the nation-emblem of Erinna; the Kymric dragon; Scota's leaping lion and Kernow's stately choughs; the Vanx triskele, that three-limbed spinning star, and the five-petalled Prytanic rose. Not only did the Throne of Scone bear up all the rulers of Keltia, it bore upon itself all the history of Keltia as well.

Fionnbarr sat upright and unmoving in the stone chair. Upon his head was the ancient Copper Crown, with its spiral plaques and conical centerpiece; across his knees lay the Silver Branch. Emer the Queen sat in the consort's throne, to the right and a little lower, for only here in the Hall of Heroes did monarch and consort not share perfect equality of rank; similarly on Fionnbarr's left was set the heir's seat, which Aeron would take as Tanista for the first time today.

But just now her eyes were all for her father, as halfway down the Hall's length she made him the first of the three formal obeisances; the second, when she came to the broad open space before the throne, and the third and last when she had ascended the seven steps of the dais and stood before the Ard-rígh; and when she had made him that final deep reverence she remained kneeling before him.

In the charged hush that had fallen over the chamber—even the faint sound of the farviewer cameras that carried this most momentous event to all the Keltic worlds and even beyond the Pale was hardly to be heard—Aeron bent her head and lowered her eyes as the King—she could not think of him, in this moment and this sacred state, as her father—placed both hands upon her head in solemn benediction.

"Be it known to all here present, and to all Keltia, and to all the worlds beyond the Pale," said Fionnbarr, his voice carrying effortlessly to all corners of the enormous vaulted chamber, "that Aeron Lassarina Angharad Aoibhell, our beloved and eldest child, is this day confirmed our heir and Tanista of Keltia, and into her hands do we therefore place, with all trust and confidence, that she shall be obeyed even as ourselves, the Scepter of Llyr, known as the Silver Branch—as token of her rule to come, and first symbol of the Ard-tiarnas, the High Dominion of Keltia that will be hers in time. So say I, Fionnbarr King of Kelts."

He leaned forward to kiss Aeron formally on either cheek, as a king to his successor, then took her hands between his for the pledge of fealty. Her voice betrayed a little her nervousness, but by the time the oath was completed her tone was as clear and carrying as his had been.

One more detail . . . "What name, as Tanista, do you choose to add to your own?"

Aeron looked up into the hazel eyes, so familiar to her, now so remote. *By all gods, but he is the King . . .* "If it please the Ard-rígh, I choose the name of Aoife."

Murmurs of approval ran round the assembly, and in the chair below Emer looked up in surprise. Though none had known what Aeron's choice of name might be—by custom she was under no compulsion to reveal it beforehand, and not even Fionnbarr had known—the King was indeed pleased with his daughter's choosing. *And, Grandmother, I have a feeling you too are pleased . . . with the chooser equally as with the choice.*

"It pleases me well," he said aloud, "that the next Ard-rían of Keltia should bear the name of her who was the latest. Aeron Lassarina Angharad Aoife, take up the Silver Branch."

Only then did Aeron rise from where she had been kneeling all this time. She raised her hands a foot apart, and Fionnbarr laid the Silver Branch across her upturned palms. A plain heavy rod of polished findruinna, the scepter—formally known as the Scepter of Llyr, though only rarely called so—had narrow bands of gold knotwork at top and base, but bore no stone or other adornment. The weight of the thing was by no means inconsiderable, and the thought crossed Aeron's mind that all symbols of sovereignty were heavy: perhaps deliberately so, in a crude, almost childish illustration of the burdens of rule.

Her fingers closed round the scepter's cold shaft, and looking up she did brief obeisance again to her father—the only one in all Keltia to whom she had now to bend the knee—and took her place upon the throne at his left hand.

She remembered very little afterwards about the five hours that followed, when every ranking noble in Keltia, every elected Senator and Assemblator, every planetary rechtair, every ambassador to the outworlds, every Protectorate delegate, every Council member, every system viceroy and vicereine and lord of the Fainne, every member of the royal family itself—beginning with her own mother and grandmother—came before her to swear homage to her as Tanista and as Ard-rían that would be. There were bright happy flashes amid the endless stream of solemn faces: her brother Rohan's hands strong and steady in hers, Rohan who had by her elevation to Tanista been himself raised to the dignity of Prince of the Name, heir-presumptive to the throne until such time as his sister did wed and produce an heir for herself; Faolan Douglas's loving paternal salute; Gwydion's grave approval, and the spark there had been when their hands met; Kesten's warm and perceptive gaze.

At last all was done, and a very weary Tanista went out on Rohan's arm, behind the tall figures of their parents. All that day Aeron had been longing for this moment, hoping for a quiet family celebration after the ceremony: It was her birthday, after all, and a significant one as well; such occasions were usually observed with a small gathering and gifting among close friends and relations—Kelts gave presents on their own birthdays, most notably to their parents and fosterers, as well as received—and Aeron had long since had her own gifts prepared for those she meant them for.

But when she emerged from the Keep into the late afternoon sun, to the cheers of the assembled crowds, she saw an aircar hovering above the stones of the Square, and her parents were beckoning her to join them inside.

The flight was a short one—only to Mardale, the spaceport that served Caerdroia, seven miles beyond the walls in a steep-sided glen of the Loom. By the time the craft touched down outside a skydock, Aeron's curiosity was almost past bearing; but she asked no questions, and Fionnbarr paid no heed to her inquiring looks, merely taking her hand in silence and leading her inside the huge domed structure.

The inner doors opened upon such a ship hanging in the stasis field of skydock as Aeron had never before laid eyes on. It was sleek and black and gleaming, as if it had been recently rained upon; not overlarge, as she could see now that the field had lowered it to the dock floor, but sizable enough, and of excellent line and proportion for a personal craft.

"That is a beauty! Whose is she?"

"Well, yours!" Fionnbarr laughed at her stunned expression. "It *is* your birthday, is it not? Time it was, any road, you had a ship of your own; you will very soon be beset with far-flung chores, and you will need a swift way of arriving at them—you may not wish always to rely upon the starfleet. Elharn and Rhain designed her; so, in part, did you yourself. Do you not recall all those questions they were forever asking you this past year, about ship design and what would be desirable to have in a personal craft?''

"Aye, well, I but thought they inquired in general." Aeron ran a hand over the shining hull, admiring its sleekness, then touched a silver plate set into the smooth black metal—síodarainn, it was called; ''silk-iron''—and a door slid silently open on the ship's interior.

"Your thoughts on design were well taken, Aeron," said her cousin Rhain, coming round the side of the ship and giving her a warm greeting. He was one of her favorite kinsmen, though she saw him but seldom. Tall, brown-haired, affable, a Druid scientist who advised the Fianna on military technology, he was a prince himself, the eldest of the four children of Fionnbarr's brother Deian.

"We used many of your suggestions in the building," continued Rhain, leading Aeron round the ship on a quick inspection. "And added a few of our own: For instance, there is a cloaking mechanism installed—a tirr. No other ship in the starfleet has one as yet, not even *Firedrake*. It might prove useful some time. As for speed, with a reasonable weight aboard her, only the courier cursals and scout sloops are in a class with her; even heavily laden, she will be faster than most.''

"What shall you call her?" asked Emer, after Aeron had finished expressing delighted thanks to all concerned.

Aeron hesitated, as if she listened for some word that had not yet been spoken. "I know not just yet," she said. "For the moment, let her use-name be *Dubhlinnseach*, 'The Black-sailed'; until such a day as she herself shall tell me her truename, and fairly earn it.''

By the time Aeron returned with the others to Turusachan, the birthday ceili she had hoped for was in full cry: wisely limited by her mother and grandmother to close friends and family only. And so among the many Aoibhells and Kerrigans there were old friends and dear ones: Morwen, and Sabia, and Dafydd Drummond, and the Camerons, and Vevin ní Talleron; and newer ones as well, that she had made on Fian service or at the Hill of Laws or in her recent travels around Keltia. Some of these, less accustomed to such company or such surroundings, seemed a little daunted by it all, but the others did their best to put them at their ease, and very soon all their discomfortableness was forgotten.

Not so, however, Aeron's own: As she had known they would be, and was both fearing and longing to see, both Roderick and Gwydion were among the revelers gathered to celebrate her day. *Well, they could scarce not have been asked; and it is not as if I have seen naught of them these past few years . . .* But she was a little shy of them all the same, and on arriving at the palace had not had nerve enough to face them at once. Instead, she had made excuse to go to her rooms and change her ceremonial attire to less stately garb; a reasonable cause for delaying her appearance at her own ceili. But she did not attempt to deceive herself: The respite had been needed to restore herself a little after the strain of the investiture, but needed still more to prepare herself a little to face the two who awaited her below.

So now Aeron threaded her way through the crush, accepting the felicitations and kisses and embraces offered her on every side, and she soon found her spirits rising to merriment almost in spite of herself. Then, in a lull, she saw Rhodri across the room, with Mared his mother, his dark-gold head overtopping most of those around him, and she knew at once she was not yet ready for him, and in her confusion she instantly turned the other way.

But there was still less peace for her in that quarter: Gwydion stood in an alcove, the center of a group of laughing friends. He had not seen her, and for a moment she had leisure to watch him unobserved.

I forget, between times of seeing him, how tall he is, and how very fine to look upon—though it is scarce a punishment to have to look on Rhodri either . . . The formal dress Gwydion had worn to the day's ceremony, and still wore now, was but a richer version of his usual attire: Instead of wool or linen, the black tunic was of velvet; the snowy white leinna beneath it of sith-silk instead of the everyday gwlan; the sapphire signet of Gwynedd was upon his hand and the coronet he so rarely wore was upon his brow. He had risen that year to the rank of full Fian general— one of Keltia's youngest ever, for he was not yet thirty-three, and one of the most gifted ever, according to those equipped to judge of such matters. And all this in the teeth of his mother's and his planet's fierce opposition, for he had been Ruling Prince barely two years, and they were unwilling to let him continue to risk himself in combat, lest they should lose him so soon after losing his father.

But he was here tonight, and Aeron's joy at seeing him was as great as her disquiet; her surprise was greater than both, to see his sister. *I did not know Ari was to be here—we have not been on the same planet, much less in the same room, these seven years past, save at the rites for Arawn-maeth* . . . She cast a covert glance at Arianeira, feeling a deep, somehow shameful, reluctance to go and greet her foster-sister, and for all her efforts she could not master it.

Arianeira decided the thing for her. Catching sight of Aeron standing there irresolute, she left the group of which she had been part and came over to join her.

"Tanista!" Before Aeron could move to hinder, Arianeira sank in an elaborate court curtsy before her fostern. "My greeting on your birthday, and your day of glory."

"Oh, get up, Ari, that is no way to do after we have been so long apart." Embarrassed and discomfited—and with the uneasy impression that that was exactly how Arianeira had intended her to feel—Aeron embraced her, but there was from the other no answering warmth; she might have been embracing a standing stone, or an unbending white tree. *Nay, not even those, for tree or stone, at least, would greet me back, and she does not* . . . Aeron stood away and took a hard look at her foster-sister, using Ban-draoi tricks that she did not like to employ with those close to her, and which use she carefully shielded from Arianeira, who was after all a Ban-draoi adept herself. *She is lovelier than ever; and colder than ever she has been to me; I wonder whyfor* . . .

"If I may make petition of the Tanista on her birthday—"

Aeron felt herself coloring, aware of the many listening ears. "Anything, Ari; you know you need but ask."

"Aye so? Well then, only a moment's private speech with you, if you can bear to absent yourself from this rout awhile. Is that too great an asking?"

Why does everything she says sound as if she holds me in the wrong . . . "It seems scarcely favor enough . . . Come, there is a withdrawing room close by; we will talk in there." Aeron led the way through the throng, where dancing was now general, smilingly declining all invitations to join the reel with promises for later. Coming to a door half-hidden behind draped gold curtains, she stood aside for Arianeira to precede her into the little chamber and closed the door behind them.

"I spoke not entirely true just now, Tanista," said Arianeira without further prelude. "There *is* a favor I would ask of you."

"Ari, you are my foster-sister; no need to call me by my title—in truth I wish that you would not."

"It is right that I should call you so," she countered, "when I am petitioning for a place in your household here at Turusachan."

Aeron's surprise showed on her face, and she spoke before she thought. "A place for you! I had not considered it; we have been so long apart, and the places are largely already spoken for—"

"Oh, do not pretend with me!" For one who was suing for a favor, Arianeira's tone was scarcely one of entreaty. "You could easily find a place for me—if you so wished. Is it that you begrudge it me? You had no problem finding offices for other of your friends: You named Sabia ní Dálaigh as captain of your guard; Morwen as your chief advisor; Struan Cameron as master of horse in your marca-sluagh. Even former lovers—is not Deio Drummond appointed one of your household officers? Am I so much less to be honored than they, so much less your friend?"

"I had not thought of you," admitted Aeron frankly.

"Nay, you had not! But that is naught new—"

Arianeira had begun to pace up and down in the room's confines; the sounds of the revel came muted in from outside, and Aeron found herself longing to escape back into it. *Better to face Gwydion and Rhodri both together than to have to endure more of this* . . . But Arianeira was speaking again, her voice vibrant now with bitterness long suppressed.

"Why *should* you have thought of me? You will be Queen of Kelts. Morwen shall have the dúchas of Lochcarron, and most like more besides. What is there for me to content myself with? I shall never be more than I now am: the sister of the Prince of Gwynedd. If Gwydion condescends to throw me some crumb of governance in my own planet, that is one thing; or if I marry some other prince or duke and rule with him over his dúchas. Otherwise, nothing."

Aeron looked down at her hands, seeing in memory the Silver

Branch as she had held it a few hours since, recalling the weight of it—and all it represented. "I had not known you felt so."

"Nor did you try to learn," said Arianeira, calmer now. "You did once promise me when we were children that you would give me whatever title or place I wished, so that you and Wenna and I should ever be together, here in Turusachan. Have you forgotten that promise?"

To my sorrow and shame, until this minute I had so . . . "It seems that *you* have not," said Aeron aloud. "When I am Ard-rían—"

But the other was not to be pacified, and all her anger kindled anew. "When you are Ard-rían! Comes *that* time and you will take all the future from me as you have just taken the past. You will take Morwen from me completely—and she was *my* sister too, Aeron, not just yours—and I think you will take my brother as well, if you have not already done so, and you who will have so much will leave me with nothing. Even from the time we were children together at Kinloch Arnoch have I known this— Do you remember my white dog Wynos? He was mine at least until *you* arrived, and then you took him also."

"I did nothing of the like, the poor puppy came to me for that you whipped him when he would play—"

"Aye, you have ever been the one to protect those not so strong as yourself—though that tender heart never seemed somehow to reach out so far to me . . . I say you will leave me nothing, and you will leave me alone."

"Ari, Ari, that is not true, it will not be—"

"*Nothing!*" she flared. "I see it all so clear— And what shall happen then, Aeron—*Tanista*—what shall come of it in the end . . . it will be upon your own head!"

The door slammed behind her, rattling the room. Aeron stood without moving in the center of the floor. *Have I been truly so selfish, then; there was so much all these years to contend with, but I should not have forgotten Ari so—only . . . only it seemed that she wished not to remember me . . .* She took a deep breath to quiet herself, in the Ban-draoi way, then flung wide the door, only to meet Rohan on the point of entering, two cups of usqueba in his hands.

Aeron took one without a word and gratefully downed it, then, after the briefest of pauses, drank off the other as well. Rohan made no comment, and she knew he had guessed much of what had happened.

"What had Ari to say?" he asked at length.

"Little enough," said Aeron, surprised at the strength of the anger she felt; it seemed somehow to have passed blazing from Arianeira to her. "Though, I daresay, more than perhaps she meant to." She shook her head and shook off the mood. "But I have missed *you*, braud; you have been much away of late. It is not like the old days with all of us here together, and I do not see near enough of any of you as I might like."

"It will be so again," he assured her. "Once we have satisfied our duties elsewhere—we will all be back here once more, you and I and Ríona and Nuala and the twins; it will be a fine thing as before."

A wistful little quiver passed over Aeron's face. "Fine enough," she said. "Though perhaps the duties will be rather different— But it is my birthday still, and I hear a strathspey being played. Would the Prince of the Name care to dance it with his sister?"

"He would indeed," said Rohan smiling, and they went out together.

Chapter 25

Aeron's Tanistry was little more than one year old before it was put to its first real test.

A challenge had been sent to Fionnbarr some time since: a question of land-rights and inheritance, one of the usual matters upon which such challenges bore, in the time-honored way among the Kelts that any subject should have the right in settlement of grievance to challenge the monarch in fíor-comlainn, the truth-of-combat, magical or military as the litigant party should choose.

And Royne Druchar, a landholder of the Venton Country on the planet Kernow, had chosen the sword.

" 'Lex est ata regis'," said Aeron, quoting the ancient maxim. She set aside the challenge-screed and looked up at her father. " 'The law is the armor of the King.' "

"That is surely seen," agreed Fionnbarr. "But in Keltia it could as easily be turned 'Rex est ata legis'—'The King is the armor of the law.' And in nothing so much as fíor-comlainn is that so clearly proved."

"You have proved it so yourself, a fair number of times."

Her father smiled. "True, though some times with more notable success than others . . . But if the King may be shield at need to the law, better still if the King's heir can be sword-arm to the King."

"Ah, now it all comes out!" said Aeron, laughing. "Well, you did warn me it should be so, once I was Tanista—and I take your point." Her smile turned wicked. "And so, if I have the luck of the fight, will this Royne Druchar take mine."

* * *

The noise of the spectators hushed dramatically as Aeron, followed by her chosen seconds Sabia and her cousin Desmond, Elharn's son, stepped out onto the compall, the dueling floor behind the Fianna Commandery across from the palace. She was clad for contest, not for battle, in the close-fitting unisuit with its protective plastron front. Both hands were gauntleted to the elbow, and her hair was bound up in braids at the back of her head.

She briefly ran her gaze over the onlookers in the stone benches that rose in tiered galleries around the combat floor: officials of the government, many of them, here as their duty commanded to observe the fight according to law, and officers of the Fianna come to see how one of their own would carry herself. But there was a fair number of plain citizens among them, though the day and hour of the contest had not been made known until that morning.

Which is only to be expected, she thought. Any fíor-comlainn against the Crown brought out those eager to watch and judge the royal participant; whether they came out of pure curiosity or out of some deeper motive—even in hopes of seeing her fail— mattered no whit to her. Today they were here to see *her*—win, lose or draw. *And* that *my father knew well; therefore did he pass this challenge over to me . . .* Still, she had to learn sometime; Fionnbarr had fought the truth-of-combat often enough himself, and would again if need demanded. All the same, Aeron had a strong suspicion that should she prove herself here today abler with a blade than her father, there would be many more of these antics in her future, before she herself even came to the throne, or had an heir of her own on which to foist them in her turn.

She accepted Sabia's ministrations of water and oxygen tablets; quite lawful, and across the ring her opponent was receiving the same. From under her cousin's arm Aeron studied her adversary, his way of moving, his height and reach and port.

"Well, do you think you can best him?"

Aeron looked up to see the humorous glint in Desmond's eye, and bent her head to hide her grin from the watching crowd.

"That bannock?" Sabia's indignation was genuine, if hardly politic in public. "Shame to you, Aeron, if you give him more than two hits in ten, and Struan Cameron will cry more than shame if you do so."

"Bannock or no," said Aeron, "that is a trained fighter over there; else he had never chosen the iron-fight. Two good blades to choose from, and—presumably—two good hands with which to wield them."

Desmond, who had picked up Aeron's own swords for her to choose, raised his brows at that.

"Aye so? Then what hand is best in this ring?"

She caught the blade he tossed her. "It is here."

"And the second best?" asked Sabia.

Aeron flipped the sword to her left hand. "It is there."

She had fought under the gimlet gaze of an audience before now, so that was of little concern to Aeron as she stepped out into the ring; she had fought to save herself and others in battle, where no polite rules of the dueling code did apply. But today there was a reason beyond personal pride or even survival for her to wish for victory. *Macha Ruadh,* ran her brief prayer to the Erinnach battle-goddess she often besought in combat, *your strength to my arm . . . if not for my sake, then for the sake of the Ard-tiarnas of Keltia I defend here.*

After the formal reading of the grievance brought against the Crown of Keltia by the litigant, Royne Druchar, of Caerhays in the Venton Country of Kernow, and the acceptance by the combat judges and the plaintiff of the Tanista Aeron to act as her father's arm in this matter, the two combatants stood forth, saluted the judges and each other, and commenced.

Aeron quickly realized that though her opponent was far from the slow-footed lumberer Sabia had scorned him for, neither was he the product of three years' hard hammering by Struan at Caer Artos. Had it been true battle, or other life-and-death matter, she could have dispatched him in a minute's exchange. As it was, an honest fight, and a real one, mattered more here than a quick triumph—though not more than the need that that triumph must of course be *hers* . . .

So it went on for perhaps twenty minutes, a respectable session with blows taken and points scored on either side; long enough for Royne Druchar to feel that honor had been satisfied and that he had received justice as he had sought, and brief enough for Aeron to be sure that all her tricks had not been revealed in one bout for the benefit of future challengers.

In the end she called upon the same speed and seeming foreknowledge that had served her so well in her Fian test: a slow parry swiftly overborne, a lunge, a remise, the blade taken; and then Royne Druchar was standing weaponless, his hand stinging where Aeron had curled her blade round to snap his own from his grip.

Amid the storm of applause and approval that rained down from the galleries, Aeron pulled off her gauntlet and clasped her opponent's forearm as was custom; a formal quit-claim by the litigant, sworn to before the attending brehons and Fionnbarr's named witness, his Taoiseach, Conn Trehere, fifteen years in royal service; and it was over.

"A strange justice," mused Desmond later, serving as esquire to help his cousin out of the dueling plastron and into the steaming pool-bath beneath the arena. "I wonder what Bres of Fomor would make of our way, or the Cabiri Emperor Strephon."

"I for one would pay good crossics to see *those* two face off on the compall," said Aeron laughing, and blissfully sank up to her chin in the pool. The hot water felt so good to her sore muscles: She had taken some sharp buffets in the fight—though no blood had been spilled by either blade—and a few grape-blue bruises were already beginning to show on her arms and sides. *Still, I have no doubt Royne Druchar is battered worse . . .* The thought pleased her, and she riffled through the water like a sun-shark at play. "As for the justice," she said after a while, "well, I for one would rather be fought against than fasted against. The trosca-mór, the hunger-strike, is a fearful thing to have brought against one . . . I'd sooner fight than starve any day."

"You would sooner fight than eat, you mean," teased Sabia, and got a palmful of hot water for it. "The justice of the fíor-comlainn is that aggrieved folk can feel there is true recourse for them. What could be more satisfying than being able by law to challenge your ruler to combat, and know him or her bound by that law to accept?"

"I admit it is a pleasing notion," said Aeron, swimming with strong strokes to the pool's far end. "However hard on Keltia's rulers—and their heirs. I am only glad so few cases ever come to it, else I might never be out of the compall myself . . . Mislike the thought as I do," she added, emerging from the pool and taking the drying-robe Sabia offered, "there may well come a day when I fight and fail, and that is a thing I must be prepared for, long before it comes."

Sabia's face was uncharacteristically sober as she helped her friend into tunic and trews. "And the better prepared you are for defeat, the less likely you will ever be defeated."

Aeron looked at her closely, startled a little by the solemnity of the tone, hearing in it more than surface meaning. "Do you speak as Ban-draoi, Sabhait? Have you Seen, then?"

Sabia's brown eyes sparkled. "Nay," she said. "I speak only as your friend, and perhaps a little as the captain of your guard. But do not forget, all the same."

It was not long thereafter that an old prophetic word of Kesten Hannivec's was fulfilled, and Aeron became Kin to the Dragon, a member of that mystic company known as the Dragon Kinship. Called by the uninitiate the Ten Thousand, though their numbers varied according to Keltia's needs and the availability of suitable candidates, of all the magicians in a realm that lived by magic those who were Kin to the Dragon were most respected and most feared.

With good reason: Though rank or birth or riches made no differ in the naming of a new recruit to the Kinship, and any current Dragon might name any he or she found worthy, those so named must be gifted indeed in sorcery, and it must needs be a more substantial gift than was the common run among Kelts, who had been a sorcerous race from their very beginnings. Though the Aoibhells had had their full share of magicians, few of the house had been tapped to join the Kinship; in recent times only Duthac, now dead, who had been brother to Lasairían, Gwyneira, the Dowager Queen, Aeron's much-loved grandmother, and Melangell, daughter of Fionnbarr's brother Deian, had been so honored; and even Gwyneira was no Aoibhell by blood but of the Clann Isla, the Lords of the Isles.

But for Aeron it had come unlooked for; and though she was herself both exalted and humbled by the honor, the rest of her kindred seemed rather to regard it as a thing foreordained, scarcely to be noted and certainly not to be marvelled at. She was the finest sorceress to come along in the Aoibhell line for many score of years; what wonder that she should also be named as Dragon Kin?

Yet they, and the rest of Keltia with them, were by no means so indifferent when Gwydion ap Arawn, Prince of Gwynedd and general of Keltia, was named to a rarer honor yet: was chosen as successor to the outgoing Pendragon, chief of the Dragon Kinship, to be himself Pendragon for the next seven years.

There were many dark mutterings when the news became public knowledge, for not in seven centuries had the Pendragon been a warrior of such standing, and those who murmured against the choice were not always to be found outside the Kinship. But the Pendragons had ever chosen themselves according to the needs they Saw must be met; there was no pattern to their choosings other than that, and though their namings must always be confirmed by the Kinship as a whole, their reasons never needed to be justified or excused or explained.

Still, though the reasons were not always set out, the othersight each Dragon possessed in full measure, and the shared superconsciousness, the fiosaiocht, that all possessed in common, gave them sufficient understanding of both chosen and choice; and in all the centuries since the Kinship's founding no naming of a new Pendragon had ever been denied.

So Gwydion became Pendragon, at the age of thirty-eight, on the word of Cadreth Emac'h, farmer and landowner of the Morbihan on the planet Brytaned, two-hundred-and-twelfth Pendragon since Taliesin who was the first; and Aeron, robed in the Kinship's black and purple, the silver dragon disk at her throat, sat with the others to see Gwydion become the two-hundred-and-thirteenth, and to hear him name Grelun O Faracháin, a Fian in his own service and a longtime Dragon, as his Summoner or chief officer.

After the ceremony, Aeron spoke briefly with the new Pendragon. The exaltation still blazed upon Gwydion's face, so that it was for the moment more than handsome, taking on the austere perfection of a beauty of spirit that matched that of the body. For a moment even Aeron could not gaze directly into his eyes; then he seemed to come back a little from where he had been, and the spark that had ever been between them leaped into new life.

"I think you had not expected this?" said Aeron, touching the great jewel of the Star and Dragon he wore now upon his breast, and it was only half a question.

His rare smile lighted his face, and he glanced down at the amethyst ring of his new office, its stone stepped like a staircase, on his left hand beside the Gwynedd signet. "I had not," he said honestly. "Nor am I by any means sure that Cadreth made the right choice in choosing me . . . Many others there are who might devote themselves more completely to such office; many more who have been Dragons, and fine ones, since before ever I was born. I know there have been doubts even among the Kindred as to my fitness for the office."

"Yet in the end none gainsaid your naming; the vote was unanimous—save for your own."

Gwydion nodded. "And it is just that which gives rise to my deepest doubts. It is as if you others do see or sense something that I do not, or cannot, or may not; something that you might not know, even, or will not say, some time to come in which the Kinship, and Keltia itself, will need *me*—I alone, of all others, to be Pendragon, and what I can give. And since my chief gift has ever lain in my sword . . . well, you of all people must understand how it fears me to think on it."

"It would fear anyone," said Aeron, then grinned. "But only think how it might have been worse: You could have been named Pendragon in the days of my Ard-ríanachtas to come, and would then have had to sit on my Ard-eis, to give me the benefit of your Sight and counsel."

At that the strangeness left him entirely, and he laughed out loud. "Name of Dôn, but it would take a good deal more than even Sight for me to counsel *you* . . . Thank gods we will never see it."

But there Gwydion's Sight did fail them both.

It was in the autumn of that year, when Aeron had celebrated both her sixth year as Tanista and her thirty-third birthday, that Emer her mother, like Gwyneira before her, reopened an old campaign in a war very dear to her heart: the battle to get the heir to Keltia safely wedded, and an heir provided to ensure the line of the succession.

To the Queen's mind, it could not, and should not, be delayed very much longer. Though Aeron had attained to her full and final majority, in the reckoning of her long-lived folk she was barely out of adolescence, and had thus in theory at least many decades ahead of her in which to breed the hoped-for heirs. All the same, she was now of full age to rule in her own right, without the cumbersome, and tiresome, machinery of a Regent and the Council to hamper her: Time now to take a lord, and embrace duty along with him. Who that lord should be had of course long since been decided in Emer's mind; what she did not yet know was that Aeron too had decided, and in a way, and for a reason, her mother would not have guessed.

Tybie was working as usual in the little kitchen-garden behind the llan, digging up some of the vegetables she had planted in the spring, when Aeron's ship *Dubhlinnseach* suddenly shadowed the valley and touched down at the base of the hill. The anchoress showed no surprise, either then or when Aeron, a little blown from the steep climb, appeared at the gate—for which lack of astonishment Aeron was grateful—but set aside her gardening tools and led the way down the sanded path, to the great water-hollowed rock beside the cataract, where of old she and her pupil had sat so often in talk, and Aeron followed after.

"So your parents have determined that you shall wed Rhodri Douglas," said Tybie, having listened to Aeron's account of everything but that very same matter, and seeing as usual into the heart of the true problem upon which Aeron had come to consult her.

Aeron did not even trouble to wonder at the swiftness of Tybie's insight, having seen it at work too often in the past.

"Nay," she said, "*I* have determined that I *shall*; my parents determined only that I *should*. There is a very great difference." She stared at the flying water, cold and white, just beyond reach of her fingers. "What they do not know just yet is that I have determined also—though this I have spoken of with Rhodri alone, and now with you—is that it will be a brehon marriage only, for one year of the moons of Tara. That will satisfy my obedience to the wishes of the Ard-rígh and the Queen, though I have no doubt my mother will push for reconsideration after the year is done."

"*Will* you reconsider?"

Aeron's smile flashed. "Only that I shall, when the time comes for it, make the Prince of Gwynedd the King of Keltia."

"That have I ever known would be so," said Tybie calmly. "And Gwydion too, I think . . . He is not troubled then by this marriage of state to Rhodri?"

"He has said not, and I would know if he said untruly. Nor is Rhodri troubled, as far as I can tell. I have adored him since my childhood, and had things fallen out other wise I could have been well contented with him as my king-consort. Or so at least I think, for as you know he is neither Druid nor Dragon, and that might make some differ. As it stands—"

"As it stands," said Tybie dryly, "I think neither one of you will lay a sword in the bed between you for this year you speak of."

Aeron laughed. "Most likely not—but nor will any heir come out of this brehon year either, as my mother so blatantly hopes. That is for later—much later." She sat silent for a while, watching the water. "When I come to rule Keltia," she began, a new hesitancy to her voice, "though by the grace of the Mother may that day be long delayed, I shall need the help of my partner in sovereignty for what I have it in mind to do. Gwydion is the only one of all those I have known who will be able to give me that help; Rhodri, fond as I am of him, is not in it."

"And this that you have it in mind to do?" asked Tybie, though she had a shrewd idea of it already.

Aeron leaned forward eagerly, face animated, arms hugging her upraised knees. "Keltia has stood too long aloof from the worlds beyond the Pale. The Curtain Wall has been our long protection, but also I think it has been a barrier—to thoughts, to ideas, to knowledge. It cannot come amiss to join more fully— though most cautiously—in the stream of the galaxy; most particularly, to make ourselves known once more to Earth. And this is a dream Gwydion shares with me full measure . . . There may be a time when Keltia will stand in need of out-Wall friends, and a friend who is also kin, however distantly removed, is the best friend there could be."

"Your father thinks otherwise—as did your grandfather Lasairían before him."

"They are wrong, though it pains me to say so; my great-grandmother Aoife was the one who had the right of this matter—though that too pains me to say. They have all been wrong, those who have kept us tucked safe away behind the Wall. Safe, aye, but stagnating, and perhaps selfish to boot; however necessary it may have been at first for our protection.''

"Are you so wise then?" murmured Tybie. "It was our own Morgan Magistra who saw the need for the Curtain Wall, and raised it in her brother's name."

Aeron gave her a sidelong look. "It is not for me to question the wisdom of St. Morgan of the Pale, though her brother may not have entirely agreed with her reasons . . . And I have no intention that the Wall shall be lowered any time soon—but wisdom is not at issue here, only plain sense. If we speak of the wisdom of saints, Brendan himself thought that the link with the Terrans must one day be reforged, and he was the one led us all from Earth to begin with . . . Any road," she added more cheerfully, scrambling to her feet to stand atop the rock like a statue on a plinth, "such a choice is far away. I shall not be Ard-rían for decades yet to come, and by then Keltia will be a very different place. Much can happen, and doubtless will." She looked down at Tybie, who still sat below her in the water-worn curve of the granite, looking more reflective even than usual. "Nor is it for me to remind my teacher of the law of the coire ainsec; but what chance is there of getting something to eat? Serious talk is hungry work, and I did see you picking fresh greens when I arrived . . ."

As Tybie, two hours and a simple daymeal later, watched Aeron depart, *Dubhlinnseach* lifting from the valley floor like a giant black falair, she was shaken by a sudden cold wind not of the ship's passing, and she caught at the gatepost for support.

You came here not to seek help in deciding but to test your own decision, she thought, watching the ship arrow up through atmosphere to the vanishing point. *And that is a thing I am very glad to see. Gladder still to see you so calm and happy in your certainty . . . But that time you speak of—my dearest child!—that time runs short. You came here today as Tanista, but it is on my heart that the next time we meet, you will meet me as Ard-rían. And it will not be in those decades you think you shall have, but in days. Be ready, Aeron, and be strong. I think you are both . . . but we shall see. All the worlds shall see.*

Chapter 26

Emer stared into her daughter's impassive face. "You will wed Rhodri, then? Oh Aeron, glad am I to hear it, and your father will be as well."

"I will wed Rhodri," continued Aeron inexorably, "next Brighnasa, in a brehon ceremony only, the marriage to last for one year of the moons of Tara. After that, I shall consider my duty to the Ard-rígh and the Queen discharged in full, and will decide for myself who is to be king-consort in the reign to come."

"And it shall not be Roderick Douglas."

Aeron held her peace, though inwardly she was longing to shout her thoughts at her mother. *You meddled yourself with the succession laws, Emer ní Kerrigan!* she thought in fury. *You defied your parents and your King and you chose your lover where you would; and now you try to deny me the right to choose mine* . . . But she kept her silence, and after a while Emer sighed and nodded.

"Gwydion. Always it has been Gwydion."

"Not always; but what if it is?" Aeron flung at her, all the pent-up anger lashing out at last. "Is the Prince of Gwynedd not fit to become the King of Keltia?"

Ah, Goddess, how swift she is to temper—just exactly like Aoife; the folk do not call her Aeron Anfa for naught . . . "Oh, alanna, it is not that . . . Your father and I have ever loved Gwydion as a child of our own; we fostered you to Arawn and Gwenedour, how could we not love their son?" *Yet that is not the truth entire*, thought Emer, careful to shield her mind. *It is Gwydion's great gift for magic gives me such pause; a sorceress*

287

High Queen is one thing, but to set a sorcerer King at her side seems needless risk. Then again, I have never held much brief for magic . . . She tried again. "It is only that—"

"—only that you and my father have conspired with Faolan and Mared," said Aeron bitterly. "And you would none of you be thwarted, and certainly not by any wishes Rhodri or Gwydion or I might have in the matter."

"You and Rhodri are agreed on this, then?"

After a moment Aeron shook her head. "Not yet; not formally. But I leave in two days' time for Caledon. I will bring the Ard-rígh and the Queen his answer—as soon as I have it myself."

Kinloch Arnoch lay in a wide-mouthed glen leading up onto a windy moor that ran for miles along the sea. No word spoken, Aeron and Roderick turned their horses' heads up that narrow trail, and after an hour's leisurely ride they drew rein atop a sheer bluff overlooking the sea, and dismounted to let the horses cool. Here rounded blue hills came down to the beaches, one after another for miles along the shore: Kirrier, the High Coast, nothing here but stone—even tough seagrass and wiry bent could find scant footing on this face. Mist rose up off the water, billowing about their knees; above them, vapor rose up off the hills, to reach the knees of giants, if any giants there had been.

It was for her to speak, Aeron knew, and it was for that Rhodri waited. Why was it so hard? They had talked of it before, and both of them knew what each would say . . .

"I have told the High King and the Queen that we shall wed," she said finally, her voice muffled by the wind. "A brehon marriage for the time we two did agree on. Unless you have had a change of mind or heart?"

Rhodri shook his head. "Nay, Aeron, I do not take back my word. It may well be that after a week, or a month, or a sixmonth, one or the other or both of us together will think the thing better ended sooner; it may be too that your parents shall see that a poet and a chaunter with no magic to his hand is no fit consort for a Domina Ard-rían. But we shall have satisfied duty, and pleased our kindreds, and that is after all the name of the exercise . . . I am but a poor political creature in any case," he added, running a hand over his blond beard. "I dreaded even the prospect of taking up my own father's coronet as Prince of Scots when he gave it over to me last Beltain. Tarsuinn my brother would make a far finer job of it than I—but Father would resign the title in my favor, thinking it not suitable that the heir of Keltia should wed with only the Master of Douglas. So now *he* may go off happily to the bards, to study as he pleases, and I must not only rule Caledon but wed with the Tanista as well.''

"I had not known you thought it such a hardship," said Aeron, unaccountably stung. "We have had no secrets from each other, Rhodri, as to how the other feels; but I think we shall be not entirely wretched for a year."

"No more do I." He kissed her hand, and she smiled, but the smile was a distracted one, and she let her glance turn out over the water.

Though the day held fair still, the wind was rising now, the sea beginning to shout upon the beaches; high above, the gath-an-dubha, the Storm-riders, were out—those torn clouds streaming upon the upper winds, heralds of the approaching tempest.

"Often I think it will be on a day such as this that Rocabarra will rise for the third time," said Rhodri behind her. "To be the end of all—"

Rocabarra . . . The name chimed well with Aeron's mood, though it was far from an auspicious omen: Rocabarra, a great gray mountain of stone that had stood in the seas of Caledon for centuries unchanging, until that day when a Druid in his wrath had set a doom upon it, and it sank beneath the waves. Twice since had it reappeared, or so at least it was claimed; the third appearance—so also it was claimed—would signal the end of the world.

"And sometimes I think I would almost welcome it," muttered Aeron, and felt his startlement as much as her own: She had not meant to sound so bitter.

But Roderick only put a hand on her shoulder. "What do you fear?" he asked presently. "I think you have never truly told me."

Aeron shrugged, still staring at the racing cloudshadows on the moving sea. "Perhaps I have simply not met it yet—my true fear. If fear be defined as that which causes one to alter one's life to avoid it, there is but little: tidal waves, fire, a bat tangling in my hair—"

"Nothing magical? Have you never encountered aught to fear in the course of your workings?"

"Well, *surely*!" she said, as if the thing were self-evident; as it would have been to him had he been Druid. "But whatever they were—and some of them were fearful indeed—they did not cause me to change my path, so perhaps I did not fear them after all. Or perhaps it was only that I did not know enough to be afraid . . ."

"And what of your geisa?" Rhodri drew her away from the overlook, back along the track to Kinloch Arnoch; the horses, reins loose, followed amiably after. "Did *they* never cause you any bad moments?"

"Not so far. My chief birth-geis was that I am not to carry war out of Tara in the Wolf-moon. Not hard; who would, in her right wits, lead an army out to fight in the winds and mires of March? And if it were some battle in space that demanded my sword, well, armies can be led out of other places than Tara, and other folk than I may lead them, and so the geis need not be broken."

"That sounds special pleading to me, Aeron," said Rhodri doubtfully. "I think it can lead only to disaster if you try to use such splintered reason; like trying to drink from Madoc's Mether. Though you may well have preserved the letter of the geis, the spirit would be done violence to; and so would you in turn, as ever befalls those who break their geisa in arrogance or hardness of heart."

"Only in songs and sagas, master-bard." But Aeron's face had clouded over. "There *was* another geis," she said with difficulty, "laid upon me at Scartanore—but I will not speak of it now. What of you?" she asked, glancing sidewise at him. "What will become of your bardery now you are Prince of Scots?"

"Oh, I shall keep it up. No musician ever wholly forsakes his calling, even amid other calls. I have ever thought myself a bard before I thought of myself a prince—much to my father's annoyance."

"Who could hold to annoyance, when the prince makes music such as you have made? There are songs and chaunts of yours that will still be sung when the name of Aeron Ard-rían is remembered by none but the Shining Ones in their hollow hills."

"Be that so or no," said Rhodri, though his face had lighted with shy pleasure at her words, "just now it is the prince and not the bard who is called for. Let us go back and tell my parents I have put up the pipes for a time."

Now that her decision had been taken, Aeron felt at the same time not only more resigned to it than she had been, but happier than she had hoped to be. Still, though House Aoibhell had been informed as well as Clann Douglas, there were two others Aeron wished to have the news from her own mouth . . .

"Well," said Morwen when she had heard all the story, "I think it a fine solution, and the more so since I myself could see no way out of your trouble."

"It was the only way I *could* see," said Aeron gloomily, "for that I love Gwydion, and I love Rhodri—oh aye, did you not think I felt so?—and I love my parents, and there was no other way to find some joy for myself amongst all that without doing violence to one or all."

Morwen nodded, her face thoughtful. "True it is you have told me yourself how you believe you and Gwydion to be marked by dán to be each other's; and it is in my mind you are not wrong to think it . . . But dán chooses its own time, and if that time be not yet, why should you not follow another road for a while, and please the King and Queen as well? I am sure, m'chara, that whatever falls out with you and Rhodri is just as much dán as the other. Can you not trust to that?"

"That sounds like something Tybie said to me," admitted Aeron. "But if you as Rhodri's sister can say so—"

Morwen cast up her eyes to heaven. "Chriesta tighearna, Aeron Aoibhell, then do as you have decided and let it rest! Do as your parents wish, and as my parents have hoped; do as I would like so much to see you do! You and Rhodri will not be so unhappy, I think, and a year is soon past." The blue eyes were suddenly soft. "But Gwydion? What of him?"

What, indeed . . . "We have spoken of it, he and I," said Aeron, in a cool little voice that forbade further questioning. "And we shall speak of it again."

But when they did speak of it, Gwydion seemed less concerned than ever, and more amused than anything else at her confusion, despite the sight of the pale, rigidly controlled face before him.

"How many times have I told you? Aeronwy, do not torture yourself, for surely I do not . . . The Tanista of Keltia must be pulled in more directions than the Prince of Gwynedd or yet the Prince of Scots. None of this makes any differ in any way that matters; I know it, and you know it—or so at least I trust, by now—and Rhodri knows it too."

"Well, that may be," she said, "but to me it seems almost as if you do not wish it other wise, by how you behave."

At that his patience broke at last, and he reached out, seizing her by hair and arm together and pulling her round to face him. "Is *this* how you would have me behave?" he asked, voice rough now, torn between passion and anger. "Do you think *I* have not wished things other wise; that you and I might be together from the first and no other to stand between, far less a beloved friend? We have all three had lovers enough over the years to know the difference now—but I have Seen, and I say it is evil and selfish and a sin to turn away from dán . . . Aye, Aeronwy—nay, *look* at me—sin to turn away, and sin to try to alter; a bitter and bootless struggle to fight against dán, for you will lose and lose, and you will only wound yourself, and all around you, with your struggles."

"So we must just give in to it, then? We are just to give *up*?"

"We are to wait," answered Gwydion, calm again. Remorse came over him as he saw the ruin his grip had made of her tunic, and the clear red prints of his fingers on her skin. He touched the marks gently, but she pulled away.

"So we wait," she said. "If not now, then when? If then, why not now? How if we choose to overset the pattern; if we run off this instant, as did my own parents, to an unsanctioned bridal, announcing to them and to all Keltia that you and I are handfast, and you my irrevocable choice for king-consort—you, and never Roderick . . . He knows he is never to take the seat at my right hand, for all this match's politics."

"Aye, he knows; he understands as well as do we, for it is all linked, Aeronwy, like a coat of mail. You cannot sever one link without breaking all those others linked with it."

"You are the only one calls me 'Aeronwy', do you know

that?'' said Aeron after a long charged silence. "No other would dare.''

"With good reason," he said, smiling now, seeing that she had accepted all he had said to her, and, more than that, all that she had been saying to herself. "Even I dare call you so only for that I know you will allow it. Did I not know, I had not dreamed of daring.''

And Aeron, looking up at him, sensed that Gwydion spoke of more than merely daring an endearment of her name.

There was little ceremony, and no pageantry, to a brehon wedding, even when the two to be joined so were of such exalted station. All that the law asked was for the man and the woman to state their names and ranks and intention, and to name the duration of the contract and the terms of tinnscra, if any, before a robed brehon and two suitable witnesses. After the time contracted for had expired, the union could be dissolved by either party's public declaration; if any children came of the match, though all involved knew that unlikely to be the case here, they were legal heirs—though not necessarily chief heirs—and as true-born as children born of any other form of Keltic marriage, permanent or no.

On Brigit's night, the February chill as sharp in the air outside as was the mood of certain persons in attendance, Aeron stood with Rhodri before Halc'hyn her father's brehon, in the Presence Chamber of Turusachan. She did not glance sidewise to where Emer stood with Fionnbarr, and Faolan with Mared, but she knew well that the rite's spareness distressed them all. Emer still cherished the vain hope that her daughter would even yet change her mind or her heart, to choose Rhodri over Gwydion, to make him the king that would be. *Small hope to her,* thought Aeron grimly, *she knows me better than that, and better than most; this today is all that filial duty and the obedience of the Tanista will have of me. When the year is gone, the bond is gone with it, and there is the end of* that . . . In the meantime, her mother and Mared could cosset whatever hopes made them happy. Rhodri—she looked up at the tall form beside her, clad in the formal Douglas colors—Rhodri understood, and Gwydion, and she herself, and they were after all the only ones who mattered.

The ceremony was a brief one: Aeron and Roderick each

spoke the contract's promises—no vows were taken at such a joining—and then came the exchanging of tinnól, the traditional gifts given between the wedded pair. Aeron took from Morwen's hands a massive torc of twisted gold set with two huge ink-blue sapphires at the finials, and reaching up she placed it about Rhodri's neck; then in turn lifted her hair from her own throat as he fastened there a heavy gold chain from which depended a cabochon ruby the size of a hen's egg, glowing purple-red against her black silk gúna.

She raised her face for his kiss—light, formal, more a salute than a caress—and then the others came crowding round to wish them well. A small enough group, immediate family and closest friends only: Aeron had had Sabia and Rohan as her supporters, Roderick his brother Tarsuinn and his friend Kiernat ní Tornaigh. None of them had expected to see Gwydion there, but when they turned from the dais to adjourn to a nearby chamber for a celebration feast, he was standing in the shadows at the rear of the room.

Aeron felt rather than saw the surprise, and worse, that seized upon some of the others—her mother chief among those last—but as Gwydion came forward into the light she saw his face, and the peace that lay upon it, and she smiled as Rhodri beside her reached out his hand to his friend. *There, you see, my mother?* she asked in her mind. *I told you we had settled all among ourselves, and any road he is here today as any friend would be—but there have been other promises made than the ones made just now, and all of them shall be kept.*

Though Gwydion's appearance had been a surprise to all but Aeron and Rhodri, in the state chamber awaited another wedding guest that even Aeron could not have dreamed of seeing . . .

She was standing with her sister Ríoghnach and Niall O Kerevan, the Duke of Tir-connell and a distant Aoibhell cousin, whom Ríona had wedded four years past—the first to marry of all the royal brood, though she had been close followed by Kieran, eldest of the twins, who had taken as his bride Eiluned of Garioch, an effervescent Scotan who brought as tinnscra lands on Caledon, at Inver in the Decies Country. They had been talking of family matters, naught of import, when suddenly the crowd shifted, and past Niall's shoulder Aeron saw a face she had not seen for long.

"*Duvessa?*" For an instant Aeron thought she had been mistaken, but then the woman turned, and Duvessa Cantelon, for it was indeed she, came gliding forward with both hands held out to Aeron.

"Tanista," she said with a deferential smile. "And Princess of Scots—"

Aeron felt a small quiver pass over her, as the leaves of the shiveroak will do at even the slightest breath of air, then it was gone. *She calls me by Rhodri's title, but by the terms of the contract it is not even lawfully mine . . .*

"Not so that last," she said then, "and no need to call me Tanista, as if we were not friends from old. But tell me of yourself, Duvessa; how have you kept yourself since our days at Scartanore?"

"Well enough. You may not know I too went for a Fian, though I trained at a humbler establishment than Caer Artos; also I was obliged to depart before it came time for the triail-triarach . . . Still, I acquitted myself creditably enough to earn a place in your new lord's guard; it is as such that I am here today. Did you not know?"

Though there was no cause, Aeron felt strangely betrayed; as if Rhodri, Morwen, Sabia, *someone,* should indeed have let her know, so that it came not as so complete a surprise. But Duvessa was speaking again.

"Come, Aeron; I'll wager you have not had a bite to eat since you came from the ceremony." She lifted a silver dish from the laden table. "Now this is a delicacy from my own home, sent here and prepared expressly to my instructions for your wedding-feast."

Aeron looked down at the silver ashet, and the savory stew it contained. "It looks delicious, Vessa; what is it?"

"Oh, only game seethed in wine and spices. Though the game was special enough: a red stag from our own estates, hunted by my mother's pack of gazehounds." She looked innocently at Aeron, who now stared at the dish as if it were a nest of nathairs. "Is aught amiss, Aeron?"

Only everything . . . I had not dreamed she could still hate me so— For it was Aeron's geis that she not refuse any dish offered her at a feast, and geis also that she not eat of the meat of the red stag; and both those geisa had been laid upon her by Duvessa herself. *She does this a-purpose, knowing I cannot escape: Which is worse to break, or to keep? For if I keep one I must surely break the other* . . .

Slowly Aeron drew the little silver sgian from its sheath on her left wrist, where she had worn it for the ceremony. *It is the lesser evil if I eat of it, though it choke me, for if I do not, I break host-laws as well; she herself does great violence to many laws, but that is her trouble and not mine* . . . She managed to force down a bite or two of the venison, not even tasting it in her mouth, but watching Duvessa's face all the while.

"I shall tell my mother to commend her houndmaster and his pack, so well did they hunt for the Tanista," said Duvessa, replacing the cover on the ashet and smiling again her tight little smile.

Aeron had no reply, but it did not matter, for all at once Sabia was beside her, and she had more than enough to say for both of them.

"I *thought* I saw your ill-found face," said Sabia, in a voice that in any hunting creature would have been the snarl before the kill. "I see too what you have wrought here; very clever, to set geisa upon one you envied and feared, and then see to it that one way or another she must break them. I recall well that afternoon in the annat of Scartanore; do *you* recall what I said to you then?"

Sabia smiled as Duvessa paled a little and began to back away, and it was not a smile Duvessa could have wished to see.

"So now I say a little more in that same vein," continued Sabia, beginning to enjoy herself. "Just a small glam-dicenn, such as we of the Ban-draoi learn to pronounce at Scartanore . . . Duvessa of the Cantelons—who were ever a tarnished kindred—may your own evil turn and stalk you and smite you down in the end. May you walk upon serpents and sleep on splinters. May you lie with a duergar, and bear him a púca, and may the seven terriers of hell sit on your shoulder and bark in at your ear all the days of your life—and may there not be many more of those. Go now, and thank the Tanista and the rest of this company and the nature of this day that I do not rip out your liver here and now and feed it to the geese."

She watched in satisfaction as Duvessa fled from the chamber, then turned to Aeron, who was staring at her aghast. "Well, what would you have *had* me do!" she challenged. "She has richly deserved it, and for long . . . For there is a thing you do not know," added Sabia in a lower tone, linking her arm through Aeron's and drawing her into a nearby oriel. "It was not by chance, as she would have you think, that Duvessa came to be in Rhodri's guard; I had it from several mouths that she is deep in love with him, and has been for some years. She engineered the duty to be near him, in what hopes I shrink to say, and when she learned that you and he were to be brehon-wed, even one year of such union was too much for her."

"So she came here to induce me to break my geis on my marriage-day," said Aeron. "A fine omen to begin that year . . . Well, it is done now. Does Rhodri know?" she added, suddenly alarmed, though for what cause she could not say.

"That she has done so, or that she does feel so? Neither, I think; would it matter?"

"Most like not; but all the same I would not have him learn of it . . . and any road, we do not long remain here. We leave tonight for our wedding-journey to Armoy, and Duvessa will *not* be in the tail that comes with us. We spend five weeks in the lake-country, and then return to bid my parents farewell on that embassy to Kuniath that has been so long planned. Rhodri is to go with them as commander of their escort."

"That seems a little hard, to take him away so soon, and to send him out-Wall as well."

"It was all settled months ago," said Aeron with a shrug, "before there was any talk of a wedding. My father offered to release him from the duty, but he would not be kept from it. Still, it is only for a fortnight; then he will be back and we will settle in here at Turusachan, and arrange terms of residence at Kinloch Arnoch also; he must be there a stated number of days each month, for reasons of governance." Aeron laughed. "All of which you very well know, for you come with us to Armoy."

"And happy to be asked; Armoy is very fair in early spring."

"The lakes are always fair no matter the season," agreed Aeron. "It will be a strange thing indeed to have naught to do there but enjoy them . . . Come, let us go and give greeting to

Faolan and Mared; I have not yet spoken to them as sinsear-
cheile, and I would not have them fault me as daughter so
soon.''

Armoy was lovely indeed when they came there; Aeron and
Rhodri and the tail they had brought—some of her folk from
Turusachan and some of his from Kinloch Arnoch—were royally
housed in a small castle, given over to their use by the lord of
Kensaleyre, that stood high on a crag above the blue chain-lakes.
For perhaps the first and last times in their lives, they had no
duties but their own whims and pleasures, and, as Tybie had
foreseen and Morwen had prophesied, neither was there any
sword between them in their bed. If there was no true-passion
either, there was surely caring, and desire, and the security of
long friendship, and for both of them it more than sufficed. But
the enforced idleness, pleasant as it was, began to work upon
Aeron, and before the five weeks were out she began to feel a
little guilt at her own inaction.

She confided as much to Sabia, one afternoon warm with the
spring that came early to that far southern corner of the continent. The two of them were sitting comfortably ensconced in
longchairs, on a sun-drenched terrace overlooking the lake; Rhodri
and most of the rest of the company had gone hunting in the
hills.

Sabia had protested, laughing, that one's marriage-moon was
hardly the time to be pining for everyday chores. But Aeron had
not been seeing it quite so.

" 'Autonomy is the price of sloth'—so said the Ard-rían
Aoife, though of course she was speaking about far different
matters. But it is all the same true, Sabhait: The lazier one is, the
more one permits others to do for one and choose for one, the
less hold one has on the reins of one's own life. Once the habit
of choosing is lessened or lost, so too is the will, even, to
choose. The less one chooses, the less one *can* choose.''

"She was a wise woman, the Shan-rían,'' said Sabia, offering
Aeron another round from the ale-keeve.

"Oh, sometimes, only,'' said Aeron, pausing to take a deep
draught. "For each time she taxed Keltia with her wisdom and
won, three times there were when she tried it with her folly, and
lost. And the worst of *those* times, I think, was Lykken; not only

did it cause much woe in her own day, but it set the pattern for this most recent enmity with Fomor.''

''We have been unfriends with the Fomori before now, and will again.''

''Truly; but, I know not how it is, there is something dark and very evil about this present feud.'' Aeron resettled herself beneath the laprobe of silver fur that covered her from toes to waist; for all the sun's warmth, the air was cool still. ''I have sensed it growing of late—almost as if Bres is preparing himself to throw something monstrous against us, and his is not the only presence I have sensed.''

''His son, then? Prince Elathan? Or perhaps the demiprince, Talorcan?''

Aeron hesitated, as a hound or wolf will that has lost the scent, then shook her head. ''Nay, not he. Strange enough, the name that comes to mind is Alphor.''

''Alphor! The Emperor Strephon—''

But again Aeron shook her head. ''Someone who is a greater sorcerer even than Strephon, though I cannot see the face.''

''Have you spoken of this feeling to Roderick, or to the King?''

''What would I say to either of them? I have not tested it; have not put it to the taghairm or the imbas-forosnai or any other divination that might prove me right or wrong. I have not even consulted Kesten or Tybie on it . . . Even did I so, even did I learn for fact that Alphor *was* in it, that the sorcerer was indeed Strephon, or his daughter Helior, or her son Jaun Akhera—what could I tell my father to do about it? We can hardly arm for war on the ground of my feeling. Nay,'' she said, and ran her hand through her hair in baffled frustration, ''we must wait. And pray gods we shall have better warning in good time.''

When Roderick returned with his attendants from the hunt, he saw them still lolling on the terrace, and detoured at once to join them. Dropping a kiss on Aeron's red-gold head, he seated himself beside her and waved off those who had followed after. Sabia, murmuring some excuse, tactfully slipped away as well, and they were alone.

Aeron, watching him as he lay back in the longchair, eyes closed, hair and beard impossibly golden in the westering sun, thought suddenly to tell him of her doubts, then as suddenly decided against it, wishing as she had a hundred times since they were wed that things might have been different between them. *For I do love him, as I told Wenna; yet not as I might have loved him, had I not come to care so for*— But she had resolved not to speak that name, nor even think it overmuch . . . As for her premonitions, if warnings they were, she would say naught of those either. *I would not cloud this time we have with such mist-begotten fears; there will be time later to speak of those . . .*

"What news from the hill?" she asked instead.

Rhodri smiled, though he did not open his eyes, luxuriating in the feel of the sun on his face and the pleasant exhaustion the hard day's hunt had brought.

"There is better news than that for your ear," he said. "The Master of Sail has sent word of the ordering of the Kuniath voyage: He gives me *Corwalch* for the command ship of the Ard-rígh's escort." Opening his eyes, he was in time to see Aeron go away for an instant—a few seconds there and back again—and leaning over to her took her hand in sudden concern. "Ansa? What is it?"

"I know not," said Aeron, stunned by the strength of the feeling. "For a moment there, when you said *Corwalch*—I had such a turn as I have never had before . . . It is gone now. But *Corwalch* is one of our best fighting ships; surely my great-uncle Elharn, as Master of Sail, does not think there is danger? Kuniath has ever been a peaceful friend to us."

"Kuniath, aye; but the road there is not the safest path through the stars. Therefore your great-uncle Ironbrow, as master of the starfleet, and Alasdair Ruthven as First Lord of War, insisted on *Corwalch* being the lead ship of the escort." But the haunted look did not leave her eyes, and Roderick tried again to cheer her. "Do not look so! Naught ill will befall. *Corwalch* alone is more than enough to guarantee the convoy's protection; and *Tuala* also has ample defenses of her own. She is your father's own ship; and any road, she is named for you—'Princess of the People.' That alone should suffice to discourage would-be brigands."

As he had meant her to, Aeron smiled at that, and lifted his hand to kiss it, and their converse turned to other matters. But the fear, and the feeling, had not gone.

Chapter 27

Fionnbarr took the big emerald ring from his finger and put it on Aeron's hand, and both of them looked down at it in silence.

"There!" he said presently. "The leas-ríocht is now yours, and you have from this moment until the moment of my return the full governance of Keltia. The Silver Branch, that you have wielded these six years past; and now the Great Seal, which signifies all the power conferred by the Copper Crown itself. In law, you are more than Regent; you stand as Ard-rían in my place, and not even I may now gainsay your edicts."

"Oh aye?" said Aeron laughing. "Then how if I banish you and my mother from Keltia forever?"

"Then we would go off in great relief and lightness of heart," he returned, laughing with her, "for that mil-na-mela we have never yet had."

Aeron looked up at him a little wistfully. "And do you still feel the need of a marriage-moon after all these years?"

"Surely; and perhaps if this embassy to Kuniath goes well we shall take some time after for holiday, and let you manage things here a little longer."

"Well, see you leave it not *too* long, then," Aeron told him. "Else I might grow a taste for power sooner than is my right, and you have something of a tussle to get this back."

But this time Fionnbarr did not rise to her teasing tone. "That, I think, is one thing you shall never need fear acquiring; nor do I fear it in you. You have not been the most biddable Tanista Keltia ever had, and certainly not the most tranquil, but power has never been for you a temptation or real desire—not so?"

"You and the Queen, and others beside, took great care that it

301

should not be," said Aeron, matching his sudden seriousness. "And you were successful; small credit to me." She glanced down again at the heavy ring, and he followed her gaze.

The ring had been made more than two thousand years ago for one of the Dôniaid kings of Keltia—Gwydion's line. After that, the High Kingship had passed to Clann Douglas, and then on to the Aoibhells, and all those reigns the ring had gone with it. It was a massive and impressive thing: a wide band of dark gold, incised with Keltic interlace, bearing an emerald two inches long by an inch wide. The huge gem weighed down Aeron's hand, and the gold band fit loose on her thin finger.

But she felt an immediate affinity with the great green stone, seeing as if for the first time, though she had always known it, that the sixfold knot of Keltia was carved into its polished table. *I have worked with crystals and lithfaens and other stones of magical properties, but this one is different from all . . .* She could sense the presence in the emerald of the others who had borne it: Arthur himself was in that stone, and St. Keina of the house of Douglas, and the great warrior queen Athyn Anfa, the one the Kelts had called Mother-of-storms; so too was Brendan Mór, first of the Aoibhell line, and all the Aoibhells after him for eight hundred years—

"You are one of those the stone cherishes."

Aeron had forgotten her father still stood there, looked up to see his smiling face touched with a certain sadness.

"Not every ruler to wear that stone is loved by it," said Fionnbarr. "Some it but tolerates; others it has been known to repudiate entirely—aye, three kings and two queens has it driven from the throne, and events did prove that it was right to do so. Even of those it deigns to suffer, not all are equally fit in its judgment."

"You speak of it as if it were a living thing."

"In many ways I think it is," he agreed. He took his daughter's hand and turned it so that light suddenly flooded through the stone's green heart. "It is more—*aware* than any of the other royal treasures: Neither crown nor throne nor scepter has the living sentience I have felt from this—surely it is a great deal more sentient than some human servants of the monarch, and even some monarchs too! It has approval for me; but you,

Aeron, will be among those few it chooses to love, and it is for those that it reserves its greatest power.''

Aeron tilted her a hand a little, seeing the flaw that lay like a flame deep within the stone. ''Power? To what end?''

''To whatever end the wearer wills: victory in war, as Arthur willed, and Athyn too, though they willed for Keltia's weal and not their personal glory; or triumph in faith, as Keina; or magic, as Brendan Mór; or knowledge, or healing, or any of a dozen different ends. It shall be you who choose, cariadol, but the stone that confirms that choice.''

''Speak of it no more,'' said Aeron quickly; she had caught something of her father's mysterious sadness, some echo of a strange and distant grief, and she would for no sake that it came any clearer or nearer to either of them. ''It will be very well,'' she said, and now she was reassuring herself as much as comforting him. ''You will see: I shall not even have grown accustomed to the weight of this thing on my hand before you are returned to wear it once more.''

She slipped her arms around Fionnbarr's neck and held him close a few moments, then stepped back and bowed and left. But as she went along the palace corridors, on her way to bid farewell to some of the others who were to accompany the King beyond the Pale, Aeron tightened her hand to a fist over the ring's unfamiliar weight, by no means so sure as she had spoken.

Long before Bres of Fomor had finished detailing his plan to Elathan, his son was struggling not so much to comprehend but to keep the horror he felt from showing upon his face; by the time his father *had* finished, that fight had long been lost, and he could control his words no more than he had been able to control his countenance.

''Have you no thought at all for the *treachery* of the thing? Nay,'' Elathan contradicted himself, with a savage laugh, ''I can see where you would not . . . Well, let me put it this way: Have you no thought for the consequences to your people—to yourself? No thought of what must surely happen when the Kelts learn that Bres of Fomor has slaughtered their King and Queen? What of the reprisals they will take?''

''If I am successful enough, they will not be capable of reprisal,'' said Bres, his face black with displeasure. He had expected his heir's support in this, as he had already had the enthusiastic approval of his elder son Talorcan.

"If your quarrel with King Fionnbarr demands such satisfaction after all this time—as I see it seems to—then face him with honor on the field, not like this . . . And what of all those folk with him on the embassy, who will die with him, all to feed your own ancient grudge?"

"I have no grudge against Queen Emer," conceded Bres. "I have never met her and have no reason to suppose her aught other than a good queen and loyal wife . . . As to her, and the others who must die with Fionnbarr, if that is their fate, then I am but the instrument."

"You are a tool!" said Elathan furiously. "I know well who it is that incites you to this; it *cannot* be merely a slight dealt you decades ago—"

"No," said Bres, watching him. "I did not think you would truly understand, Prince Elathan; though I had hoped you might . . . So. You think I am encouraged in this solely by your brother—"

"*Half*-brother!"

"—by your brother Talorcan. He is of course one of my heirs, and as my eldest child, he has the same right as do you to speak his mind to his father, as well as to counsel his King. I will not say that he approves or opposes the course I have fixed upon, but the idea is mine alone, and the time at last is right. Fionnbarr has not come out from behind the Curtain Wall for many years. And those few times that he did were times when I was not in a position to take advantage; but now all that is changed, and, whether I have your approval, your neutrality or your active opposition, I intend to avenge myself on Fionnbarr Aoibhell." Bres paused to collect himself. "I will not prolong the suffering," he said in a quieter voice. "It will be a clean end and a quick one for all of them. And that I can promise you."

"And can you also promise me, and the rest of the Fomori, not to mention the Phalanx and our chancy friends the Cabiri Imperium, that we will be safe from retaliation afterwards?" Elathan was running out of arrows, and both of them knew it; but he kept his tone one of reason. *Or as near as I can make it, to reason with a madman* . . . "Though Fionnbarr, as you never tire of pointing out to me, is perhaps not the greatest of warriors, he has many loyal servants—not to speak of friends and relations—who are. Moreover, there is his heir to think of. Aeron has made herself over the past ten years a certain reputation in war as well as in temper; I need not remind you of how she has fared in her martial actions against us in defense of Keltia's Protectorates. And she has just taken a lord whose name in the field is at least the match of hers. Do you tell me *they* will sit idly by and let Fionnbarr's murder go unavenged?''

''They cannot prove it.''

''They will find a way to prove it,'' said Elathan, suddenly sure. ''At least, Aeron will—Father, I beg you, let the past enmity between you and Fionnbarr—whatever the cause may have been, I do not know and nor do I wish to—let it *be* past. Let *it* die, not him.''

Not even for an instant did it seem that his son's powerful plea had found some mark: Bres turned on his heel and went to the door.

''Never.''

Why do I even bother, thought Bres with no small bitterness as he strode from his son's chambers. *This sheep-hearted appeasement of his is nothing new, it has been so for years—every time I would take any action against Keltia or Keltic interests. One would almost think him suborned by some Keltic spy . . . But not this time; this time he must be with me or risk his rank as my successor. I could do it; could have him set aside—it would not be easy, but it could be done. And if Elathan does not very speedily show something very much more to my liking than this—* forbearance, *by the gods I will have him unseated, and quickly too . . .*

But it was a good plan he had worked up with his generals, and it would be successful; of that he was quite sure. It had taken rather longer than he might have liked, or could have thought, back there on Ganaster, when he had first vowed he would have his vengeance if it took him the rest of his life and cost him crown and queen and heirs and kingdom. But now it was almost within his grasp, and in the end it had proved so absurdly simple—

Bres leaned against a window embrasure, staring down over Tory far below, though in his mind's eye he saw a very different

picture. When word of Fionnbarr's out-Wall journey had been
brought to Bres by Fomorian spies, and the destination of Kuniath
made public, Bres had mapped out the route of the Keltic king
and had then sat back, well pleased. For the way Fionnbarr
would take to Kuniath went within striking distance of a Fomorian
garrison world called Bellator: a small moon of a barren planet in
the Alcluith system; not near enough to Fionnbarr's route to
cause the Kelts undue alarm—especially with a military escort—
but certainly near enough for a killing strike to be launched from
the base Fomor had long maintained on that planet.

And so now it was all in place, waited only on his word. So
confident was he of the secrecy and successful outcome of the
ambush to come that he had even sent his youngest son, Tharic,
to Bellator to watch his father's triumph. Basilea had of course
protested, he recalled now with disgust, but the boy was past
twenty; time it was he saw a little of what it meant to be a
prince, and a prince of Fomor. It would not be a pleasant thing
for him to have to watch, but it was something all princes must
grow accustomed to; the boy would be safe enough in the care of
the garrison commander.

Bres went on his way, a little slower now. Whatever else
came out of this attack, did only Fionnbarr perish it would all be
worth it. It would mean, of course, total estrangement from his
own queen; but he and Basilea had lived apart, in their hearts as
well as in their persons, for a good many years now. She did not
yet know what he intended, though she knew something of
reverberant consequences was toward. Even Thona might turn
against him when the deed was accomplished; and at that thought
Bres balked more than a little. *Well, if it must be, then it will be,*
he thought reluctantly, *though I had not believed there was
anything under heaven that could come between us* . . .

Yet he knew that even Thona could not turn him from the way
he had chosen. Of course Fionnbarr's death would only serve to
make his daughter Queen; but this young Aeron was scarce out
of tutelage, younger even than Elathan. He was not even certain
if Keltic law would permit her to take the throne herself; she
might well have to suffer the guiding hand of a regent—which
by all accounts he had heard of her she would detest—and that
too could only prove well for him. *Either an unsurely seated
regent or an untried girl: It must be good for Fomor either way.*

Very soon, he would learn just how good for Fomor it would be.

So the Keltic embassy departed for Kuniath: Fionnbarr Ardrígh, and the Queen Emer ní Kerrigan, and a hundred of their folk aboard the *Tuala*, and a military escort of three destroyers commanded by their daughter's lord Roderick Douglas, just returned that morning, with Aeron, from Armoy.

From the windows of her rooms in Turusachan, Aeron watched the steel-colored needles stitch upward through the blue sky: shuttlecraft ferrying the royal party to the starships waiting in orbit beyond the Criosanna. At any other time she would have gone out to Mardale Port with them, to bid them gods'-speed and watch them depart. But she had been for once unsure of her ability to command her composure, and so her goodbyes had been said privately, here in the palace precincts.

Her parents had been high-spirited and merry, she recalled now, as if they were in truth going on holiday instead of on a dull diplomatic errand, and all her father's strange mood of that morning, when he gave the Great Seal into her keeping, seemed vanished like snow under sun. Her farewell to Rhodri had been more strained, for she had not managed to dispel the aura of disaster to come that had gripped her in Armoy. But she had hidden it well enough from him, she reflected, for he had given no sign that he had noted her unquiet. She had sent him off lovingly, banishing her fears from her own heart with the cold light of logic: If Rhodri were in peril, then so too were her parents, and she had had no premonition of *that*; therefore there could be *no* danger, and she was a thickhead indeed to think there might be.

With a flex of her shoulders, as if she shook off portent like an ill-fitting gúna, Aeron drew closed the window casements and went to find Rohan and Morwen. *If I cannot free myself from this mood, I would wager those two between them can manage my deliverance within the hour; if not—well, did not my father say I stand as Ard-rían? If they fail to cheer me up, I shall banish them both . . .*

The first real chore of Aeron's leas-ríocht was not slow in coming: a Council meeting at which she must preside, the next morning; a routine session, such as she had conducted often before in her father's absence. There was naught of real significance to discuss, and once she had opened the session, and one Councillor after another took the floor to drone interminably on, Aeron began to fidget just a little.

She could never afterwards say precisely just when the disquiet became known to her; perhaps it had been silently growing for hours, and only then had pierced the barrier of her conscious mind, some plant rising up through thick black earth to meet the light at last.

Whatever might have been the truth of it, after half a morning's discussion, bored and a little peevish, Aeron leaned back in her chair, one hand toying with the pendant jewel that hung from its gold chain round her neck: the great ruby that Rhodri had given her five weeks since, upon their marriage-day.

She touched the cold stone to her lips. *Where is the fire said to sleep in these? This jewel might be comet-ice; is it some sort of omen, then, for our year together?* No sooner did she think it than she felt it: She turned the ruby to catch the sunlight streaming in through the skylights, but the red depths did not kindle, and her unease began to grow.

Closing her fingers over the stone, Aeron sat up in her seat, oblivious to the sidelong glances thrown in her direction by others at the long table, and, in the way she had learned at Scartanore, sent her spirit to seek after her lord, as easily as she might stretch out her hand to him had he been by. But for all her effort she caught only a trace of him, far away and moving fast. *Farther and faster than I like . . .* Her alarm rose now to small panic. *I do not usually have to reach so far to find him; nor any other I do love . . .* Mere distance alone would not account for the distance she sensed; some other thing was afoot, and now real fear took root and began to bloom like an evil pale flower.

But the Council must meet, and the Tanista must conduct the meeting; any fears however consuming would have to wait upon duty at least a little while longer. *After the meeting is done,* she thought. *Then I will have the time and undivided mind I need to make a proper search for him; after the meeting. After, I will know.*

And so she would; but sooner rather than later, and not as she had thought.

Chapter 28

Aeron's hand was still closed upon the ruby when Rohan, all unannounced, entered the room. All those at the table looked up at the Prince in surprise, and surely he must have known they were there, but if any had asked him afterwards, he would have sworn he saw no one in that chamber but his sister.

From her place at the table's head, Aeron smiled at him as he came round to stand beside her; though her smile held a question in it, for Rohan was not one lightly to interrupt state business, and had indeed been summoned earlier to his own seat on the Council, and none had been able to say why he had absented himself.

"Brother?" she said, the smile fading a little, to be replaced by puzzlement, and, though she tried to quash it, fresh fear.

But before Rohan could draw breath to speak the words that he knew, and she was beginning to suspect, must be spoken, there came a sound from outside the palace, an eerie descant rolling down from high above them on the slopes of Eagle; a sound that struck like a knife and hung like doom in the air—the utterly mournful, lamenting howl of a wolf.

For a long time it seemed that no one moved; indeed, while the dreadful keen throbbed round them, it seemed that none had power even to breathe. Then there was silence, and into that terrible silence Rohan spoke.

"Ard-rían," was all he said, and went to one knee before his sister.

Aeron's face, that had gone white to the lips at the first note of the keen, went paler still, and she put out a hand to him as if in entreaty—one that must be denied, for she knew as did all of them that from that keen there was no appeal.

"*Nay,* Rohan, it is *not*—"

He rose then from his knee, holding himself straight as a spear, reciting the formal words without inflection. "My sorrow to bring to the Ard-rían Aeron and to the Ard-eis Keltannach the tidings of the death of the Ard-rígh Fionnbarr XIV, together with the Queen Emer and Roderick Prince of Scots and all their party, in an ambush on their way to Kuniath, near the planetoid known as Bellator in the Alcluith system, at the hands and by design of the Fomori. The word comes to the Fianna by way of Falias station on the Curtain Wall and cannot be doubted." He paused an instant, then, his face a mask, methodically completed the dreadful formula. "Gods save Aeron Queen of Kelts."

The silence was even more profound than before; the stricken Councillors seemed in their shock to have resolved into eyes only, and all those eyes were fixed now on Aeron. To judge by her expression, she herself saw nothing, seemingly, and her face bore no emotion in it at all.

Down the table's length, Elharn stirred, and as if he had somehow commanded her, with a slowness beyond words Aeron dragged her glance up to meet his at last. *Nay,* he thought through his own blinding pain, *she must not be permitted to give in to it now, for if she does she may well never come out of it again* . . .

"Ard-rían?" he said, clearly and deliberately. "What is the High Queen's will?"

That seemed to register on her, pulling her back, however brutally, from wherever she had been. Aeron flinched as at a whip-crack across her face, but she stood up, and all the others at once followed suit.

Son of Aoife, she thought, *you do well—very well—to remind your new Ard-rían of her duty* . . . She glanced at the rest of them. *But my true duty is rather otherwise, and what you do not know of, you cannot hinder; though naught short of physical restraint, and perhaps not even that, should keep me from it* . . . She left the room without a word to any of them, not even Rohan, and in her wake there was at first stunned silence, then a frenzy of query. But as Aeron left the chamber, she spoke to a page who hovered outside.

"Tell the portmaster at Mardale to make my ship *Dubhlinnseach* ready for space. I will sail within the hour."

Aeron encountered no one else as she strode through the halls of the palace to her own rooms. It was as if all Turusachan had been suddenly unpeopled, though a small corner of her brain told her that the palace folk had but gone to each other for comfort as word of the calamity spread, seeking to ease their grief and shock in the company of friends as devastated as they.

For herself she had no such option. In the round bedchamber, she put on the black battle dress of the Dragon Kinship, tearing Rhodri's jewel from her neck—*Better it is that what I am soon to see, and to do, should not cling to this token of happier times*—and leaving her weapons in their places, for the vengeance she had in mind would require different weapons altogether.

Until that moment's thought of her vengeance to come, Aeron had by force of will managed to keep any picture or image of what had happened out of her mind's eye. *Nay, I must not think of them now, for if I do I will surely break, and if I break I will not be able to do what I mean to do* . . . But it was too great for anyone's strength to bear, and for a moment she reeled under it. *My father, my mother, my lord, my friends—ah, Mighty Mother, not* all *of them!* But only for a moment, ten heartbeats, no more; then she was heading to the landing-pad several floors below, where an aircar always stood ready and which would take her now to Mardale and her ship.

Running footsteps sounded behind her, and then Morwen had seized her arm, and was pulling her to a halt.

"Aeron—oh, Aeron, I do not know what you mean to do, but whatever it is, surely it will be better done after time for thought!"

"*That* I doubt!" said Aeron, a little surprised to find that she could converse, that her mind and mouth and voice obeyed her will. "Any road," she continued, "I myself do not yet know what I shall do; do you know me so much better?"

"Sometimes, aye, I think I must," said Morwen unflinching. "Your duty is to stay here, with the folk, to keep yourself safe, to wait and see what further word may come before you act. Aeron, you are Ard-rían now, gods help you—your life is no longer solely your own, and your duty—"

"Duty!" Aeron's eyes blazed green, and for all their long

loving friendship Morwen stepped back a pace. "We will see soon enough about my duty! A creagh-rígh, as new-made rulers did in ancient times, is now my chiefest duty: to my parents, to Rhodri—and you his sister would surely not deny him that—to all the others with them . . ."

"Well, if you will not remember your duty," said Morwen desperately, though she had nearly broken when Aeron spoke Rhodri's name, "then do you remember your geisa! Not to take war out of Tara in the Wolf-moon—"

It is March, thought Aeron, surprised even in her turmoil of heart. *I had forgotten. All the same—*

"It is not war I shall take; it is revenge."

"That is splitting it too fine by any measure! In the name of Nia, then, Aeron, I beg you—"

Aeron checked at that, without question caught more truly by that plea than by the other. For that too was her geis, not to refuse any who asked of her in Nia's name. *But, given what has befallen, Wenna cannot think even that could hold me; though Nia is not one I would willingly deny. But be that so or no, I will not be denied my intent.*

With an effort she made as if to move away, but Morwen clung to her arm, like a drowning swimmer to the last spar of a foundered ship.

"If you do this—if you do this thing, Aeron, you will prove that everything folk have said about you is true, that they have called you aright all these years when they called you Aeron Anfa—and that you have no more temperance or self-control than does . . . than does Bres himself."

'Aeron Anfa' . . . it was Rhodri called me 'Ansa', to make play on the words . . . But even through the stab of pain and joy combined at the tender memory, even through the spasm of fury that seized her on hearing Bres's name, so strong and so violent that for an instant she lost her power of sight, even in her haste to be gone and her anger that even her beloved sister-in-law dared detain her, Aeron laughed.

"And was the King of Fomor all so intemperate, then—to wait near seventy years for his one perfect chance, and to take it so completely when it came? In *my* book that is cold patience, or nothing is." But when Morwen still barred her path: "Let me by, Lochcarron. Who rules here now?"

"Ard-rían?" said Morwen flatly; but she stood aside.

Aeron dropped her eyes, shouldering past in silence, and Morwen did not try again to hold her back.

Summoned by Rohan's frantic message from his maenor of Llys Dôn a few lai from Turusachan, Gwydion reached the field at Mardale just in time to see *Dubhlinnseach* race overhead, like a thundercloud running low upon a hurricane wind. The beautiful black ship swept down the valley and passed over the city beyond, then turning sharply out over the sea shot upward thousands of feet in a few seconds, vanishing into hyperspace barely past atmosphere. Gwydion caught his breath, swearing, at the elegance and utter recklessness of the maneuver. It had been superbly flown, but to go into hyperflight so close in to a planet was foolhardy, and dangerous in the extreme.

Though she is well past caring . . .

"I could not make her stay," said Morwen, coming up beside him where he stood with Rohan and some others. Her face was pale and haunted; the succession of hammer-blow shocks had worked the same upon them all, and as she stared after Aeron's vanished ship, Morwen's grief began at last to overtake her, and she leaned sobbing into Gwydion's side. "Oh gods—she heard not a word I said to her . . ."

Gwydion put his arm around her shaking shoulders, closing his eyes and his mind against his own grief. "She would have heard me no better."

For all its swiftness in flight, even the Black-sailed took a few hours to come to the scene of the disaster. So hard had Aeron pushed her craft, though, that only two other ships, both of them Keltic warships that had been on out-Wall station in that sector, were there before her. The ships hovered now near the blasted wrecks of the embassy craft, like dumbly grieving beasts who cannot comprehend what has befallen their comrades at the hunter's hands.

When Aeron emerged from her shuttle into the main companionway of the *Tuala,* there was a somber knot of people awaiting her: officers from the two warships, strangers to her mostly, but some of whom she knew, and one of whom, her old Fian comrade Vevin ní Talleron, she knew very well indeed. She paid no heed to any of them, not hearing their murmured condolences, not seeing the salutes paid to her new rank, but moved impatiently through their midst, and they stood aside for her to left and right as she came at last to her parents' quarters.

They lay in each other's arms, faces down, Fionnbarr uppermost, as if he had attempted to shield his wife with his own body from the shattered vitriglass and twisted metal beams that had come crashing down upon them. They had died quickly, for their faces were peaceful; Emer's bore even yet the trace of a smile, as if she had looked up into her husband's face for a last loving farewell. Someone, perhaps one of the officers from the newly-arrived destroyers, had closed their eyes, to spare her that task at least, but they had not otherwise been touched or shifted.

Aeron knelt beside them, taking her father's hand in her left hand and her mother's in her right, and bowed her head. For all her Ban-draoi training in the holy words such a moment demanded, naught came to her now but the simplest farewell she knew, the first she had ever learned to speak: '*S é do bheatha, King of Kelts; 's é do bheatha, Queen of Keltia* . . . 'Life to you': Not a priestess's farewell, nor yet a High Queen's, but a child's.

Setting their hands down again, one in the other, Aeron tugged gently at the black-and-silver ring upon Fionnbarr's midfinger—the Unicorn Signet of the House of Aoibhell, that had been the personal seal of Brendan Mór, first of that line. *Fifteen before me, Ard-rían and Ard-rígh alike, have taken this ring from the dead hand of the one who bore it before them: father, sister, mother, brother. They have mourned, and they have claimed this ring—as I do now—to set beside that other ring—as I do now—and claiming those they have claimed the Crown—as I have already done. And one day someone shall mourn me, and shall take the rings from my hand in my turn; and that is very much as it should be. And so is this, but—oh gods, tasyk, mamaith!—I cannot feel it just yet* . . .

Aeron held the ring clenched in her hand a moment longer, then in one violent move thrust it onto her right forefinger, as the Great Seal already glowed green upon her left, and fisting both hands rose again to her feet.

There will be time enough later for those holy words, and holier hearts than mine to give them wings. But time is now for a rite rather more to my heart. And turned away.

*   *   *

On the bridge of the *Corwalch*, it was much the same, save that here they had at least died fighting: dead Fians and dead Dragons, dead kerns and dead officers, and somewhere their dead captain . . . but where *was* that captain—*Rhodri? Where are you?*

Aeron stepped onto the bridge, and those whose sad task had already begun of straightening and identifying and bearing the dead away in honor snapped to instant attention for her, and then withdrew, to leave her alone with her lost.

I know he is here; but I cannot see him . . . She stared round her at the destruction, far worse than that on the *Tuala*; though the end was the same, these had died much harder. *As well they should have, for they were warriors; no red for these lions of mine.*

Moving cautiously past a projecting spar of jagged metal, Aeron found herself looking down on the dead face of Duvessa Cantelon. *So, Vessa; in the end the geis you laid upon me, and then caused me to break, did work against us both. You it destroyed, and me it may yet destroy, and perhaps Sabia's glam-dicenn helped to hasten it along; my sorrow for all of it, any road. Go well now, and come again happy.* She paused, knowing that only perfect honesty was due to such a moment. *Glad am I he had one who loved him to join him on his way* . . .

Then suddenly he was there, half-hidden by the wrecked command console, lying where he had been thrown by the ship's convulsions, dying there alone and in silence, as she knew he would have preferred. There was fiber-dust from the crushed hull plating dulling the bright hair, and blood too, though not very much, across his forehead. His eyes were closed, and his face was turned away.

As she had done on the *Tuala*, Aeron went slowly to her knees here too, heedless of the sharp metal shards that littered the decking; watched him for a while before putting out a hand to touch his cheek, where the gold hair met the darker gold of the beard. He was not there, of course; he was far upon his way already, as she had sensed hours since, when she had sought to reach him in the Council chamber of Turusachan. She let her fingers move down to touch the sapphires in the torc that still circled his throat, thinking to capture some last memory or thought or picture from the blue stones; but there was nothing. *This torc I gave you for tinnól, my Rhodri; but it has not been part of you long enough to hold any message for me now . . .*

She knelt there a while longer, until the metal splinters cut through the fabric of her trews and her knees bled upon the floor, feeling neither the pain of that nor the pain of the greater wound nor even the smallest inclination to weep for her loss, wondering in some far corner of her mind how such a thing might be. The answer would not come to her until much, much later, and by then her demeanor would have spawned legend among her people, and not among them only: how Aeron Ard-rían had conducted herself as she knelt by the body of her dead lord. In their awe they would think it the exercise of a powerful will, a mighty control: The truth of it was that Aeron was locked in the iron jaws of the most profound anger of her life, this life or indeed any other; an anger that totally consumed bereavement and grief and pain, that fed on them to fuel its flames, leaving nothing to her but the strangely pure wish for an equal annihilation of revenge—which she would have, or herself perish in the trying . . .

Dán, my Roderick, she said to him. *You were never King of Keltia, nor would have been had we been wed a hundred years— but I will give you a king's sending all the same. You will not go alone, I promise you; not you, nor any of these . . .*

And still Aeron knelt there, dimly aware that behind her the others were gathering in the corridor, growing more uneasy with each moment she tarried, fearing only for her safety: For who knew whether this disaster were not part and prelude of a greater and still more dreadful plan, and Aeron too should be a target?

She did not trouble herself to ease their fears, though she knew them unfounded. What was in her mind now was not the terrible present nor the unimaginable future; not even the recent past of her five weeks' marriage, but the far past of her young womanhood: one summer day at Caerdroia, when the four of them, she and Gwydion and Rhodri and Morwen, had gone up into the high mountains of the Stair, to where a stream came leaping from the cliff face and ran down over the plain to join the Avon Dia near to its mouth. She had stood knee-deep in the icy water, one bare leg raised, balancing like a heron to spear them a salmon for their meal; Rhodri lolling on a sun-warmed rock, singing, stringing his voice to fit the measures of the stream; Gwydion and Wenna watching amused and carefully dry-shod from the bank.

She touched his face one last time, then bent to kiss him. "You were ever better at song than I, my hawk," she murmured. "Now we shall see how *I* may prove, at that craft that I have chosen for my own."

She rose and stepped away from him, and the senior officers who had been waiting for her to complete her farewell—though they would not have dreamed of hastening her along—came forward in haste of their own.

"Ard-rían—" began one.

"Athiarna—" said another.

Aeron raised her head to look each of them in the eyes, and they flushed and fell silent, waiting for her to speak to them, for they could not speak to what they had seen in her face.

But her voice came as it had always done, even and unstressed. "What is the count of our dead? My lord Fearghal?"

The Fian captain Fearghal mac Tíre answered at once. "No survivors, athiarna. One hundred dead on the *Tuala* and here on the *Corwalch*; another hundred on the two escort craft—those ships were vaporized; there is nothing left of them. Therefore it is but a rough tally—I do not have an exact figure, nor names as yet, to give you—"

"Two hundred dead is a close enough count for me . . . There will be other ships following me from Tara—my uncle Elharn most like. Arrange with him, when he comes, the returning of the dead to Turusachan. Tell him it is my wish that all be given state funerals, not the Ard-rígh and the Queen only but down to the lowliest kern and cabin-page, and rites too for those whose bodies cannot be brought home."

"*I* am to tell him?" gasped mac Tíre; the thought of telling the fearsome Elharn Ironbrow anything at all was chilling enough, let alone this message with its implication that Aeron would not be here to tell him herself. "But you, Ard-rían?"

Aeron allowed the full weight of her gaze to rest upon him, and mac Tíre began to wish he had not spoken. "I have somewhat to attend to before I myself return to Tara, and I cannot tarry to speak to Ironbrow beforehand. Do you see to it that all is done seemly here, my lord. I will come in my own time; you may tell the folk as much."

She started through the press, heading for the hatchway where her shuttle was still moored to the docking chute. None dared intercept her, for they had seen her face as she turned from Roderick's body, and seen her eyes as she spoke to mac Tire; none save one only.

"Aeron?" Vevin ní Talleron reached out to touch Aeron's shoulder. Save for the sake of old friendship and Fian comradeship she would not have ventured even that; and she was at once sorry she had done so, for Aeron rounded on her with a freezing green stare, as if some stranger had dared familiarity.

"Ard-rían—" she stammered instead, as Aeron threw off her hand as she had thrown off Morwen's, back at Turusachan. "I am sorry—"

Some bladepoint of remorse pierced Aeron's armor then, for the glacial stare softened. "Nay, Vevinnach, it is I who am sorry . . ." She gripped her friend's arm a moment, then a thought came to her, and she removed something from her finger.

"Here; take it." She thrust the thing at Vevin, who took it without even daring to look to see what it might be. "Now by your oath as feinnid of the true Fianna," said Aeron, "I charge you deliver this into the hands of my great-uncle Prince Elharn, when he arrives here, as he will do very soon now. Bid him hold it for me against my return—or my failure to return, in which event he must give it up only to my heir and brother Rohan, or to whoever else of the rígh-domhna shall win the election, to be Keltia's next Ard-rían or Ard-rígh upon my death proved."

Vevin, and the other Fians who stood by, stared down appalled at the Great Seal of Keltia that now rested in her hands, the emerald winking blue in the ship's artificial light. She shook her head in horror.

"Aeron, I *cannot*—"

"Vevin," said Aeron, "you must." And she swung herself through the port into her waiting shuttle.

Chapter 29

Not since leaving Turusachan had Aeron had what could in any honesty be called a thought as to her ultimate intent. All the same, never once to her deep instincts had her course been in doubt: The idea of revenge had seemed to form of itself, first as she listened to the keen rise over Caerdroia, the lament of the Faol-mór on the death of a chief of the line of Aoibhell; then again as she looked upon the faces of her dead on the *Tuala* and the *Corwalch,* and stared into empty space where the two ships of the escort, and their crews, had been reduced to glowing dust. And now *Dubhlinnseach* answered to her touch upon its helm, turning to point like a hunting-dog straight at Bellator, again almost of itself, by no will of Aeron's.

Though very much by wish *of Aeron's,* she thought with a certain snap, and activated the long-range scanners. One of the few things mac Tire and his officers had managed to convey to her—for in truth she had done very little listening—was the certain knowledge that the ambush had been effected by Fomori harrier ships out of that realm's base on Bellator, operating just as certainly under the personal command of that realm's king. *Oft before has a long sword been in a coward's hand; therefore I very much doubt Bres himself is nearby, even to witness his long-awaited triumph. Which absence may save his own personal neck, but nothing will save his soldiers . . .*

She glanced down at the scanboards. *Bellator . . .* The small garrison planet formed on the main screen, a glowing cloudy pearl not yet visible through the ports, for Aeron was still a very long way off, but on the viewers plain for what it was: an armed moon.

Those upon that moon should have no more warning or chance to save themselves than their harrier ships had given her parents and the rest; on that Aeron was as iron. But there were few strategies open to her: She could sail there through hyperspace, the usual method; but ships could be detected entering and leaving that dimension, even tracked across it, and that would suit her not at all. Or she could go in full-tilt through space-normal, relying on *Dubhlinnseach*'s speed and her own skill of pilotry to get her close enough, but there was the chance that the Fomori ground scanners and sentry ships would observe her coming, and blast her out of the stars before she came within striking distance; and that too was not good enough. So she would have to do the only other thing there was: She would have to go in to Bellator through subspace.

Even in her passion of revenge it was a chilling thought. So far as Aeron knew, the sailing of subspace had never been achieved, or even attempted, and there was no guarantee that she could succeed in such an attempt now. Space-normal, and the hyperspace regions above it, though each dangerous enough in its own fashion and each with its own particular hazards, held no such terrors; they were travelled as a matter of course, well-charted oceans that vessels of many civilizations had crossed for centuries. But subspace, that mysterious stratum traversed only by radio waves, was very much—and very literally—a leap in the dark, and it was also every bit as much her only choice.

Theoretically possible, though . . . That she knew from her Fian studies. Some adjustment to the ship's main enginery would be required—a matter of perhaps an hour's work—and then she would be on her way to Bellator and none to mark her coming; or to forbid her going. Not a living soul nor the most sensitive devices would know she was there, not until she came up out of subspace and stood off Bellator itself. And then Bellator would die; that too she knew. As to how it would perish . . . *One fence at a time*, she thought, clasping her hands to calm the shaking that threatened to convulse her entire frame. *True in the hunting-field, and true here; for this is but another kind of hunt* . . .

As her fingers tightened, Aeron became aware of the ring she still bore upon her hand: Brendan Mór's signet, forgotten amid the press of other matters since she had taken it from her father's midfinger and set it upon her own. She had not given it into

Vevin's keeping as she had done with the Great Seal, for reasons on which she was even now not entirely clear, for if she perished on this foray, as well she might, the ring and all its history would be lost with her.

But this is in truth my own creagh-rígh, and I wished Brendan and all the other Aoibhells who have worn this ring to ride this reiving with me. He of all those forebears would have understood— and, I think, would have well approved . . . Her great-grandmother Aoife would certainly have approved; Aeron could sense *that* without even trying, and a smile came to her lips at the thought. *It seems you were right after all, dama-wyn; I am indeed child of your blood, as you did See so long ago, and it seems too that I am not at all unhappy to be so. This then is the dán you Saw for me and named me for, and I am well pleased to concur in its unfolding. But, Lady, it is* my *dán; I would for no sake drag the rest of Keltia into this with me. Surely the Six Nations would avenge our loss as gladly as do I, but I am Ard-rían now, and I say no more Keltic lives shall be lost to Fomor and to its duergar-king for this quarrel—save mine alone if that must be. But I think that it is not: Whether that thought be traha or an-da-shalla, we shall all know soon enough.*

The adjustments to *Dubhlinnseach,* carried out hiding behind a distant moon so that no cruising Keltic warship might detect Aeron's plan or presence, took less time than she had feared; a few more moments to match her mood to her mind, to call to her hand the weapons she would need when she arrived at Bellator— weapons more fearful far than *Dubhlinnseach's* guns—and then she reached out to take the helm once more.

At once the ship shuddered as if caught in a high wind or a tiderip, wrenched in several directions at once. The síodarainn hull seemed to ripple with the terrible strain, and there was a roaring in Aeron's ears, and a high singing note that seemed to transfix her as surely and painfully as a spear. Just as the pitch became intolerable, and she thought she must either perish or go mad, there came a mighty jolt—whether of the ship or of space itself, she could not tell—and then *Dubhlinnseach* and Aeron dropped together through a rift in the familiar interstellar black- ness, into a place where they had never before been.

And nor had anyone, perhaps . . . Aeron looked round, then out through the ports. Subspace . . . it seemed that her mind held no reference points for this silent eerie locum. It was a place of phosphorescent milky grayness shot with sparks, utterly disorienting, and she felt unbalance roil her inner ear, nausea constrict the back of her throat. It reminded her of nothing so much as things she had done in childhood: spinning round and round like a whiptop, faster and faster, until at last she fell down sick and dizzy, or lying awake in the dark with her fingers pressed to her closed eyelids; there was the same heaving vertigo, the same whirling fire and expanding cross-hatched ripples of phosphene light, the same feeling of floating unbodied in the void, all in a ghastly cottoned silence. She could not even hear herself breathe.

If it was a silent world she had fallen into, it was a turbulent one: The fierce tide that had buffeted *Dubhlinnseach* upon entry seemed now to have caught the ship in its tremendous pull, and yet the craft seemed standing still, all unmoving, while beyond the viewports gray oblivion streamed past like a sick aurora. It was a place to lose one's mind long before one lost one's courage; but in the dreadful purposiveness of her errand Aeron was long past fearing for either. It was as if some other thought for her, and another sailed the ship, and another breathed and moved and looked out from behind her eyes, and yet another wove the pattern of her revenge to come: Aeron, as 'Aeron', seemed somehow not to be there at all.

Which may very well have saved her sanity: If she could not fear, and did not think, neither could she tell time passing or feel the full horror of this place where no living being had ever been meant to be. She had set the ship on autohelm for the voyage—it had seemed the prudent thing to do—and so it sailed itself on its computed course; but it was time that seemed to her most strangely altered.

It is a different face of the time in the space above . . . it seems somehow stretched, and yet also racing past. Aeron drew a breath to calm herself. *Yet even so I know not how much more of this I can bear easily, if at all, and still come to my journey's end in fit mind to fight . . .*

But by either standard it seemed to her only a little time indeed before a beacon signalled her that Bellator, somewhere above her in space-normal, was nearby.

And none too soon . . . Aeron pulled back sharply on the helm, reclaiming control of the ship, her fingers dancing over the board in the sequence she had calculated; now she would learn if her design had been successful. *Here it begins, or ends; now I shall see if I have in truth the power they have been forever telling me is my own; now we shall know whose dán prevails here: Fomor's, or mine* . . .

The ship bucked and broke from its strange fixity, rolling violently to deosil as if pitched by some giant hand, what way a child might swamp in play a toy birlinn in a pond; but this play was a far grimmer enterprise. For a moment it seemed that the ship must be torn in pieces between two mighty forces, spilling Aeron out into the starless void. Then *Dubhlinnseach* surged forward with a roar, bursting through a skin of strangely plastic light, back into the old familiar brilliance of space-normal. All at once Aeron could hear again, and breathe, and move, and she let out a cry that was at once triumph and malediction, for before her, hanging it seemed only an arm's-length before her in the spangled dark, was Bellator.

For the moment, she knew, the folk below her were unaware of her presence, but that ignorance would not last long. Honor required that she announce her coming, and pronounce their doom, before they themselves discovered her. But she needed a little time to prepare that doom's launching, and touching a stud on the console she activated the tirr—the cloaking mechanism, half magic, half technology, with which the foresight of her uncle Elharn and cousin Rhain had thought to furnish her ship. *Pity it is this tirr can be used only when the ship is at rest; else I should not have had to trouble myself with subspace* . . . *though I must say it went well enough.* But the brief elation Aeron allowed herself, and the triumph she might have felt in another moment at the spectacular crossing she had just achieved, were engulfed alike in the urgent demands of the moment, as Aeron began to call in her power to shape her revenge.

They shall know why they perish, and the moment of it, as my dear ones did not; and whose hand it is that strikes them down. Beyond that, nothing. But so all the galaxy may likewise know, I shall make a sending of this, sound and picture both, to Keltia, and to Fomor, and to any other worlds the transmission may reach. This may be, very like, the greatest éraic ever claimed, and I want no doubts in any quarter as to my action and my cause to take it. Whether it be the last thing I do as a private person, or the first as Ard-rían of Keltia, let there be no mistake as to what I do, and why, and that it is I who do it; so that later, if sanctions are brought, and well they might be, they will be brought against me alone and not against my folk or my realm. Be it so, and let it now begin . . .

Aeron had used the moments of her passage through subspace— minutes or hours or days, she still did not know, and would not consult the chronodials to learn, lest the knowing distract or distress her—to call up from her store of Ban-draoi learning the working she would use against the planet still spinning calm and unsuspecting beneath her. *My magic—my one surest weapon. It would take an armada of ships the like of* Firedrake *itself to do what I shall do to Bellator with one lifted hand. I should not have learned this rann; but in my traha I wished in those days to know all that could be known, and now I am glad I did wish so.* No matter that she must now, to use that knowledge, override all the controls and inhibitions set upon the use of such a magic; no matter that it was by all laws of man and nation, all laws of mortals and gods, utterly forbidden: Aeron was prepared to accept all consequences and would not count the cost. *For cost there will surely be, and a high one: my crown or my reason or my life—perhaps even all three . . . but I will pay it, whatever.*

She sat back in her blastchair as if that seat had been the very Throne of Scone, her hands gripping the contoured arms, feeling herself begin to move inward as her power started to build. She had none of the usual tools for such a working, and for an instant her concentration wavered as she regretted the lack. But then the words of one of her Ban-draoi preceptresses came echoing back, one time at Scartanore when Aeron had lamented a similar want of magical trappings: *'You may stand in the riomhall of Broinn-na-draoichta, Aeron, robed in oréadach and with Fragarach itself to cast the circle, or naked in a ring of stones with not even a table-sgian to your hand: If the power is not in you it makes no differ wherewith you are clad or how armed—and if the power is in you it makes no differ still more . . .'*

And it made none now; her teacher had had the right of it, though she could not have imagined in her darkest dreams the use to which Aeron meant to put that power: It rose around her, filling the cabin, thickening the air like palpable mist, a manifestation of her will and being, so that she did not need even to touch the transmitter key but only thought the touch, and all other signals died away for lightyears around; the tirr faded like fog before a gale, so that *Dubhlinnseach* stood revealed to Bellator's eyes. Then they heard her voice, on that world below, and in Keltia far away, and for many star-miles beyond, even to Fomor itself.

"Fomori of Bellator, it is Aeron Queen of Kelts who speaks . . ."

A brief unemotional statement delivered in a clear neutral voice, scarce half a minute long, to tell them that their deaths had come upon them, and for what cause that vengeance came— though they were soldiers down there for the most part, and had presumably known their peril.

Then Aeron ceased to speak, and raised her hands before her face, wrists set back to back in form of the sacred sun-cross—its use here anything but holy—and turned all her power down the forbidden path, the path she had never been taught at the Thicket of Gold but had learned all the same, shutting out the cry of her own deep soul in protest, and the voices of all those other souls that clamored suddenly all about her: the spirit-presences of those she loved, all gainsaying her action. Kesten's voice rang clear amid that tumult, and Tybie's; Gwydion's she heard, and Morwen's, and Rohan's; and, aye, her parents' voices too called to her not to do this terrible thing, and Rhodri's, and even Duvessa's. *Do not,* they begged her; *not even for us,* they said. *I do not hear you!* she cried in answer, *I will not hear you!,* and they were then silent.

And in that enormous silence Aeron began to chant aloud the words of the working, like a child's counting-out rhyme, and what it counted were the seconds that Bellator and all its thousands had yet to live.

"Ger niutri, ter niutri, yso haneth dhe'n—"

At Caerdroia time had not been stretched and speeded, as it had for Aeron in her passage through subspace, but had spooled out at its accustomed pace, or perhaps if anything somewhat slower, as the first numbness of shock began to give way and slow unendurable pain began to throb.

Even as a wound taken in battle, thought Gwydion, as he waited at Mardale with the others for Aeron's return. *First there is only surprise, and one feels nothing; then with realization comes the pain. I have known both that and this, and I would a thousand times liefer take the battle-hurt . . .*

So would all of them who waited there; waited there because they could think of nowhere else to go, waited for a return that might never come. Earlier—it seemed years ago—Elharn had sent word that he had reached the ruins of the *Corwalch* and the *Tuala* only an hour behind Aeron. Finding her already gone where none knew to follow, he had instead done her bidding— had received the Great Seal from Vevin's shaking hand, and was now bringing home Keltia's dead, to lie in honor as Aeron had commanded.

But no, Gwydion thought now, *that had happened; that was true past and not yet to be . . .* He himself, with Rohan and Trehere, Fionnbarr's Taoiseach, had met Ironbrow on the landing-field, as the ruined hulks so carefully and tenderly brought home settled to earth within their protective scathachs. He had himself looked upon those who had perished within those ships, brought back aboard *Firedrake* and decently disposed as befitted their ranks—Fionnbarr, as dear to him as his own father had been— *well, they ride together again now*—and Emer, still so very fair; and Rhodri— *Ah, braud,* he thought again now as he had thought at that moment, *dán or no, this was* not *how it should have been . . .*

Yet for all that, they had had no real word of Aeron. Elharn, stone-faced and weary, had shown Rohan the Great Seal that Aeron had delivered to him by Vevin—the new heir of Keltia had blanched at sight of it—and had then informed them all that their new Ard-rían had apparently chosen her own vengeance and a fearful path to it: The devices aboard *Firedrake* and the other ships had tracked her craft for a while, and then she was gone, as if she had fallen through some hole in space itself, and only then had they realized what her plan had been.

Subspace, thought Gwydion with a shudder. *How had she dared . . . I knew she must be desperate, but*— He did not waste his strength torturing himself as most of the others were doing:

lamenting and bewailing that they should never have let her leave the palace. *As if they had had any say in the matter . . .* No, she would have gone even if all Keltia had flung its arms about her knees; nothing could have kept her, and perhaps nothing should have. At least it was better to have let her go unhobbled by *their* fears; she would have enough of her own to deal with, and one less distraction, in a moment when distraction could mean death, might make all the difference . . .

"Still," Rohan had said, "she must come back sometime; and when she does she will come here." His words had sounded right and reasoned, and in their hope and fear they had put aside the thought that she might not come back at all, and had agreed, and lingered on here in the portmaster's tower. But if she did not come soon—and this they all knew though not even Rohan spoke it—someone would have to step into her place, if only to hold Keltia together until such time as she *did* come, or they had certain word of her fate, for in the absence of certain knowledge the realm was beginning to fear the worst.

Then word did come, and it came from the planetoid known as Bellator, and it was by no imagining the word they had thought or hoped to have: a transmission sent by Aeron herself, a terrifying testament to her power and her grief, and though they had not believed that it could be possible, by the time the sending ended they saw that indeed it was so; and they continued to wait.

And then, even as some were beginning unwillingly to depart, for their duties had grown beyond urgency, there came a flash far above them, the blur and smudge of light that announced a ship exiting hyperspace, and lifting their heads they saw, appalled, Aeron's ship spinning out of control, twenty miles up and plunging straight for the high barren peaks of the Loom.

When the word came at last for which he had waited all day in fevered patience, Bres of Fomor was sitting with his sons and his advisors and his generals in the Council chamber of the palace at Tory, and as Vaemond, the Prime Minister, entered the room, all eyes flew to his face.

Old Vaemond looks perhaps not so pleased as he might, observed Elathan. *I wonder if this treacherous venture were not secretly as little to his liking as it is to mine . . .* Then, as he saw the minister's face more clearly: *Nay—there is more here than simple loathing for the ill-advised policies of an ungovernable king. What has happened, to make him look so?*

Vaemond stood now before Bres. "Majesty—"

"No ceremony, dear friend." Bres's expression shone indecently eager, at least to the mind of his heir. "But tell us of our success. Fionnbarr of Keltia is dead?"

Vaemond gave a curt nod. "He is, and all his party with him—not sparing his queen or his daughter's new-wed lord."

"Then why is it you look as if we have failed?"

The chief minister could hold it back no longer. "Because Bellator too is dead! Because Aeron Aoibhell, by your dubious grace Keltia's new queen, did not choose to sit quietly in Caerdroia and send polite protests to Ganaster over the murders of her parents and her lord, but went instead to Bellator and burned it down to bedrock! Because the entire garrison and their families and everyone else who had been on or near that planet is destroyed with it! Including—*Majesty*—your own son Prince Tharic, whom you yourself sent there in your arrogance to witness your 'triumph'!" Vaemond fell silent, and passed a hand over his face, then sank pale and sweating into his chair at the table.

No one seemed to breathe; it was as if they themselves had all died of the telling, struck dead on the spot by Vaemond's words. And none dared even to *think* of looking at Bres . . .

Vaemond made a supreme effort and collected himself. "I am sorry, King, for your loss; but I too have lost a son in this futile quarrel of yours."

In the terrible quiet Elathan leaned forward. "My lord Vaemond," he began, ignoring the stabbing pain—*my brother! Ah, Tharic, my dear lad; you did not want to go, and I should have tried harder to keep you here*—"My lord, how do we know this to be true fact? I do not doubt your word, but only so that we may know."

"A handful of the sentry ships, being on station in deep space when Aeron attacked, managed by some miracle to escape." Vaemond closed his eyes for a moment, unable himself to escape the picture his own words had conjured: His eldest son, a captain of the Bellator garrison, had been on-planet at that same moment Aeron struck. "She hunted them ship to ship, after she had—had finished with the planet. She destroyed most of them, but eight—

eight! out of near *fifty!*—were able to elude her, and made it limping to our base on Fasarine. It was a long hard pull for such small ships, but the nearest haven—and the only place they could go, for there is nothing left of Bellator.''

''But surely there is some—'' one of the generals protested.

''*Nothing left!*'' Elathan looked away, for Vaemond's voice had been a scream. ''Oh aye,'' he continued, with a harsh unmirthful laugh, ''there is still something there, but you cannot imagine . . . But I am forgetting, you do not *have* to imagine. Aeron was thoughtful enough to provide us with a record of the entire event.''

He took a crystal block from some fold of his tunic and inserted it into a slot into the table. At once a hologram formed in the center of the polished wood: Aeron's face clearly visible, as she sat in the command cabin of a ship; beyond the viewports, Bellator just as plain.

They stared fascinated and horrified as the projection dimmed and blurred away from her for a few moments as she appeared to speak the words of some spell—*lest our own sorcerers should learn her trick,* thought Elathan—but the picture came clear again as the spell began to work on the unshielded world below her.

Unbelievingly they saw—and knew too that they *must* believe—the atmosphere of Bellator waver like a curtain caught in a sudden breeze; then horror moved beyond even that horror, as the air itself kindled and burned. The surface of the planet charred from green to black, then burst into pure orange flame that mantled the little planet from pole to pole. But still that was not all, though by this time surely the folk had perished: The fire went deeper, seeming to soak like water into the soil and rock of Bellator's crust, and they could see dreadfully distinct the rock beginning to melt, the small oceans flashing in an instant to clouds of steam, the whole planet glowing as it must have done in the moment of its birth. And then just as suddenly it was over: Where an incandescent sphere had been, there was now only the nickel-iron slag of the planet's shriveled core, the clinkered ashen orb of a dead moon, as dead as if it had never once known life.

But it had! cried Elathan in silent anguished protest. *That was a living world-home to near two million people! All dead now, and my brother among them, all at Aeron's hand*. But even in his pain, a small voice in his mind spoke more justly: *Not by her hand alone but by my father's also . . .*

All this time Bres the king had said nothing, but now he looked up at Vaemond, and he seemed to those who dared glance at him to have aged fifty years in the past ten minutes.

"How?" was all he said.

Vaemond shook his head. "Sorcery, how else? As you have just seen, she went through subspace—aye, subspace; she dared it and she won through—to reach Bellator undetected; that is how she was able to take them so completely unaware."

"Then they had no warning? The attack was a treacherous surprise?"

Vaemond raised his eyes to stare at his king. *YOU dare speak of treachery?* he thought, wondering not for the first time how Bres seemed so easily able to divide his words from his actions, and his actions from those of others. *Well, he does not get away with it so smooth, not this time; not though it costs me my office and my lands and my life—little pleasure left in any now that my Chanos is lost . . .*

"They had no more warning than your harrier fleet gave to King Fionnbarr," said Vaemond deliberately, and was grimly pleased to see Bres flush an ugly dull red and drop his eyes. "Where they used laser artillery, Aeron used magic—both seem to have been equally effective. The sorcerers tell me they felt the backwash of her working even here—she is a very great sorcerer, even the best of them admit it. Not since the Wizard-king himself, Arthur of Arvon, came against us all those centuries ago—" Again Vaemond buried his face in his hands, control beginning to crack as his grief at last overcame him.

Bres looked up again, his glance going not to Elathan but to Talorcan. His eldest son seemed as stunned as the rest of them, but no more than that; the components of grief and outrage and anger that had so ravaged the rest of them seemed to have bypassed Talorcan, and Bres was for the moment too stricken to wonder why.

"Who could have known?" he murmured, half to Talorcan, who had been his chief confidant and encourager in the attack on Fionnbarr, and half to himself. "Who could have known what she would do—or could do . . ."

"You should have known!" That was Elathan, who had stood out against the raid from the first, and whose anger and grief now broke over him like a red wave. *Small hope now of ever seeing my dream come to pass of peace and friendship with Aeron and the Kelts* . . . "You are the *King*, Father, and you were *warned*! I myself—"

At that Bres's glance sharpened to a bright narrow point. "Speak no further, Elathan, for if you say 'I told you thus' now, I think that I may kill you, and I have already one son dead this day."

Elathan's mouth thinned with contempt. "I thought perhaps you had forgotten," he said in a cold clear voice. "All your mourning has seemed to be until now for the imperfect success of your plan." He stood up as a gasp of horror, plainly audible, went through the room. "But I leave you to it. As for me, I go now to the Queen my mother, and try to comfort her on the death of her child."

But as he went alone through the stricken palace to Basilea's chambers, hearing all around him the muffled weeping of the palace folk, Elathan found that he himself was weeping. *And not all these tears are for you, Tharic my dear; some are for me, and some even for my father, and not a few, I think, are for Aeron Aoibhell.*

Chapter 30

When Aeron's ship fell spinning into sight, those who had waited at Mardale for her return—though such a return as this had never entered even their blackest thoughts—raced to the portmaster's tower, where great windows of polarized vitriglass looked out over the landing-field and the mountains of the Loom beyond it.

Eyes narrowed not against sunblink alone but in horror of the sight before them, they stared upward into the swimming blue of the March sky. Aeron's craft was plainly visible now without the use of field-glasses, falling faster, a black swan pierced through the heart by some more than mortal arrow.

"She will crash if she does not correct declination," said Ruairc O Barraigh, who was portmaster at Mardale, and though he spoke unemphatically the control it cost him to speak so was plain to be heard.

Elharn, who had returned from supervising the lying-in-state of the dead High King and his companions in the Hall of Heroes, and was waiting for Aeron with the rest, glanced briefly away from the plummeting starship.

"I helped design that craft myself; it was built to withstand stresses no other ship might endure."

"Even so, Ironbrow," said O Barraigh sympathetically, for Elharn was an old friend, and his devotion to his great-niece was well known, "though the ship survived the impact, what way could Aeron do so? Still, we have lost neither just yet." He made rapid adjustments to a board before him. "Let us see if tractor fields may slow her fall."

Though all could see the immediate effect of the fields upon the speed of *Dubhlinnseach*'s precipitous descent, they could see as well that the ship continued to tumble toward the sharp-toothed peak of Garvelloch, a mile or two to the south of the spaceport. Even the full force of the tractor devices seemed not to be able to halt it, and some in the room began to turn away, not wishing to witness what seemed now so inevitable. Gwydion had instinctively lifted his hand in an attitude of magic, as had some other sorcerers present, thinking to use his art to try to bring the ship and its pilot safely to earth. But he knew, as did they, that time was too short even to make the attempt, and he let his hand fall again to his side.

Then suddenly *Dubhlinnseach* moved of herself within the grip of the fields; the nose came up, the tail settled back, and with barely a lai to spare the black ship touched down in a near perfect landing.

Morwen and Gwydion were first out upon the windswept field, the others like a following tide hard after. But all came as one to a sudden halt, as if commanded: The doorseals had opened in the ship's side, and Aeron stood there framed in the hatchway.

Gwydion closed his eyes at the sight of her, in pain at her pain as much as in thanksgiving for her safe return. *But is she safe returned, in truth? She looks as if she had been burned alive, and that I do not wonder at, after what we saw her do to Bellator; and just now it must have taken what strength she had left, to pull the ship out of that spin and into a landing . . .*

He realized in that moment, as did they all, that only the door's metal frame was keeping Aeron on her feet. He moved forward, thinking to help her, but she waved him off, looking at him, and the rest of them, as if she had never before laid eyes on any of them in any life.

"From now," said Aeron, her voice clear and overcarefully controlled, "let this ship be known by the truename she has earned this day: She shall be called *Fragarach*—the Retaliator."

Stepping down from the doorway, Aeron found to her great surprise that her legs would not support her, and the ground came spinning up to meet her as she pitched forward into Gwydion's arms.

But save for that one instant of giddiness she had full possession of her senses, and when they arrived at Turusachan, she gave brief orders to Rohan and Elharn and Trehere as to what they must tell the people, and what they might tell them, and against all protests disappeared up the great curving double staircase.

"How is it with her?" Rohan, haggard and hollow-eyed, met Gwydion at the door of the Council chamber, where many of Fionnbarr's aides and advisors had assembled, for lack of direct command from their new High Queen.

"No one knows for sure. She is in the Presence Chamber, has been there since her return."

"That was six hours since!"

"Truly," said Gwydion, his own face showing all the strain of the day's events. "She sits in her chair beside her father's, and she does not move, or speak, or seem to hear; only sits there alone. She will not even have the sconces to be lighted, but sits there in darkness."

"Has she been told of the treaty?" asked Rohan after a while. Barely an hour after Aeron's return, a pact of nonaggression, its terms more than favorable to Keltic interests, had arrived for Trehere, as Taoiseach: It had been sent by subspace beacon on emergency frequencies, and it had been sent from Fomor. *No doubt much against Bres's will,* thought Rohan, fury blazing up again at the mere thought of that king's name. *But I think he can have been given little choice, after what my sister encompassed this day . . .* He shook his head, still staggered. The communication from Fomor, though terse in the extreme, had indicated that the count of the dead on Bellator had been near two million; not warriors alone, but their mates and children and servitors, merchants and farmers, artisans and techs, all those who had made up the fabric of a living, thriving garrison world—and Bres's own son, a lad barely twenty, had been among them. *How will she live with this,* he wondered, *when the shock and the pain have been blunted a little, and she must* think *on what she has done—or will the guilt of it destroy her altogether?* But all his reflection took place in an eyeblink of time, for now Gwydion was shaking his shaggy dark head in answer to his friend's question.

"She has not; though judging from the tenor of the treaty's

phrasing the Fomori are in clear terror to have her sign straightway, lest she perhaps decide that Bellator was not enough to satisfy her vengeance after all.''

''And do *you* think it will suffice her?''

Gwydion was about to answer when Aeron's cousin Slaine came up to them where they stood. Both men gave her their full attention, for Elharn's only daughter was not only a First-rank Fian warrior but a gifted healer, and on her face now was a look neither had seen her wear before.

''I think you both had best come with me to Aeron,'' she said. ''You may be needed.''

''It was my father grew anxious at last,'' she explained, as the three of them hastened along the gallery that led to Aeron's rooms in the Western Tower. ''He thought it a very bad sign that she stayed so long alone in the Presence Chamber, and, though she had given order that she was not to be disturbed, he went in himself, with Melangell and me and one or two others. Doubtless he should have consulted you first, Rohan, as heir of line, but—''

Rohan waved away the apology. ''My great-uncle is senior of the family here at Caerdroia; whatever he thinks it right to do, that is for my part what will be done. But Aeron?''

''It was as well he went in when he did,'' resumed Slaine. ''She had fallen into a trance such as I have never seen, near as deep as the taghairm; but she was half-aware of us, and in her delirium she was lashing out with magical strength as well as with physical. It took six of us to control her—you might have managed it better, Gwydion, but we dared not tarry on your coming—and get her to her chamber. In such a state she might have done great harm to herself as well as to others, so the Dragon healers have placed her under a restraint field.''

''Delirium!'' repeated Rohan. ''But she is not ill? No fever—she took no wound?''

Slaine gave her head a small tight shake. ''Not of the body.''

''Madness?'' asked Gwydion, and his voice was very quiet.

''It might be so,'' admitted Slaine after a moment or two. ''But see now for yourself.''

Within the white-walled round room that served her as solar and office and bedchamber, Aeron lay pale and still and appar-

ently asleep under the restraint field that the healers had reluctantly fastened down upon her. The force-field was set as close
as possible, Rohan now saw; she could breathe, and turn her
head, and move an inch or two in any direction, but no more, for
as Slaine had said, her struggles and the accompanying wild
volleys of undirected magical power had been fearful—dangerous
to herself, and to all about her.

And maybe more dangerous even than that, thought Rohan,
staring down at his sister's shuttered face. *If she could destroy
Bellator in her fury of revenge, what might not she unleash now,
in a passion of guilt and repentance?* For that it *was* remorse and
guilt, he saw quite plainly. *She must have wrestled with this
those six hours alone in the dark. To know that she used her
powers unlawfully to avenge, and that compounded with the loss
that provoked her to do so—small wonder she lies here in such a
state; if she is even here at all . . .*

"Can grief do this?" he heard himself asking. "The deaths
alone?"

Gwydion shook his head, his own eyes veiled as he watched
Aeron's face. "She is a Ban-draoi trained, and a Dragon also.
Life and death are to her no more than a passing from one room
to another in a many-chambered brugh; had those she has lost
died more usual deaths, she would of course sorrow for herself,
but not for those who had gone."

"But?"

"But these are not usual circumstances, as you hardly need to
be told. We all saw what Bellator—which is to say Fomor—did
to us, and what Aeron—which is *not* to say Keltia, for she made
that very clear by the manner of her going—did to Bellator.
What she suffers from now is the return blow: the reaction to her
own action. As a blade will recoil from another in a duel, the
weight of blow and parry added together, both coming back
upon the blow's deliverer: That is how it is with her now."

"But Bellator did not resist her," objected Rohan.

"Nay," said his cousin Melangell, speaking for the first time
from where she stood by the head of the bed. "It had not the
time to do so, so swift and final was Aeron's strike. And the
very unjustice of that strike is what gives the return blow such
power over her now. For all the validity of her pain and loss,
Aeron struck wrongly, and she knows it; she knew it when she

struck, knew it even before she struck—and she struck regardless. And that knowledge multiplied by all the thousands who perished by her hand is what is on her now. If she cannot make her peace with their souls, then she will die.''

Rohan, feeling as if he had taken a spear through the heart, stared in horror at his cousin. For all her youth and air of pale pretty frailty, Melangell was a soul-healer of the Dragon Kinship, trained to do battle against sickness of the mind. *And as such, she is about as frail as pressed findruinna . . . If she says this, then it must be; but I have today lost my parents, and my King and Queen, and my brother-in-law—that is enough dead Aoibhells for one day. I will* not *lose my sister also . . .*

He turned again to Gwydion. ''Can you not call her back? You are a gifted sorcerer—you are the *Pendragon,* come to that—and her beloved as well. Surely she would come back for you?''

Gwydion made no answer, and after a swift glance at his face—a glance involving more senses than sight alone—Melangell answered for him.

''Whether that be so or no,'' she said gently, ''his is not the hand she can take just now. She is half in love with the idea of slipping away, to join those she loves; and half of that again is purely guilt, so that if she thinks she might atone for Bellator by her own death, in her present state of mind that to her seems good. If she can even be said to *have* a functioning mind just now . . . She loves Gwydion, I know that it is so; but I know too that she carries a still heavier guilt for that: To her, if she had not loved Gwydion as she does, and had wedded Rhodri as and when her parents wished it, perhaps none of this would ever have happened.''

''That *is* madness,'' said Rohan.

''As to that, who can say? But there is little can be done just now to mend it.'' Melangell took Gwydion and Rohan each by an arm, drew them gently out of the chamber; behind her, Slaine moved quietly into her post by the bed-head to keep vigil a while. ''And there is not little but naught that either of you can do . . . She has gone so far into herself, shutting off her magic in her guilt for so misusing it, that none of us has yet been able to reach her.''

''But you will not stop trying?''

Melangell's face changed, as if she would have smiled, or wept, and dared do neither, and she gave Rohan's arm a little shake. "Nay, we will not stop trying . . . Go now and take something to eat and drink, and then rest if you can. I will call you both if there is need—or change."

There had been nothing but pain at first, pain blinding and deafening, and so heavy that it seemed to Aeron that never could she find the strength within her to stand up beneath it, so harsh and hard it bore her down. Then all at once it had passed, the pain, and she was beyond it, alone in a vast hollow crowded darkness, that, though she had never been there before in conscious life, she recognized all the same.

Annwn, the Abyss of the Unformed . . . or the misformed? Have I come here to be unmade, then; or remade? All according to Arawn's will . . . Even as she hovered, herself silent, in the murmuring dark, Aeron knew that her body—as it had been in Broinn-na-draoichta, as it had been in the Fian clochan—was firmly anchored in the upper world, this time pinned beneath the confines of a restraint field under the gimlet vigilance of assorted healers. *They think me close kept . . . but they cannot know how very far I am from them. And I say that they shall not find me unless I do wish it—the which I do not just yet, and maybe not for long, and maybe not ever . . .*

Yet she was aware of them all so far above her, calling her name, employing every trick of magic that they could devise. But she knew the tricks, she recognized those who called the clearest: Melangell, Slaine, Ríoghnach, her aunt Keina; Brychan, a talented Fian healer she had known at Caer Artos; Druids who had been near at hand in the city and Dragons who had come at Gwydion's command; others who did not call, but whose presence she could sense: Rohan and Sabia; Morwen—*ah, Wenna, I am so sorry! Rhodri dead and I not even there to comfort you*—her uncle Conor and grandmother Gwyneira. Of them all, Melangell came the nearest; time and again Aeron felt her cousin's mind daring to plunge down through the darkness, some sharp shining hook, coming closer each time.

And yet the one voice she would have been bound to obey had not been heard to pronounce; and she knew that she would not hear it. *He could bring me back swifter than most, and surer*

*than any; but he will not do it, for he knows I must come back on
my own or not at all—with my shield or upon it, as the Spartannach
did say of old . . .*

How long she remained so Aeron could not say; she would
learn afterwards that she had lain as one dead for three days and
nights together, her body barely functioning, her mind inaccessible to all those who had sought so desperately to reach it.

What she did know was that for all that time she was battered
by winds out of the Abyss and voices out of nowhere, or
everywhere. She was by no means alone: There were small quick
darting creatures, like sleek black otters, that flashed chattering
past her and were gone; and Presences, huge silent majesties
striding tremendously by, whose galactic calm she could never
hope to trouble—the light of their eyes stabbed through her as
though she herself were the phantom in this realm; as perhaps
indeed she was. There were cold fires that burned her with
flames of blue ice when she tried to warm herself, and dry
waters that parched her with heat when she tried to drink. She
was poured out like metal for the casting, hammered like a blade
upon some titan's anvil; but never sight nor sense did she have of
Rhodri, or her parents, or any other of those who had gone out
with Bellator.

*I seek them in the wrong place . . . this is not the path that
they have followed. They are not in Annwn, and I am barred
from Gwynfyd; for a time, only for a time—one life or ten, it
makes no differ; and then we shall meet again, on the Wheel or
beyond it. But I am here now . . .* And in that far extremity
Aeron came face to face with herself and with her pain and with
her deed; and embraced them all three, and in that moment she
began to live again. She felt herself turn again to the world, once
more a return to Hollfyd, rushing through the darkness, rising up
out of spinning colors, leaving the winds and the voices behind,
coming back into her body, donning flesh once more like a
favorite old tunic; surprised somehow to find it still fitted her so
well, half-remembered, yet unfamiliar enough for her to test its
working, flexing hands, arching shoulders and shifting hips.

Aeron opened her eyes to meet Melangell's blue-green gaze,
so loving, yet at the same time so considering. *As if she is not
yet sure just who it is that has come back from—from wherever I
have been; as if she is not sure it is even I who has returned.*

And I blame her not at all, for I do not think I am quite sure myself . . .

"Well, cousin," said Aeron aloud. "I am home."

"She seems hale enough physically," remarked Melangell later to Kesten Hannivec, after Aeron had been given a light supper and a draught from the Fianna healers to permit her the blessing of a true sleep. The Ban-draoi Magistra had arrived at Caerdroia only a short while since; Rohan, thinking perhaps his sister's old mentor might be able to reach her where everyone else had failed, had begged her to come, and, though ill herself, and concealing it, Kesten had made the journey from Erinna at once.

"What then?" asked Slaine wearily.

"She is still of course shadowed by what she did, and by what was done to her . . . That shadow is diminished now, for she knows she has tasks to fulfill in the next days, but after that it will grow again, and it may be that it will darken beyond her ability to lift. I am a soul-healer; I should know how to take that shadow from her, and yet I do not."

"It is not yours to take," said Kesten, with such a weight of authority in her voice that Melangell, and all the others who heard, looked at her in surprise. "She called her dán upon herself, and now she alone must lift it. You may help her, of course, as you wish—and it is in my mind that you, Melangell, and you also, Slaine, will be chief of those who will help her to heal—but the greater part of the labor must be done by Aeron alone."

"That is a hard saying, Magistra," said Slaine respectfully.

"But a true one; and she knows the truth of it herself."

When the Ard-eis Keltannach, the High Council of Keltia, convened the next morning, the last person they expected to see at the table was their Queen. But just as Trehere was beginning to outline the plans he had made with various court officials and the royal household officers, concerning the funeral rites for Fionnbarr and Emer and the rest, the door of the Council chamber opened and Aeron stood upon the threshold.

She looked like the bansha herself, her hair disheveled, her face chalk-white, save where blue shadows had painted themselves like bruises beneath her eyes. She said no word, and they were too staggered to speak, but she met the glance of each in turn, and went to her place at the head of the table. For an instant they saw her hesitate, then she seated herself in the tall carved chair, and looking at none of them she spoke to all.

"Tell me."

When the quiet command was met with silence only: "Must I tally each of you in turn? I will not ask again: Tell me what was done at Bellator. Nay," she corrected herself at once, sparing neither herself nor them the euphemism, "tell me what I did."

Of them all, only her great-uncle Elharn could look at her, and it seemed too that only he could speak. "Since you ask, Ard-rían, of warriors garrisoned, near a quarter million dead; of their dependents and the other dwellers on that world, perhaps five times that again; perhaps more. We are not certain, and the Fomori have not told us."

Aeron had closed her eyes briefly as the numbers sounded in the room like An-Lasca, the Whip-wind itself—though Elharn had not emphasized them or raised his voice in any way—but that was the only indication that the magnitude of the slaughter had registered.

"And we did lose two hundred . . . it seems the proper ratio, of Fomori to Kelts." She heard the shocked gasps, felt the wave of revulsion pass through the room, ignored both.

"You cannot mean that, Aer—Ard-rían," remonstrated Trehere soberly. He had been Fionnbarr's Taoiseach for the past twelve years, and a Privy Councillor before that, and of all the dead King's servants he found it hardest to accept—this change that had made a High Queen out of one he still looked on as a much-loved if willful child. "You cannot mean it," he repeated, "for you will surely be damned for it."

Aeron met his eyes, then looked away again. "I can, and I shall not be . . . But to our work, my lords and ladies—I have heard of a certain compact the Fomori are something eager for me to sign?"

Silently Trehere pushed a treaty diptych over in front of her, and without glancing at the terms imprinted upon the matrix Aeron extended her hand to Elharn. In silence too her great-uncle dropped into her outstretched palm the Great Seal of Keltia that she had left to his safekeeping aboard the *Tuala*, and slipping it home upon her midfinger Aeron set the carved emerald to the matrix.

She looked up at them then, saw the emotions plain upon their faces, and those behind their eyes, that they tried with varying degrees of skill and success to conceal from her othersight: shock and pity, approval and disapproval—and perhaps what stabbed her the cruellest, a kind of hopeful desperation, as though those who looked so saw in her their last and only hope, that only she could help them across an appalling abyss they could not hope to cross themselves.

Ah, Name of Dâna, I can deal with none of this just yet— they must fend for themselves a while longer . . . if I can bear it, surely they can do no less.

"And now I will hear," said Aeron without a tremor to her voice or her soul, "what arrangements have been made as to my orders for the speeding of Fionnbarr Ard-rígh and Queen Emer and Roderick Prince of Scots. Trehere, do you begin."

Chapter 31

It was not Keltic custom to stage elaborate ceremonials on the passing of even the royal dead; a plain simple rite at the stones, never overlong, conducted by Druid priest or Ban-draoi priestess or Dragon Kin, or, not infrequently, by no hierarch at all but clann chief or dúchas lord or family member, was held to be both sufficient and desirable, for those who remained behind as well as for the one—or the many—who had gone on.

And that was all in keeping with the tenets of the Keltic faith, that death was but a change of life, and that every man and every woman should deal directly with the gods of their race, should work their own dán for themselves and save their souls alive. Formal intermediaries between the people and the gods were guides, not dictators, and their utterances and interpretations had not—as in some perhaps less enlightened faiths that ruled by fear and shame—the force of divine law, but carried all the favor of divine love.

Indeed, thought Aeron, *how could it be other, and it is at such times as these that we see the reality of our faith in our gods; and theirs in us* . . . She stood at that moment with many others at the foot of the Way of Souls, the steep path that wound up from Turusachan into Calon Eryri, the Heart of Eagle, that high green valley where stood the hallow of Ni-maen. Though that ring of stones had been a holy place ever since its raising, also it had served as a royal barrowing-ground from the reign of Arawn, Arthur's son; and many, though by no means all, of the rulers of Keltia since Arawn's day, and their kindred also, lay there in the green-turfed mounds beyond the bluestone ring, blessed in the sight of the gods.

But what had lain between them and their gods, as it lay between any god and any man, was no matter for the general, being instead a thing for each man—and each god—to resolve each time anew; and as a Domina of the Ban-draoi the new High Queen of Keltia knew it better than most. Only when the voyaging soul has crossed into Gwynfyd for the final time, to stand naked in the presence of the Shepherd of Heaven, is that soul able to see itself as it is, and was, and will be, and to judge itself in that fierce final light. Not until then is it fit to make such judgment; and certainly no other, mortal or immortal, could make that judgment for it.

For even Kelu does not judge, thought Aeron, the joy of that certainty flooding through her like a tide. *But in His—or Her— perfect wisdom leaves it to each of us, for the Shepherd of Heaven knows well that we will judge ourselves in that hour more exactly, more harshly, more correctly, than any other judge could do. And no judgment there is ever a false one: whether it be to stay in the peace and perfection of Gwynfyd forever, stepping for all time out of time, or to take yet another round in the body and upon the Wheel. The soul in the presence of the Highest knows what it must do, and not even the Highest may gainsay its knowledge or its choice . . .*

Aeron straightened, clearing her mind as from far above her a faint horn-cry signalled the cortege's arrival at Ni-maen: the cortege that bore the bodies of Fionnbarr, Emer and Rhodri to rest among the other royal dead. *And it is for us who remain to do them this one last service: to speed them with love through that passage. True it is they are far along their road by this time, but 'time' is the least of it, and that distance is by no means a barrier insurmountable. Let us touch once more across it, as is right and fitting, and then let us go peacefully on. Neither law nor love is well served by more.*

As the sound of the horn faded on the air, Aeron gathered herself in, as a rider will collect her horse before they face a jump together, and without so much as a glance at those who waited to follow her to the stones, she set her foot upon the Way of Souls and began to climb.

To those who waited above in the nemeton for the Queen to arrive, it was a quiet time under the gray skies of March: time spent in memory and musings alike—sorrowful yet smiling recollection of the past, and cautious hopeful thought for the future.

That future approaches even now, thought Kesten Hannivec, as she stood with Teilo the Archdruid and with Gwydion the Pendragon at the pillared entrance to Ni-maen. A sudden gust of bitter wind rocked her; ill and frail as she was, though so far she had managed to hide it from even Aeron's lynx's-eye, she shivered a little, grateful for the strength of Gwydion's arm on which she leaned, and for the scallan that Teilo had thrown about her, to shield her somewhat from the cold and wind. But as the line of mourners came into view at last, Kesten drew herself up, standing free of the support of her companions. *I would face my Queen on my own feet alone; for the future now is here, and it is she herself* . . .

The line, two abreast, wound up from Turusachan far below: members of the kindreds of Aoibhell and Kerrigan and Douglas; the councillors who had advised the dead Ard-rígh, and other officers of state; bards and warriors, friends and comrades, those who had served Fionnbarr and those whom he himself had served in youth; the fellows of a lifetime, walking together now, with no regard for rank or precedence, all equal in their loss.

And ahead of that long line came Aeron walking alone, wrapped in a terrible triple solitude of newmade widow and orphan and queen. The unrelieved white of formal royal mourning was not her best color, and she looked gaunt and tired. By custom her hair was loose and her face unveiled, and she bore no ornament or jewel save the two rings she would wear always from now on: the silver and onyx seal of Brendan Mór, and the emerald seal of Keltia; the one taken from Fionnbarr's hand on the *Tuala*, and the other given from his hand in Turusachan.

The three who had waited upon her coming looked keenly at her as she drew near to them at last, looked with more than eyes alone. To most of her folk, Aeron appeared simply to be suffering the natural effects of so violent and multiple a sudden bereavement: very dreadful, to be sure, but to be accepted, and to be triumphed over in the end. But to those whose Sight saw more and deeper, who knew the true tale of Bellator and the three days and nights that followed—and Kesten and Teilo and Gwydion were by no means the only ones who saw so—Aeron looked reborn.

Though she herself does not know it yet, thought Teilo, returning his Queen's bow of greeting, *and may well not know it for some time to come, either little or long; and so the trouble is not yet done with. But she speeds today not only her own dead but all those thousands who died on Bellator; and that, I think, she does know* . . .

But Aeron had turned from him, and was now giving Gwydion the same formal bow she had given first to Kesten as Ban-draoi Magistra, and then to Teilo as head of the Druid order. She had not seen the Prince of Gwynedd since her return from Bellator—had not in fact seen him since her marriage-morning six weeks since—and though it had been to the Pendragon of Lirias, chief of the Dragon Kinship of which she herself was one, that Aeron made her reverence, as she straightened from her bow it was Gwydion only to whose face she lifted her gaze.

The relief she felt at what she saw there almost stunned her: Aeron had been expecting she knew not what but had feared the worst—blame, or revulsion, or even condemnation. But the gray eyes were clear as always, and as always showed plain to her mind that which lay behind them; and thus supported by what she read in his face, as if it had been by the strength of his hands, Aeron passed between the pillars to the circle's heart, to begin the rite of sending for her beloved dead.

"I cannot reach her, wherever she has gone."

It was a week after the funeral rites, and in a high chamber of Turusachan it was Morwen Douglas who had spoken.

And it was of course Aeron of whom she spoke: In the sevenday since the new High Queen had conducted the death-ceremonial at Ni-maen, Aeron had seemed to retreat as far within herself as she could manage and still remain alive to the world. She kept to her rooms in the Western Tower, took no part in any of the kingdom's affairs, and would not permit herself to be approached by any, not kin nor friend nor minister. Though they could come near her in their own persons—she had not barred her doors against their presence, either with magic or with steel—they were in fact *nowhere* near her; her mind and soul were beyond that area in which she allowed them to venture, as if she had drawn a line in the dust with her sword and defied them to cross at their peril.

"Did I not see her walking and talking—such little of both as she does—I would think her back where we could not find her at all," added Morwen. "Back in Annwn—"

"Ah, nay!" said Melangell swiftly. "Not so far as *that*! But true it is she is not here; and it may be some time yet before we can lure her back."

"Do you know, she has not once spoken Rhodri's name to me," said Morwen after a while, and her voice betrayed all her hurt and sorrow. "Neither has she wept, that we know of—she is lapped round with grief like a tower in the sea, but she herself does not grieve . . . or will not."

Melangell cast a professional eye over Morwen at that, noting with the detached empathy of the soul-healer the other's own grief and care.

"And it is *that*, I think, pains you the most," she said softly, seeing Morwen's startled look and reaching out with her skills of mind to comfort, at least, the one she could. "I can read little of my cousin's heart and mind in this; she has her guards raised again, higher and stronger than ever before. But from what I *can* read, I think it is not grief that so besets her."

"What then?"

"She is angry with herself, for that she allowed her emotions to lead her into inappropriate action, and so now she will not permit herself any emotion at all. She has accepted the deaths as all Kelts accept all deaths of those they love, that is not the difficulty; it is rather that she fears to admit her loss to herself, lest she be tempted to commit some new and greater horror."

"She cannot go on so! Or can she—in sanity?"

"As long as she feels the need," said Melangell with a small shrug. "She will keep an iron hand over it; and she has the strength to do so a very long time indeed."

"Well, there seems little more we can do for her now," said Rohan, speaking for the first time. "Our father trained her up to be Ard-rían, and now the people have confirmed her by the election; and by so doing they confirmed her actions at Bellator."

"Aye," said Morwen darkly, "and I am not altogether sure which would have been the worse: to have set her aside and had you, Rohan, or another, in her place as sovereign, or to have so sanctioned and sealed what she did."

"Not I for Ard-rígh!" said Aeron's brother with some heat. "That is a thing I have never envied Aeron in all our lives."

"Yet I think you would by no means make aught other than a good king," remarked Melangell consideringly, "should it ever come to it."

Rohan laughed and gave his cousin a mock bow. "Which by all gods may it not, though I thank your grace for the thought . . . A good king, perhaps; a great one never. If ever it was time for Keltia to have herself a ruler who might truly be named among the great, that time is now, and Aeron, gods help her, is that one. As for what she has done, it is done and paid for; though I wonder if all the price is yet accounted."

"Not yet," said Melangell, and the other two turned to look at her in surprise, so clear had rung the certainty in her voice. "Though it will be . . . But there will also come a day, doubt it not, when something shall befall her to match this just past, but of opposite nature. Instead of harming, it will heal; instead of striking, she will bless; instead of seeking, she will find. And then, I tell you both, Aeron will be free of her sorrow, for then she will choose to be."

"What in all the worlds would ever equal that which she has endured here?" asked Morwen wondering.

Melangell shrugged again, and shook her red-blond head. "I know not. But by every law of dán, it will come to her. And of that, at least, I am sure."

But for all Melangell's words of hope, the days of Aeron's self-commanded exile in her own palace lengthened to weeks; and the weeks became one month, then two, and still she did not emerge from the stronghold of her guilt. Rohan and Elharn and Trehere among them managed to run the day-to-day affairs of state, praying every instant that nothing would arise, either within Keltia's borders or beyond them, that might be beyond their writ or their wits to deal with. But Fomor seemed chastened, and the Cabiri Imperium made no move, and Keltia itself was subdued and quiet.

And that was well for those three, for they had little of the help they might otherwise have relied upon: Gwydion, to exorcise his own ghosts and guilt and pain, had quitted Caerdroia directly following the funerals, to go into cloistered retreat at a

Druid monastery on his home planet of Gwynedd. And Morwen, shut out by Aeron, deserted by Gwydion, denied the chance to grieve for her dead brother with the other two who had been closest to him, found for herself a surprising source of comfort: Aeron's cousin Fergus mac Hallion, Lord of the Isles, grandson of Gwyneira's brother Corlann.

More surprising still, she wedded him barely six weeks after Rhodri's death, to the shock and dismay of many folk, and the understanding and warm sympathy of many more—including her parents. But though Aeron attended the small ceremony—held at the maenor of Fergus's family, for no one would have inflicted upon Aeron any further memory of her own recent marriage-day than the event demanded—she did not preside nor even assist; and after bestowing brief congratulations and a suitable tinnscra on the couple she withdrew again to her tower, and Morwen went with her new lord to his seat at Duneidyn on Caledon.

There followed then a cold dark time indeed, as Aeron seemed to sink deeper and farther into her private well of guilt; nothing seemed to stir her, and rumor was rife throughout the kingdom that the deaths and her unlawful use of magic to avenge those deaths had unhinged Aeron's mind, that perhaps she should indeed be set aside as Ard-rían, or even put in mercy out of her pain.

But it was not her wits that had been injured, it was her will; and to one who had never before known a hurt of that sort, the lack of will was devastation beyond imagining. At times she thought the only thing to do was to die herself; that the losing her parents, and losing her lord, great though those losses were, were merely an outward echo of the loss she now felt: the loss of her springs of action.

In that encompassing darkness, only Melangell, and to a lesser degree Slaine, could reach Aeron at all; and even they could but reach her as she chose to allow herself to be reached. They would sit with her by the hour, as anxious parents might sit vigil with a sick child, sometimes speaking, more often silent, but always there. Never for an instant did their spirits flag or their strength falter, never once did they fail to hold out to their cousin their very souls as a bridge, across which she might make her long painful way back to find her own again. And for all her seeming distance, Aeron was well aware of their presence and their efforts, and the cost to themselves, grateful beyond words for their sustaining love; nor did she forget it, or them, after.

Then, one day which had begun in no fairer hopes than any other day of that long bleak season . . .

Aeron heard the words as from across a great empty plain, a plain upon which she had been wandering for it seemed a long time; it seemed too that she knew the voice—was it Melangell's, perhaps?—and that she knew of whom it spoke.

Kesten, it had said to her; *your teacher Kesten Hannivec lies at Scartanore near to her passing, and she wishes you to come to her.* And though some had thought that Aeron should not be told this news, that the death of yet another much beloved of her might serve only to drive her soul past hope of recall, others had argued that Kesten's wish and wisdom must be obeyed. Rohan, as the one such a risk most closely concerned, had consulted with Melangell and with Elharn and with his sister Ríoghnach, and it was decided among them that the risk, if risk there were, must be taken.

Rohan was there now, in Aeron's chamber of magic, where she spent near all her waking hours, watching as Melangell put forth all her powers as soul-healer to touch Aeron's mind. *Wherever she has gone,* he thought, shivering a little. He was himself but an indifferent sorcerer, though like almost all his family he possessed somewhat more than the usual Keltic talent for magic; but over the past weeks, as he saw Aeron grow more and more distant, he had wished passionately that he knew more of sorcery than he did, for perhaps he might have reached his sister where others could not.

Though that too is a sleeveless wish, for our own sister Ríona is a Ban-draoi Domina, and even she has not been able to break this wall of darkness Aeron has constructed . . . yet somehow I think I might have been granted the grace to do so—

He left off his bitter reflections as across the room, where she sat as she had done for weeks now in the great black basalt cathaoir, the ceremonial stone throne in the north of the chamber, Aeron's head slowly turned to them, turned so slowly that it was as if some other turned it and not herself at all; but when she looked at them they could see by her eyes that she was back.

Her voice when she spoke was unsteady, a little hoarse, as if in all her days of silence she had forgotten how a voice must be used; but her words were plain enough.

"Ready a ship to take me to Scartanore."

Rohan in his joy to hear her speak did not pause to think. "I will have them prepare your own ship—"

His sister's eyes flashed with something very near their full fire. "Nay, not *Retaliator;* this is not an errand for her to sail, nor for me to pilot. Any ship will do, so that it is a swift one, and any competent captain." Aeron leaned back in the cathaoir, resting her bright head against the smooth dark stone. "And let it be done at once; when I return we will have much to do."

"When you return—" breathed Melangell.

The first faint hint of a smile then; the merest softening of the planes of her face. "Oh aye," said Aeron. "It seems I am here to stay."

"Goddess, look at you! You look like the Gwrach y Rhibyn herself, the Hag of the Dribble—all eyes and hair and bones."

Aeron knelt beside the low bed, set upon the dais in Broinn-na-draoichta. "My sorrow to say it, but you look little better yourself, Magistra of all the Ban-draoi—"

Kesten snorted in disdain, or what would have been had she had the strength. "I at least have the excuse of my years—and my present state."

But Aeron shied from that jump. "When you are healed of this small passing malady, I expect to see you in Turusachan at my Council table. I have few enough in that room I can count upon; I shall need every friend I can find as members of my government."

"I shall not much longer *be* a member of your government," said Kesten smiling, and Aeron's face contracted briefly in pain at the words. "Nay, Aeron-fach, you know better; you were certainly taught better than that, and I think you have learned better than that, too, over these past few weeks."

"That I have; but is it so, truly?"

Kesten shifted against her pillows. "Truly; the Mother Herself has told me . . . I am only sorry I cannot promise you a successor to share my visions for you, alanna. It is the only thing I envy the Archdruid, that he has the right to name his own successor before he goes out. Tybie will do her best with the conclave preceptresses, of course, but the election will go as it must.''

Aeron's eyes fell. ''This is my fault only, it is but more grief caused by my traha—had I not broken my geis at the wedding-feast, none of the rest of it would have happened: not my parents' deaths, not Rhodri's, not Bellator's . . .''

''Now that is foolishness, and self-indulgent wallowing, and I will not allow it,'' said Kesten, and her voice was as sharp as it had been of old, when her favorite student had had need of correction—as it seemed she did now. ''There was no way out of that corner; Duvessa Cantelon saw to that—for which she herself will have to answer. She set the geisa on you that day here in the annat—yes, yes, I know all about it—then saw to it that you would be forced to break one or the other of them. She has earned thereby much dán for herself; but though doubtless your own dán is part of it, to my mind it is Bres of Fomor, and he alone, who is to blame; if blame there be. No fault to you, and what is between Bres and you will play itself out upon a greater field.'' She fell silent, struggling for breath, for the little speech had wearied her.

Aeron found her powers rallying all unbidden, sending energy sparkling down her arm through her hand and into the strong old hand she clasped so tightly; and she was rewarded to see her teacher smile with proud approval.

''Now that is not so poor a showing; but wasted on me, child. Save your strength for your own needs—they will be upon you very soon. Such needs they will be as Keltia has never seen before, and it will be your task to meet them. At least, by the mercy of the Mother, you are healed for it.''

Aeron's tone was strangely urgent. ''Am I? Am I truly healed?''

''Healed enough,'' came Kesten's voice, suddenly distant. ''Healed in Annwn, healed in Ni-maen, healed in the corner you have curled up in for the past weeks—nay, I do not chide; the lioness needs to lick her wounds no less than the lap-dog—and better healed in future. And in the end—in the end only the scar to remind you, like that one you bear from young Vevin's sword,'' she added, opening her eyes and smiling up at her pupil.

''That was rather less deep a wound than this.''

''Without doubt; but the shallowest cuts, though they are the most immediately painful, are the quickest mended. It is the deep wounds that heal the slowest, for we may not even know for some time that we have been wounded at all. Let it have the time it needs, Aeron, and it will find its own way of mending. You will see.''

But you will not . . . Aeron could see Kesten fading visibly now, as the spirit pulled away within itself, preparing to cast off from its earthbound vessel and voyage on its own, and for a moment her knowledge deserted her and she reached out in her panic and her pain.

''Do not leave me! Stay a while yet—I have such need of you *here* . . .''

''And I will still have help for you, *there;* do not fear so. You are already on a path of brightness, Ard-rían; I have Seen it. It began in darkness, and it will pass through still greater darkness, but it will end in a greater light than Keltia has seen for long. My joy to know that Gwydion will walk it with you; it could not have been other, not without great violence being done to the fabric of dán, though it came to the balance of a feather. You and he will never be apart.''

Aeron's peace had returned. ''Nor you and I, mathra-chairde.'' *'Heart-mother'*: of all the many Keltic words for foster-mother, the deepest-meaning, and the deepest-felt.

Kesten lifted her hand in the old gesture of blessing, laid it gently on the shining copper head. ''Beannacht leat,'' she said clearly. ''Beannacht deithi 's mhuintire—'' *'My blessing of farewell on you; the blessing of the gods and the people. . . .'*

''May your journey thrive,'' murmured Aeron, head still bent, and Kesten smiled.

''We will meet again; never doubt it. And what things we shall have then to tell each other . . .''

Then Kesten was silent, and when Aeron raised her head she was gone. But gone with such a radiance of peace upon her face, such a light left behind in the room, that Aeron could not weep.

Weep! she thought with wonder. *Nay, such joy is here—would that I might dance.*

Chapter 32

It had begun to rain again, fine sweeping mists that blew like smoke across Caerdroia on a strong southwest wind. For all the weeks since Fionbarr's death and Aeron's accession, there had been but little rain upon the city; as if the heavens, like Aeron herself, could not let down to weep. The prolonged siege of dry air with its positive ion charge had strung tempers to the snapping point; but as the front had moved through that morning, coming up out of the great bay with the rain riding upon it in irregular successive waves, one could feel the tensions ease from the Stonerows up to Turusachan, as if a terrible strain that had been for a long time upon a knotted rope had suddenly slackened, and the knots unloosed, and now the rope was free to run out smooth and unhindered.

Five months, thought Aeron. *That is long to be so tightly ravelled up; and the folk no less than myself. And had it not been for Melangell and Slaine, and Kesten in the end, I had still been there in that prisoning darkness. But, please gods, all that now is done with . . .*

She had been sitting in the window-bench of her solar, watching the rain approach; the casements opened on a little turret walk that gave a view over both the bay to one side and the palace grounds to the other. Now she unlatched the mullioned frame to let in the damp air, with its flinty smell of water falling on sun-heated stone, and over all a waft of the sea. *The tide must be in, down below . . .*

Through the veils of rain she caught sight of a cloaked figure crossing the courtyard below the tower's landward side, a tall figure with a swift purposeful stride. Aeron knew him at once, even hooded and mantled as he was against the rain, and the breath slammed out of her with the abruptness of it, for her instinct and her othersight had given her no warning of his coming.

She was halfway across the chamber before her judgment reined her back, and with an effort she forced herself back to the seat in the window embrasure. *Nay; it is he must come to me, this time; and if he does not—* But she knew that even did he never come to her again, that too she could face and master; she would love it not at all, but it was a thing that could be borne. *And that I would not have thought possible, five months since; but it is so, and I will wait.*

Aeron did not have to wait very long: Though the rain grew heavier, and the wind stronger, she did not close the casements and she did not move from the window-bench; and when the heavy oak door of the solar opened quietly behind her, she did not move then either.

"You were not here, when I came back," she said; it was not her return from Bellator she spoke of, and he knew it was not. Neither did she speak to reproach him, nor did he take it so.

"I was not sure you wished me to be," said Gwydion at once, in the deep bard's voice she remembered with her whole body. "And as I had hurts of my own to be healed, I thought it best that I was gone before you could send me away. There was naught I could have done; and any road you did not call me."

She had not looked at him, did not look at him now. "You were at Diamor; your mother told me."

"A Druid monastery, in a lonely corner of Gwynedd; a good place to go for healing."

"And you found it?"

Gwydion nodded, though she did not see. "Even as you did find healing for yourself, these past months here at Caerdroia."

Aeron shrugged. "I do not know if I should call it so myself," she said. "And in the event it was not I who found it, but Slaine and Melangell who forced it upon me—Kesten too, before she went . . ." She was silent, aware of the almost physical constraint that was between them. *Never in my life have I found it hard to speak to him of what is on me; why is it so different and difficult now? Like trying to run in the ocean . . .* But she knew very well why: This was the moment of setting foot upon the path that Kesten had spoken of with almost her last breath; now that it had come, there was no going back for either of them from what should happen in the next moments. *For either do we walk it together, or do our paths diverge; there is no middle way. And since that divergence is a thing I will not have nor can imagine—*

Aeron raised her eyes to look at him at last. *Why trouble ourselves with the treachery of words, when our thought will serve us truer and better?* But of that too she was afraid, though she had never lacked for courage in the past: In the weeks since her recovery and return to herself, Aeron had had both fears and hopes in abundance of the moment when she and Gwydion should meet again; had feared that once he too had recovered from the events that had so nearly destroyed them all, he might blame her or damn her; or worse, that he might demand from her a full accounting and a full explanation, and neither of those was she prepared to give just yet, not even to him. *Especially not to him . . . perhaps in time, but not now; and aye, perhaps not ever—who can say?*

But as her thought reached out to unite with his, in that old intimacy of theirs that was more and deeper and greater than any intimacy of the body could be, Aeron saw with inner vision—the only valid kind—that this he would never do. Whatever she wished him to know of what she had endured—before Bellator or after—that was all he wished to know; whenever she chose to tell him, that was when he chose to hear. He would not press her for more, or other; if she wished to tell him, that was well, and if she never wished to speak of it with either mind or voice, that too was well. The choice was hers, and he would bide her choosing.

And how could I ever have feared he might think other . . .

But in the night, behind the drawn curtains of the great fourposted bed, Aeron found courage in the darkness and in the solid warmth of Gwydion stretched beside her to speak of it a little.

"It was my own fault only," she said, in a plain, unstressed, almost conversational tone. "For that I broke my geisa—"

His arm that lay beneath her head tensed and shifted. "Many

folk have broken many geisa, and they were not punished so hard for it."

"That is as may be for them. Some seem able to walk ironshod over their souls and consciences and suffer not so much as a bad dream; while for others to set a single foot off their path means pain and damnation. Unfair, to be sure—or perhaps not so, as dán is reckoned—but there it is. And not my birth-geisa only," she added after a short silence, "but the ones that Duvessa, gods rest her, was moved to put on me. I broke those, and then to compound my sins I disavowed Nia's name and I went out of Tara with war in the Wolf-moon, as I was forbidden to do. Small wonder it took five months, and Kesten's passing, before I could find my way back to my self and senses—and to you; and even now I wonder if the coil is truly run."

The arm came up to pull her closer. "Is this a thing you do often, to punish yourself so? You must leave it, Aeronwy, for you will only make yourself ill again, and Keltia will sicken with you."

"Or *at* me—"

"Nay, never that. The folk confirmed you as Ard-rían; that is sanction enough for your deeds. By their vote they have said you acted in correctness for their part, and they said so of their own unforced choosing. Now sleep awhile; it is hours yet till morning."

But she persisted. "You have said you knew when I wished you to be gone from me; how did you know when I wished you to return?"

Gwydion seemed astonished that she should ask. "How not?"

"How not . . ."

When Aeron's chamberer came in to wake her at her usual time of rising, for the first time ever Aeron was not alone in the curtained bed. Gwydion lay beside her, both of them still asleep, his sword-arm outside the fur coverlets and her unbound hair beneath his hand like a drift of red leaves.

And though there was a full day's schedule ahead for the Ard-rían, and one but little less full for the Prince of Dôn, Blanid carefully closed the thick oak doors behind her again, and went away down the passage to the head of the gallery stairs, and gave quiet orders to the Fians who stood guard there.

*   *   *

Aeron came gradually up to wakefulness, a little startled to find that the dream she had been lost in was no dream after all. He had thrown off the fur coverlet in his sleep, and before she pulled it up around him, for the windows had stood open all night long and the air was cold for summer, she studied him shyly; she had had little chance simply to look at him during the night. Tall he was, a full head taller than she herself, and she was tall even for a woman of the Kelts; broad-shouldered too, with the deep chest and high ribcage of a singer; in the classical idiom, more Roman-bodied than Greek. The shoulder-length dark hair fell forward to mingle with the new beard, and the gray eyes were closed.

She nestled down against him, sensing that he was beginning to awaken. It was strange to wake so, with him beside her; never before had they had a whole night to spend together in a chamber of their own, and all the morning to lie in undisturbed. Still a little shy of him, Aeron reached out to touch the beard, dark and flecked with gray, that edged the strong line of his jaw.

"Do you like it?" The deepness of his voice went through her bones; it held laughter, and she smiled in answer.

"It suits you. Not of course that the crimbeul alone did not, but this— Bearded men have ever— I like it very well indeed," Aeron finished, coloring a little as she saw him grin. "Whose idea was it?"

Her fingers had brushed his lips, and he kissed her palm before replying. "No one's. It seemed a good thing while I was at Diamor among the monks, and then when I came away it seemed good also to leave it. But I admit it took some getting used to.'"

"Well, if you managed, no doubt but so shall I."

Gwydion laughed and drew her hair across his chest like a banner. "Your chamberwoman was here a little earlier," he said then. "And though I would like nothing better than not to set foot beyond the bedcurtains until noon, other folk have other plans for us. Blanid may have left us in peace and privacy, but she will surely burst of it unless she may tell your ladies, and they likewise unless they may tell your household lords and the Fians of your guard and the palace cooks—"

"—and all Turusachan will know before the daymeal," she finished for him, "how the Ard-rían has passed the night, and with whom. Well, *I* care nothing if they know. Or is it that you selfishly fear for your own good name?''

For answer he pushed her head into the pillows, and laughing Aeron struck back at him. "Nay, I see that you do not! That you are already lost to all decency of 'havior and comportment. So much then for the race of Kymry; but we Erinnach do things more seemly." She leaned back against him. "We could not have hoped to keep it to ourselves for long in any case; nor do I think we had been wise to try, for many know what has been between us these many years. Let folk make of it what they please: *I* do not think it unseemly, or untimely, or a slight upon Rhodri''—her voice was clear and steady on the name she had not spoken aloud for five months—"or a disrespect to my parents, or aught else unfitting or unmeet. Our coming together is a thing apart, and does by no means signify that we hold our loss any less dear. But, all the same, it is you who shall be King of Keltia, sooner rather than later, and that they must accept."

"Shall it distress you if they may not, or if folk might think what you have just now spoken?"

"Nay, they *will* think it, at least some folk will; and they may very well *not* accept it, at least not straightway. For my part they may think or balk as they please; it will change nothing. You and I know the truth of the one; and for the other, now I am Ard-rían I shall do as I like."

Though her words had given him joy, Gwydion turned to look at her consideringly. "Even the Ard-rían may not do entirely as she likes."

"Now that is a strange thing, your sister Ari once said much the same to me—it must be near thirty years since. Still"— Aeron sat up in an energetic flurry of tumbled hair and silkwool sheets and fur blankets—"this Ard-rían shall please herself in some things at least, and you are first and chiefest among those. After that, the next matter upon which I will not be thwarted is that of the appointments to my new High Council. While I was—that is to say, over the past five months I could not give thought to it; but now I have done so, and my choices have been made this sevennight past. I shall announce them today."

Gwydion's gray eyes sparked with interest. "Oh aye? There was much interest even in Diamor on those namings, most particularly as to who shall be Taoiseach and who First Lord of War."

"And well there might be," said Aeron grimly, "for after the Crown itself those are the two most important posts in the realm." She gave him a sidewise glance. "Whom did the wagering favor?"

"And does the Ard-rían suggest, then, that Druid monks do most irreverently wager upon worldly matters? —Well, since you seem to know all about it, there was even money being laid on your keeping Conn Trehere as Taoiseach, and three-for-two on Alasdair Ruthven remaining as First Lord of War. Shall I take the bet?"

"If you wish to make some real crossics, I shall give you a better tip than that." Aeron bent her head until her lips touched his ear. "Morwen Douglas for Taoiseach," she whispered, "and Gwydion Penarvon for First Lord of War."

Gwydion shot up beside her, staring down into her smiling face. "Have you lost your wits? Do you know what sort of brangle will break loose across all Keltia the instant folk get wind of this?"

Aeron nodded, green eyes wide and dancing, her fingers pressed to her mouth in purest delight. "I do indeed; and I'd not miss it for worlds! But first my choices must accept their being chosen. What says the Prince of Dôn?"

Gwydion lay back down again among the scattered pillows. "You have thought, I take it, of all the objections that will be raised against me? That I am already overmuch honored—or taxed—as Prince of Gwynedd, and as Fian general, and as Pendragon; and more, that it is not fitting for the Ard-rían to choose her—"

"—her beloved," said Aeron firmly when he hesitated. "What of it? As Prince of Gwynedd these nine years you have learned governance; as general and Pendragon, war and magic; and as for that last—who better to know the Queen's mind and wishes than he who is to be King? No one could find aught amiss in that."

"Many will find much in it," he said presently. "I myself have no an-da-shalla, to See that far ahead; but even a talpa could envision an interesting reign to come."

"Well, and so I hope! Else why should I trouble myself . . .

But I asked for straight talk, and you give me sweet talk. If I did not think you were the best choice, I would not have offered you the post; nay, nor Morwen neither.''

"What has Wenna said to this? To be Taoiseach is a heavier burden even than to be First Lord.''

"I have not yet spoken to her of it.'' Aeron seemed all at once bored with the topic. "But I expect that when I do, and I shall do so within the hour, she will answer much the same as you have done—demur, and decry, and deny—and in the end I expect she will accept, also as you have done. For you *have* accepted, not so?''

"Dôn help me,'' said Gwydion after a while, and not without piety. "But I think I have.''

While Aeron bathed and dressed and prepared herself for her morning Court, Gwydion had done as he had earlier threatened, and not so much as one foot did he set out of bed. Instead, he had lain there in contented idleness, watching her as she moved to and fro across the chamber, choosing boots, choosing jewels, talking to him all the while; watched her much as she had watched him as he had slept, seeing her beauty as for the first time: the tallness of her; the build of a dancer or a fencer, slim though full-breasted; the knee-length flood of flaming hair, and the ambling grace of a blood-mare in her stride.

Aeron had chaffed him mercilessly for his sloth, but she could not shame him into stirring, and at last, with a laughing warning that he should be in the Council chamber by noon if he knew what was best for him, she had kissed him tenderly and gone out.

At the door she turned to deliver one parting shot. "And see too, Gwnedd, that you are there in good time; I would not have my First Lord of War to miss the first battle of my reign.''

The door closed after her, and Gwydion stretched luxuriously down in the great bed. *And this, then,* he thought with amazement, *is how it will be from now onwards. What a thing of wonder and terror, to get what one has wanted for so long . . .* He smiled then, thinking of what she had chosen to call him by way of farewell. *Gwnedd, indeed!*

Unfond of her own name being so altered, Aeron in all the years she had known him never once had used a diminutive of

Gwydion's, though the name carried several, as did most Keltic forenames, according to the degree of intimacy the user shared with the name's bearer. But early in their courtship she had taken to using his title itself for pet-name, and 'Gwynedd' had it been ever since, even in the bedchamber; while he himself called her 'Aeronwy,' though never before others, as none else in all her life had dared.

So the sudden shortening of the word had caught him by surprise. *'Gwnedd':* She had given him a teasing twist to his title, making it into an ancient Kymric word that carried the meaning of "battle" or "passion."' *Either of which was appropriate comment on the night just past . . .* Gwydion laughed outright. Well, it was far to the fore of certain other names she had seen fit to bestow upon him in less loving mood: 'Gwyddon,' for one, which according to its inflection could mean either "sorcerer" or "weevil." *And when she calls me so, seldom is there any doubt as to which she has in mind . . .*

He threw back the coverlets, fishing his boots and trews and tunic from the floor where they had been flung in haste the previous evening, and padded into the adjacent pool-room, to the swimming-baths almost every home in Caerdroia could boast. *Time it is I readied myself to face the Council; I would not hear myself called laggard before such ears as theirs.* He hesitated, then dived into the steaming water, surfacing again halfway down the pool's length. *Still—for Aeron's sake only and not my own—I could hope that such might be the worst thing they can think to call me.*

While Gwydion nerved himself to appear before the Ard-eis of which he would so soon now be a ranking member, second only to the Taoiseach, Aeron had summoned Morwen to the state office on the ground floor that she was accustoming herself to use, and there beneath the lovely coffered vault she offered her sister-in-law and foster-sister the post of Taoiseach, First Minister of Keltia.

"For what else did you spend all those years at the Hill of Laws? And did I not tell you, years and years ago, that we would both be glad of your training, when that I came to be Ard-rían? True it is that I have come to it sooner than any of us could have looked for, or longed for, but now I *am* Ard-rían, and it is as Ard-rían that I ask the Duchess of Lochcarron to be my Taoiseach.''

Though Morwen protested, even as Gwydion had done, as best she could in her staggerment, in the end she too bent to Aeron's will—even as Gwydion had done, and as Aeron had foreseen, and as more and more folk would bend in time to come—and she had accepted. Then she too went off, to tell Fergus her lord, and attire herself appropriately for the announcement in an hour's time, and try to calm herself, and Aeron was alone.

And now that she was alone, she permitted her delight to well up around her at last, hugging her arms and flinging back her head to let her smile blaze to the frescoed ceiling. *Is this what power may mean? Small wonder then that folk do love it . . . I think I have never in my life been so happy. I have the lord of my choosing, who has for his own part chosen me; and I shall have very soon now the Ard-eis that will give me strength and guidance to build the reign I shall design for myself and for Keltia.*

She glanced down at her hands where they cupped round her elbows: at the two rings that gleamed there: the onyx and silver of the one, the green flame of the other. *These signify the realm and the folk I am bound to serve and shield, and at my coronation this autumn I shall take oath before the gods and the people to do so. But that is it: From the moment that my father was struck down, that oath, though not yet spoken, has bound me; it has bound me, even, from the moment of my birth. And, being bound so, I must set myself to perform the article of that oath. Though the dates will be reckoned otherwise in the histories, the true reign of Aeron Ardrían begins from now.*

The noon sun beat down through the skylight into the Council chamber, as Fionnbarr's Councillors fidgeted in their accustomed places, waiting on their Queen's arrival.

When she did enter, unattended except by Rohan, they scraped back their chairs to rise for her, and she nodded in acknowledgment, making her way round to the tall carved chair that stood with its back to the north windows. She paused imperceptibly before seating herself—she had of course occupied that chair many times in her father's absence, and even once as Queen herself, before she fell into her five-months' darkness—but now that it was hers absolute, and her father absent forever, it seemed newly daunting. But she took the chair in silence, and the others followed suit.

Gwydion and Morwen, who with others that Aeron had commanded here now occupied places along the wall, watched her closely and possessively, and with real concern.

Though I know she is otherwise, thought Morwen, *she is looking very ill.* The plain red of everyday Keltic mourning was Aeron's worst color, for it drained her face to a ghastly pallor and clashed jarringly with the copper hair. But the period of official Court mourning was nearly done now; in private, even Aeron had already returned to her favored hues of green and brown and black. Morwen shook herself. *What in all the hells am I thinking of? Aeron is about to launch the lightning here in this room, and I am fretting about her garb . . .*

She looked sidewise in sudden gratitude: Gwydion, sensing her state of mind, had taken her hand and pressed it to give her heart. But he was not looking at her; he had not once taken his eyes from Aeron since she entered the chamber, and she for her part had not once met his.

"There is no civil or easy way to do this," Aeron was saying, and though there was strain in her face there was none in her voice. "But I have made my decisions as to who shall make up my High Council and Privy Council, and I have summoned you here to know my choices." She paused to allow to die down the murmur that rippled through the room. "I wish to say first and last that all you here present did serve the Ard-rígh Fionnbarr most well. Better than that: There is not one of you whose services I had not been proud to retain. But my reign will demand differences, and I have had to determine by whom shall those differences be best served. I thank all of you for your acceptance and understanding, in especial over the months of my—incapacity; and certainly there is no reflection upon any whom I have elected to replace."

Again she paused. "Well, then, no more suspense. To continue in their offices from the reign of Fionnbarr XIV Ard-rígh: Master Alun Dyved, Home Lord; Mistress Kelynen Gwennol, Rechtair; Prince Elharn Aoibhell, Master of Sail; Gavin Earl of Straloch, Lord Extern. Also of course to continue, those heads of orders whose election the sovereign does not command: Master

Teilo ap Bearach, Archdruid; Master Auster Tregannic, Lord Chief Brehon; Master Idris ap Caswyn, Chief Bard; Mistress Ffaleira níghean Enfail, who has but recently been named in conclave to succeed our beloved Mother and Sister Kesten Hannivec as Magistra of the Ban-draoi; and Prince Gwydion Penarvon ap Arawn, Pendragon, chief of the Dragon Kinship.''

Aeron surveyed the room, noting the pockets of relief and pleasure, the apprehension that still chilled the air. She touched minds briefly with Gwydion—a fleeting smile of thought, strong and steady with love and approval—and made a notation on the computer pad at her right.

"And now for my new appointments: To replace Mistress Tryssa Pendeven, who has requested retirement, as Earl Guardian— Lord Illoc mac Nectan. As Earl Marischal, Lady Douglass Graham shall follow Kerrec, Duke of Morbihan, who has succeeded to his new lordship by the same unhappy circumstances which elevated me to my own; and to replace Mistress Elowen mar'Dyth, also requesting retirement, Sir Lodenek of Gorlas as the new Sea Lord. My thanks to the departing Councillors, my welcome to the new.''

Now it seemed as if all the chamber held its breath. "And as to my two chiefest appointments, to which I have given much thought and consideration: For First Lord of War, I name Gwydion Penarvon, Prince of Gwynedd, Chief of the House of Dôn; and for Taoiseach, First Minister to the Crown, I name Morwen Mariwin Douglas, Duchess of Lochcarron and Lady of the Isles.''

There was a pause electric in intensity for ten full seconds, the silence yelling like a bansha in their ears; then uproar unparalleled. Conn Trehere and Alasdair Ruthven, the deposed Taoiseach and First Lord of War, sat white-faced and still in their chairs: not so much out of dismay at their dismissal—for Aeron had been frank with them about the matter and they had known their service was to end—but at the identities of their young successors. In their maddest dreams or darkest nightmares, never had they thought to hear such names as those.

Against the wall where they sat just as pale and unmoving, Gwydion and Morwen were but little less stunned themselves. Though they had known Aeron's full intent, the hearing it pronounced in full Council made it real in a way it had not been before. But beside them, Rohan was grinning from ear to ear, and from a few places away, Gwyneira the Dowager Queen smiled upon her granddaughter with grim satisfaction.

Aeron herself sat with her elbows planted on the table and her chin cupped in her hands, watching the eddies of emotions and complex comings-to-grips with an almost amused detachment. She had of course known perfectly well that these two appointments would cause more upheavals and heartscaldings than all the others put together. In truth, there was nothing whatever to enrage anyone in her other namings: The carryovers from her father's Council were good, solid, experienced officers of state, who knew their jobs warp and weft; the replacements for those who sought retirement—and if they had not sought it of their own wish or need she would have kept them on as well—were inspired choices, and no one could find fault with any of them.

But to name Morwen and Gwydion had been her great gamble; even now she was by no means sure she had thrown a winning cast, though of her two choices themselves she had not the smallest doubts. She could see that one of the prevailing thoughts in the room was "How could Aeron dare!"; but daring had nothing to do with it, nor had courage, nor even imagination. For these two offices, of necessity the right and left hands of the reigning monarch, she had wanted souls she could rely upon as her own—better than her own—friends and advocates, auxiliars she could trust as her sword-arm and with her life, and she had known from the first who those two must be.

It was not even as if they were inexperienced in such matters: Gwydion was after all a Fian general, and not lightly did the Fianna give such rank; and Morwen had taken her seat in the House of Peers five years since, as Duchess of Lochcarron to follow her grandmother Raighne. Too, Aeron had wanted helpers who would be with her for all the years of her reign. *And if I live to reign longer than the Shan-rían Aoife herself, still shall I have these beside me. With Gwydion and Wenna and Rohan, how can I fail? We are as the Four Watchtowers of the World, waking and warded, armed and guarded, on all points of the Circle . . .*

Rollow of Davillaun, one of the rising young Assemblators, here today at Aeron's bidding, had been trying to catch her eye, from his seat near Gwyneira over against the wall.

"Aeron—Ard-rían, rather . . ."

" 'Aeron' will suit very well, Rollow," she said mildly. "It has ever done so before."

He refused to bend. "*Ard-rían*, I beg you reconsider. It is not that your last-named choices are unacceptable or unworthy in themselves"—he faltered a little as Aeron, who had been studying some notes in front of her, suddenly lifted her eyes to his, a green flash of warning visible clear across the chamber—"but I must put it to you that I do not know how the Senate and Assembly and House of Peers will vote upon these namings."

The green flash kindled then to fire, though Aeron's voice stayed pleasant and unemphatic. "It makes no differ, my master of Davillaun, for that those bodies you mention have but a vote only, and no final authority over the Ard-rían's choice. Though naturally we would prefer that our choices be respected, it is of no great consequence to us if they are not. We have chosen as we have seen fit, and there's an end of it."

She had not stressed the word, but not an ear in the room had failed to mark her unprecedented shift to the royal plural, and not a mind failed to note its significance: Like it or loathe it, from now on it was Aeron Ard-rían, first of that name, and the rueful shock of that realization was plain on many faces.

"If you wish to make of it an issue in the Houses," added Aeron, rising as she spoke and grimly pleased to see them all scramble obediently to their feet, "you have of course the right to do so. The duty too, if you feel so strongly. And if you do, know that I shall never hold it against you; not this nor indeed any loyal and honest opposition, now or in time to come, and gods willing, we shall be together a good many years. But know this too before you begin: It will change nothing. For in that if in naught else, sirs and ladies, I am indeed my father's daughter. I give you all good day."

She collected Rohan, Gwydion and Morwen with her eyes, and went out with them following after.

"Why do they *do* this!"

It was afternoon of that same day, and Aeron was in her solar with her two new chief ministers; Rohan too was there, having been earlier named Tanist, heir to the Throne of Scone until such time as Aeron produced one to supersede him; and Ríoghnach, who by his elevation had herself become Princess of the Name and next heir of line, with her husband, Duke Niall O Kerevan; and assorted other intimates.

"*Why?*" repeated Aeron. "Half the galaxy knows, having learned the harsh way, how qualified Gwydion is to be Keltia's war-leader; and doubtless the other half will learn soon enough . . . And Morwen's maiden term in the House of Peers, when she took up her seat five years ago—how many measures did you carry through, Wenna? Well, I cannot recall how many, but it was more than any maiden peer in recent history; and how? By politics, and by reasoning, and by knowledge of the law, and by diplomacy: just exactly what is wanted in a Taoiseach. Chriesta tighearna, what would the pigheads have me to *do*!"

"I saw old Trehere before he left for Erinna," offered Sabia into the uncertain silence. "So cross was he with you that he was kicking badgers out of his toes."

"I cannot help that," said Aeron, still a little cross herself. "I told him weeks ago what was to happen; it is hardly as if it comes to him as a skybolt."

"Perhaps he and the others think you mean to name your friends and your kindred exclusively to posts of power," said Rohan.

Aeron began to laugh, shaking her head at the absurdity of it all. "And if I do, what business is it of theirs, the toads . . . But they had best grow used to it, for there is going to be a good deal more of it before I've done! Ríona, Sabia, Macsen, Melangell, you are all named Privy Councillors; also my cousin Shane, and Donal mac Avera, and my uncles Estyn and Deian, and my grandmother the Queen-Dowager, who sits on both Councils by dower right as widowed consort. Slaine shall be my personal healer; Niall, you shall be master of the household troops, and Denzil Cameron shall be master of fence, if we can winkle him out of Caer Artos as featly as we did his brother Struan to be master of horse."

"Aeron," remonstrated her brother-in-law Niall, only half-laughing, "is this not perhaps a little overmuch, merely to prove your point—or your power?"

His tone was light, but he spoke for them all, and Aeron gave him a very sharp glance before she answered. "It might be; but aught less would only confirm them in their opinion that I am unsure of myself, and uncertain that I acted rightly." She favored them all with a grin and a flash of characteristic candor. "Which, perhaps, a little, sometimes, I am; but that is not for them to know, and certainly not for them to dare to tax me with . . . Any road, are we not forever hearing from them about the sacredness of the clann in Keltic society? Well, let them see then their own words at work, right here in Turusachan. Now, can any of you think of others I might appoint? I should hate to have it said of me that I overlooked either friend or kin when it mattered."

Chapter 33

The brehon laws, that had been brought from Earth to Tara with the first ships of Brendan's immram, held that the sovereignty of Keltia was never vacant: No sooner did one king cease to breathe than the next queen drew her first breath as ruler; should a queen's heart be stilled, a king's pulse struck the next beat unfaltering. According to that ancient code, then, Aeron had been High Queen, the seventeenth monarch of her house to rule since the crown had come to them from the Douglases eight hundred years since, from the instant her father's spirit had peacefully passed in an untranquil time.

But to the folk of Keltia, and to the worlds beyond the Pale as well, her queenship would not be complete, not the tangible thing it must be, until she had been crowned; had been acclaimed publicly by the folk who had already attested to her by the election. And not until she bore the Copper Crown upon her brow, with the Silver Branch that was already hers in her hand, and took her seat upon the Throne of Scone would it be complete to her.

To that end, then, preparations had been afoot ever since she had returned to herself and gathered up the reins of her rule. In the days following the appointment of her Council—stormy days, in which she was already proving she knew well how to weather such blasts—Aeron had given order that her coronation should take place, as did most crownings, upon her birthday. Her order did not leave much time for the readying of such a solemn rite, for her birthday was in the early days of October and here it was already summer's end. But she had resolved that it should be then, that another year was too long a wait for her sacring, and so those whose duty it was to arrange such matters were already hard at work.

"Any road," said Aeron to Tybie as they walked in the palace gardens, "there is not so much pomp attached to a crowning. More ceremony went into my making as Tanista, and the oaths sworn to me then are binding now. They need not be taken again save in mass affirming; only those newly come to their lordships, who have not yet sworn to me personally, must now take their oath between my hands. As for the rest of it—"

Tybie glanced swiftly at her beloved charge. *Aye,* she thought very privately, *That 'rest of it' is what we have come here to speak of; and a good deal more to it than just the Copper Crown upon her head . . .*

"Is it the thought of the vigil to come that troubles you?" she asked, thinking that perhaps to Aeron the unknown terrors of the dusk-to-dawn vigil that she, and all rulers of Keltia, must undergo would seem less fearful to one such as Tybie, whose whole existence was spent in just such focused solitude.

But Aeron shook her head. "Nay; *that,* strangely enough, I am eager to face . . . What I *would* know," she went on with a dogged hesitancy, "is how I may take what I have learned at Lundavra, and at Scartanore, and carry it with me to Turusachan; and bring it to the rest of Keltia, in the end. Now you, who are a holy anchoress—"

Tybie's clear laugh rang through the gardens. "Very easy to be 'holy,' as you name it, well away from the world's woes and wonders!" She grew grave again at once, for she knew Aeron's difficulty. "To lead a life of the spirit, as you have been trained to, and as you have come to love to do, in the full stream of the everyday and the royal—that is what you are asking, and it is a tremendous asking. So I ask *you* in return: Whom would you count the holier, one like myself, say, or one like the Ard-rían St. Keina Douglas? And I say to you, Aeron-fach, there is no question— I, and all who choose as I have chosen, live a life that if of no less complexity than others' is at least less worked-upon from the outside, and therefore perhaps less difficult to order. But Keina—now *she* lived in the heart of worldly pomp and power; indeed she was the living heart's-blood of it, as you shall be, and indeed are already. Yet she was also one of the greatest saints who ever blessed our realm, and if she could live so, so also can you.''

"Well, I do not aim anywhere near so high!'' said Aeron fervently. "I wish only to find for myself, and thus pass on to the people, some of that which you and Kesten so freely gave me: to give it in turn to Keltia, and perhaps even to more than Keltia, if that be not traha past all pride.''

"Then do not fear, for it is yours already, and so theirs, and I have no more advice to give you: I shall be returning to Lundavra, as you know, once you are safely crowned, and this time for the last time— As for what else you may need as Ard-rían, you must look to yourself, and to your vigil. That it will be given, and you will find it, I have not the smallest doubt; and that you will give it back again still greater and more blessed, I doubt even less.''

After Tybie had taken loving leave and gone to her rooms to rest—at Aeron's beseeching, the anchoress had come to Turusachan only for her pupil's crowning, to fill the place of spiritual advisor that would have gone to Kesten Hannivec, to bless and guide and pray with the new-crowned Queen—Aeron crossed the gardens and went in at the terrace doors of her state office on the palace's ground floor.

Though the chamber was far too opulent for her own tastes, Aeron was training herself to use it, conforming to association and tradition alike. Her father had worked here; indeed, one of Aeron's earliest memories was of being in this room as a child of perhaps two years, sitting upon her father's lap while he and her grandfather Lasairían, whose office this had been also, had spoken to outworld ambassadors—the first galláin she had ever seen, though she could not now recall their race.

Her great-grandmother Aoife too had had this chamber for her own workplace, the center of the great and lasting web she had spun over Keltia and beyond. *And she in the middle of it like the royal spider she was* . . . Still, it was a room of perfect proportion, a double cube, with great loveliness of line and adornment, and the tall windows she had just closed behind her gave an unparalleled view of the bay that was Caerdroia's western boundary.

Far below her as she watched, sun-sharks leaped in formation out of the calm blue waters, six silver curves flashing in the light, breasting the waves in perfect unison and vanishing below, to leap up again farther from shore, looping across the Bight in a path as straight as any tântad drawn upon the land.

Aeron found her hand going to an object she kept on her desk: a small woven basket with a hooped lid. There were a few personal oddments inside—a broken earring, a worn coin, a seashell picked up one day on the strand—but it was not for random storage that Aeron had kept it so carefully all these years.

Lifting the little basket to her face, she sniffed the woven grasses, and found herself back on a long-ago plain: There was sun on grassland in those dry woven splints, sun and wind and the smell of horses, blue sky and huge silent cloudshadows, hay drying for miles in the high light. Black ash, red armot, aromatic sweetgrass, woven by a craftsman of the western clanns into a pattern of ribs and diamonds . . . A small girl who had dwelt near Caer Artos had given Aeron the basket—a shy private presentation one afternoon, no ceremony to it though much love, and no one else about—as welcome-gift on the Tanista's coming to the Vale of Arvon as a Fian novice, sixteen years since.

Sixteen years! Strange what small pictures the mind will refuse to part with, when other, greater, memories have fled beyond recall . . . She could still call up that child's face, smiling shyly up at her from beneath a tangled glib of honey-brown hair. That child was long grown, perhaps a Fian now herself; but the basket, still faintly fragrant, had stood amid other loved clutter on every desk of Aeron's all those years, and would continue to stand so, now, on this desk, now that she was Queen. *Even more so now, for a queen needs more than any to remember that such things, such days, such memories, can be; it is just such that she swears before the people and the gods to uphold and protect, a great planting that began long since, and that will still be long after I am gone.*

Aeron smiled, and set the little basket down again, with tenderness and resolve both. *And if I am to do so with any hope of harvest, time it is that I began to prepare my fields.*

As the day of Aeron's crowning drew near, gifts began to flow in from all quarters of the kingdom, and from beyond the Pale as well: rich gifts, such as queens and empresses might properly be offered, and humble ones alike. Aeron, who cared but little for silks and laces, and only for such jewels as held for her significance either magical or personal, dutifully accepted the grand tributes from the hands of bowing ambassadors, and received with greater and genuine pleasure the small offerings from the ordinary folk of her realm. Her kindred and friends knew better what would please her, and for the most part their gifts did so, but there was one in especial that did more beside . . .

Sabia, with Morwen's connivance, had finally managed to drag Aeron off to the stables for a long-postponed ride out to the mouths of the Avon Dia, as the three friends, and indeed each of them alone, had done often for pleasure and exercise in time past. At first reluctant, Aeron had at last made time and inclination come together, and now she stood in the stableyard impatiently waiting for her horse to be fetched out to her. Sabia and Morwen, already mounted, seemed to be sharing some secret, but she paid no heed to it.

"Ah, here is your mount, Aeron."

Turning, Aeron came up short with surprise at sight of the beast that had been led up by the horsemaster. It was certainly not her old white faithful Foven . . .

"Do you like her?" Sabia was asking with unconcealed glee, and Morwen too was grinning.

Aeron could only stare. The tall black mare stood three hands and a half over Foven, with a long silky mane and a tail that touched the ground; the white star beneath the forelock was echoed in a tiny snip upon the velvet muzzle.

"Who would not! She is magnificent—is she yours, then?"

"Nay," said Sabia, with a fine offhand air. "Yours."

"Mine!"

"A coronation gift from the O Dálaigh." Sabia was enjoying her friend's staggerment. "Her lineage is from that Glora strain that you like to put so many crossics on at the race-meets."

"And which wins me so many crossics more on my wagers . . . But I have never seen one of even that line as fine as she." Aeron held out a hand to the lovely creature, and the mare snuffed at it, analyzing, ears and nostrils working to sort and register the stranger.

"One of the best we have ever bred; the Chief of the Name,

my mother and I made the final choice, though the gift comes from all our clann. She is war-trained—what else for a Fian's mount—and parade-trained too, so that you may use her at march-pasts and such.'' Sabia leaned forward to touch the mare's shoulder, and the horse bowed her head, bending one foreleg in what looked so much like a curtsy that Aeron burst out laughing.

"A courtier already! Nay, nay, lassie''—for the mare, startled by the sudden peal of sound, had crabbed sidewise a few steps, snorting in alarm—"my sorrow to fright you so, come up now . . .'' Still murmuring soft words, Aeron held out her hand again. After a delicate hesitation, the horse thrust her sculptured head against Aeron's front, wanting to be scratched between the eyes, and she was instantly obliged. "I shall call you Brónach.''

'The Sorrower' . . . Sabia smiled, knowing what had moved her friend to name the horse so, but the smile was the one that springs from long-ago memories, and she leaned over again in her saddle.

"Think of her as gift from that world you so longed for—do you remember—back at Caer Artos, when we saw the lights of the farmstead through the snow.''

Aeron met her smile. "I remember well,'' she said then, and swung lightly up into the black mare's saddle. "And I thank you—for this, and for then.''

They rode out in silence, Brónach moving smooth and silken under Aeron's hand and knee as if they had gone together so for years. After a pleasant detour through the City's northwestern quarter, they went out through the Seagate and onto the machairs that bordered the shores of the huge western bay. Once on the wiry seagrass they urged the horses to a gallop, but the beasts smelling the salt wind needed no urging, and with their riders knee to knee they thundered through the surf.

After a mile or so Aeron drew rein, and the others came up to her in a few moments, for Brónach had outpaced their mounts by a good score of lengths.

"I was something lonely for a time there,'' she said, patting the mare's gleaming neck. "This one is a distancer.''

"Distance is no new thing for the Ard-rían of Keltia,'' said Morwen, and though Sabia looked a little shocked Aeron only laughed.

"There is distance and distance," she agreed, and throwing her right leg over Brónach's neck she slid to the ground and began to walk, to cool down the lathered horse, and her companions did the same.

After a while they came to a place where an inlet of the bay and a stream branching off the Avon Dia made a web of waters over the machair, sweet and salt mingling amid reeds and the thick seagrass. At the water's edge, Aeron halted, to look out over the sparkling semicircle of the bay, then back southwards to where the City shone white below the Loom, a jewel in the lap of Eagle.

"I have been thinking much on distance of late," she said then. "And of all those distances, that which most concerns me is the distance Keltia has kept in time past from the worlds beyond the Wall, and of how it now falls to me to maintain, or diminish, that breadth."

"Which shall you?" asked Morwen quietly, for this was a matter of high policy, and she was Taoiseach, and though they had spoken of it before Aeron had never yet declared clearly to anyone, save perhaps Gwydion, her true and ultimate intent.

But it had long been thought throughout Keltia that if any sovereign, Ard-rígh or Ard-rían, would be disposed or destined to lead the kingdom to a greater closeness with the outworlds—though perhaps "greater" was scarce the word to use, since the closeness had been historically nil, and even the smallest increase would be seen as sweeping and unprecedented change—that sovereign would be the one who now reigned. But none knew for sure, and so—

"Which, then?" repeated Morwen.

Aeron stroked Brónach's nose, and the mare gave a gentle whickering sound, ruckling down her muzzle and mouthing the cuff of her mistress's gauntlet.

"I must introduce this one to my hounds Cabal and Ardattin when we come back to the City—the four of us shall be much together from now on . . ." She glanced up at each of her friends in turn. "From our time on Earth, there has been the law of the maigen," said Aeron slowly, and now her eyes were on neither of them, but rested on the City seven miles behind them. "That a lord or lady was responsible for the inviolate peace and sanctuary of the lands surrounding each's maenor or brugh, to a certain limit set by law according to the rank of each, that all the folk and their homes and beasts and goods should be untroubled. And, by that same law, as you know well, Wenna, from your time on Arvor, all Keltia is the Ard-rían's maigen—all the worlds and all the stars and all the space of the Bawn, everything that lies within the Pale—and I will do what I must to ensure that the peace of my maigen is kept unbroken, and all who dwell within its bounds happy and safe.''

"That is not what I did ask," said Morwen.

"Nay, it is not." Aeron vaulted back into Brónach's red leather saddle, and turned the mare's head for home. "But—for now—it is all that I shall give for answer.''

The black ship settled like a falling feather on the high moor where it lifted from the plains below, and Aeron, stepping from the main hatchway, looked up at the holy mountain—Mount Keltia—towering before her. It was the first time since her return from Bellator that she had piloted her own ship—or indeed any other ship—and it had taken her some little time back at Mardale Port before she could bring herself even to set hand to helm. *And that too will be conquered here today,* she thought, staring up at the double horns of the peak above. *It is right that* Dubhlinnseach *is no more, and that it is* Retaliator *should have brought me on this errand. It brought me on one just as necessitated though utterly unholy; but both of those errands were bound upon me, and now my ship must be cleansed even as I myself must be . . . and shall be, by tomorrow's dawn.*

But that cleansing would be only part of what awaited her here. For Aeron had come to Mount Keltia as had every ruling king and ruling queen before her, back to Brendan himself. They had come on the days before their crownings, as she had come on the day before her own, all to serve the same high obligation: to keep vigil from dusk to dawn, alone, unarmed, unsustained by so much as a rusk of bread or sip of water, in the great stone circle that stood beneath those double horns, that was known as Caer-na-gael.

A nemeton, a sacred circle of the same pattern and purpose as Ni-maen or any other of those that linked together across Keltia like bright beads of power, Caer-na-gael was all the same unlike all others. It was first, and oldest, and holiest of all: Here it was that thanks had been given by Brendan for Keltia's very discovery, the great gift of a safe harbor and a new home among the stars for those who had come as refugees from Earth. He had ordered the stones hewn and carved and set in place, and when they had been raised his mother, Nia, had consecrated them, and awe and power had lain upon them ever since.

Though to come here was by no means forbidden to the folk of Keltia—as it was rather required of their rulers—few indeed ever found courage enough, or a need urgent enough, to do so. But if Caer-na-gael, unlike the other nemetons, had few visitors, it was commonly believed to have no lack of other visitants: The Sidhe, the Shining Folk themselves, were thought to gather here, what time Gwyn the son of Nudd would call up his Hunt to ride the wild winds, coursing his white hounds upon the slopes of the upper air, and fear kept mortals far from there on such nights.

But Aeron, who had been instructed in Nia's own knowledge by votaresses of the order Nia herself had founded, had no such fears; and if she had, still it would have made no differ, for what she sought here was by custom less for herself than for her folk, and in that cause—and that too was custom, and for her more than custom—there was nothing she would have stood away from.

According then to the ancient tradition, the monarch must make the ascent to Caer-na-gael on foot, and Aeron had come to the mountain in good time to begin; it was not yet afternoon, though sunset came earlier now these October days, and the shadows were already beginning to stretch downslope. The climb was not a difficult one—for all its altitude, Mount Keltia could be climbed with one's hands in one's pockets, along a broad switchbacked road up the mountain's western face. It was an easy road, an ancient processional way up the Holy Mountain for such pilgrims as might come; and it was as a pilgrim that Aeron would go now.

So she bathed and purified herself in the clochan that had been built for that purpose at the mountain's foot, divesting herself of her weapons and her jewels, all the metal that was upon her—

even the two signets of her royal rank were left behind; none would dare touch them in such a place, or indeed in any place, and in any event no other Kelt would be tarrying within fifty miles of the mountain once the sun had set—and unbound her hair so that it fell loose to her knees. Emerging from the clochan, she paused to make brief reverence at the little shrine to the Mother that stood nearby, then set foot upon the rising road.

Teilo and Kesten and Tybie and Ffaleira and Gwydion had all counseled her on what to expect upon this path; but though they had spoken from their wisdom and their magic—and their love— they were for all their knowledge as ignorant as she. They themselves had never walked such a road, and so they could not know what she might meet upon it. Fionnbarr, who had walked it in his time, had died before ever speaking to her of the matter; and even had he not perished so unlooked-for, he might have foreborne to instruct her, for what had been true for him might be far otherwise for his heir.

But all the advice, and she had had goleor of it and more beside, had come down to this: that all ordeals were different, according to what was brought to them by the one tested, and according to what would be demanded of that one in days to come; and this was a truth of which Aeron had already knowl- edge of her own twice over, from her immram when she became Ban-draoi and her test of soul as a Fian. True, she came to this third test with bloody hands, though perhaps no bloodier than certain of her predecessors' had been. *But they in their time and truth, I in mine . . . I have no right to make comparison, for they may well have been right to do as they did, and I may well have been in deadly error. Let the moment judge the moment, and me.*

In the old, long-practiced way, she set her mind to quiet blankness as she walked, a smooth slate upon which might be inscribed the knowledge to come, and in that state ascended the mountain. If she was being taught along the way, it was no teaching she was aware of, and she might or might not recall later on with waking mind what it was that she had learned.

Then all at once, as if indeed she wakened from walking sleep, Aeron stood before the western gates to Caer-na-gael, with no memory of how she had come there, or how the road had been, or how long it had taken her to climb the mountain's face; though when she glanced behind her she saw Grían going down in fire at the world's edge, and her boots, when she bent to remove them to enter the holy place, were worn near through the soles, the shafts slashed and cut as if by thorns or daggers.

A harder road than I thought, then . . . Aeron looked up at the pillar-stones that marked the gateway. 'Three times the height of a tall man,' that was how it was set down in the old texts; the close-grained bluestone surfaces were carved with symbols whose meaning eluded even the scholars of the Ban-draoi and the Druids and the bards. The wind, from which the mountain's breast had shielded her during her climb, now streamed over the plateau like liquid silver, and she had to turn aside a moment to catch her breath, before facing resolutely into the blast from the east.

From where she now stood at the circle's edge, her view into its center was cut off by the inner ring of tall trilithons. But Aeron knew, as did all in Keltia, who had lain there all these centuries: St. Brendan, the mighty Astrogator himself, who had raised this circle, barrowed beneath the bluestone altar at the circle's heart. His Danaan mother, Nia, had made his tomb here, before she went off into solitude and exile, or back to her Sidhe kin as many believed, or to her own ending. None knew for sure, even now. But when last she had been seen, by her great-granddaughter Morna, her face had been toward the Hollow Mountains.

Aeron's glance was drawn that way now, almost against her will or wish. If Caer-na-gael was a haunt of the Shining Folk, then the Hollow Mountains were for them their homeplace: Many miles to the north and west, those peaks still glowed in the sunset light, or perhaps by some other light from within their depths, or of their own. *Yet not not so many miles, either, as would hamper any who dwelt there and might wish this night to ride the winds from there to here . . .* As she stared at the rose-touched crags, almost Aeron could sense a Presence and a Power in those hills, a mind or a spirit that was aware of her as she stood revealed to its sight beneath the stars, perhaps even judging her as she did stand so.

She shook herself, feeling anew the bite of the wind. St. Brendan did not sleep here alone, she knew; St. Morgan rested beside him, Arthur's sorceress sister, architect of Keltia's mightiest achievement, the Curtain Wall that had so long been their sure protection; though Taliesin her mate, her brother's dearest comrade, had chosen the Fian way, to be disembodied by the scadarc upon the wicker bier.

And for the great King himself . . . Taliesin's enigmatic words, learned long since and never forgotten, sang now in Aeron's mind: 'Not wise the thought, a grave for Arthur.'

For a moment Aeron allowed that thought to run: Arthur of Arvon, greatest ruler that Keltia had ever known; he who had struck down the malignant blight of Edeyrn's Theocracy, and put an end to that bent Archdruid as well; who as Rex Bellorum had routed the invading Fomori and Fir Bolg, and who as High King had destroyed the Coranians who had come after; who in his ship *Prydwen*— 'Fairface'—had disappeared in the final battle, taking his enemies with him, sending his promise to his Kelts that he would come to them again in time of need.

And that was a reign of such splendor, of deed and spirit both, and he a soul of such matchless excellence, as would be sin and affront alike even to dream of coming near to; and none since Arthur's day, High King or High Queen, has been vain enough or vaunting enough to so presume. Yet am I of Arthur's own blood, and if all goes as I will have it, my heir to follow me will be doubly of Arthur's line . . . I think I may dare hope, with no violence to dán, that at the very least I might bring no dishonor to that lineage. And is that not part of what I have come here to attest to?

Slowly Aeron passed between the trilithons that rose up around her like trees in a granite grove, rooted in concentric rings, and came at last to the huge stone chair, scaled seemingly for one of more than mortal frame, that faced the altar. Almost the only thing on which her advisors could agree among them was the charge, many times repeated, that, chance what might, Aeron must remain in this seat of stone until the first light of Grían returned to Tara through the Gates of the Sun—those double horns of the peak above her. But it would be a long cold autumn night before the dawn would bring deliverance, a night without food or water or rest or sleep, and only the unknown for company.

With a farewell flash, Grían was gone in the west, the last of her flame dying beyond Caerdroia far away, as Tara moved deeper into its own shadow. And in that long blue twilight, so soon now to give place to true night, Aeron seated herself in the stone chair, to await what might befall, and to return as a queen in the morning.

Chapter 34

For all her fear and doubt, and the bite of the midnight air, Aeron must have half-drowsed for a time, or so it seemed to her, for all at once she came alert with a terrible start, her heart pounding and every instinct she possessed bidding her strike out at danger. *But I am not to leave the chair, and any road I can see no danger here against which I might strike . . . Had* there been someone, then—or something? Or had it merely been a natural sound of the night that had roused her, if indeed she had slept at all? Or not so natural—a shout or cry, or something like the belling of hounds a long way off, or had it been the far music of a hunting horn?

With a tremendous effort of will she quieted her pulse and evened her breathing, resettling herself more comfortably, and more watchfully, in the great stone seat. *How long have I been here, I wonder? It feels something like forever . . .* She glanced up to gauge the hour by the stars and Tara's two small moons, but now for the first time the magic that was on Caer-na-gael, or in it, or of it, was seen to be at work, for not moons nor stars nor even the arching ribbons of the Criosanna could be observed in the heavens, though the night was crystal-clear.

Aeron smiled a little and hitched her cloak closer against the chill. *Very well then; I see that that is to be the way of it . . . Whatever the hour in truth, though, I daresay there is still a fair chunk of night to get on the other side of, and a fair span of time in which many things may happen; though it has been peaceful enough thus far.*

But until that peace—largely temporary, she suspected—did end, there was always thought with which to busy herself, and that was a thing for which Aeron had had little leisure of late, so crammed had her hours been with doing. *No doubt but that I should now be holding solemn converse with myself on my crowning tomorrow, and my rule to come; but what seems to want to be thought of is very different* . . . Bres of Fomor, for one, and the inescapable link to Bellator: Though it seemed sacrilege to contemplate either in so holy a place and time, Aeron found to her considerable surprise that she could face both; if neither gladly nor willingly, and in no case without pain, at least steadily. *And that is one prayer answered that I had not even known I had asked: Never do I wish to flinch from facing an act of mine, and never do I wish the memory of that act to cease to cause me pain, so that never am I tempted to commit its like again* . . . *But there has been strange dearth of news from Fomor these past months; not since I did sign the treaty that they petitioned for has there come any formal word. And all the spies can tell us is that Bres has gone to ground in Tory like a wounded stoat, mourning his losses, or, more like, lamenting his strategy. Well, please gods, he will stay so, until I have had at least a chance to put my reign upon a straight course, or, even more like, to set my spear against the rock for his next attack.*

But Bres was not the only one who came to Aeron's mind just then: The more she tried to turn her thought from them, the more vivid they grew to her inner sight—all those whose own thoughts were even that moment fixed firm upon her, with love and fear and confidence—Gwydion, Morwen, Rohan, Sabia, Tybie . . . She could feel the weight of their attention—indeed the attention of all Keltia, for few that night would not be thinking of their Queen; could feel it laid across her shoulders like a friendly arm, or a burdensome yoke. *For it is all in how one perceives of it* . . .

She could call up their images, Aeron knew, to comfort and cheer herself through the remainder of the night; even use that same art of hers to warm herself, or furnish herself the illusion of meat and ale and a soft feather-cushioned couch. But she knew too that such would be gravest error, and instead she turned her strength to the clearing of her mind, and the lowering of those defenses of the spirit she had trained and labored for long years to raise up, knowing surest of all things that this night of all nights her soul must stand unveiled, that the immanence all about her now—the air had grown thick with it, as with a sudden mountain mist—might have its own dominion.

Aeron did not have long to wait. The east wind that had been raking Mount Keltia since afternoon had some time ago backed round into the north, and now it seemed to be coming from every quarter at once, and it was filled with voices. She leaned forward in the stone chair, straining to hear the words embedded in the blast, but the rushing air turned all to light instead, a helix of blue fire with an opal at its heart, and centered atop the altar not five paces from Aeron's chair.

As she watched in wonder, the flame arched and hollowed, until it stood in shape of a tall pointed doorway, its frame and lintel limned in splendor, and within the space thus bounded was a silver mist. *An Doras Lasrach*, she thought, awed. *I have seen the Flaming Door . . . It opens here for me this night. But who shall enter Caer-na-gael by so holy a portal?*

And as if in answer to Aeron's question, a face formed in the silver mist, and a pair of hands was held out to her. For an instant the face was no face Aeron had ever seen, waking or sleeping, dreaming or entranced; then it changed, and it was Dâna's; changed again, and now it was Dôn's, Fionn's, Nia's, Brendan's; was Morgan Magistra's, was even Arthur's. And the last change of all—

At sight of the One who stood now before her in the Door, Aeron half-rose from her chair, out of deepest instinct, and respect, and an awe that seemed bred in her bones. But she fell back again, in the knowledge that she was not to stir from that seat, and the Goddess—for it was She who was framed in the flaming portal—bent a bright and loving gaze upon her.

"Ban-dia," murmured Aeron, head bowed and hand to heart in the only obeisance she could make. *'You shall know Her when you see Her,'* that had been Dâna's promise long ago, in the annat of Scartanore, made to a shy and skittish seventeen-year-old: Aeron's memory, bound fast for seventeen years more to forget, was loosed now in the light from those eyes, and understanding flooded her being, and was a torch to her soul.

"I know what, and who, you would see, Queen of Kelts," came that calm and lovely voice, "and perhaps later you shall see all that you do wish to. But for now, you are here not to see but to be seen: Tomorrow you will put on the Copper Crown in Turusachan as Queen of Kelts, but here in Keltia you are not queen over Kelts alone. Others there are who will make themselves known to you this night; others who though they swear no fealty to you or any mortal ruler do all the same uphold your reign as surely as any, man or woman, silkie or merrow, prince of the blood or humblest urrad of the townlands.''

Aeron had regained her confidence a little, dared now to look up into the shining countenance, so bright that her eyes dazzled and fell again; and she spoke soft and humble to the Goddess.

"Who are these, then, Mother, that I may know them and greet them when they come?''

The Ban-dia raised one long white hand, though She said no word, and a torrent of prodigies poured out of the Door behind Her. Vision or reality, Aeron could not say; so many and so numinous that her mind could not sort them, far less fix them in memory's eye: red-cloaked banshas with long flowing hair, their faces wet with tears, their voices lifted in the eternal keen of their kind; hawk-headed warriors, gray-pinioned and steel-taloned, fierce marigold eyes gleaming from under their feathered helms; a tall man clad in black, with the great antlers of a royal stag scything upward from his dark tousled hair; a fair woman at his side in a robe all of flowers . . .

And beasts as strange companioned them: water-horses and elf-bulls, afancs of Kymry and cait-sith from Scota; horned horses with skulls for heads, whose hoofs were white bone and whose flanks shadow; the midnight Púca with eyes of fire and the snow-colored hounds that belonged to Gwyn himself.

Can this then be what my father saw, and all those others who have come here before me? Or is this rather for my seeing only, a thing that Aeron Ard-rían must witness, for her own weal and that of her worlds? And—whichever it be in truth—does it make any differ?

As the white hounds loped past her, silent now, their red ears pricked and long tongues lolling, Aeron saw behind them something approaching that seemed to sail upon the winds as a birlinn on the waters; it appeared as ribbons of light, a long stream of watered wildfire that bloomed and swayed and rippled as it drew near to the sacred peak. And when it had curved round the summit, seeming to pause there hanging in the heavens, Aeron could see that it was no light-tide but a cavalcade of bright riders, each distinct in beauty: tall proud princes belted with silver, swan-necked queens whose plaited hair was roped with pearls, and the lords as fair to look on as were their ladies; the horses they rode were shod with silver before and gold behind, and paced upon the air as sure-footed as Aeron's own Brónach did cover the ground.

In the splendor of the sight Aeron had almost forgotten the Ban-dia's presence; it was too much wonder for one mortal mind, however trained to magic, to hold at one time, and she already suspected that, as with her vision of Dâna in the annat, the memory of this too would be taken from her when she departed Caer-na-gael. *Therefore the more reason to store up as much of it as I can, so that perhaps it may not be entirely lost to me in the deep places of my soul . . .* And, lost so in her own hopes of remembering, Aeron startled back to full awareness when the Goddess spoke again.

"The Shining Ones," said the divinity, Her voice clear and thrilling as a horn-cry. "The Hidden People that you call the Sidhe, under Gwyn their king and Etain their queen." She bowed a little in acknowledgment of the salutes the faery host had given Her; it was as if a flame had bowed, or a wave of the sea. "They have made this rade from their home in the Hollow Mountains to greet you, Aeron, and to honor you as Ard-rían over Keltia. For Keltia is their homeland as much as it is the Kelts', and though the Shining Folk pay no homage to any mortal sovereign, they would think scorn to fail of courtesy to the one who guards the maigen for the peace of all within."

Aeron, looking upon the face of the faerie king, thought it strangely like to Gwydion's—the same strong brow and sculptured bone, the same shaggy dark hair to the shoulder, though the king's eyes were peat-brown where Gwydion's were sea-gray—and, still mindful of the compulsion put upon her that chained her to the chair, bowed then to Gwyn as she had bowed to the Goddess.

A ripple of approval ran over all that sky-borne company, as Gwyn, though he spoke no word to Aeron as she had spoken none to him, returned the bow from his high-backed gilded saddle. Then, with no sign given, the rade swept round to follow as he spurred out again upon the air, back to his stronghold in the Hollow Mountains, and the wind of their going sent Aeron's hair streaming behind her like another cloak.

The Sidhe-gaoithe, she thought, watching as the riders diminished once again to a silver stream in the dark sky, then faded altogether to her sight. *The faerie blast that ever blows where the Shining Ones do ride* . . . She took a long deep breath, and then several more, for it seemed to her now that she had neglected entirely to breathe while the Sidhe were yet at hand. But for all that, her vigil was not yet ended, and Aeron turned again to the One who still stood quietly beside the door of flame.

"So then," said the Ban-dia, and now for the first time Aeron heard the laughter in Her voice. "You have kept the rule well, much though it did chafe you; thrice you would have left your seat, and thrice you have obeyed the command against it. But now the test changes, and we shall see if you can change so featly with it. You have been seen, and now you will See; if you wish, and if you dare."

"There is a choice, then?"

"There is ever a choice, Aeron; did you not learn so long since, in the clochan at Caer Artos? But—as you have also learned—there is ever a price for knowledge."

"I am no stranger to éraics, my Mother."

"That you are not; and will be still less so in a time not too far distant." The tall form of the Goddess began to grow less solid, to fade back into the flame from which She had taken shape, and Aeron, clenching her hands on the chair's granite arms, called out in protest with the inner voice.

Do not leave me! What price must I pay for my Seeing? Only name it, and I shall tell it out gladly . . . but do not leave! But the divinity withdrew through the arch of fire, back into the realm from which She had come; and as She did so, Her words came echoing back to Aeron's ear.

"Feed the stone . . ."—and She was gone.

Aeron sank back defeated in the chair, cold and sad, more than a little appalled that she should feel so. *What a graceless wretch I am in truth: Have I not been granted such a holy wonder as few in Keltia have ever been blessed to behold? Dishonor indeed to crave more, like an importunate mannerless child . . . I did not even give proper thanks for that She did so bless me.*

She shifted uneasily within the swathings of her furred cloak, and pondered what she had just been witness to. With the departure of the Ban-dia, and the going of the Sidhe, Caer-na-gael seemed now darker and lonelier and colder than ever. *I am no more alone than I was before the Mother came, yet somehow I do feel so, now the Door has shut behind Her and the fire has died into darkness; and the words She did give me were dark also, if any utterance of Hers might be said to be dark . . .*

" 'Feed the stone,' " said Aeron aloud. Surely the stone was the bluestone altar-slab before her, where the Door had flamed and the Mother had stood; but to *feed* it? Aeron glanced about her, baffled: She had as custom demanded brought nothing with her by way of food or drink; the nearest such lay thousands of feet below, with the rest of her gear in the pilgrims' clochan at the mountain's foot, or in her ship that she had left not far from there.

Then it came to her that food and drink and warmth and sleep, and even movement itself, were not the only sacrifices to be made for this vigil. *This,* this *is what none could tell me; for those who are never called to face it know not of it, and those who are called may never say. Aye, Mother; I know now what is the price You spoke of, and how the rule may change in an eyeblink from breaking to keeping—and I think I may yet summon up that which will pay the price and bide the issue.*

With a calm deliberate certainty that was almost a smile, Aeron rose from the chair where her will had so long kept her, and turned that same will to a new need, knowing that she was right to do so. Shaking the stiffness from her cold and cramped muscles, glad of the chance to move again, she stepped forward to stand beside the bluestone altar.

For this is the price of my knowing, and the price is blood for the stone. 'Feed the stone'—aye, it is ever so, and in truth I would spend of my blood more than that for Keltia—and may yet. But the price is a fair one and a true, the price of all solemn covenants . . . When Gwydion and I are wedded, there shall be a few drops shed by each of us to make sacred the bond and the oath; tomorrow I wed Keltia in a rite no less binding, taking an oath no less enduring—shall the price of that be any the less?

But how to pay it out . . . She had no blade upon her—that too was custom—not even a sharp-edged flint upon the circle's floor that she might use. She checked for a moment, feeling hobbled by the lack, a little angered that it should prevent her. Then memory came to help her, and she laughed aloud at the solution it presented: *If my power could heal a wound, then surely it can make one. 'The power is not in the blade, but in the arm that wields it'*. . .

Or in the hand: Baring her left forearm, Aeron closed her eyes, summoning what power was needful, unsurprised that it came so readily to her call. Then, looking down, she drew the forefinger and midfinger of her right hand—the pads of the fingers only, not the nails—across the smooth skin of her inner forearm, and where the light touch brushed blood followed after.

Only a few drops, a thin scarlet stream across the blue-veined whiteness; then Aeron quickly pressed the wound to the stone and lifted her arm away again. She used no further magic to heal the shallow score, as once she had done at Caer Dathyl long time since, ignoring the small stinging pain as the cold air flowed over the wound, and stood back to await what would happen.

She was not surprised to see that neither mark nor stain was to be seen upon the flint-grained rock of the altar; it was as if the stone had drawn the blood into itself, had drunk it down as a thirsty land will lap up the least drop of rain. *But the stone is paid . . . now let us see what my blood has bought me.*

A cry rent the darkness above her head, and she looked up quickly to see its source. Nothing to be seen; but the words hung in the air:

"It is not day, nor yet day; it is not day, nor yet morning; it is not day, nor yet day; for the moon is shining brightly."

Before Aeron could begin to think what this might mean, a shadow seemed to sweep over the circle, and with a single shiver that rocked her from head to foot she recognized the great mantled form that loomed above the stones: the Alterator, whose lifted hand changed worlds and lives and destinies.

Then both god and circle alike seemed to vanish, and Aeron looked out upon darkness like a cleft in space itself. There came then a flood of faces, as there had been at first; but these faces she knew not at all, or at least not yet. A young man's face looked back at her; he was of her own age, and of an impossible beauty, with dark-gold hair and deep-set dark eyes; then another's, near as fair, though this time it was the eyes of him that were gold and the hair that was dark. Aeron saw witch-power in those eyes, and felt her own power rise in answer, as the hackles will rise on a hound's neck when danger is at hand.

But the faces were already gone by her; she swayed on her feet a little, for the stream of images was dizzying, and it did not slacken. She saw galláin warriors in outlandish armor, and Kelts—*Kelts!*—who fought them; strange creatures with scaled skin, a sense of a hot barren world of dust and fire; then a cool green forest, and other creatures small and delicate, with fur, or feathers, the color of the leaves in which they lived. Also she saw those she knew, who were ever in her thoughts as she in theirs: Gwydion first of all, in many aspects, in war and love and wrath and magic; Morwen, Rohan, Sabia; even Rhodri and her parents and Kesten; and though these seeings brought her to joy and tears alike she did not wish an end to them.

But then there was a pause, and the darkness deepened, and it came to Aeron's mind that what she now beheld was the Alterator's work and warning: These faces, when she came to look upon them in waking life, would signal a new age for Keltia, and though she struggled not to see she was at the same time desperate for whatever glimpses she might be granted.

Foreign faces, all of them . . . A man's first, older, perhaps her father's age, his almond-shaped eyes bright and black as jet, his skin as yellow-gold as mead. Then a young woman looked out of the darkness; there was a Keltic air about her, something that lay in the eyes and mouth, though without doubt she was gallwyn; again a man's face, this one long and weedy, with watery blue eyes and straggling wisps of dun-colored hair. And now a black man's face, full of intelligence, generous and humorous, and close upon it another woman's, fine-boned and small, shy but strong.

And last of all, so that the surprise of it nearly sent Aeron reeling against the altar, came the face of Arianeira, cool, moon-pale, smiling slightly. *Ari?! In the midst of all these warnings? How should* that *be?*

But then all faces were gone into the dark, and there was no answer to her question. Even so, Aeron knew that the visions that had been granted her were all part of one doom, all masks that would be worn by a great and terrible dán, the human cat's-paws of a destiny that would be not hers alone but all Keltia's; knew too that try as she might she would never recall this seeing with her outer awareness. *That is not part of the bargain; the Seeing is all that was bartered, and there is not blood enough in my body to purchase anything greater . . .* She could but pray, as she did now, that something of what she had Seen would remain with her for warning, however dim and distant, so that she might not be caught entirely unawares when dán came down upon her. *And surely that is all anyone may rightly ask . . .*

And even as Aeron prayed so, the darkness thinned and faded around her, and far above, the first light of Grían struck through the Gates of the Sun.

Though they knew perfectly well that Aeron, tired and hungry as she must surely be after her long vigil, would take some hours to make the descent from Caer-na-gael, and that even *Retaliator* would take some time to fetch her from the holy mountain back to her capital, and not forgetting the time differential, Gwydion and Morwen, all the same, were standing on the field at Mardale Port before the sun was fairly up.

Shivering in the October chill, wishing he were still in the big curtained bed in the Western Tower and Aeron with him, or at the very least that he had thought to wear a warmer cloak, Gwydion cast a sidewise glance at Morwen, and both of them smiled a little sheepishly, knowing the other's thought, and said nothing.

They had no need of explanation: Arriving separately, neither aware of the other's like intent, they had not been surprised in the slightest to see each other there; the care and anxiety that had driven each to rise from a sleepless bed in the cold and dark and come to Mardale was shared and understood. And when Rohan turned up with Ríoghnach and Niall half an hour later, and Fergus with Sabia and Struan and half a dozen more an hour after that, beyond a word or two of friends' greeting still nothing was said, and nothing needed.

About nine in the morning, Sabia, the most long-sighted of all there, spied a black smudge in the eastern sky that resolved almost at once into a ship. As at an ungiven signal, they trooped out upon the field, where even now *Retaliator* was lightly coming in to land.

Anxious as he was to see the ship's pilot, Gwydion spared a

moment's admiring glance for the craft, noting again the lines and sweep, recalling the range of armaments that Elharn and Rhain had built into her. *And even so, none of those were needed, for the killing of Bellator, in the end* . . . Then all dark thoughts vanished as the morning mist had burned off the Loom, for Aeron had emerged from the ship's hatch, and was looking down at him.

For an instant, in spite of the radiance on her face, the shared thought in their linked minds was of that other return to Mardale in *Retaliator*; then it was gone, and she jumped down, and let her smile embrace all her welcomers.

"Is this how you do, then—my Taoiseach, my First Lord of War, my Tanist, my guard-captain, all the rest of you whose duties of state I know well—when the Ard-rían is not at hand to keep you to your tasks? Dawdling away the morning here in the open air, while all the time back at Caerdroia I am told there is a crowning to prepare for . . . Well, join me to breakfast; there is much to tell you—or so at least I *think*, it was a strange night—and any road I have such a hunger on me as requires notable feeding."

Chapter 35

Aeron came barefoot to her queenmaking that day at sunset. As she had herself remarked to Tybie, there was little pomp, though great solemnity, to the crowning of a Keltic sovereign—a survival perhaps of old rituals, old purposes, brought from Earth by Brendan, upon whose own crowning all those to follow were patterned.

In the hush of the circle of Ni-maen, she came to stand before another thing Brendan had brought from Earth: Lia Fail, the Stone of Destiny, lying at the circle's western edge as the Helestone stood in the east. A great monolith of gray granite, the Lia Fail was rough-dressed, shapen to an oblong of perhaps twelve feet, waist-high, unadorned by carving or interlace as were most of the nemeton's other stones, and there was a slight hollow in the center of its length, as of the print of a human foot.

Looking past the stone, Aeron could see the clustered members of her family and Court and government, their faces joyful and expectant, free at last of the fears and cares that had plagued them so long. *Indeed, since my accession, and nor do I blame them; but now there is no more need for fear—or at least not the same fears—and though the true crowning was for me last night at Caer-na-gael, this sets the seal on it for all of us.*

She lifted her head and composed her features, as out of the splendidly robed knot of household officers stepped Conaire Donn, chief of the Clann Diarmada who had served since the reign of Lachlan of the Battles as heredity inaugurators and deposers to the line of Aoibhell. In his hands Conaire carried the white rod of his office, and for all his long friendship with Fionnbarr—and Fionnbarr's daughter—his countenance now was stern and unsmiling as he addressed himself to his new Queen, to perform his kindred's ancient task.

"For what is a prince chosen over the people?"

"For the excellence of mind, and blood, and heart, and body," responded Aeron as gravely. "For wisdom, and for knowledge; for full lawfulness in soul and in act"—(had there been a hesitation there? Gwydion glanced sharply up at her, but Aeron was continuing serenely to speak)—"for valor on the field, and justice in the high seat, and grace in utterance; to be generous and righteous to the people, and to be served so in return, and so will all prosper."

"It is so said, and well said," answered Conaire. He held out to Aeron the white rod he bore; she took it, held it briefly, and gave it back again.

And now he spoke in the High Gaeloch, the ceremonial tongue of old, for all Keltia to hear: "Wilt thou go back, Aoibhell?"

"I will not."

"Then go forward, a queen."

She moved like flame through the circle, three times sunwise, three times widdershins, and came again to the Lia Fail in the west. But this time Aeron did not stand before it, but leaped unassisted to the top of the stone, high above the throng, feeling as she stood there a terror and strength and joy such as she could not compass. Then, very stately and deliberate, knowing that she was doing exactly as she chose to do, and as sixteen of her House had done before her, she stepped forward and placed her right foot in the footprinted hollow at the stone's heart.

There was silence in the circle, and perhaps all who were watching the rite on Keltia's many worlds were silent too. Then a wind began to rise, flattening the grasses in an ever-growing spiral round the stone, and there was a sound upon that wind like a deep-mouthed horn crying in the valley's walls: a sound that grew to a singing roar, a sonorous clamor that shook the stones in their seatings and caused the ground beneath to tremble, a sound surely heard by all folk near and far—the Kelts who stood by, the merrows and silkies in the bay that lapped Eagle's foot, the Shining Ones who were no strangers to that valley, even the royal dead barrowed nearby in their long green beds—as the kingstone of the Keltic peoples proclaimed the Kelts' true ruler.

And Aeron, standing atop the stone, feeling the vibration in every bone of her body, as if she had been but the instrument for the voicing of the mightiest of shouts, took oath amid that holy thunder to preserve Keltia at her life's cost. Her heir and brother Rohan then giving into her hands the Copper Crown, Aeron set it upon her head, its color as it caught the sunset light making a match for her unbound hair.

And in that moment the cry of the Lia Fail died away, and that of the jubilant throng superseded it.

"Gods save Aeron, Queen of Kelts!"

They were still shouting it late that night in the stone streets of Caerdroia; Aeron could hear it faintly even through her closed windows, as she stood alone in her chamber, divesting herself of her royal trappings and attire before her intimates came to join her, by invitation, for a last small private family revel before retiring.

She cast her mind back over the events of the day. Much of what had taken place after the roaring of the stone was a blur to her. But they had put the Silver Branch into her hands, while she had yet been standing atop the Lia Fail; that she did recall. She had borne the scepter through all that had followed, and now she turned it over in her hands before setting it down at last.

This at least is no stranger to me; we have been friends these seven years past. Brought from Terra like all the other Treasures of Keltia, those that had been lost and those that yet remained, the Silver Branch had ever gone with the Copper Crown, though it was nowhere near so ancient, and in the sequence followed for all those centuries, it was the first symbol of royal power to be taken up—and first to be wielded.

And after that . . . Aeron let her glance rest on the diadem of hammered red metal she had just now taken from around her aching brows, seeing as for the first time the intricate pattern of spirals and whorls and bosses. *And that is the second of the steps to sovereignty, coming to the monarch upon acclamation, as today it came to me. If seldom worn, the power of the Copper Crown is translated to everyday by means of the Great Seal.*

And the third of those steps was the Throne of Scone itself, and that step, last and greatest, Aeron had taken only hours before. She had come down from Ni-maen with those who had earlier accompanied her there, after a most untraditional—though most characteristic—stop of homage at the barrows wherein lay her parents and Rhodri. Coming again to Turusachan, she had entered the Hall of Heroes in the great Keep, and there, before the assembled nobles and commons and all the watching billions, she had for the first time taken her seat upon the Throne of Scone.

Though that and what came after is no part of the true crowning ritual, but added later; and an addition I could have well done without . . . but she knew the reasons better than most: a statement of politics as well as power, an opportunity for fealty to be reaffirmed, or sworn openly in those cases where it had not yet been personally attested; time too for formal homage to be paid Aeron, the homage "of hand and heart"—the kissed hand and bent knee that the monarchs of Keltia required of their lieges on this day and in this place alone, and then never again for all their reigns—and all that had taken some hours, and for those hours Aeron had sat straight-backed and still in the tall stone throne.

Not unlike the chair in which I passed the night previous—but though the Throne be assumed upon my crowning, fully to earn my right to it will take far longer than one span between dusk and dawn: all my reign, or all my life, which will from now be one and the same. For barring abdication or deposing, she was Keltia's from today forward, and Keltia was hers.

Aeron threw back her head and stared unseeing at the ceiling. *Ah gods, I am too young for this!* she cried despairingly, and had for comfort only the crown's cold red glitter. *I should have had years and years yet, decades to grow in my duty, to watch my father and learn rule from him, to live with my chosen lord in love and peace, to breed an heir or two of my own before I did relinquish my own heirship to be Queen* . . .

But now all that was changed utterly: She would be the youngest monarch that Keltia had ever had. Youngest in her own right, to rule unregented: In all history only Prince Arawn, Arthur's son, had been her junior at accession. For him a Regency had been created, and for Regents he had had three of the most formidable personalities in Keltic annals: his mother, Gweniver the Queen, daughter of Leowyn Prince of Dôn; his aunt, Morgan Magistra, sister to Arthur and beloved of Taliesin

Pen-bardd; and his grandmother, Ygrawn Duchess of Kernow, widow of the slain Uthyr.

I have no such help to me, thought Aeron, wondering not for the first time how young Arawn had managed caught amongst those three; for he had managed, in the end, very well indeed. *Though perhaps it is just as well that I do not; I had been as set upon my own road as they on theirs, and there would have been such battles right here in Turusachan as would have made it superfluous to seek battle out-Wall* . . . Yet she knew also that she was by no means without the best of supporters and auxiliars should she choose to call upon them, and had indeed already named some to her councils. And above them all she had Gwydion and Morwen and Rohan, and above all again she had Gwydion . . . *A terrible manner in which to get my own way, to lose Rhodri and my parents before I could have things as I did wish them. But, hear me all gods, now that I have them so I will keep them so, if it kills me and everyone else beside, and if it be sacrilege to pray it I care not.*

All the same, it was with great reverence that Aeron returned the Copper Crown to its velvet-lined leather casket, and set the Silver Branch as gently into its own wooden case. *Well and good; an end to pomp and mystery, I think there has been goleor of both these past two days to last me long. And I think too that I have worked hard enough these same two days to merit some time of celebration more to my mind than the great ceilis folk have wished for. Enough pomp, and too much mystery, and the morning will see duty enough for all of us; let tonight at least be without demand. That cannot be too much to ask for, surely?*

Though all across Caerdroia bonfires had burned and revels honored Aeron's crowning, Turusachan itself had been quiet. No great celebrations or glittering balls had graced the state apartments or filled the huge banqueting-hall of Mi-cuarta; Aeron had given permission for the palace dwellers to hold what ceilis they pleased or go out to the public revels, but she had ordered no festivities herself, saying only that such things were not really to her liking, and the manner of her accession, and the memory of the months that had followed, did not dispose her to any great show of merrymaking.

Which had been keen and bitter disappointment to many who

had been eagerly anticipating so grand an event, a palace ball for the Queen's crowning; but those who knew their Queen were not surprised that she should shy from a display of that sort, and sympathizing with her reasons, they lifted their methers instead in her honor at revels of their own.

For all her reluctance to submit herself to a public celebration, Aeron by no means wished to be alone that night, and had no intention of so being; all day she had been waiting and wanting to be with those she loved best, and one by one they came now to her chambers in the Western Tower, though Tybie had already taken ship back to Lundavra: Gwydion, Rohan, Morwen and Fergus—who that day had announced the news of their expected daughter to their delighted friends—Kieran and Eiluned, Declan, Sabia, the Cameron brothers, Ríoghnach and Niall, Slaine, Desmond, Deio Drummond and his new wife, even Aeron's youngest sister Fionnuala, sweet-faced and sleepy; a few others—Gwyneira the Dowager Queen had come and gone early, saying the gathering was both too late of hour and too young in years for her, but leaving her granddaughter with her loving goodnight kiss and no less loving blessing—to make up a party of perhaps two dozen, and all of them heroically drunk.

"And if the Ard-rían of Keltia may not down a fair drench on the night she has been crowned," Aeron was saying, with tremendous care of enunciation, "then when?"

"When indeed," agreed Sabia. "Aeron, we have not yet finished the keeve—"

"Have we not! Nay, then everyone drinks—Niall, do you and Desmond be cupbearers—Kieran, do not look so sour! Ah, your mether is empty, have mine instead . . ."

Her brother grinned. "My thanks, Ard-rían—as to my demeanor, I had a disagreeable chore to finish off today, and one I delayed too long as it was."

Aeron settled herself comfortably against Gwydion's knees. "Tell us all, and pray you make it entertaining."

"A small squalid tale at best: One of my retainers, a man from Ruabon on Gwynedd, was discovered by my rechtair to be indulging in influence-selling and other petty crimes. I should have dismissed him straightaway, but I felt sorry for the rogue and he begged to keep his place, so I kept him on, though Luned was at me morn and night to send him packing. Any road, he is gone now; my sorrow that it troubled so happy a time.''

''Was his wrongdoing proved?'' asked Morwen, her brehon's interest roused. ''If so, you may sue to recover honor-price damages.''

Kieran laughed. ''That babe of yours will be lawyering before the birth-cord is fairly cut . . . But nay, there was no proof to be set before a brehon; and Kynon—that is the wretch's name—would only revel in a false suit. Best simply to discharge him, and give him such a letter of character as will neither help nor hinder him finding a place elsewhere, perhaps with some friend of ours on some other world.''

In after days, Gwydion and Aeron, and others beside, would wonder that they had no memory of Kieran's idle complaint; would wonder too that no othersight had warned them, no sense of unease or of danger to come; would ponder what dán—or whose—had been at work here . . .

But Eiluned's tart reply to her husband—''Do what you will, so long as the pig-dog is gone from Inver by the time we come home again''—had caused general amusement, and amid the laughter a call went up for music, and the thing was forgotten as Gwydion reached for his telyn, and others produced borrauns and bones and even a set of pipes or two . . .

When at last all had gone, Aeron toppled laughing across Gwydion's lap; in the light from the fire, she looked flushed and happy and very young.

''I cannot even keep my crown on—well, I *could* not were it in fact on my head this moment, which then of course it would not be—and nor can *you* hold a harp, never in my life have I heard so many jangled strings. Ah, Gwynedd, I have not been so ale-mazed in many years, and yet I think it is not all the ale . . .''

''I know it is not—Aeron, you must sit up a little, my foot has gone to sleep—nay, not that far . . .'' He settled her back against his chest, resting his chin upon the top of her head. ''A good day's work,'' he said presently. ''Not only does Keltia have a High Queen crowned and her Tanist proclaimed, but a new Prince of Thomond and two new countesses as well.''

''Aye,'' agreed Aeron. ''I had been wanting to reward Rohan

and Slaine and Melangell for what they did to aid me in my dark days; to name them Prince of Thomond, and Countess of Ralland and Countess of Gwent, seems little enough, but they say they will take no more. I would have given your sister some dúchas as well," she added hesitantly, "as for peace offering, but she barely stayed at Caerdroia past my enthronement."

"And ran grave risk of incurring not only displeasure but honor-price violations as well," said Gwydion, vexed anew. "What *is* it with Arianeira of late? Her behavior has barely qualified as civility . . . if you wish it, as Prince of Gwynedd I could—"

"Nay, I would for no sake make matters worse!"' said Aeron quickly. "And I have hopes that things may improve with time . . . But she has cause for anger, or believes herself to have such: She is still angry with me for that I gave her no place in my household or on my councils as Tanista, nor have I done so now as Ard-rían. Perhaps I cannot blame her; she is after all still my foster-sister."

"That is not what she holds most against you," he said quietly.

Aeron shifted a little in his arms. "That too I know: I have deprived Ari of Morwen by making Wenna Taoiseach, and I have deprived her of you by making you First Lord of War."

Ah, cariad, that still is not the whole of it, he thought behind deep shields, for he had no wish to distress her further on this day of all days. *And I think you yourself are well aware of it, but let us leave the matter to seek its own time . . .* He brushed back the hair from her face, and turned the topic.

"Well, now that you are Ard-rían, what shall be policy for the realm?"

Aeron laughed. "Now did I not hear someone, I forget just who, warn me not too long since that even the Ard-rían cannot have everything her own way? I will tell you a thing I have told you before, and apart from you only Tybie has heard me say it: Soon or late, this reign will see an alliance with Earth. It is long past time we renewed those ancient bonds, and though many have held against it—even my own father—Brendan himself saw that it must come in time. All the same, I do not know if the folk will much like it, and I very much doubt my Councillors will . . ."

"Well, there is no doing without *some* rueing; better it be theirs than yours."

"Spoken like a true counselor," she teased. "Which is of course to be expected from one who is First Lord of War, *and* Prince of Gwynedd, *and* Pendragon"—the teasing note was gone now from her voice—"and who will be King of Keltia when the Ard-rían can find the courage to make him so, for that seems to be his dán and hers . . ."

But even that was too near what they had not yet been able to speak of save in thought-speech or glancing reference—that loss which alone had brought them to this chamber and this moment—and again they shied away from it into silence.

"Not only a High Queen crowned, as I said before," remarked Gwydion after a while, and his tone was merrier now, though that might have been his bardcraft at work. "But that High Queen is a full year older as well."

"My birthday!" Aeron sat up in indignant surprise. "I had clean forgot—"

"I dare say most of Keltia has done the same—there was much else to think on today—though doubtless tomorrow they will all remember, and then there will be odes and ballads and flowery pronouncements in spate. But tonight, perhaps, in all the kingdom you and I are the only ones to recall it."

"And an excellent thing, too. Where then is my gift?"

Her air had been mock-demanding, but the laughter faded from her face to be succeeded by wonderment, as she stared down at the shining thing in Gwydion's hands. He had apparently produced it from his harp-satchel, it seemed as if by magic: a delicate gold torc, each finial end shaped like the flower of the rhosyn-y-mynydd, which was another name for the peony, the serrate petal tips of each gold flower cradling a great ruby.

"This has a feel of more than birthday-gift," she said presently.

He nodded. "Tinnól, if you will take it so; or at least a pledge for it."

Aeron looked up at him then, her mouth caught between pain and laughter, eyes sparkling with tears and joy in equal parts.

"We think more alike than is safe, or perhaps even lawful . . ." She rose then, and going to the chest beside the bed opened a carved casket and took somewhat from it. Returning, she caught his hand to draw him to his feet, and sprung onto his arm above the elbow a massive arm-ring of red gold, wrought into the likeness of the Gwynedd stag facing the Aoibhell wolf. "The goldsmith brought it me just three days past, though I ordered it made a month since."

Gwydion said no word, but covered her hand with his as she rested it on his sleeve; then lifting the hair from her neck, he set the torc about it. Aeron felt the gold cold against her skin, but then the circlet settled to the contours of her neck so perfectly that she felt neither the weight of it nor discomfort at the fit. Gwydion touched the stones, and the rubies flared to sudden fire under his fingertips.

"Swords are too much in our hands for rings to be a good choice for tinnól—I can hear Struan even now on *that* old tune—and too obvious perhaps to be a wise one. This way none shall know, and it will be better that they do not just yet; there is enough stour already for that I am First Lord of War. Let the folk grow used to the one before we face them with the other."

"And let them be quick to do so; for I serve warning now I shall be a less patient ruler than my father." She looked up again, and he would hold the image in his heart for the rest of his days and hers: the firelight, the green eyes and copper hair and smiling face, the flame of the rubies at her throat.

But later, when they had set the fields on the double doors to keep out intruders, and set the seals on the chamber to keep out evil influences, and were lying drowsing under the fur coverlets, Aeron suddenly laughed.

"What then?"

"I was but thinking of what my birthday wish might be, if such wish were not greed and purest vengefulness."

"What would be such a wish?"

She did not answer him straightway. Then: "Fomor and Alphor. To spit their hearts on my sword and roast them over a slow flame and feed them to my hounds."

Gwydion was startled at the venom in her voice, for he had never before heard her speak so, and it was utterly at variance with her mood thus far; he was not at all sure that it might not be ill omen even to think so on such a day. She noticed, and smiled grimly.

"*Or* I could draw out their guts and twist them round a pirn like silk from a spool; or push their heads through a winepress and then dance upon their flattened faces . . . it makes little differ, so that they suffer long and greatly. You are shocked to hear me say it?"

"It does not sound like you," he replied cautiously.

"Does it not? Then what *would* sound like me? A Crann Tarith across Keltia, to call for war? The aim and end of Bellator was all to keep Keltia *out* of war."

"Which you did."

"Which I did, so, for now at least . . . Well," added Aeron with a sigh, "I shall launch no more bolts against either of them, so long as they raise no hand against us. But if they do, even the least littlest finger—"

Gwydion waited for her to finish the thought, but she said no more.

Epilogue

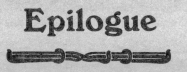

In a room not a mile from where Aeron and Gwydion lay so late awake, a man was sitting at a desk composing a coded message for his distant master.

He had come to Caerdroia as a minor member of an embassage from a friendly nation, one of the many delegations sent to witness and celebrate Aeron's crowning; but he was neither a diplomatist nor yet one of the race he feigned to represent, and to get him into Keltia under cloak of stealth had taken much gold—and several lives.

He had reported duly on the week's events—the public splendor, the mood of the Kelts, the outworlders in attendance—and now he was writing of Aeron.

"She is much of an age with your highness, some eight years younger, no more; and between her and her kindred there is great closeness which by all accounts is genuine. Though I have heard of a bitter rift that has opened between the Queen and her foster-sister Arianeira, who is a princess of Gwynedd; and that is a thing we might turn to our own purposes, if the chance presents itself—or if it can be made to do so.

"Most else that we have heard of Aeron appears also to be true: her prowess in magic and with the sword, her quickness of mind and greater quickness to anger, her certainty of the rightness of her course whatever it might be and her obduracy in keeping to it once she has chosen.

"And as to that last, she has as your highness will already know demonstrated it in her chief appointments: Morwen Douglas, her other foster-sister, as First Minister of State; and for First Lord of War, Gwydion Prince of Gwynedd, brother to that

Arianeira I just now spoke of, who is like to be king-consort in time to come, if one can credit palace gossip—and one would be unwise not to.

"It will not be possible to come at her, to slay her by treachery as your highness did suggest; she is herself most aware and alert to such things, and also she is far too carefully guarded; but I have had the beginnings of a thought as to a way in which we might, if we manage it well enough, bring down not only Aeron but all Keltia with her . . .

"There is beyond the Curtain Wall the trading planet of Clero, which as all know is the Kelts' only place of contact with the outworlds. Half the galaxy comes there to trade, out-Wall folk freely coming and going and mingling with the Kelts. If I, or another whom your highness might deign to trust with such an errand, were to go there, I think it not unlikely that we might find one we could bend in time to our use.

"Though Kelts cannot be bought to betray their chiefs, for some there may be reasons more compelling even than gold—I will say no more of this now lest it miscarry, nor shall I let any know, lord, that the plan has origin with you.

"I would ask your highness bear in mind, too, that it is believed Aeron thinks more kindly on an alliance with Earth than any monarch before her, and it has been our long fear what such an alliance might mean to our Cabiri Imperium.

"But a plan that turns on Clero, and on our old friend Bres of Fomor, who has done us second's service in the past, and on this wish of Aeron's to covenant with Earth, and perhaps even on that disaffected princess Arianeira, who might in her wrath against her Queen be induced to turn her cloak entirely—I will speak in greater detail when I may speak direct in your highness's ear. Though I say this now: It is absolutely certain, to judge by what I myself have heard and seen, that Bres pulled down upon his head the roof and king-post of his own house, when by slaying Fionnbarr he thought to pull down Keltia.

"And now more of Aeron, and today's crowning: She is just now descending from the magic stone, but her countenance changes not . . ."

In the silence of the night, in the heart of Aeron's realm, no winds of dán or dreaming to carry his words to her he spoke of, the Imperial spy wrote on.

(Here ends *The Silver Branch*, a book of THE KELTIAD. The sequels are *The Copper Crown* and *The Throne of Scone*. Forthcoming in the tale of Aeron and Gwydion will be *The Shield of Fire*, *The Sword of Light*, and *The Cloak of Gold*.)

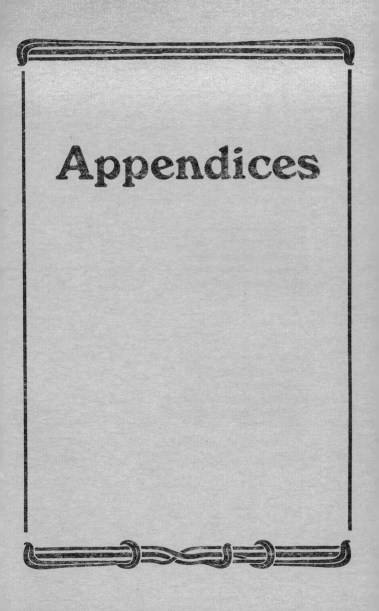

Appendices

History of the Tuatha De Danaan and the Keltoi

The Tuatha De Danaan, the People of the Goddess Dâna, arrived on Earth, as refugees from a distant star system whose sun had gone nova. They established great city-realms at Atlantis, Lemuria, Nazca, Machu Picchu, and other centers of energy. It was an age of high technology and pure magic: lasers, powered flight in space and in atmosphere, telepathy, telekinesis and the like. There was some minimal contact with the primitive Terran native inhabitants, who, awed, regarded the lordly Danaans as gods from the stars.

After many centuries of peace and growth, social and spiritual deterioration set in: faction fights, perversion of high magical techniques, civil war. The Danaan loyalists withdrew to the strongholds of Atlantis, or Atland as they called it, there to fight their last desperate battle with those of their own people who had turned to dark ways. Atlantis was finally destroyed, in a fierce and terrible battle fought partially from space, and which resulted in a huge earthquake and subsequent geologic upheaval that sank the entire island-continent. (The battle and sinking of Atlantis were preserved in folk-myth around the world; obviously the effect on the Earth primitives was considerable.)

The evil Atlanteans, the Telchines, headed off back into space: their descendants would later be heard of as the Coranians. The Danaan survivors made their way as best they could over the terrible seas to the nearest land—Ireland—and to the other Keltic sea-countries on the edge of the European landmass. There had long been Atlantean outposts in these lands, and they made a likely refuge.

411

*   *   *

But the refugees had yet another battle to fight; with the Fir Bolg and the Fomori, the native tribes currently in occupation of Ireland. Atlantean technology carried the day, however, and the Danaans settled down to rebuild their all-but-lost civilization.

After a long Golden Age, the Danaan peace was shattered by invasion: the Milesians, Kelts from the European mainland. War exploded; the new race was clever, brave, persuasive and quarrelsome. The Danaans, at first victorious in defense, were at last defeated by the strategies of the brilliant Druid Amergin. They conceded possession of Ireland to the sons of Miledh, and obtained sureties of peace.

The peace and amity between Danaans and Milesians lasted many hundreds of years; there was much intermarriage, informational exchange, joint explorative and military expeditions against raiding Fomori and Fir Bolg. Then a period of Milesian distrust turned to outright persecution, and the Danaans began to withdraw to live strictly isolated, although even then there continued to be marriages and friendships and associations. With the coming of Patrick to Ireland, bringing Christianity, the persecutions resumed with redoubled intensity, as Patrick and his monks called upon all to denounce the Danaans as witches and evil sorcerers.

Brendan, a nobleman of the House of Erevan son of Miledh, was also half-Danaan by birth—and more than half one in spirit. His mother was Nia, a Danaan princess, and he had been taught by her in the old ways. He rebelled against the persecutions, the narrow-mindedness and prejudice and condemnation of all the high old knowledge, and he resolved to relearn all the ancient lore, to build ships and take the Danaans back out to the stars, to find a new world where they could live as they pleased. All who felt as Brendan did might go, and did: Druids, priestesses of the Mother, worshippers of the Old Gods and followers of the Old Ways, all now so ruthlessly put down by the Christians.

After much study, instruction, construction and a few short trial runs, Brendan was ready at last, and the Great Emigration began. Following the directions of Barinthus, an old man who was probably the last space voyager left on Earth, Brendan and his followers left the planet. After a two-year search, they discovered a habitable star system a thousand light-years from Terra. He named it New Keltia; eventually Keltia, as it came to be known, would command seven planetary systems and a very sizable sphere of influence.

The emigrations continued in secret over a period of some eight hundred years, with Kelts from every Keltic nation participating in the adventure, and not human Kelts alone; the races known as the merrows and the silkies also joined the migrations.

After the first great voyage, or immram, Brendan himself remained in the new worlds, organizing a government, ordering the continuing immigrations, setting up all the machinery needed to run the society he had dreamed of founding: a society of total equality of gender, age, nationality and religion. He personally established the order of Druids in New Keltia; his mother, Nia, who left Earth with him, founded the Ban-draoi, an order of priestess-sorceresses.

Brendan, who would come to be venerated by succeeding generations as St. Brendan the Astrogator, became the first monarch of Keltia, and his line continues to rule there even now.

By about Terran year 1200, the Keltic population had increased so dramatically (from both a rising birthrate and continued waves of immigration from Earth) that further planetary colonization was needed. The Six Nations were founded, based on the six Keltic nations of Earth: Ireland, Scotland, Wales, Man, Cornwall and Brittany, called in Keltia Erinna, Scota, Kymry, Vannin, Kernow and Brytaned. A ruling council of six viceroys, one from each system, was set up, called the Fáinne—"The Ring." The monarchy continued, though the Fáinne had the ultimate sovereign power at this time.

This was the Golden Age of Keltia. The mass emigrations ended at around Terran year 1350, and the dream of Brendan seemed achieved. There was complete equality, as he had intended; a strong central government and representative local governments; the beginnings of a peerage democracy; great advances in magic, science and art.

It could not last, of course. By Terran year 1700, increasingly vocal separatist movements sprang up in each nation, and, a hundred years later, the Archdruid of the time, Edeyrn, saw in the unrest the chance to further his own power, and the power of the Druid Order. A fiercely ambitious and unquestionably brilliant man, Edeyrn succeeded in engineering the discrediting and ultimate dissolution of the Fáinne, in forcing the monarchy into hiding, and in installing those Druids loyal to him as magical dictators on all levels. Civil war broke out all over Keltia, and the realm was polarized by the conflict.

This was the Druid Theocracy and Interregnum, which was to endure for nearly two hundred unhappy years. Edeyrn and his Druids were joined by many politically ambitious and discontented noble houses, who saw in the upheaval a chance for their own advancement.

There was of course a fierce and equally powerful resistance, as many Druids remained loyal to the truths of their order, and joined forces with the Ban-draoi, the magical order of priestesses, the Fianna, the Bardic Association and some of the oldest and noblest Keltic families.

This resistance was called the Counterinsurgency, and it opposed Edeyrn and his Druids with strength, resource and cleverness for two centuries. Consistently outwitting the aims of the Theocracy, the loyalists managed to preserve the fabric of true Keltic society. Through the efforts of the Bardic Association, they also succeeded in salvaging most of the important lore, science, art and records of the centuries of Keltia's settlement, and the records from Earth before that.

The terrors of the Theocracy raged on for two hundred years, with the balance continually shifting between Theocracy and Counterinsurgency. The general population was sorely torn, but most did in fact support the loyalists, in their hearts if not in their outward actions. Then full-scale alien invasion, by the races called by the Kelts Fomori and Fir Bolg after their old Earth enemies, hit Keltia, causing enormous destruction and loss of life. But even in the face of this appalling new threat, Edeyrn continued to dominate, and some even said he was responsible for the invasions. Though he himself was by now ancient beyond all right expectation, his adopted heir Owain served as his sword-arm, and Owain was as twisted as ever Edeyrn was.

Though their most immediately pressing need was to repel the

Fomori and Fir Bolg invaders, the Kelts had first to break free of the grip of the Theocracy; and in the midst of that chaos, a mighty figure began to emerge.

Arthur of Arvon, a minor lordling of a hitherto minor noble house of the Kymry, rallied boldly the forces of the Counterinsurgency. Arthur proved to be an inspired leader, and more importantly, a military genius, and he quickly smashed Owain's Druids in the Battle of Moytura. The Theocracy, its military power broken, caved in, and Arthur was named Rex Bellorum, War-Chief, by the hastily reconstituted Fáinne and the newly restored monarch Uthyr. Arthur then led the Keltic forces out against the invaders; the aliens were not prepared for such a concerted counterattack, and Arthur succeeded in utterly crushing the invasion.

But King Uthyr had died in battle. Arthur married the royal heir, Gweniver, and with her assumed the sovereignty of Keltia by acclamation. The wars behind him, at least for the present, Arthur turned his genius to political and social reform, establishing elective bodies of legislators, the Royal Senate and Assembly, restoring the House of Peers, formulating a new judicial system on the remains of the old brehon laws, and laying the groundwork for a standing battle force. He commanded a purge of the Druid Order, setting his closest advisor and old teacher, Merlynn Llwyd, to undertake the task, and he gave new power and prestige to the loyal orders of the Ban-draoi, the Fianna and the Bardic Association.

Arthur and Gweniver reigned brilliantly and successfully for nearly fifty years, and had two children, Arawn and Arwenna. Then, in Terran year 2047, he was betrayed by his own nephew, Mordryth, and the infamous Owain's heir, Malgan. Their treachery let in the invading Coranians, descendants of the Telchines, who had evolved into a race of sorcerous marauders whose savagery made the Fomori and Fir Bolg look like sheep. This was Arthur's first chance to test his reforms, and he was well aware that it might be his last also. He dealt with Mordryth and Malgan, then led a space armada against the Coranians, with devastating success. Tragically, he disappeared in the climactic battle, sending his flagship *Prydwen* against the Coranian flag-ship and taking both vessels and all aboard them into hyperspace forever. His last message to his people was that he would come again, when he was needed.

In the absence of proof positive of Arthur's death, he is still King of Kelts, and all succeeding monarchs have held their sovereignty by his courtesy and have made their laws in his name . . . for who knows when Arthur the King might not return?

The monarchy, after Arthur's disappearance, became a Regency, the only one in Keltic history. Arthur's sister Morgan, his wife Gweniver, and his mother Ygrawn ruled jointly, until such time as Prince Arawn should be old enough to take the crown.

All three women were strong characters, skilled in magic, but Arthur's sister Morgan, called Morgan Magistra, was the greatest magician Keltia would ever see.

After taking counsel with the Ban-draoi, Merlynn's newly rehabilitated Druids, the Fianna and the Bardic Association, and with her own co-Regents, Morgan undertook the immense achievement of the raising of the Curtain Wall. There was no other feat like it, even back to the days of the High Atlanteans.

The Curtain Wall is a gigantic force-field, electromagnetic in nature and maintained by psionic energies; it completely surrounds and conceals Keltic space, hiding suns, planets, satellites, energy waves, everything. Once outside its perimeters, it is as if Keltia does not exist. Space is not physically blocked off, and radio waves and the like are bent round the Wall, but any ship attempting to cross the region is shunted into certain corridors of electromagnetic flux that feed into the Morimaruse, the Dead Sea of space, and now no one goes that way, ever.

So the Keltic worlds and their peoples became a half-legend of the galaxy, a star-myth to be told to children or to anthropologists. But behind the Curtain Wall, the Regency carried on Arthur's work, and when in time Arawn became King, he proved almost as gifted as his parents. The dynasty he founded was followed in peaceful succession by the closely related royal house of Gwynedd, and that by the royal house of Douglas.

*   *   *

For fifteen hundred years Keltia prospered in her isolation—not a total isolation even then, for still there were out-Wall trading planets and military actions, and ambassadors were still received.

In the Terran year 2693, the Crown passed to the House of Aoibhell. Direct descendants of Brendan himself, the Aoibhells have held the monarchy in a grip of findruinna for eight hundred years, according to the law of Keltia that the Copper Crown descends to the eldest child of the sovereign, whether man or woman.

In the Earth year 3512, the probe ship *Sword* arrived in Keltic space. The Ard-rían Aeron Aoibhell, seventeenth member of her House to occupy the Throne of Scone, determines on an alliance with the Terran Federacy, and Keltia is plunged into war as a result of it. The tale of that war, and what followed, is told in *The Copper Crown* and *The Throne of Scone*.

Glossary

Words are Keltic (Gaeloch) unless otherwise noted.

Abred: "The Path of Changes"; the visible world of everyday existence within the sphere of which one's various lives are lived.

aircar: small personal transport used on Keltic worlds

Airts: the four magical directions to which sacred circles are oriented: East, South, West and North

alanna: "child," "little one,"; Erinnach endearment

amadaun: "fool"

amhic: "my son"; used in the vocative

an-altram: Keltic custom of fosterage; children of all social classes are usually exchanged between sets of fostering parents, beginning at the age of five and continuing in most cases to age thirteen

anama-chara: "soul-friend"; term for those close and strong friends limited to one or two in a person's life

an-da-shalla: "The Second Sight"; Keltic talent of precognition

anfa: "storm"

An-Lasca: "The Whip"; the ionized northwest wind at Caerdroia

annat: place of formal public worship or contemplation; indoors, as opposed to **nemetons** (q.v.); usually attached to institutions such as convents or monasteries, but frequently to private homes as well

Annwn: (pron. *Annoon*) the Keltic religion's equivalent to the Underworld. ruled over by Arawn, Lord of the Dead

ansa: "sweetheart"; Erinnach endearment

anwyl, anwylyd: "sweetheart"; Kymric endearment

ap: Kymric; "son of"

Ard-rían, Ard-rígh: "High Queen," "High King"; title of the Keltic sovereign

Ard-ríanachtas, Ard-ríghachtas: "high queenship," "high kingship"

Ard-tiarnas: "High Dominion"; generic term for supreme rulership over Keltia

athair-talam: "father-of-the-ground"; magic herb used by the Fianna, among others, with narcotic/analgesic properties; related botanically to aquilegia, archmain and other hallucinogenic healing herbs

athiarna: "High One"; Fianna form of address to superior officer

athra: "father"; a formal style

athra-cheile: "father-in-law"; lit., "mate-father"

athro: Kymric; "teacher" or "master"

banacha: spirit of the air, usually malevolent (also **bonacha**)

ban-a-tigh: woman householder (*far-a-tigh,* male householder)

Banbha: sun of the planet Erinna

Ban-dia: the Mother, the Great Goddess

Ban-draoi: lit., "woman-druid"; Keltic order of priestess-sorceresses in the service of the Mother Goddess

ban-laoch: woman warrior, female hero

bannock: thick, heavy biscuit or muffin bread

bansha: (also **banshee**) female spirit, often red-cloaked, that sings and wails before a death in many ruling Erinnach families; often seen as a wild rider in the air or over water

bards: Keltic order of poets, chaunters and loremasters

Bawn of Keltia: the space enclosed within the **Curtain Wall** (q.v.; *bawn:* the area enclosed by the outer barbican defenses of a fortress)

Beltain: festival of the beginning of summer, celebrated on 1 May

birlinn: elegant, galley-type ship, usually oared and masted

bodach: term of opprobrium or commiseration, depending on circumstances

bonnive: young pig, piglet

borraun: wood-framed tambourine-shaped goatskin drum, played by hand or with a small flat wooden drumstick

braud: Kymric, "brother"

brehons: Keltic lawgivers and judges

Brighnasa: feast of the goddess Brigid or Briginda, celebrated on 2 February

bruidean: inn or waystation, maintained by local authorities, where any traveller of whatever rank or resources is entitled to claim free hospitality

Cabiri: (Hastaic) Coranian magical order of adepts, similar to the Druids or Ban-draoi

cantrip: very small, simple spell or minor magic

caoine: "keen"; lament or dirge of mourning, usually sung (cf. *coronach*, a lament that is played only, on the pipes)

cariad: "heart," "beloved"; Kymric endearment (**cariadol:** variant used to a child)

cathbarr: fillet or coronet; usually a band of precious metal ornamented with jewels

cath-milid: Fianna captain, with command of a **cath** or several **catha** (**cath:** military unit of 5,000 warriors)

ceili: (pron. *kay-lee*) a dancing-party or ball; any sort of revelry

ceo-draoichta: "druids' fog"; a cloaking spell used by Ban-draoi, Dragon Kin and Druid adepts

Chriesta tighearna!: lit., "Lord Christ!"; name of the Christian god, used as an expletive

cithóg: "port," as on board ship (cf. **deosil**)

claymore: Erinnach/Scotic, *claideamh mor*, "great sword"; two handed, double-edged broadsword, sharp at the point and edges and often weighted at the hilt

clochan: dome- or yurt-like structure used by the Fianna in the field; also, a similar structure built in unmortared stone and used for trance-ordeals by the Fianna and the bards

coelbren: magical alphabet used by the Druids

coire ainsec: "the undry cauldron of guestship"; the obligation, in law, to provide hospitality, shelter or sanctuary to any who claim it

compall: dueling-ground used by Fianna and others, especially for **fíor-comlainn** (q.v.)

Coranians: the ruling race of the Cabiri Imperium, hereditary enemies of the Kelts; they are the descendants of the Atlantean Telchines, as the Kelts are the descendants of the Atlantean Danaans

coron-solais: "crown of light"; personal aura

corp-creidh: doll or poppet, usually made of cloth or clay, used for magical purposes, benevolent or not as the maker intends

Crann Tarith: "Fiery Branch"; the token of war across Keltia. Originally a flaming branch or cross; now, by extension, the alarm or call to war broadcast on all planets

creagh-rígh: "royal reiving"; in very ancient times, the traditional raid led by a newly crowned monarch to consolidate his rule

Criosanna: "The Woven Belts"; the rings that circle the throneworld Tara

crimbeul: lit., "droop-mouth"; mustache

crochan: magical healing-pool that can cure almost any injury, provided the spinal column has not been severed and the brain and bone marrow are undamaged; cap., also refers to **Pair Dadeni,** the Cauldron of Rebirth, one of the four chief Treasures of Keltia

crossic: unit of Keltic money; small gold coin

curragh: small leather-hulled boat rowed with oars

cursal: very fast light warship of the Keltic starfleet

Cúrsa-nan-coillte: "The Running of the Woods"; ancient Fianna ordeal, part of the **triail-triarach** (q.v.)

Curtain Wall: artificial energy barrier that encircles and conceals the seven Keltic star-systems (also known as **the Pale**)

Cwn Annwn: (pron. *Coon Annoon*) in Keltic religion, the Hounds of Hell; the red-eared, white-coated dogs belonging to Arawn Lord of the Dead, that hunt down and destroy guilty souls

daer-fudir: "outlaw"; a legal term, used in banishment of a malefactor

damacho-andra: (Hastaic) co-wife; legal second wife, who possesses most of the rights and privileges of the senior wife according to this polygamous (and, occasionally, polyandrous) system (*damacho-zarak:* co-husband)

dama-wyn: "grandmother," "great-grandmother"; a formal style

dán: "doom"; fated karma

deosil: on board ship, the starboard side (cf. **cithóg**); also sunwise (clockwise)

dermasealer: skinfuser; medical tool used to repair flesh lacerations by means of laser sutures

dewin-arwydd: magical symbol or totem chosen by a sorcerer upon initiation

draighean: thorn, usually from the blackthorn shrub

Dragon Kinship: magical-military order of Keltic adepts

draoichtas: generic term for the body of arcane knowledge shared by adepts of the Ban-draoi and Druid orders

droch-shuil: "evil eye"; baleful influence or malign magical attention

Druids: magical order of Keltic sorcerer-priests, in the service of the Lord-father, known variously as Hu-mawr, Ollathair or Dagda

dubhachas: "gloom"; melancholy characterized by causeless depression and inexpressible longing for unnameable things; often afflicts Kelts

dubh-cosac: stimulant herb usually taken in powder form; burned as incense, it is a powerful hallucinogen

dúchas: lordship or holding; usually carries lands and a title with it

duergar: in Kernish folklore, an evil elemental or place-spirit

dûn: a stronghold of the Sidhe, the Shining Ones (also *liss* or *rath*)

earthfasting: a simple magic, often the first a child will learn, whereby the practitioner causes the victim to be rooted to the ground, unable even to lift up a foot until released

enech-clann: brehon law system of honor-price violations

Englic: tongue of Terran Federacy; unofficial galactic Common Tongue

éraic: "blood-price"; payment exacted for a murder or other capital crime by the kin of the victim

-fach (masc. **-bach**): Kymric, suffix added to a woman's name to denote affection; used to all ages and stations but especially to children

faha: courtyard or enclosed space in a castle complex or encampment

Fáinne: "The Ring"; the six system viceroys and vicereines of Keltia

falair: winged horse whose species is native to the Erinna system

feinnid: a fully accepted Fian who has passed all tests and who is acknowledged to have done so by the Fianna Captain-General or duly appointed deputy

fetch: the visible form taken by the spirit-guardian of a Keltic family

Fianna: Keltic officer class; order of military supremacy

fidchell: chess-style game

findruinna: superhard, silvery metal used in swords, armor and the like

firead: quick, sleek-furred animal similar to a weasel or stoat

Fionnasa: feast of the god Fionn, celebrated on 29 September

fíor-comlainn: "truth-of-combat"; legally binding trial by personal combat

fiosaoicht: "overknowledge"; shared superconsciousness or telepathic unity common to members of magical orders

fith-fath: spell of shapeshifting or glamourie; magical illusion

Fomori: ancient enemies of the Kelts; sing., **Fomor** or **Fomorian**

Fragarach: "The Answerer." Also translated "Retaliator." Historically, the magical sword borne by Arthur of Arvon; also, the moon-size laser cannon emplacement or sun-gun that defends the Throneworld system of Tara

framach: brown-skinned root vegetable found throughout Keltia; a food staple

fudir: "criminal," "outcast"

galláin: "foreigners"; sing., **gall** (fem. **gallwyn**); generic term for all humanoid non-Kelts and often used for non-humanoids as well

galloglass: Keltic foot-soldier

garron: small, sturdy horse, 13–14 hands high, usually gray in color

gauran: plow-beast similar to ox or bullock

geis, pl. geisa: prohibition or moral injunction placed upon a person, often thought to be divinely inspired; many are revealed at birth

glaive (from Erinnach, *claideamh*): lightsword; laser weapon used throughout Keltia and much of the civilized galaxy

glam-dicenn: formal curse placed on a person by a practicing sorcerer

glib: hair above forehead; bangs or forelock fringe

goleor: "in great numbers," "an overabundance"; Englic word *galore* is derived from it

grafaun: double-bladed war axe

grianan: "sun-place"; solar, private chamber

gúna: generic name for various styles of long robe or gown

gwlan: fine, strong wool-linen weave, used for everyday apparel

Gwynfyd: the Circle of Perfection; eternal afterlife to be attained to only after many cycles of rebirth

hai atton: "heigh to us"; the horn-cry that rallies an army

Hastaic: language of the Cabiri Imperium

hedge school: informal, unstructured places of learning, run in summer, often outdoors, by journeyman bards; not meant to replace formal schooling but to augment; anyone may come and go at will

hippocamp: "sea-horse"; aquatic herd beast, semi-amphibious, that bears a strong resemblance in appearance and function to an ordinary horse; often domesticated by **merrows** (q.v.)

Hollfyd: the visible, imperfect, physical universe

imbas-forosnai: "foreordering"; deep divinatory trance

immram: "voyage," pl. **immrama;** the great migrations from Earth to Keltia; also, initiatory trance of Druid and Ban-draoi training sequences

Inadacht-na-laithe: "the path to the kingship"

(I) 's é do bheatha: lit., "life to you"; traditional Keltic salutation, used on both meeting and parting

Justiciary: voluntary interstellar court, located on the neutral planet Ganaster, to which systems may make petition for arbitrated settlement of grievances short of war; all participants must agree beforehand to be bound by the decision

Kelu: "The Crown"; the One High God above all gods; also addressed as **Artzan Janco,** "Shepherd of Heaven," and **Yr Mawreth,** "The Highest"

kenning: telepathic technique originally developed (and now used almost exclusively) by Ban-draoi and Druids

kern: Keltic starfleet crewman

kilvach: small formal garden-alcove often found within larger gardens

Lakhaz: language of the Fomori

lai: unit of distance measurement, equal to approximately one-half mile

leas-ríocht: "half-rule"; formal governance given over to an heir or named deputy; not a regency, but an actual substitution of persons and power

leinna: long, full-sleeved shirt worn under a tunic

lithfaen: "lodestone"; quartz crystal, piezoelectrically charged, that can be keyed to various objects and acts as a homing device

llan: retreat-place; cell or enclosure for religious anchorite

lonna: light hydrofoil-type vessel used by Keltic sea navy

Lughnasa: feast of the god Lugh, celebrated on 1 August; by custom, marks first sexual encounter for most young Kelts

machair: "sea-meadow"; wide grassland tracts bordering on the sea and running down to the high-water mark

Madoc's Mether: a philosophical argument, on the order of "eating one's cake and having it"; trying to drink from Madoc's Mether results in wine in one's lap

maenor: hereditary dwelling place, usually a family seat, in the countryside of Keltia

-maeth: suffix used with name for one's foster-father (**-methryn,** suffix for foster-mother)

maigen: "sanctuary"; border, fixed by law and its extent according to rank, that surrounds a noble's lands, within which that lord is responsible for the peace and safety of all folk and their goods

mamaith: child's word for "mother"; equivalent to Englic "mama" or "mommy"

marana: "meditation"; thought-trance of Keltic sorcerers, lighter in degree than most others

marbh-aisling: "dreaming-death"; profound trance

Master: Scotan; title of heir to clann name (as **Master of Douglas**); *Mistress* for a woman heir

mathra: "mother"; a more formal style (cf. **athra**)

mathra-chairda: "heart-mother"; style sometimes used to one's foster-mother, nurse or teacher; a style of deep affection

Mathra'chtaran: "Reverend Mother"; ancient form of address used to the Ban-draoi Magistra

m'chara: "my friend"; used in the vocative

merrows: (Na Moruadha) the sea people originally native to Kernow, amphibious, red-skinned and green-haired

mether: four-cornered drinking-vessel, usually made of wood or pottery

mil-na-mela: marriage-moon, honeymoon journey

nemeton: ceremonial stone circle or henge

Nevermas: a time that never comes

ní, níghean: "daughter of"

nithered: trembling with cold

ollave: master-bard; by extension, anyone with supreme command of an art or science

oréadach: cloth-of-gold (*arghansadach*, cloth-of-silver)

pastai: small handmeal; a turnover consisting of a pastry crust filled with meat or vegetables or both

Pheryllt: class of master-Druids who serve as instructors in the order's schools and colleges

piast: large amphibious water-beast found in deepwater lakes on the planets Scota and Erinna; the species was known to Terrans as the Loch Ness Monster

pishogue: small magic, cantrip

plomine: element, chemical symbol Pl; bright blue gas of the halogen family, used in the manufacture of hyperspace enginery

púca: mischievous, sometimes malevolent spirit of darkness; *cap.*, a spirit-dog, terrifying of aspect, the size of a pony, black-coated, with flame-red eyes

quaich: low, wide, double-handled drinking-vessel

rann: chanted verse stanza used in magic; spell of any sort

rechtair: steward of royal or noble households; title of planetary governors; title of Chancellor of the Exchequer on Keltic High Council

rígh-domhna: members of the Keltic royal family, as reckoned from a common ancestor, who may (theoretically, at least) be elected to the Sovereignty

riomhall: magical circle used for ritual or protective purposes

saille: Erinnach, ''willow''

saining: rite of Keltic baptism, administered anywhere from seven days to a year and a day after a child's birth

saining-pool: another name for **crochan** (q.v.)

Samhain: (pron. *Sah-win*) festival of the beginning of winter and start of the Keltic New Year, celebrated on 31 October (Great Samhain) and continuing until 11 November (Little Samhain)

scallan: ''shelter''; magical shield that can be used as a protection against wind, rain, cold and the like

scathach: ''shadow''; protective force-field generated by starships to convey other craft to safety

schiltron: military formation much used by the Fianna; very compact and organized, it is extremely difficult to break

sea-pig: semi-intelligent aquatic mammal, friendly, noisy and playful

sgian: small black-handled knife universally worn in Keltia, usually in boot-top

shakla: chocolate-tasting beverage brewed with water from the berries of the brown ash; drunk throughout Keltia as a caffeine-based stimulant

Shan-rían: ''The Old Queen''; epithet for Aoife Ard-rían, who reigned longer than any other Keltic monarch (more than a hundred and fifty years), and was older than any monarch before her at her death at age 202

Sidhe: (pron. *Shee*) the Shining Ones; a race of possibly divine or immortal beings; their king is Gwyn ap Nudd

silkies: (Sluagh-rón) the seal-folk originally native to the Out Isles

sinsear-cheile: lit., ''mate-parents''; in-laws

síodarainn: ''silk-iron''; extremely strong, smooth black metal often used for starship hulls

sith-silk: very fine, very costly silk fabric

Six Nations: the six star systems of Keltia (excluding the Throneworld system of Tara); in order of their founding, Erinna, Kymry, Scota, Kernow, Vannin and Brytaned (or Arvor)

skiath: "shield"; a force-field/pressure suit worn in hard vacuum, it generates for its wearer all necessary oxygen, gravity and protection against harmful or poisonous atmospheres

slán-lus: "heal-herb"; specific often used in herbal compounds

slat-draoichta: druid's wand; magic staff usually made of ash or rowan wood

sluagh: a hosting, as of an army (**marca-sluagh,** a cavalry force)

Spancel: magical spell of binding, much favored by the **Sidhe** (q.v.), for use on trespassing mortals or those they wish to steal away to their dúns

Spartannach: the Spartan people of ancient Greece

Spearhead: the polestar of Tara

Stonerows: the lower circles of Caerdroia, the Keltic capital

stour: uproar, tumult, outcry

streppoch: term of opprobrium; roughly, "bitch"

summerbye: chrysanthemum

sun-shark: species of dolphin native to most Keltic oceans. Friendly and gregarious, they are intelligent beings who can communicate with not only each other but with humans, silkies and merrows; they are therefore accorded full civil protection under law against being harassed, hunted or slain

taghairm: "echo"; magical trance technique common to Druids and Ban-draoi

tailstar: comet or meteor

talpa: blind, blunt-snouted digger animal native to the planet Kernow

Tanist, Tanista: designated heir of line to the Keltic throne

tântad: "The Path of the Fire"; lines marking out routes of terranic electromagnetism; land-tides

Taoiseach: the Prime Minister of Keltia

tasyk: child's word for "father"; equivalent to Englic "daddy"

telyn: Kymric lap-harp

thrawn: stubborn, unreasonably perverse

Timpaun: "The Drumhead"; a vast flat plain on the planet Erinna, home of many horse-breeding establishments

tinna-galach: "bright-fire"; the will-o'-the-wisp, occurring over marshy ground; especially noted for its appearances in the great marshlands of Gwenn-Estrad, on the planet of Arvor in the Brytaned system

tinnscra: marriage-portion given to a man or woman by their families, clann, or (in the cases of royalty or high nobility) the reigning monarch (**tinnól:** the marriage-gift each partner gives the other)

tirr: cloaking effect, part magical, part mechanical in nature, used on ships, buildings, and the like

togmall: "lap-dog"; a teacher's pet or other favorite

traha: "arrogance"; wanton pride, hubris

triail-triarach: the three-part ordeal which must be passed by those who seek admittance to the Fianna

trosca-mór: "great hunger"; the hunger-strike. A fearful method of compelling justice, in which the aggrieved party fasts against the party who has allegedly wronged him (who has in turn the right by law to fast back against his accuser)

tuathal: antisunwise (counterclockwise); also **widdershins**

urrad: townsman, usually landless; lowest social class in Keltia

usqueba: "water of life"; whiskey, generally unblended.

vitriglass: crystalline substance, its molecular structure reinforced by metallic ions; used in starship viewports for its extreme hardness and resistance to shattering

Notes on Pronunciation

The spellings and pronunciations of the names and words in THE KELTIAD are probably unfamiliar to most readers, unless one happens to be thoroughly steeped in things like the Mabinogion or the Cuchulainn cycle. The Celtic languages (Irish, Scots Gaelic, Welsh, Cornish, Manx and Breton) upon which I have drawn for my nomenclature are not related to any tongue that might provide a clue as to their derivation or spoken sound. Outside of loan-words, they have no Latin root as do the Romance tongues, and they are in fact derived from a totally different branch of the Indo-European linguistic tree.

Therefore I have taken certain, not always consistent, liberties with orthography in the interests of reader convenience, though of course one may deal with the names any way one likes, or even not at all. But for those who might like to humor the author, I have made this list of some of the more difficult names, words and phonetic combinations.

One further note, to those (and they are legion) whose Celtic linguistic scholarship exceeds my poor own: The words used herein are meant to be Keltic, not Celtic. I have appropriated fairly evenhandedly from most of the Celtic languages—and from Elizabethan English and Lowland Scots (Lallans) as well where it seemed good to do so—both archaisms and words that are in common modern usage, and in not a few cases I have tampered with their meanings to suit my own purposes. Therefore do not be unduly alarmed should familiar words turn out to be not all they seem. Words may be reasonably assumed to change over time and distance; Keltia is very far away by both measures, and who is to say (if not I) what words they shall be speaking and what meaning these words shall have.

But just in case that does not suffice to avert the wrath of the purists, I hereby claim prior protection under the Humpty-Dumpty Law: "When *I* use a word . . . it means just what I choose it to mean—neither more nor less." Now you are warned.

Vowels

Generally the usual, though *a* is mostly pronounced "ah" and *i* never takes the sound of "eye," but always an "ee" or "ih" sound. Thus: "ard-ree" for *Ard-rígh,* not "ard-rye." Final *e* is always sounded; thus: "Slay-nee" for *Slaine,* not "Slain."

Vowel Combinations

aoi: "ee" as in "heel"

ao: "ay" as in "pay"

au: "ow" as in "cow," never "aw" as in "saw"; thus *Jaun* rhymes with "crown," not with "fawn."

ae, ai: "I" as in "high." Exceptions: the proper names *Aeron* and *Slaine,* where the sound is "ay" as in "day."

á: The accent gives it length. Thus, *dán* is pronounced "dawn."

io: "ih" if unaccented. If accented (*ío*), then "ee."

Consonants

c: always a "k" sound. (To avoid the obvious problem here, the more usual *Celt, Celtic, Celtia* have been spelled *Kelt, Keltic, Keltia,* throughout.)

ch, kh: gutturals as in the German "ach," never "ch" as in "choose"

f: in Welsh-derived words, pronounced as "v"; "ff" is normal English "f"

g: always hard, as in "get" or "give"

bh: pronounced as "v"

dd: pronounced as "th" in "then," not as in "thin"

Some of the more difficult names:

Aeron: AIR-on
Aoibhell: ee-VELL
Gwydion: GWID-eeon
Fionnbarr: FINN-bar
Ríoghnach: REE-oh-nakh
Slaine: SLAY-nee
Taliesin: tal-YES-in
Melangell: mel-ANN-gel (hard "g")
Jaun Akhera: jown a-KHAIR-a
Aoife: EE-fa
Lasairían: las-a-REE-un
Caerdroia: car-DROY-a
Ard-rían: ard-REE-un
Ard-rígh: ard-REE
Taoiseach: TEE-shokh
Turusachan: too-roo-SAHK'N
Ban-draoi: BAN-dree
Sidhe: shee
Annwn: a-NOON
Gwynedd: GWIN-ith
Scone: properly, skoon; but, as you please

Keltic Orders and Societies

The Dragon Kinship

The Dragon Kinship is a magical and military order of adepts, under the authority of the Pendragon of Lirias. Members are the most accomplished adepts of all Keltia, elected strictly on the basis of ability. All professions and ranks are equally eligible.

All those of the Kinship are equal under the Pendragon; no formalities are observed, no titles are used, no precedence of rank is followed. The only other office is Summoner; chosen by the Pendragon, this officer is what the name implies—the person responsible for calling the Kinship together on the Pendragon's order.

The Pendragon is chosen by his or her predecessor to serve for a term of seven years; this choice must be confirmed by a simple-majority public vote and may be renewed only by a unanimous secret vote of the entire membership (not surprisingly, such a renewal has never taken place). At the moment, Gwydion Prince of Dôn is Pendragon; he was preceded by a farmer from the Morbihan, a poetess from Vannin, a weaver from the Out Isles and a bard from Cashel.

To call someone ''Kin to the Dragon'' is the highest tribute possible. Most members are public about it, some prefer to keep it a secret, but all possess a certain unmistakable and indefinable air of apartness and assurance. It is a severely demanding society: More than any other power, save only the Crown itself, the Dragon Kinship is responsible for the well-being, the welfare and the quality of life and spirit of Keltia, on all levels. As a magical order, the Kinship takes precedence over all other factions: much of its membership, in fact, comprises members of other orders such as the Druids, Ban-draoi or the Bardic Association. It is truly a cross-section of Keltic society, for it reaches from royalty to farmers to artists to techs to soldiers to artisans to householders. There are no age limits either upper or lower, and no entry requirement save the possession of psionic Gift.

That Gift must include all psionic talents, and feature supreme proficiency in at least one: healing of body or mind; seership; broad-band telepathy, either receptor or sender; magical warfare—attack, defense or strategic; energy control; psychokinetics; retrocognition or precognition; shapeshifting; transmutation; pure magic; or any other magical discipline or talent. Members are recruited through observation and direct approach by a current Dragon. There are generally no more than ten thousand members at any one time, though in time of war or other great emergency the membership may be increased, if acceptable candidates are available.

The Dragon Kinship have their own brugh in Turusachan and rich lands on Brytaned and Dyved; their main training establishment, Caer Coronach, is in a remote part of Caledon. A Dragon is by tradition named the sovereign's Magical Champion, as a Fian is always named Military Champion.

The Druid Order

The Druid Order is, with the Ban-draoi, the oldest order in Keltia, founded by St. Brendan himself in the direct tradition of the Terran Druids. The Order is limited to men only, who may present themselves for membership beginning at thirteen years of age. As with the other orders, preliminary training is begun as soon as a child begins to show promise of talent, sometimes even as early as three or four years old.

The Druids are an immensely powerful body; they concern themselves with sorcery and politics, not necessarily always in that ranking. There are three degrees of Druidry: Novice, Ovate, Master. Head of the Order is the Archdruid, who is chosen by his predecessor upon his deathbed, and who then rules until his own death. The Archdruid sits in the House of Peers as Lord of Carnac, and is a member of the High Council which advises the monarch.

The training is long and intensive: all forms of magic, lore, herbalism, alphabets, correspondences, alchemy, psionics, chants, music, healing, seership, trance mediumship, and other occult disciplines. A fully qualified Druid is a master of magic, and very few can manage to withstand him when he puts forth his power.

There have been a few doubtful passages in the history of the Order, most notably the appalling two-hundred-year period known to infamy as the Druid Theocracy and Interregnum.

At a time of unusual political polarity and turmoil, the Archdruid, a brilliant and devious man called Edeyrn, saw in the divisiveness a chance to seize power for his Order—which is to say, for himself. A series of battles and massacres called the Druids' Wars followed, effectively demolishing all semblance of civil order in Keltia, and Edeyrn installed himself as magical overlord. He was supported in this by his fellow renegades and quite a few equally opportunistic noble houses. He was opposed by the remnants of the Fáinne, the Ban-draoi, the Bardic Association, the Fianna, most of the noble houses and many of his own Druids who had remained loyal to the teachings of their Order. This opposition was the Counterinsurgency, and they were very, very strong.

This horrific state of affairs existed for nearly two centuries, with the balance of power continually shifting from one side to the other, until the invasion of Keltia by Fomori and Fir Bolg space fleets resulted in enormous destruction and panic. The Theocracy, now led by the ancient Edeyrn's heir Owain, tried to make a deal with the invaders but failed, opening the way only for full-scale war.

Arthur of Arvon, himself a Druid, rallied the Counterinsurgency in one great desperate throw and defeated Owain's forces at the Battle of Moytura. With the help of his chief teacher and advisor Merlynn Llwyd, who assumed the Archdruidship, Arthur went on to pull Keltia together and become King of Kelts, as has been told elsewhere. But throughout his long and glorious reign, Druid precepts remained Arthur's guide to action.

The Druids, under Merlynn Llwyd, began a period of severe purge and purification, and eventually were restored to their former high standards.

The current Archdruid is Teilo ap Bearach; the ranks of Master-druids include Gwydion Prince of Dôn, Aeron's uncles Deian and Estyn, and her cousins Alasdair and Dion.

The Druid Order has a brugh of its own in Turusachan, and its chief college is at Dinas Affaraon on Gwynedd.

The Ban-draoi

Equal in rank and antiquity with the Druid Order, the Ban-draoi are the evolvement of the incomparably ancient Goddess-priestesses of the most deep-rooted Keltic tradition. The Order was founded in Keltia by St. Brendan's mother, Nia daughter of Brigit, who many said was of divine parentage herself, and who became the ancestress of the House of Dâna in Keltia.

Divine or not, Nia of the Tuatha De Danaan was brilliant, beautiful, foresighted, and incredibly gifted in magic, and the Order she established had power, respect and influence right from the start.

Open only to women, the Order of the Ban-draoi (the name is Erinnach for, literally, "woman-druid") has as its chief purpose the worship of the Lady, the Mother Goddess; but they are sorceresses as well as priestesses, and their magic matches that of the Druids spell for spell. All women, whether initiates or not, participate to some degree in the ways of the Ban-draoi, as do all men in the ways of the Druids, since both systems are at their deepest hearts paths of worship. But the mysteries of the Ban-draoi are the Mysteries of the Mother, the things of most awe in all the Keltic worlds. Priestess or not, every Keltic woman shares in this awe, and every Keltic man respects it.

The Ban-draoi were never so politically oriented as the Druids, but when the Theocracy began, they became the chief focus of the Counterinsurgency and gave the resistance movement much of its force. Later, Arthur's mother Ygrawn and sister Morgan, and his wife Gweniver, were all three high priestesses of the Order, and gave him invaluable aid in his task of defeating both Druids and aliens. After Arthur's departure, it was Morgan who raised the tremendous energy barrier of the Curtain Wall, thus protecting Keltia from the outside worlds for fifteen centuries.

Obliged by circumstances to assume a critical political role, the Ban-draoi adapted, and have retained a position of political pre-eminence down to the present day. Aeron Aoibhell holds the rank of Domina, or a High Priestess of the Order, as does her sister Ríoghnach.

The training of a Ban-draoi (the word is both singular and plural) is as intensive as that of a Druid, and includes the same body of magical knowledge. Due to the heritage of Nia, however, it also emphasizes many branches of arcane lore known only to the priestesses. It is not so hierarchical as the Druid Order; an aspirant to the Ban-draoi is initiated as a priestess once her training is judged complete. If she wishes, and if her teachers agree, she may then seek the rank of high priestess, which carries with it the deepest knowledge of all and the title Domina.

The Chief Priestess is elected for life by a conclave of all the high priestesses; she bears the title Magistra, sits on the monarch's High Council, and sits in the House of Peers as Lady of Elphame. The office is currently held by Ffaleira níghean Enfail.

The Ban-draoi have a brugh of their own within the walls of Turusachan, and their chief training school is at Scartanore on Erinna.

The Fianna

The Fianna is a purely military organization, comprising the most skilled and talented warriors of Keltia. To become a Fian, a candidate must pass a series of incredibly rigorous tests of his or her warrior skills: a test of knowledge, in which he or she must demonstrate mastery of a specific body of lore; a test of soul, in which the candidate must face psionic examination by a qualified inquisitioner, who may be Druid, Ban-draoi or Dragon; and finally a formal combat with a chosen Fian of the First Rank.

So rigorous are these tests, in fact, that it seems astounding that anyone at all ever becomes a Fian; but many do indeed succeed, and rightly are respected. Membership is open to all ranks, ages and professions; candidates must be at least eighteen years of age, for physical reasons, though training may often begin at age six or seven if a child shows talent.

Skills a Fian must learn include all forms of combat and martial arts: sword-mastery, both classic and lightsword techniques; fencing; archery; wrestling; four forms of unarmed combat approximating to Terran judo, karate, kung-fu and foot-fighting; boxing; riding; marksmanship with all forms of weapons; tracking; running; spear-throwing; and the piloting of all types of vehicles from starship to snow-yacht.

The test of knowledge requires extensive study in the fields of history, both Keltic and Terran; literature; brehon law; the arts; heraldry and genealogy; politics; and science, both pure and applied. Fians are expected to be able to speak all seven Keltic tongues, Latin, and as many alien tongues as possible (the minimum is three, and Hastaic, the Imperial tongue, is mandatory). In addition, Fians are taught the secret Keltic battle-language, Shelta Thari.

The test of soul could well be called an ordeal. It involves deep-trance, telepathy, and astral travel, and no candidate, whether pass or fail, will ever speak about it afterward.

The final formal combat is determined on an individual basis by the Captain-General of the Fianna; choice of weapon and combat form will vary, but there is always one armed and one unarmed duel for each candidate. The Captain-General also selects the First-Rank Fian who will oppose the prospective member. No allowance is made for sex or physical size: Women, for instance, are expected to know how to defeat a male warrior who vastly outmeasures them in height, weight and strength.

The Fianna have their own training establishment, Caer Artos in Arvon, and their quarters in Turusachan, the Commandery, are directly across from the royal palace. Military champions for trial-by-combat are always selected from the ranks of the Fianna; the Royal Champion is always a First-Rank Fian, and the monarch's personal bodyguard is made up of Fians.

The current Captain-General of the Fianna is Dónal mac Avera.

The Bardic Association

The Bardic Association has a long and honorable history. From its founding in Keltic year 347 by Plenyth ap Alun, the society of bards has held without stain to its high principles and rigorous requirements, and bards of all degrees have traditionally been granted hospitality, honor and semi-royal precedence throughout Keltia.

Although bards receive a good deal of magical training in the course of their studies it is not emphasized; the primary training of bards is words. Any and all literary disciplines: poetry, sung or spoken; satire; history, sagas; ballads; myths and legends; drama; genealogy; precedent—all belong to the bardic tradition. Unlike magical schooling, the bardic discipline may begin at any age; there are records of peers in old age handing over their titles to their heirs and going to the bardic colleges to end their lives in study.

Bardic aspirants spend five years as apprentices; five years as journeymen; five years as institutional bards. Having completed the fifteen-year training program (which does not preclude other study; Gwydion of Dôn, for instance, is both Druid and master-bard), they are then permitted to take the examination for the rank of ollave, or master-bard, if they so wish. If they are successful in this bid, they may then represent themselves as master-bards of the schools and seek the very highest employment. Not all bards choose to seek the status of ollave, however; and many do not remain even to become institutional bards. Any bard who has successfully passed the examination at the end of the journeyman term may serve as a teacher of children, and many choose to leave at this level to work in such capacity.

Bards of all degrees, whether journeyman, institutional bard or ollave, are much in demand throughout Keltia; they are employed by royal or noble families, or by merely wealthy families, as poet of the house and artist in residence, encouraged to recite the old lore and to compose creatively on their own. Exceptional bards of high degree are often entrusted with delicate diplomatic or social missions, including—not to put too fine a point on it—spying; though the last is done only in cases of the gravest national importance, for if too many bards did it, all bards would be suspect. The Ard-rían Aeron makes great use of bards, and gives them greater honor than they have had from the monarchs of Keltia for some years.

Bards have by law and custom several odd privileges: A bard may demand the nightmeal from anyone, in exchange for a song or a poem; the royal ollave (or ríogh-bardáin) has the right to a seat at the high table in Mi-Cuarta not more than seven places from the monarch's right hand; an ollave is permitted by law to wear six colors in his cloak (only the reigning monarch may wear more—seven, if desired).

The Chief of Bards is chosen by a vote of senior masters; he serves until death or retirement, and sits on the monarch's High Council. Chief of Bards at present is Idris ap Caswyn.

The Bardic Association has a brugh of its own, Seren Beirdd—"Star of the Bards"—within the walls of Turusachan, and the Bardic Colleges are located on Powys.

Partial Chronology

3400	Fionnbarr born at Caerdroia
3405	Bres born at Tory
3434	Emer born at Coldharbor
3442	Quarrel of Bres and Fionnbarr
3455	Fionnbarr and Emer marry
3467	Jaun Akhera born at Escal-dun
	Roderick born at Kinloch Arnoch
3470	Gwydion and Arianeira born at Caer Dathyl
3472	Desmond and Slaine born at Drumhallow
3473	Elathan born at Tory
3475	Aeron born at Caerdroia
	Morwen born at Kinloch Arnoch
3476	Rohan born at Caerdroia
3477	Ríoghnach born at Caerdroia
3479	Fionnbarr's reign begins (death of Lasairían)
3482	Kieran and Declan born at Caerdroia
	Melangell born at Bryn Alarch
3489	Fionnuala born at Caerdroia
3509	Aeron's reign begins (deaths of Fionnbarr, Emer and Roderick)

Dates given here are in Earth Reckoning (A.D.); to find the date (A.B.) (*Anno Brendani*) or A.C.C. (*Anno Celtiae Conditae*), subtract 453 and 455, respectively.

Note on Age

The average Keltic lifespan is 160–175 years, and many individuals reach, even surpass, the two-century mark in full possession of their faculties both physical and mental. Physical development occurs at the same rate as in shorter-lived races, with full physical maturity coming between the ages of 18 and 21.

There is no single legal majority age. At 18, all Kelts, both male and female, are liable for military service; the mandatory term is three years. They may also vote in local elections and assume minor titles.

At 21, citizens may marry with consent (though marriage at this age is almost unheard-of—thus the scandal of Emer ní Kerrigan's elopement with Prince Fionnbarr as he then was; most marriages occur at around ages 30–35), vote in planetary elections and hold minor public office.

At 27, Kelts may marry without consent, vote in major (system and national) elections, hold major public office and succeed to major titles.

And no one under the age of 33 may hold the Copper Crown unregented.

Righ-Domhna: The Royal Family of Doibhell and Collateral Kinships

Brychan = Mauern   Copanc = Fiona   Giksym = Somharle   Greham = Dorfe

Gwennan   Ales = Farrell   Conall = Rohan   Corlann Gwynevra = Lassairian   Revelin   Surhec   Elharn = Yynysa   Seven

Dulyus

Mesenn = Carlach   Dlascaar = Kenwyn

Solais   Dion

Finnabhair = Drogal

Senghin   Capadhe (Shape)   Desmond   Slaine   Maesen = Tioch

Emer = Fronnbarr   Orlarch = Conor   Sean = Rhosynna   Garalc

Dlascaar   Mahon   Kereisa

Morlaus   Tamhna   Escyr   Keina = Riada

Suhan   Scora   Inbec   Tryscan

Rhan   Rhys   Maboc   Melangell

Rohan   Rioghnach   Kieran = Eilunyed   Declan   Fionnuala

Aewyn = Gwenedour   Copmal   Drolach

Faolan = Mared

Fergus = Morien   Caersunn   Roderek (1) = Guvybion (2)   Aeron   Arianrna   Elveo

Arianna

PARTIAL DESCENT
OF THE HALDANE KINGS
From the Royal and Noble Keltic Houses

House of Odin House of Arjdor

Gwennyr = Arthur Morgan

Gwenhlaech = Ayaun   Ayuenna = Madoc

(not every generation shown)

Ayauwen = Maesen Iluyo

Gwieper (1) Marawaun (2) = Sempela

Brennal = Keirios   Margfal = Corynec
(not every generation shown)

Princes of Gwynedd

Gwydion

Celery = Rhydian
Lord of Powys

Lords of the Isles

Glesny = Somharle

House of Háya
(Royal line of Torenthall)

Malen = Brennan 1768 Aoibhyell

Kieron XVI   Erthe = Lachlan par Cathal

Declan VIII Ranall II Ayaharex Cryseyrach = Sorcha

Kennrec or Gwladys = Teynot Fall V

Briónor-Brennyr = Lessaruna V

Brennan XVIII = Elowen

Siosa = Declan IX

Kinnan = Rohan

Sultain = Fromhbarg XIII

Gresham = Aoife VI Conn Lunes

Gwynnera = Lesarian III Revelin Dustfac Elharn

Morlaus Tamhyra Eocyn Emer = Fromhbarg XIV Orlaith Deian

Aeron Rohan Ríoghnach Keren Declan Fionnuala ...

Lords of Orecotpes   **Prynces of Leinster**

Brychan = Marwyn Corane = Fiona

Gwennan Abes = Farrell Copall Corlayn

Morlaus Tamhyra Eocyn Keira Emer = ...

*(In early generations,
not all issue shown)*

The Books of THE KELTIAD

The Tale of Brendan
*The Rock beyond the Billow
*The Song of Amergin
*The Deer's Cry

The Tale of Arthur
*The Hawk's Gray Feather
*The Oak above the Kings
*The Hedge of Mist

The Tale of Aeron
The Silver Branch
The Copper Crown
The Throne of Scone

The Tale of Gwydion
*The Shield of Fire
*The Sword of Light
*The Cloak of Gold

* forthcoming

About the Author

Patricia Kennealy was born in Brooklyn and grew up in North Babylon, New York. She was educated at St. Bonaventure University and Harpur College, taking her degree in English literature. For three years she was the editor-in-chief of JAZZ & POP magazine, a national publication devoted to rock and progressive music in the late 60's and early 70's, and she has written extensively in the field of rock criticism.

She is an award-winning advertising copywriter; a former record company executive; and a member of Mensa, the Richard III Society and The Society for Creative Anachronism (where she is known as Lassarina Douglas of Strathearn). In 1970 she exchanged vows with the late Jim Morrison, leader of the rock group The Doors, in a private religious ceremony. Her leisure pursuits including riding, fencing and playing the violin.

She lives in New York City and Stephentown, N. Y. Her ambition is to christen a warship.